ROSE OF THE PROPHET
Volume Three

THE PROPHET OF AKHRAN

MARGARET WEIS AND
TRACY HICKMAN

BANTAM BOOKS
NEW YORK • TORONTO • LONDON • SYDNEY • AUCKLAND

THE PROPHET OF AKHRAN
A Bantam Spectra Book / September 1989

ISBN 0-553-28143-7

Published simultaneously in the United States and Canada

*Bantam Books are published by Bantam Books, a division of Bantam Doubleday Dell
Publishing Group, Inc. Its trademark, consisting of the words "Bantam Books" and the
portrayal of a rooster, is Registered in U.S. Patent and Trademark Office and in other
countries. Marca Registrada. Bantam Books, 666 Fifth Avenue, New York, New York 10103.*

PRINTED IN THE UNITED STATES OF AMERICA

RAD   14 13 12 11 10 9 8 7 6 5 4

THE PROPHET
OF AKHRAN

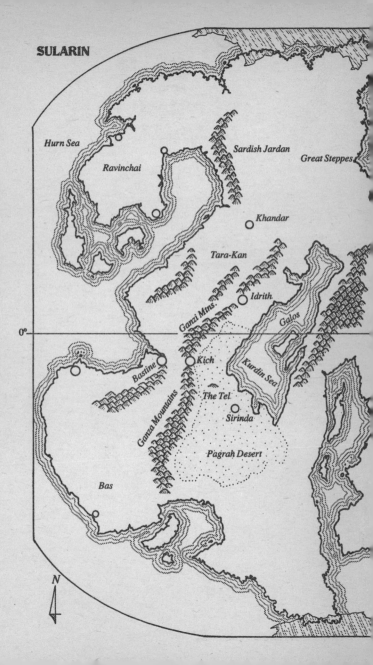

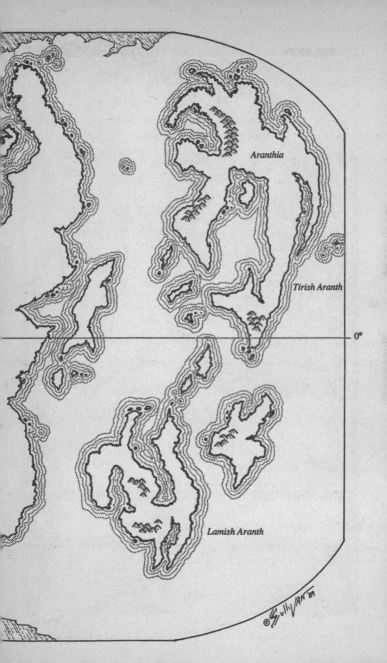

Aranthia

Tirish Aranth

0°

Lamish Aranth

© SulliVAN '89

THE BOOK
OF QUAR

Chapter 1

The desert burned beneath a summer sun that blazed in the sky like the eye of a vengeful god. Beneath that searing, withering stare, few things could survive. Those that did so kept out of the god's fiery sight, burrowing into their holes, skulking in their tents until the eye closed in night's sleep.

Though it was early morning yet, the heat was already radiating from the desert floor with an intensity that made even the djinn, Fedj, feel as if he been skewered like *shishlick* and was being slowly roasted over the coals of an eternal fire.

Fedj wandered disconsolately through the camp around the Tel—if camp it could be called. He knew he should be in attendance upon his master, Sheykh Jaafar al Widjar, but given the Sheykh's humor these days, the djinn would have preferred attending an imp of Sul. It had been the same every morning for the past few months. The moment Fedj sprang from the ring upon his master's hand, it began.

First, the whining. Wringing his hands, Jaafar wailed.

"Of all the children of Akhran, am I not the most unfortunate? I am cursed, cursed! My people taken captive! Our homes in the hills destroyed! The sheep that are our lives scattered to the winds and the wolves! My eldest daughter, the light of my old age, vanished!"

There was a time and not long ago, Fedj always thought

3

sourly at this point, when that daughter's disappearance would have been considered a blessing, not a curse, but the djinn—not wanting to prolong the torture—always forbore mentioning that.

The whining and handwringing escalated into loud exhortation and breast-beating, silently punctuated by the inward comments of the long-suffering djinn.

"Why have you done this to me, *Hazrat* Akhran? I, Jaafar al Widjar, have faithfully obeyed every one of your commands without question!"

Without question, master? And I'm the son of a she-goat!

"Did I not bring my daughter, my precious jewel with the eyes of a gazelle—"

And the disposition of a starving leopard!

"—to be wed to the son of my ancient enemy—may camels trod upon his head—Sheykh Majiid al Fakhar, and did I not further bring my people to live around this cursed Tel by your command, and further, did we not reside here in peace with our enemy as was your will, *Hazrat* Akhran, or would have lived in peace had not we been pushed beyond provocation by the thieving Akar—"

Who, for some reason, took it into their heads to be outraged by the Hrana's "peaceful" stealing of Akar horses.

"And have we not suffered at the hands of our enemies? Our wives and children swept from our arms by the soldiers of the Amir and held prisoner in the city! Our camp destroyed, the water in the oasis dwindling daily before our eyes—"

Fedj rolled his eyes, sighing, and—knowing there was no help for it—entered the tent of his master, catching him in mid-harangue.

"—and still you insist that we stay here, in this place where not even Sul could long live while we wait for some accursed plant—whose brown and dried-up appendages are beginning to look as wasted as my own—to bloom? To *bloom?* Roses will sprout from my chin sooner than they will from that sand-sucking cacti!" shouted Jaafar, shaking a feeble fist at heaven.

The temptation to actually summon forth blooms from the old man's grizzled chin was so acute that Fedj squirmed in an agony of torment. But now the exhorting and fist shaking had ceased. It was always followed by sniveling contrition and groveling. Fedj tensed. He knew what was coming.

"Forgive me, *Hazrat* Akhran." Jaafar prostrated himself, nosefirst on the felt floor of his tent. "It is only that your will is harsh and difficult for us poor mortals to understand, and since it seems likely that we will all perish from the harshness and the difficulty, I beg of you"—a beady eye, peering out from the folds of the *haik*, fixed itself intently upon the djinn—"to release us from the vow and let us leave this accursed place and return to our flocks in the foothills. . . ."

Fedj shook his head.

The beady eye became pleading.

"I await your answer most humbly, *Hazrat* Akhran," Jaafar mumbled into the tent floor.

"The God has given you his answer," said Fedj in grim and dour tones. "You are to remain camped at the Tel, in peace with your cousins, until the Rose of the Prophet blooms."

"It will bloom on our graves!" Jaafar beat his fists into the ground.

"If so, then so be it. All praise to the wisdom of Akhran."

"All praise to the wisdom of Akhran!" Jaafar mimicked. Leaping to his scrawny legs, he made a pounce at the djinn. "I want to hear from Akhran himself, not from one of his messengers who has a full belly while I starve! Go find the God. Bring him to me! And don't come back until you do!"

With a meek *salaam*, Fedj took his leave. At least this command was a change and gave the djinn something to do, plus leave to be gone a long time doing it. Standing outside the charred and tattered remnants of what had once been a large and comfortable dwelling place, Fedj could hear Jaafar raving and cursing in a manner that would have done his wild daughter credit. Fedj stole a glance across the desert, on the opposite side of the Tel, where stood the tent of Majiid al Fakhar, Jaafar's old enemy. The sides of Jaafar's tent heaved and quivered with the old man's anger like a living, breathing entity. By contrast, Majiid's tent seemed a husk whose life juices had been sucked dry.

Fedj thought back to the time, only months before, when it had been the giant Majiid—proud of his people and his warrior son—who had thundered his rage to the dunes. Now Majiid's people were imprisoned in Kich; his warrior son was at best dead, at worst a craven coward skulking about in the desert. The giant was a broken man who rarely came forth from his tent.

More than once Fedj wished he had not been so quick to carry to his master his sighting of Khardan, eldest son of Majiid and Calif of the Akar, slinking away from the battle of the Tel, hiding from the soldiers in the rose-colored silk of a woman's *chador*. Certainly if he had foreseen the wreckage of spirits and valor that would follow after—far worse than any damage done by the Amir's soldiers—the djinn would have peppered his tongue with fire ants and swallowed it before he spoke.

Wholly dispirited, Fedj wandered aimlessly in the desert, soon leaving the Tel far behind. The djinn might have acted on his master's order and gone out to search for Akhran, but Fedj knew that the Wandering God could be found only when he wanted to be found, and in that instance, Fedj would not have to look very far or very hard. But Akhran had not made himself visible for months. Fedj knew that something was going on in the heavenly plane. Just what, he didn't know and couldn't guess. The tension hung in the air like a circling vulture, casting the shadow of its black wings over every act. It was extremely unfair of Jaafar to accuse the djinn of feasting while his master starved. Fedj hadn't dined well in weeks.

Drifting through the ethers, far from camp, absorbed in gloomy thoughts and forebodings, the djinn was jolted out of his grim contemplations by the sight of unusual activity on the desert floor beneath him. A sparse scattering of tents had sprouted during the night where the djinn could have sworn there had been no tents yesterday. It took him only a moment to realize where he had traveled. He was at the southern well that marked the boundary of Akar land. And there, camped around the well, using Majiid's water, was another old enemy— Sheykh Zeid!

Thinking that this encroachment upon Majiid's precious water might bring the dispirited Sheykh back to life, the djinn was just considering how he should impart the news to one who was not his master and, moreover, an enemy, when he caught sight of a form coalescing in the air in front of him.

"Raja?" questioned Fedj warily, his hand straying to the hilt of the huge saber at his side.

The heavily muscled, dusky-skinned body of Sheykh Zeid's djinn, also with hand on sword hilt, shimmered before Fedj in waves of heat rising from the sand.

"Fedj?" queried the other djinn, floating nearer.

"It is Fedj, as you well know, unless your sight has taken the same path as your wits and fled!" Fedj said angrily. "That water you drink is from the well of Sheykh Majiid! Your master is, of course, aware that all who drink that water without the Sheykh's permission soon find their thirst quenched by drinking their own blood."

"My master drinks where he will, and those who try to stop him will end their days filling the bellies of jackals!" Raja growled.

Scimitars flared yellow in the sun, gold flashed from earrings and arm bracelets, sweat glistened on bare chests as the djinn crouched in the air, watching, waiting. . . .

Then suddenly, Raja hurled his scimitar from him with a bitter curse. It went spiraling, unheeded, down through the sky to land with a thud, carving a sword-shaped ravine in the Pagrah desert that remains a mystery to all who see it to this day.

"Slay me where I stand!" shouted Raja. Tears streamed down his face. Spreading wide his arms, he thrust forth his dark-skinned chest. "Kill me now, Fedj. I will lift no hand to stop you!"

Though the effectiveness of this display was somewhat blunted by the fact that the djinn was immortal and Fedj might run his scimitar through Raja a thousand times without doing him any harm, it was a noble gesture and one that touched Fedj to the core of his soul.

"My friend, what does this mean?" Fedj cried aghast, lowering his weapon and approaching Raja, not without a certain degree of caution. Like his master, Zeid, the warrior djinn Raja was a cunning old dog who might still have a tooth or two left in his head.

But as he drew nearer, Fedj saw that Raja was truly little

more than a whipped pup. The husky djinn's despair was so obvious and real that Fedj sheathed his weapon and immediately put his arm comfortingly around the massive, heaving shoulders.

"My friend, do not carry on so!" said Fedj, distressed by the sight of this grief. "Matters cannot be this bad!"

"Oh, can't they?" cried Raja fiercely, shaking his head until his huge, golden earrings jangled against his jaw. "Tell Sheykh Majiid that Zeid is stealing his water! Bring him to fight, as would have happened in past months, and he will have the very great satisfaction of watching my master slink on his belly back into the desert where he will shrivel up and die like a lizard!"

Fedj could easily have sworn that he would do just that. He could have gloated over Zeid's downfall and glorified Majiid to the skies. But he chose not to. Raja's pitiable plight was deeply akin to his own, and Fedj guessed that Raja must know something of the true circumstances of his enemies, or he would not have revealed such weakness, no matter what his own inner turmoil.

The djinn heaved a sigh that shifted the location of several sand dunes.

"Alas, friend Raja. I will not hide from you that Sheykh Majiid would not raise his voice in anger if your master came into his tent and gouged out his eyes. And *my* Sheykh has taken to cursing the God, which does no one any good since we all know that the ears of *Hazrat* Akhran are stuffed with sand these days."

Raja lifted a grim face. "So it is true, what we have heard—that Majiid and Jaafar are in a situation almost as desperate as our own?"

"Almost!" said Fedj, suddenly indignant. "No situation can possibly be more desperate than the one in which *we* find ourselves. We have taken to eating the camp dogs!"

"Is that so?" said Raja, with growing anger. "Well, camp dog would seem a treat to us! We have taken to eating snake!"

"We ate the last camp dog yesterday, and since *we* have devoured every snake in the desert, we shall soon be forced to eat—"

The air was split by what to a mortal would have appeared to be a tremendous bolt of lightning streaking from heaven to the ground below. The two djinn, however, saw flailing arms and legs and heard an explosive curse boom in a voice of thunder. Recognizing one of their own, both djinn swallowed their words (more nourishing than either snake or dog) and immediately accosted the singed and smoking stranger who lay on his back, breathing heavily, at the bottom of a dune.

"Arise and declare yourself. Name your master and tell us what he is doing in the lands of the Akar and the Aran!" demanded Raja and Fedj.

Undaunted, the strange djinn rose to his feet, his own sword in his hand. Noting the richness of this djinn's clothing, the jewel-encrusted weapon he bore, and his air of superiority that was not put on as one puts on a caftan, but was inborn, both Fedj and Raja exchanged uneasy glances.

"My master's name is not important to the likes of you here on this plane," stated the djinn coolly.

"You serve one of the Elders?" asked Fedj in subdued tones, while Raja instantly made the *salaam*.

"I do!" said the djinn, glaring at them severely. "And I would ask why two such able-bodied men as yourselves are skulking about down here below when there is work to be done above?"

"Work? What do you mean?" said Raja, bristling. "We skulk down here below in service to our masters—"

"—when there is a war in heaven?"

"War!" Both djinn stared at the stranger.

"The plane of the immortals has erupted in fire," said the strange djinn grimly. "By some means, the Lost Immortals were discovered and freed from their imprisonment. The Goddess Evren and her counterpart, the God Zhakrin, have also come back to life and both accuse Quar of attempting to destroy them! Some of the Gods support Quar, others attack him. We fight for our very existence! Have you heard nothing of this?"

"No, nothing, by Akhran!" swore Fedj.

Raja shook his head, his earrings clashing discordantly.

"It is not to be wondered, I suppose," reflected the

stranger, "considering the chaos up there. But now that you know, there is no time to be lost. You must come! We need every sword. Quar's 'efreet Kaug grows in strength moment by moment!"

"But if all immortals leave the mortal realm, what dreadful things will happen down here?"

"Better that than if the immortal realm collapses," said the stranger. "For that will mean the end of all."

"I must tell my master," said Fedj, his brow knitting.

"As must I," stated Raja.

"And then we will join you."

The strange djinn nodded and leapt back into the heavens, creating a gigantic whirlwind that swept the sand into a billowing cloud. Exchanging grim glances, Fedj and Raja both disappeared, their going marked by two simultaneous explosions that blasted holes in the granite and sent concussive waves throughout the Pagrah desert.

Chapter 2

The lookout ran wildly across the desert sand, often stumbling, falling, picking himself back up and running again. As he ran, he shouted, and soon every man remaining in the decimated tribes of Sheykhs Jaafar and Majiid had left the shelter of their tents and was watching the lookout's approach with tense interest. He was an Akar, a member of Sheykh Majiid's tribe, and he was on foot rather than horseback. The few horses remaining—those who had been found wandering in the desert after being cut loose by the soldiers of the Amir—were considered more precious than all the jewels in a Sultan's treasury and were rarely ridden.

One of these horses was Majiid's own, the story being told that after the stallion's master had fallen in battle, the gallant horse stood guard above the body of his rider, fighting off the soldiers with vicious, slashing hooves. Another of the horses remaining was Khardan's. No man could get near him. Any who tried were warned away with a flattening of the ears and bared teeth and a low rumbling sound in the massive chest of the black charger. But Khardan's horse remained near camp, often seen at dusk or at twilight, a ghostly black shadow among the dunes. The fanciful claimed this meant that Khardan was dead, his spirit had entered the horse, and

11

he was guarding his people. The practical said that the stallion would never wander far from his mares.

The lookout stumbled into camp. He was met with a *girba* filled with tepid water, which he drank thirstily but sparingly, being careful not to waste a drop. Then he approached Majiid's silent tent. The flap was closed, a sign that the Sheykh was not to be disturbed. It had been closed almost continuously since word came of Khardan's disgrace and his father had broken his son's sword and declared him dead.

"My Sheykh," cried the man. "I bear tidings."

There was no reply.

The lookout glanced around uncertainly, and several of the other men motioned him forward, urging him with gestures to continue.

"*Effendi*," continued the lookout desperately, "Sheykh Zeid and his people are camped around the southern well!"

A low murmur, like wind among the sands, ran through the Akar. The Hrana, led by Sheykh Jaafar who had come out of his tent to see what was transpiring, glanced at each other wordlessly. This was war. Surely, if there was one thing that could rouse Majiid from his grief, it would be this unwarranted invasion of his territory by his ancient enemy.

The mutterings of the Akar swelled to angered talk of defiance, accented by loud calls for their Sheykh, and at length the tent flap opened.

Silence descended so abruptly, it seemed the men must have had the breath sucked from their throats. Those who had not seen Majiid in some time averted their heads, tears welling up in their eyes. The man had aged a decade, it seemed, for every month that had passed since the raid upon the Tel. The tall, strong frame was bent and stooped. The sharp, fierce gaze of the black eyes was bleary and lackluster. The bristling mustaches drooped beneath the hawk nose that was now as white and wasted as bare bone.

But Majiid was Sheykh still, respected leader of his tribe. The lookout fell to his knees, out of either reverence or exhaustion, while several of the *aksakal,* tribal elders, stepped forward to discuss this news.

Majiid cut their words off with a weary movement of his hand. "Do nothing."

Nothing! The *aksakal* stared at each other, the men of the Akar glowered, and Jaafar frowned, shaking his head. Hearing the unspoken defiance, Majiid glared round at them, the dark eyes flashing with sudden fire.

"Would you fight, fools?" he sneered. "How?" He gestured toward the oasis. "Where are the horses to carry you to battle? Where is the water for your *girba?* Will you fight Zeid with swords that are broken?"

"Yes!" cried one man passionately. "If my Sheykh wills it!"

"Yes! Yes!" shouted the others.

Majiid lowered his head. The lookout remained on his knees, staring up at him pleadingly, and it seemed for a moment that the Sheykh would say something more. His mouth moved, but no words came out. With another weary, hopeless gesture of a wasted hand, Majiid turned back to his tent.

"Wait!" called Sheykh Jaafar, striding forward on his short, bandy legs, his robes flowing about him. "I say we bid Zeid come speak with us."

The lookout gaped. Majiid glared, his lips meeting his beaky nose in a scowl. "Why not invite the Amir as well. Hrana?" he snarled. "Exhibit our weakness to the world!"

"The world knows already," snapped Jaafar. "What's the matter, Akar? Did your brains leave with your horses? If Zeid was strong, would he skulk about the southern well? Wouldn't he come riding in here to take this oasis, which all know is the richest in the Pagrah? Tell us what you have seen." Jaafar turned to the lookout. "Describe the camp of our cousin."

"It is not large, *Effendi,*" said the lookout, speaking to Majiid, though he answered Jaafar. "They have hardly any camels. The tents of our cousins are few in number and are put up halfheartedly, straggling about the desert floor like men drunk on *qumiz.*"

"See? Zeid is as weak as we are!"

"It is a trick," Majiid said heavily.

Jaafar snorted. "For what purpose? I say Zeid has arrived for this very reason—to talk to us. We should talk to him!"

"What about?"

The words fell from Majiid's lips as meat falls from the hand of a man baiting a trap. All there knew it, including Jaafar, and no one spoke, moved, or even breathed, waiting to see if he would nibble at it.

Jaafar did more than that. He calmly swallowed it whole.

"Surrender," the old man answered.

"One by one," said Sheykh Zeid, "the southern cities of Bas have fallen in the *jihad*. The Amir is a skilled general, as I have said before, who weakens his enemy from within and hits them with the force of a thunderbolt from without. Those who surrender to Quar are treated with mercy. Only their priests and priestesses are put to the sword. But those who defy . . ." Zeid sighed, his fingers aimlessly plucking at the hem of his robe as he sat cross-legged on the frayed cushions in Sheykh Jaafar's tent.

"Well," prodded Jaafar. "Those who defy?"

"In Bastine," Zeid said in low tones, his eyes cast down, "five thousand died! Man, woman, and child!"

"Akhran forbid it!" Jaafar cried, shocked.

Majiid stirred. "What did you expect?" he asked harshly, the first time he had spoken since Zeid had ridden into camp. The three men sat together, sharing a meager dinner that only two of them made even a pretense of eating. "The Amir means to make Quar the One, True God. And perhaps he deserves it."

"The djinn say there is a war in heaven, as well as down here," offered Jaafar. "At least that is what Fedj told me before he vanished three days ago."

"That is what Raja told me as well," Zeid agreed morosely. "And if that is true, then I fear *Hazrat* Akhran is being hard-pressed. Not even the *sirocco* to plague us this year. Our God lacks spirit." Sighing, the Sheykh shoved his food dish aside; its scant contents were instantly snatched up and devoured by what few servants Jaafar had remaining.

Majiid seemed not to hear the sigh. Jaafar did, and gave Zeid a piercing glance but said nothing, it being considered impolite to interrogate a guest.

The conversation turned to the dark events of the tribe.

Zeid's people had fared much the same as the rest of the desert nomads in the battle with the Amir.

"All the women and children and most of my young men, including six of my sons, are being held captive in the city of Kich," said the Sheykh, whose clothes hung loosely on a body that had formerly been rotund. "My men eat their hearts out with worry, and I will not hide that I have lost more than a few—gone to the city to be with their families. And who can blame them? Our camels were captured by the Amir and now serve his army. I note that your horses are few. Your sheep?" He turned to Jaafar.

"Butchered," the little man said, eyes rimmed red with grief and anger. "Oh, some survived, those that we were able to hide from the soldiers. But not nearly enough. What I don't understand is why the Amir didn't just butcher all of us as well!"

"He wants living souls for Quar," said Zeid dryly. "Or at least he did. Now, from what I hear, that's changed. And not with Qannadi's wish or approval, if rumor be true. The Imam, this Feisal, is the one who has ordered that all who are conquered either convert or die."

"Humpf!" Majiid sneered skeptically.

Zeid shook his head. "Qannadi is a military man. He does not relish murder. I am told that he refused to give the order for his troops to kill innocent people in Bastine and that the Imam's priests were forced to do it themselves. I heard also that some of the soldiers rebelled against the slaughter, and that now the Imam has an army of fanatical followers of his own who obey him without question. It is said, Majiid," Zeid chose his words carefully and kept his eyes lowered, "that your son, Achmed, is very close to Qannadi."

"I have no son," said Majiid tonelessly.

Zeid glanced at Jaafar, who shrugged. The Hrana Sheykh was not particularly interested in this. He knew Zeid was purposefully withholding bad news and wished impatiently he would spit it out.

"Then it is true that Khardan is dead?" asked Zeid, treading more cautiously still. "I extend my sympathies. May he ride forever with Akhran who, it seems, may have taken him specifically to be at his side in the heavenly war." The

Sheykh paused, expecting a reply to what everyone in the tent knew was a polite fiction. Zeid had heard—as he heard everything—the story of Khardan's disappearance, and had circumstances been less dire and he not been a guest in the camp, the Sheykh would have taken grim delight in pricking the flesh of his enemy with gossip's poisoned dagger. But with a much larger sword at their throats, there was no sense in that now.

Majiid said nothing. His face, so heavily lined it might have been scarred by the slashing strokes of a sabre, remained unchanged. But it seemed from the glitter in his eyes that he was listening, and so Zeid continued, though whether he was spreading balm on a wound or rubbing salt into it, he had no idea.

"But it is Achmed of whom I have heard reports. Your second son, it seems, though captured with the others, now rides with the armies of the Amir. Achmed has become a valiant warrior, I hear, whose deeds have won the respect and admiration of those with whom he rides—those who were once his enemies. They say he saved Qannadi's life when the general's horse was killed beneath him and the Amir was left on foot, surrounded by the Bastinites who were fighting like ten thousand devils. Qannadi had become separated from his bodyguard in the confusion, and only Achmed remained, sitting his horse with the skill for which the Akar are famous, fighting single-handedly all attackers until the Amir could mount up behind him and the guard was able to break through and rescue them. Qannadi made Achmed a Captain, a great thing for one only eighteen."

"Captain in an army of *kafir!*" Majiid shouted, bursting out with such pent-up rage that the servants dropped the food bowls they had been licking and cowered back into the shadows of the tent. "Better he were dead!" he thundered. "Better we all were dead!"

Jaafar's eyes opened wide at such blasphemy, and he instantly made the sign against evil, not once but several times over. Zeid made it, too, but more slowly, and as his lips parted reluctantly to speak, Jaafar knew his cousin was going to impart the news that had been resting so heavily upon his heart.

"I have one other piece of news. Indeed, it was in the hope—or fear—of relating it to you that I came to camp at the southern well."

"Out with it!" Jaafar said impatiently.

"In a month's time the army of the Amir returns to Kich. The Imam has decreed that we must come into the city and reside there in the future, and furthermore that we give our allegiance to Quar or—" Zeid paused.

"Or what?" Majiid demanded grimly, irritated at the Sheykh's dramatics.

"In one month's time, our people will die."

Chapter 3

Kneeling beside the *hauz*, Meryem threw the goatskin *girba* into the public water pool with an irritable gesture that sent the water splashing and brought a disdainful glare of disapproval from a wealthy man watering his donkey near her. Flicking imagined drops from the fabric of his fine robes, he trotted off toward the *souk* with muttered curses.

Meryem ignored him. Though her bag was filled, she lingered by the *hauz*, indolently dabbling her hand in the water, watching the passersby and basking in the obvious admiration of two palace guards who happened to be sauntering through this part of the city of Kich. They did not recognize her—one reason she was using this *hauz* located at the far end of town instead of the one near the palace—for which Meryem was thankful. Last week several of the Amir's concubines and their eunuch, visiting the bazaars, had seen her and recognized her. Of course they had not given her away. They knew she was doing some sort of secretive work for Yamina, wife of the Amir and ruler of Kich in her husband's absence. But Meryem heard their giggles. The veils covering their faces could not cover their smiles of derision. The eunuch had smirked all over his fat body and, under the excuse of pretending to assist her, had the effrontery to lean down and whisper, "I understand the dirt of

18

manual labor, once ground into your pores, never washes out. You might, however, try lemon juice on your hands, my dear.''

Lemon juice! To a daughter of the Emperor!

Meryem had slapped the man who was no longer a man, causing one matronly woman to come fluttering to her aid, waving her hands and shouting at the eunuch to be off and leave decent women alone. Of course this brought only more laughter from the concubines and an affected stare of offended dignity from the eunuch, who flounced off to regale his charges with his cleverness.

Since then Meryem traveled far out of her way each day to fetch water. When Badia questioned the girl about the unusual amount of time she was taking in her task, Meryem said only that she had been harassed by soldiers of the Amir. Badia, mindful of Meryem's supposed history as the wretched daughter of a murdered Sultan, said nothing more to the girl. Meryem gnashed her teeth and plotted revenge. The eunuch especially. She had something very special planned for him.

But that was in the future—a future that held for her . . . what? Once she had thought she knew. The future held Khardan, *she* held Khardan. Khardan was to be Amir of Kich and she his favorite wife, ruler of his harem. That had been her dearest dream only months before when she was living in the nomad camp and saw Khardan every day and yearned after him every night. One of the hundreds of daughters of an Emperor who did not even know her name, given as a gift to the Emperor's favorite general, Abul Qasim Qannadi, Meryem was accustomed to giving herself to men without pleasure. But in Khardan she had discovered a man she wanted, a man who gave *her* pleasure, or at least so she dreamed, having been thwarted in her attempts to bring Khardan to her bed—a circumstance that had added red-hot coals to her already raging fire.

But the Amir's attack on the nomad camp had wreaked havoc on hundreds, not the least of which was Meryem. At first it seemed ideally suited to her plans. She had given Khardan a charm that caused him to fall into a deathlike sleep in the midst of battle. Spiriting him away, she had intended to bring him to Kich, where she planned to have him all to

herself and gradually lead him—through ways in which she
was highly skilled—to help her overthrow the Amir. But that
red-haired madman and the black-eyed witch-wife of the
Calif had literally knocked Meryem's plans right out of her
head. They had taken Khardan away, somewhere beyond
Meryem's magical sight. Now she was back among the nomads, pretending to be captive as they were captive in the
city of Kich, living a dreary life of drudgery and toil, and
spending each night looking into her scrying bowl, hoping to
see Khardan.

She no longer burned with lust when she spoke his name,
however. Without his physical presence to fan the flames, the
fire of her passion had long since cooled, as had her ambition. The only emotion she felt now upon speaking his name
softly when she looked into the bowl of enchanted water was
fear.

*Know this, my child. If I hear his name on the tongue of
another before I hear it on yours, I will have that tongue torn
from your mouth.*

Thus had spoken Feisal, the Imam.

Staring into the water of the *hauz*, Meryem heard those
words again and shuddered so violently that ripples of water
spread from her shaking hand. It was *aseur*, after sunset,
nearing evening. She could hear the sounds of the bazaars
closing for the night—the merchants stowing wares away,
endeavoring to politely hurry the last few straggling shoppers
before slamming shut their stalls. Badia and the others would
be waiting for her; the water was needed for cooking dinner,
a task with which she would be expected to help. Sighing
bitterly, Meryem hefted the slippery goatskin and began to
lug it back through the crowded, narrow streets of Kich to the
hovel in which the nomads lived by the grace of the Amir.

She looked at her hands and wondered if what the eunuch
had said was true. Would the filth and dirt ever wash out?
Would the hard spots on fingers and palms fade away? If not,
what man would want her?

"This night, I *will* see Khardan!" Meryem muttered to
herself beneath her breath. "I will leave this place and, with
Feisal's reward, return to the palace!"

*   *   *

The house was dark and silent. The six women and their numerous small children who were crowded into the tiny dwelling were wrapped in their blankets, asleep. Squatting on the floor, hunched over a bowl of water that she held in her lap between her crossed legs, Meryem sat with her back to the others, the folds of her robes carefully concealing her work. Occasionally, in a murmuring voice, the girl would speak a prayer to Akhran, the God of these wretched nomads. Should any of the women waken, they would see and hear Meryem bowed in pious prayer.

In reality, she was working magic.

The water in the bowl was black with the shadows of night. If the moon shone, no ray of its light could penetrate for there were no windows in the buildings that piled up on top of each other like toys thrown down by a child in a tantrum. There was only a door, carved into the baked clay, that stood always open during the day and was covered by a woven cloth at night. Meryem did not need light, however.

Closing her eyes, she whispered—between the tossed-off empty prayers to Akhran—arcane words, interspersed at the proper intervals with the name of Khardan. When she had recited the spell three times, taking care to speak each word clearly and properly, Meryem stared into the bowl, holding her breath so as not to disturb the water.

The vision came to her, the same that came every night, and Meryem began to curse in her heart when suddenly she halted. The vision was changing!

There was the *kavir*—a salt desert, glittering harshly in the blazing sunlight. And there was that incredibly blue body of water whose gentle waves washed up on the white sand shore. Often she had seen this sight and tried to look beyond, for she knew in her heart that Khardan was here, somewhere. But always before, just when it seemed she would see him, a dark cloud had fallen before her vision. Now, however, no cloud marred her sight. Watching intently, her heart beating so she feared its thudding must waken the slumbering women, Meryem saw a boat sailing over the blue water to land upon the salt shore. She saw a man . . . the red-haired madman, it was, curse him! step from the boat. She saw three djinn, a little dried-up weasel of a man and one other, dressed in strange armor. . . .

Yes! Khardan!

Meryem shivered in excitement. He and the red-haired madman were helping to lift someone else from the floor of the boat. It was Zohra, Khardan's wife. Meryem prayed to Quar it was Zohra's corpse they were handling with such gentleness, but she dare not spare time to find out. Her hands trembling with eager delight, she quietly rose to her feet, dumped the water onto the dirt floor, and—wrapping her veil closely about her face—slipped out into the empty streets. Glancing around, to make certain she was alone, Meryem reached into the bosom of her robes. She drew forth a crystal of black tourmaline, carved in the shape of a triangle, that hung around her neck on a silver chain.

Lifting the gem to the heavens, Meryem whispered, "Kaug, minion of Quar, I have need of your service. Take me, with the speed of the wind, to the city of Bastine. I must speak to the Imam."

Chapter 4

Achmed climbed the seemingly endless marble stairs that led to the Temple of Quar in the captive city of Bastine. Formerly the Temple of the God Uevin in the free capital of the land of Bas, Quar's usurped place of worship was—to Achmed's eyes—extremely ugly. Massive, many-columned, composed of sharp angles and squared corners, the Temple lacked the grace and delicate loveliness of the spires and minarets and latticework that adorned Quar's Temple in Kich. The Imam, too, detested the Temple and would have had it torn down on the spot, but Qannadi intervened.

"The people of Bastine have been forced to stomach enough bitter medicine—"

"For the good of their souls," Feisal interposed piously.

"Of course," returned the Amir, and if there was a twist to the corner of his mouth, he was careful that only Achmed saw it. "But let us cure the patient, not poison him, Imam. I do not have the manpower to put down a rebellion. When the reinforcements from the Emperor arrive in a month's time, then you may tear down the Temple."

Feisal glowered; his black eyes in the sunken hollows of his wasted face blazed with his anger, but he could say nothing. By making the matter of the Temple's destruction a military one, Qannadi had snatched it neatly out of the priest's hands. Though a religious man, the Emperor of Tara-kan was also a very practical man who was enjoying the wealth of the newly acquired territory of Bas. What's more, the Emperor trusted and admired his general, Abul Qasim Qannadi, implicitly. Should Feisal choose to appeal the Amir's decision, the Imam would receive no support from his Emperor, and that was the priest's final authority here on earth.

As for appealing it to the Highest Authority? If Feisal had been praying to Quar for an enemy arrow to embed itself in the Amir's chest, no one knew of it but the Imam and the God. And apparently the God, too, was satisfied with the work Qannadi was performing in His Holy Name, for the only time the Amir had been in serious danger during the entire campaign, the young man Achmed had been there to rescue him. The Imam had publicly offered thanks to Quar for this heroic feat, but both priest and God must have found it ironic that a follower of Akhran (albeit former follower) had been instrumental in saving Qannadi's life.

Pausing upon the fifth landing in the long line of stairs leading up to the Temple, Achmed turned to look at the crowd of people waiting patiently in the heat of late morning to hold audience with the Imam. The young man wondered at Qannadi's decision. There were no signs of rebellion that he could see, as in former cities they had captured. There were no threatening slogans scrawled on the walls in the night, no defacing of Quar's altars, no mysterious fires started in abandoned buildings. Despite the fact that her soldiers had fought a bitter and bloody battle and lost, the city of Bastine appeared only too pleased to be under the rulership of the Emperor and his God. Undoubtedly the immediate reopening of trade routes between Tara-kan and Bastine and the subsequent flow of wealth into the city had something to do with it, as did the other blessings of Quar that were being showered upon the heads of those who converted to him.

That was the honey the people of Bastine fed upon now. The bitter herb they had been forced to swallow was the slaughter of five thousand neighbors, friends, relatives. As long as he slept the dream-troubled sleep of the living, Achmed would remember that awful day. And he knew that no one in this city would ever forget it either. But were these people ruled by fear? The young man looked at the lines of suppliants and shook his head. Climbing the remaining three flights of stairs, he exchanged greetings with the Amir's guards posted there and, entering through a side door, walked into the cool, shadowy confines of the Temple.

Seated upon his throne of carved *saksaul* wood that had been carted the length and breadth of the land of Bas, the Imam was holding his daily *divan*. Behind him, mounted upon a dais, the golden ram's head of Quar gleamed in the light of a perpetual flame that burned at its base. Smoke drifted up in lazy spirals, and although the fresco-decorated ceiling was high above them, the odor of incense in the closed confines of the Temple audience chamber was heady and overpowering. Feisal's newly formed soldier-priests were stationed at the main entrance to the audience chamber, keeping the crowds of suppliants in order, permitting each to advance only when the Imam gave the sign.

Although Achmed kept himself invisible in the shadows, he had the uncanny impression that Feisal knew he was here; he could even swear that when he looked away, the burning black eyes fixed their intense, soul-searing gaze upon him. But whenever Achmed confronted the priest, the Imam's attention seemed centered solely upon the supplicant kneeling before him.

What fascination draws me here? Achmed could not say, and every day when he left, he vowed he would not return. Yet the next day found him climbing the stairs, slipping in through the side door so regularly that the guards had become accustomed to his visitations and no longer even raised their eyebrows at each other when Achmed walked past.

The young soldier took up his usual position, leaning against a cracked pillar near the side door; a position where he could see and hear, yet remain unseen and unheard; a position that was generally isolated. Today, however, Achmed was startled to find someone else standing near his pillar. His eyes growing accustomed to the darkness after the glare of the sun outside, the young man saw who it was, and the blood mounted into his face. Bowing, he was about to withdraw, but Qannadi motioned him near.

"So this is where you spend your mornings when you should be out drilling with the cavalry." The Amir spoke softly, though the chattering and praying and occasional arguments among the waiting supplicants was such that it was unlikely he could have been overheard if he had shouted.

Achmed sought to reply, but his tongue seemed swollen and incapable of producing coherent sounds. Noting the young man's discomfiture, Qannadi smiled the wry smile that was little more than a deepening of the lines on one side of the thin-lipped mouth. Achmed moved to stand beside the general.

"Are you angry, sir? The cavalry is doing well without me—"

"No, I'm not angry. The men have learned all that you have taught them. I drill them only to keep them alert and ready for"—the Amir paused and glanced at Achmed through shrewd eyes surrounded by a maze of wrinkles—"for whatever may come next."

Now it was Qannadi who flushed, the color deepening in his sunburned skin. The general knew that the next battle might be against the boy's people—Achmed's people. His gaze shifted from Achmed to the Imam. This was a subject neither discussed, though it was always there, following them as carrion birds follow an army.

The Amir heard the buckles attached to the young man's leather armor jingle as he shifted restlessly.

"Why don't you let the Imam tear down this ugly place, sir?" Achmed said in an undertone, his voice covered by the shrill arguments of two men accusing each other of cheating in the sale of a donkey. "There is no hint of rebellion in this town. Look, look at that!"

The young soldier nodded his head in the direction of the two men. Quar only knew how, Qannadi thought in grudging admiration, but Feisal had settled the argument to the satisfaction of each, apparently, to judge by their smiles as they left the presence of the priest.

"These people worship him!"

"Think about what you said, my son, and you will understand," replied the Amir as the Imam, seated on his throne, raised a frail hand in Quar's blessing.

"You are right, of course," Qannadi continued. "Feisal

could tear the city down around their heads, stone by stone, and the citizens would cry their thanks to him. With his words, he turned murder into a benediction. They praised him as he butchered their friends, their neighbors, their relatives. Praised him for saving the souls of the unworthy! Do they line up to bring their problems to me to judge? Am I not Governor of this wretched city, proclaimed so by the Emperor? No, they bring their dealings with donkeys, and their quarrels with their wives, and their disputes with their neighbors to him.''

"And would you have it any other way, sir?" Achmed asked gently.

Qannadi cast him a sharp glance. "No," he admitted, after a moment. "I am a soldier. I've never been anything else, nor do I pretend to be. No one will be more grateful than I when the Emperor's regent comes to take over this city and we can return to Kich. But in the meantime, I must make certain that I have a city to turn over to him."

Achmed's eyes opened wide. "Surely the Imam would not—" He hesitated to speak. The thought alone was dangerous enough.

Qannadi spoke it. "—defy the Emperor?" The Amir shrugged. "Quar's power in heaven grows. So do the number of the Imam's followers. If Feisal chose to do so, he could split my army today, and he knows it. But it would be only a split. He could not gain the loyalty of the entire force. Not yet. Maybe in a year, maybe two. There will be nothing I can do to stop him. And when that day comes, Feisal will march triumphant into the capital city of Khandar with millions of fanatics behind him. No, if I were the Emperor, I would not sit easy on my throne. Why, boy, what's the matter?"

Achmed's face was pale, ghostly in the shadowy darkness. "And you?" he said, his voice cracking. "What will— He wouldn't commit—"

"Murder? In the name of Quar? Haven't we seen that done already?" Qannadi laid a comforting hand on the young man's trembling shoulder. "Do not fear. This old dog knows enough not to take meat from Feisal's hand."

That much was true—a simple precaution. Qannadi never ate or drank anything that had not been tasted first by some man paid well enough to risk poisoning. But a knife thrust from behind—that, no one can fight. And it would surely be the work of a lone fanatic. No one would appear more shocked at an assassination than Feisal himself.

"There is no dishonor in retreating from a fight with God," Qannadi continued, lying to put to rest the boy's fears. "When the day comes that I see I am defeated, I will pack my *khurjin* and ride away. Perhaps I will go north, back to the land of the Great Steppes. They will soon have need of soldiers—"

"You would go alone?" Achmed asked, his heart in his eyes.

Yes, boy. God willing, I will go alone.

"Not if there are those who would bear the hardships with me," Qannadi replied. Seeing Achmed's pleasure, a true smile, a deep smile, warmed the Amir's dark expression. But it lasted only briefly and then disappeared, the sun shining for an instant before the storm clouds banished its rays. "In many ways, I look forward to that, to the freedom, to being rid of the responsibility," he said with a soft sigh. "But that time will be long in coming, I fear. Long for all of us." And bitter, he added, but once again only to himself.

Does the boy know the horror he faces? Does he truly comprehend the threat to himself and to his people? I have adopted him as son in all but name only. I can protect him, *will* protect him, with all the power I have left. But I cannot save his people.

Qannadi did not regret attacking the nomads; that had been a sound military decision. He could not have marched south on Bas with his right flank unprotected, thousands of those wild desert fighters yearning after his blood. But he did regret falling into the Imam's scheme of bringing the people into the city and holding them captive. Far better that he had fought them to the death. At least they would have died with honor.

Ah, well, thought Qannadi wryly. If Khardan is dead—as he surely must be, despite the Imam's misgivings—the soul of the Calif will soon rest easy enough, seeing me fall in defeat as well. And perhaps his soul will forgive mine, for—if it is my last act—I will save the younger brother the nomad Prince loved.

Or at least, I will try.

Putting his hand on Achmed's shoulder, Qannadi turned and walked silently with the young man from the Temple.

Chapter 5

The Imam saw the Amir's departure from the Temple without seeming to see it or care about it, although in actuality he had been waiting for it with extreme impatience. When the side door had shut behind the two men, Feisal gestured immediately to one of the under priests and said softly, "You may bring her now."

The priest bowed and left.

"The morning's audience is concluded," Feisal said loudly. This started a hubbub among the waiting supplicants. None dared raise his voice in protest, but all were determined that the soldier-priests remember each man's position in line, and clamored for attention. The priests took names and calmly, firmly, forcefully herded Quar's worshipers out the door.

Other priests had hurried outside to impart the news to the supplicants waiting upon the stairs and to swing shut the huge wooden Temple doors. Shrill cries of beggar children rose into the air, offering to hold the places of supplicants in line in exchange for a few pieces of copper. Wealthier citizens took advantage of this to leave the Temple and sustain themselves with a midday meal. The poorer worshiper sought what shade he could while still holding his place in line and munched on balls of rice or hunks of bread, washed down with water supplied by the priests.

30

When the huge doors boomed, shutting out the noise and the daylight, and the room was left to the silent, incense-scented darkness, Feisal rose from the *saksaul* throne and stretched his legs.

He approached the golden ram's head. The altar flame glistened in the unblinking eyes. Looking about him carefully, making certain he was alone, Feisal knelt before the altar, so near the flame that he could feel its heat upon his shaven head. Raising his face, he stared up at the ram. The heat of the coals beat upon his skin; sweat beaded on his lips and rolled down his thin neck, staining the robes that hung on his wasted body.

"Quar, you are mighty, majestic. In your great name we have conquered the land and people of Bas, driven their God into hiding, destroyed his statues, taken his treasure, subverted the faith of his followers! The wealth of these cities goes to further your glory! All is as we dreamed, as we hoped, as we planned!

"So why is it, *Hazrat* Quar—" Feisal hesitated. He licked his dry, cracked lips. "Why is it . . . what is it . . . that you fear!" The words burst out—a hushed, awed gasp.

The fire flared, flames leaped up from the white-hot coals. Instantly, the Imam collapsed, hunching his body as if in pain. Crouching before the altar, he shivered in terror. "Forgive me, Holy One!" he chanted over and over, clasping his thin hands together and rocking back and forth in agony. "Forgive me, forgive me. . . ."

A voice called his name softly. "Imam!" Lifting his eyes, he stared at the ram, thinking for one wild moment that its mouth had moved. But the voice repeated itself, and the priest realized with a pang of disappointment that the sound came from behind him and that it was a mortal who called him, not the God.

Rising shakily to his feet, having forgotten in his religious fervor that he had issued orders, Feisal glared angrily upon the one who had dared interrupt his prayers. Trembling visibly, the young priest shrank before the Imam's wrath. The woman who accompanied him was likewise stricken with terror. The blue eyes above the veil glanced about wildly, and she began to sidle back toward the secret way through which they had entered.

Reveling in the ecstasy of heaven, Feisal realized that he had not been interrupted—the God was choosing to speak to him through human lips.

"Forgive me," the Imam said, and the young priest mistakenly thought his superior was speaking to him.

"It is you who should forgive me, Imam!" The priest sank to his knees. "What I did was unpardonable! It was just . . . you said it was urgent that you talk with the woman—"

"You have done well. Go now and assist your brethren to make easy the waiting time of those who have come to us with their burdens. Meryem, my child." The Imam took her hand, starting slightly at the chill feel of the fingers. His own skin was burning hot. "I trust you have had refreshment after your fatiguing journey?"

"Yes, thank you, Holy One," Meryem murmured inaudibly.

The Imam did not speak again until the young priest had taken himself, bowing and walking backward, from the Temple. Meryem stood before Feisal with lowered eyes. She had removed her hand from his grasp and was nervously twisting the frayed gilt hem of her veil. When they were alone, the Imam remained silent. Meryem lifted her eager, still half-fearful gaze to meet his.

"I have seen him!"

"Who?" Feisal asked coolly, though he knew well enough of whom the woman spoke.

"Khardan," Meryem faltered. "He is alive!"

The Imam turned slightly, with a glance for the ram's head, almost as if to assure himself it was listening. "Where is he? Who is with him?"

"I . . . I don't know where he is," Meryem said, a break in her voice as she saw the Imam frown with displeasure. "But the witch-woman, Zohra, is with him. And so is the red-haired madman. And their djinn."

It seemed to Feisal that the eyes of the ram flickered.

"And you don't know where they are."

"It is a *kavir*, a salt desert, surrounded by blue water—

water that is bluer than the sky. I did not recognize the place, but Kaug says—"

"Kaug!" Feisal looked back at Meryem, his brows lowered ominously.

"Forgive me, Imam! I did not think it would be wrong to tell the 'efreet!" Meryem's tongue ran across her lips, wetting the veil over her mouth. "He . . . he made me, Holy One! Or he refused to bring me here! And I knew you wanted this information most urgently—"

"Very well." The Imam contained his ill humor that was, he realized, nothing more than jealousy of the 'efreet and the honored and trusted position Kaug held with the God. "I am not angry, child. Do not be frightened. Go ahead. What did Kaug say?"

"He said the description matches that of the western shores of the Kurdin Sea. When I saw Khardan, Imam, he was stepping out of a boat—a fishing boat. Kaug says there is a poor fishing village on the northeastern side of the sea, but the 'efreet does not believe the nomads came from there. He said to tell you that he thinks it probable, from certain signs he has seen, that they were on the Isle of Galos."

"Galos!" Feisal paled.

"Not Galos!" said Meryem hastily, seeing that this news was unwelcome and knowing that bad news generally garnered little reward. "That was not the name. I was mistaken—"

"You said Galos!" Feisal cried in a hollow voice. "That is what the 'efreet said, wasn't it?" The priest's eyes burned in their sunken sockets. "That is what he told you to tell me! He is warning me! Thank Quar! Warning me!"

This was good news, then. Meryem relaxed. "Kaug said something about a God called Zhakrin—"

"Yes!" Feisal cut her off, not liking to hear that name spoken aloud. His thoughts went to Meda, to the dying man's bloodstained hand gripping the priest's robes, the curse spoken with the body's last shuddering breath. "There is no need to go into this further, my child. What other message does Kaug send?"

"Good tidings!" Meryem said, her eyes smiling above the veil. "He says there is no need to fear Khardan any longer. He and the witch-woman are trapped on the shores of the Kurdin Sea. To return to their tribes, they must go west—across the Sun's Anvil. No one has ever performed such a feat and survived.''

"But they have their djinn, after all."

"Not for long. Kaug bids you not worry."

The Imam cast a suspicious glance at Meryem. "Why does this news please you, my child? I thought you were in love with this nomad.''

Meryem did not hesitate. She had known this question must come, and she had long been prepared with her reply. "I came to realize, living among the *kafir* as I have these past few months, Imam, that such a love is an abomination in the sight of Quar.''

Her eyes lowered modestly, her voice trembled with the proper tone of religious fervor, and she didn't fool Feisal in the least. He recalled the calluses he had felt on her fingertips; his gaze flicked over the tattered remnants of her fine clothing.

"I want only to return to the palace and regain my former place there,'' Meryem added, unconsciously answering any lingering doubts the Imam might be having.

"Your former place?'' Feisal asked dryly. "I thought you were more ambitious than that, or has your sudden interest in religion taught you humility?''

Meryem flushed beneath her veil. "Qannadi promised to make me his wife,'' she said stubbornly.

"Qannadi would as soon think of bedding a snake. Have you forgotten? He suspected your little plot to use the nomad Prince to overthrow him. He would not take you back, even as concubine.''

"He would if you told him to,'' Meryem countered. "You are strong! He fears you! I know, Yamina told me so!''

"It is not me he fears, but the God, as should all mortals,'' rebuked Feisal, adding humbly, "I am but Quar's servant and an unworthy one at that.'' Having said this, he continued thoughtfully. "Qannadi might take you back, if I asked him to. But, Meryem, consider. You left the palace once because you feared your life was in danger. Has the situation changed, except perhaps to grow more perilous for you? After all, you have lived with Qannadi's enemy for two months or more.''

Meryem's feathery brows came together above the blue eyes. The hands, which had never ceased twisting the silken fabric since she first entered, gave it an involuntary jerk that tore the veil from her face. Biting her lip with her white teeth, she gazed at the Imam defiantly. "Then find me some place to go! I have done this for you—"

"You did it for yourself," Feisal stated coldly. "It is not my fault that your lust for Khardan has dwindled to ash and blown away. Still, you have proven your value and I will reward you. After all, I do not want you selling this information to Qannadi.''

Eyes cast down, Meryem covered her face with a shaking hand and wished she could draw the veil over her brain as well. It was uncanny the way this man could see into her mind!

Feisal turned his back upon the woman and, walking over to the altar, sought help from the ram's head. The golden eyes shone red with the burning charcoal.

"We need to keep the girl nearby," the Imam muttered. "She can see the followers of Akhran and Promenthas in that scrying bowl of hers, and I want to know the moment the *kafir* draws his final breath. I must keep her near, yet I must keep her presence secret. Qannadi believes Khardan to be dead. Achmed believes his brother is dead. The nomads believe their Calif is dead. Their hope dwindles daily. They must not discover the truth, or they will gain strength to defy us! If Qannadi found out Khardan was alive, he would tell Achmed and word would get back to the nomads. I—"

The ram's eyes flared briefly, brilliantly. Feisal blinked, then smiled.

"Thank you, Holy One," the priest murmured.

Turning back to Meryem, who was watching with narrowed eyes, her hand holding her veil over her face, the Imam said gently, "I have thought of a place for you to stay. A place not only where you will be completely safe, but where you will continue to be most useful.''

Chapter 6

When the daily meeting of the officers concluded, Achmed lingered behind while the others, laughing and joking, left—those off duty heading for the city, the others going to take up assigned posts and to set the evening watch. Achmed remained behind, ostensibly to study a map. His brow furrowed in concentration; he might have been planning to face an onslaught of ten thousand foes at next day's dawning, so intently did he seem to consider the lay of the land. As it was, the only foe he was likely to face in the morning was the soldier's perennial enemy—the flea. Staring, unseeing, at the map was just an excuse. Achmed stayed behind when the others departed because it was easier being lonely when he was alone.

The young man had joined Qannadi's army in the spring. Now it was late summer. He had spent months with the men in his division, the cavalry. He had trained with them, learned from them, taught them what he knew. He had saved lives, he had been saved. He had gained their respect, but not their friendship. Two factors kept him from being included in the groups that went into the city seeking its pleasures. The first—Achmed was and always would be an outsider, a nomad, a *kafir*. The second—he was Qannadi's friend.

There was much speculation among the ranks concerning this relationship. Everything was guessed from a love interest to the somewhat wilder theory that the boy was really the Crown Prince of Tara-kan who had been sent away from the court of the Emperor for fear of assassination. No matter where the young man walked in the camp, he was certain to overhear conversations like the one he'd listened to only days before.

"Peacocks, that's what Qannadi's sons are, the lot of them. Especially the oldest. Waving his tail in the Emperor's court and picking up crumbs that fall at his feet," grunted one.

"What do you expect?" said another, watching with a critical eye the roasting of a lamb upon a spit. "The boy was raised in the *seraglio* by women and eunuchs. The general saw him maybe once, twice a year between wars, and then he took no interest in him. Small wonder the youth prefers the easy life at court to marching about all day in the heat."

"And I heard his wife, the sorceress, made certain the general took no interest in the boy," added a third. "The son will pull the boots off his father's corpse and measure them to fit his own feet as the saying goes. And when that day comes, Quar forbid it, that's the day I'll go back to that fat widow in Meda who owns the inn."

"Perhaps the *Kafir* will be the one wearing the boots," said the first in an undertone, his eyes darting about the camp.

"At least they'd fit him," muttered the second, giving the spit a half turn. "The *Kafir*'s a fighter, like all those nomads."

"Speaking of boots, if I was in the *Kafir*'s, I'd keep mine on day and night. A *qarakurt*'s a nasty thing to find in between one's toes in the morning."

"And no need to ask how it got there. Yamina's not his deadliest enemy," said the third softly. "Not by half. The general's being careful, though. Not favoring the *Kafir* above others, not keeping him about during the day, not even sharing his meals. Just another young hero. Bah, let me take over! You're burning it!"

The *Kafir*. That was what they called him. Achmed didn't mind the name any more than he minded the danger that Hasid, an old friend of Qannadi's, had taken care to explain to the young man. At first Achmed scoffed at the thought that anyone might view him as a threat. But as time went by, he found himself shaking out his pallet every night before he slept, upending his boots every morning, eating his meals out of a cooking pot shared by others. And it wasn't Yamina's eyes he saw staring at him from the darkness.

The eyes he feared were the burning eyes of the Imam.

Yet Achmed accepted it all—the danger, the ostracism, the whispers and sidelong glances. He had affirmed this to himself that terrible day when Qannadi fell in the midst of his enemies, and Achmed had stood prepared to sacrifice his life for this man who had come to be father, friend, mentor. Yes, he would sacrifice his life for this man, but what about the lives of his people?

I can't prevent their deaths. Neither can Qannadi. They must convert or at least pretend to. Surely they will be able to see that! I will talk to them.

Talk to them. Talk to someone who understood him. Talk to friends, family. The empty, hollow pit within the boy deepened and widened. He was lonely—bitterly, desperately lonely. Tears stung his eyelids, and he very nearly threw himself down among the rugs and the saddles that were used as backrests and wept like a child. The knowledge that at any moment one of the officers might take it into his head to have another look at the route to Kich forced the sobs back down Achmed's throat. Choking, wiping the back of his hand over his eyes and nose and rebuking himself severely for giving way to unmanly weakness, the young man strode hastily from the tent.

He wandered aimlessly, restlessly, among the soldiers' encampment. It was late evening, he had no duties to perform. He could have returned to his own tent, but sleep was far from him, and he had no desire to spend another night staring into the darkness, holding memory at bay and scratching at fleas. He continued to roam, and it was only when he heard soft voices, muted groans, and deep laughter that Achmed realized where it was his feet had taken him.

Known as the Grove, it had other names in the soldiers' vernacular—names that had brought a flush to the young man's cheeks when he'd first heard them. That had been months and battles ago, however. Now he could grin knowingly when the

Grove was mentioned. He'd even—out of curiosity and desire—availed himself of its dubious pleasures one night. Too bashful and ashamed to "examine the wares," he'd purchased the first merchandise offered him and discovered too late that it was old, ill made, and had undoubtedly known many previous owners.

The experience sickened and disgusted him, and he'd never—until now—gone back. Perhaps he had truly come here by accident, or perhaps his loneliness had led him here by the hand. Whatever the reason, the young man had heard enough talk among his elders to know now how business was conducted. Disgust vied with desire and, most burning, the need to talk, to touch, to be held, and at least—for the moment—to pretend that he was loved and cared for. A soft voice called to him, a hand reached from the shadows of the trees.

Clutching his purse, Achmed swallowed his nervousness and tried to appear hardened and nonchalant as he stepped farther into the Grove. Rustlings and glimpses of shadowy forms and the sounds of pleasure-taking increased his desire. He ignored the first who grabbed at him. They would be the professionals, the women who followed the troops from camp to camp. Deeper within the Grove were the ones new to this business—young widows from the town who had small children to feed and no other means to earn their bread. Their families would kill them if they discovered them here, but stoning is a quick way to die, compared to starvation.

Achmed was moving among the deepest, darkest part of the stand of trees, trying to push the image of his mother out of his mind, when he concluded with certainty that someone was following him. He had suspected it when he'd first entered the Grove. Footfalls that moved when he moved, stopped when he stopped. Only they didn't stop soon enough, and he could hear soft, padding footsteps through the cool, damp grass behind him. He moved forward again, heard the faint patter upon the ground, came to a sudden halt, and heard the patter continue—one step, two, then silence.

Fear and excitement banished desire. Slipping his hand to his belt, he felt for the hilt of his dagger and gripped it reassuringly. So this was it. He had supposed the Imam would hire someone more skilled. But no, this made sense. They would find his body in the Grove and assume he had been lured here by a woman, then murdered and robbed by her male accomplice. Such things were not uncommon. Well, he would give them a fight at least. Qannadi would not be ashamed of him.

Spinning on his heel, Achmed jumped at the hint of movement he saw in the darkness behind him. His hands, grappling for the neck, closed—not on male muscles and sinew—but on perfumed silk and smooth skin. A gasp, a scream, and Achmed and his pursuer fell heavily to the ground. The body beneath his went limp. Startled, shaken by the fall and his own fear, Achmed heaved himself off the inert form and peered at it intently in the starlit darkness.

It was a woman. Reaching out his hand, Achmed drew the veil from her face.

"Meryem!"

Chapter 7

The woman stirred at the sound of his voice. Too astonished to do anything except stare at her, Achmed remained crouched over her, the veil clutched in a hand that had gone as limp as the unconscious body. Her eyelids fluttered; even in the dim light, Achmed could see the shadows they cast upon the damask cheeks, delicate as the wings of dragonflies. Blinking dazedly, not looking at him, keeping her eyes lowered, Meryem sat up.

"Young sir," she said in a low, trembling voice, "you are kind, gentle. I . . . will give you pleasure. . . ."

"Meryem!" Achmed repeated, and at the sound of her name and the shock and anger in the voice, the woman looked fully at him for the first time.

A deep flush suffused the pale skin. She snatched the veil from the young man's hand and covered her face. Rising swiftly to her feet, Meryem started to flee but slipped in the wet grass. Achmed caught her easily.

"Let me go!" She began to weep. "Let me take my shame and cast myself into the sea."

Her crying became frenzied, hysterical. She tried again to break away from Achmed's grip, and the young man was forced to put his arms around the slender shoulders and hold her close, soothing her. Gradually, Meryem calmed down and lifted blue eyes, shimmering with tears, to gaze into his.

"Thank you for your kindness." She gently pushed him away. "I am better now. I will leave and trouble you no more—"

"Leave! And go where?" asked Achmed sternly, alarmed by her talk of the sea.

"Back to town." Meryem lowered her lashes, and he knew she was lying.

"No." Achmed caught hold of her again. "At least, not right now. Rest here until you feel better. Then I will take you back. You should not be wandering out here alone," the young man continued firmly, acting—for both their sakes—as if he had not heard her all-too-clear solicitation. "You have no idea what this place is."

Meryem smiled—a sad, wan smile that touched Achmed to the heart. A tear crept down her cheek, sparkling in the starlight like a precious jewel. Unconsciously the young man raised his hand to catch it.

"Thank you for trying to save me," Meryem said softly, her head drooping near but not quite touching his breast. "But I *do* know what this place is. And you know why I am here—"

"I don't believe it!" Achmed said stoutly. "You are not like . . . like these!" He gestured.

"Not yet!" Meryem hid her face in her hands. "But I soon would have been if not for you!" Looking up suddenly, she grasped hold of his tunic. "Achmed, don't you see? Akhran sent you! You saved me from sin! This was my first night here. You . . . would have been my first . . . first . . ."

Her skin burned; she could not say the word. Achmed put his hand over her lips. Catching hold of the fingers, she kissed them fervently and fell to her knees before him. "Akhran be praised!"

The woman's beauty dazzled him. The fragrance of her hair, the perfume clinging to her body, intoxicated him. Her tears, her innocence, her sweetness, mingled with the knowledge of where they were and what was going on around them inflamed Achmed's blood. He staggered like a drunken man, and it was the weakness in his limbs that made him sink down beside her.

"Meryem, what happened? Why are you here? You were in Kich, the last I heard, living with Badia, Khardan's mother—"

"Ah! Do not mention her name!" Meryem pressed her hands over her bosom, clutching at the silken gown, rending it in her despair. "I am not worthy to hear it spoken!" Rocking back and forth on her heels, moaning in grief, she let her hands fall, the torn fabric of her gown parting to reveal creamy white skin, swelling breasts.

Achmed drew a shivering breath. Taking hold of her chin, he turned her face to his and concentrated on looking into the wide, tear-shimmering blue eyes. "Tell me, what has happened? Is Badia, are my people—" Fear chilled him, his grip tightened. "Something terrible has happened, hasn't it?"

"Not that bad!" Meryem said hastily, catching hold of the young man's wrist. "Badia and all your people living in Kich have been taken from their homes and put into the Zindan. But surely you knew of this? It was by Qannadi's order."

"Not Qannadi," Achmed said grimly. "The Imam. And are they all right? Are they being mistreated?"

"No," said Meryem, but her eyes faltered before Achmed's gaze. His grip on her hand tightened.

"Tell me the truth."

"It is so shameful!" Meryem began to weep. Her tears, falling on Achmed's flesh, burned like cinders. "I was in a cell with Badia and her daughters. One night the guards came. They said . . . they wanted one of us . . . willingly . . . or they would take all by force—" She could not continue.

Achmed closed his eyes, pain, anger, desire, surging through him. He could visualize the rest and, putting his arms around Meryem, drew her close. At first she resisted him but gradually let his strong arms comfort her. "You sacrificed yourself for the others," he said gently, reverently.

"When the guards tired of me," she continued, sobbing against Achmed's chest, "they sold me to a slave trader. He brought me here. I . . . escaped, but then I had nowhere to go, no money. Akhran forgive me, I thought I could sink no lower, but—praise his name—he set you in my path.''

Achmed stirred uncomfortably, not liking to hear the name of the God, liking still less the thought that Akhran might have used him to save this poor girl.

"Coincidence," he said gruffly.

But Meryem shook her head firmly. The veil over the golden hair had slipped; the pale strands looked silver in the starlight. Achmed caught hold of one of the tresses that was damp from the girl's tears. Soft, silken, it smelled of roses. The words he said next stuck in his throat, but they needed to be said.

"Khardan will be proud of you—"

Meryem looked up at him in wonder. "Don't you know—" She halted, confused. "Didn't they tell you? Khardan is . . . is dead. Majiid sent word to Badia. They found his body. The stories about him fleeing the battle were false—lies spread by the Imam. Khardan was given a hero's burial."

Now it was Achmed who lowered his head, now it was Meryem who reached her hand out to brush away his tears.

"I am sorry. I thought you knew."

"No, I am not crying for grief!" Achmed said brokenly. "It is thankfulness, that he died with honor!"

"We both loved him," said Meryem. "That will always be a bond between us."

Quite by accident their cheeks touched. The sweet night breeze cooled skin wet with tears and flushed with passion. Their lips met, tongues tasting salt mixed with sweetness.

Meryem pushed Achmed away and tried to stand, but she was entangled in her clothing. Achmed drew her near. She kept her head averted, turned from him, straining away from his grasp.

"Leave me! I am defiled! Let me go! I swear, I will not do what you fear. You have saved me. I will pray to Akhran. He will guide me."

"He has guided you. He has guided you to me," Achmed said firmly. "I will take you to my tent. You will be safe there, and I will go to Qannadi—"

"Qannadi!" The word came out shrill and harsh, and Achmed flinched in response.

"Have you forgotten?" Meryem whispered hurriedly. "I am the Sultan's daughter! Your Amir murdered my father, my mother! He sought to have me put to death! He must not find me!" Panic-stricken, she scrambled to her feet and began to stumble through the darkness, tripping over the long skirts of her robes.

Achmed pursued her and, grabbing hold of her wrist, pulled her close to him. Her body trembled in his arms. She wept and shivered in her fright. He pressed her near, stroking the golden hair.

"There, I didn't mean it. I forgot for the moment. I won't tell him, though I'm certain that if I did, he would not harm you—"

"No! No!" The girl gasped wildly. "You must promise me! Swear by Akhran, by Quar, by whatever God you hold sacred—"

Achmed was silent for a moment. He could feel warm, soft skin swelling out of the torn bodice, heaving with her rapid, catching breaths against his bare breast. His arms tightened around her.

"I swear by no God," he said thickly. "I believe in no God. Not anymore. But I swear by my own honor. I will keep you safe, keep you secret. I will guard you with my life."

Meryem's eyes closed. Her head sank against his chest, her hands stole up around his neck, and she sighed a sigh that might have been relief but seemed to whisper surrender.

Achmed stopped the sigh with his lips, and this time Meryem did not push the young man away.

Chapter 8

Promenthas summoned the One and Twenty.

His purpose—to discuss the current war raging on the plane of the immortals.

When the One and Twenty came together this time, no longer did each God and Goddess view the others contentedly from his or her facet of the Jewel that was the world. Now only a very few of the strongest Gods were able to maintain their dwelling places. The others found themselves standing meekly in Quar's pleasure garden, being eyed curiously and aloofly by the tame gazelle.

Promenthas was strong still. He stood in his cathedral rather than the garden, but the sounds of shipbuilding echoed through the cavernous chambers and disturbed his rest. God of the lands and peoples of Aranthia, far across the Hurn Sea from Tara-kan, Promenthas's followers were—for the time being—safe from the *jihad* that was raging in Sardish Jardan. The pounding of nails into wood was soon going to end their peace. The Emperor of Tara-kan had wealth enough and material enough from the southern realm of Bas to proceed with his designs for an armada. Within the year his fleet would be ready to cross the Hurn. Hordes of fanatical followers of Quar would storm the walled cities and castles of Aranthia.

A sparsely populated land divided into small states, Aranthia was ruled by kings and queens who kept the peace by marrying off their sons and daughters to each other. The land was heavily wooded, difficult to traverse except by the rivers and streams that were the country's blood, and it could hold out long against the Emperor's troops. In the end, however, Promenthas knew his people must be defeated, overwhelmed by sheer numbers if nothing more. The teeming capital city of Khandar alone contained more people than the entire population of Aranthia.

Seated in a pew near the altar, Promenthas watched grimly as Quar leisurely entered the cathedral. So large had the God grown, he was forced to duck his head and turn his body sideways to squeeze through the doorway. His magnificent robes were of the most rare and costly fabrics. All the jewels of the world adorning his body, Quar shone more brilliantly than the stained glass of the cathedral windows that had, of late, become grimy and dust covered from lack of care. Mincing along behind Quar, chatting merrily with him and inwardly calculating Quar's worth at the same time, was Kharmani, God of Wealth.

No matter that another facet of the Jewel might shine brighter, Kharmani's facet gleamed with its own light—a golden light. No God—not the most evil, not the most good—dared try to dim that light. Every other of the One and Twenty might crouch at Quar's feet. Kharmani would sit at his right hand—as long as that hand kept flipping golden coins in Kharmani's direction.

Behind Quar, Promenthas saw a shadowy figure sneaking into the cathedral under cover of the God's flowing robes. Promenthas frowned and sighed over the fate of the Poor Box, knowing without doubt that there wouldn't be a penny left after the departure of this God—Benario, God of Thieves. Kharmani might sit at Quar's right hand, but Benario would be at his left, if the God didn't steal Quar's fingers first.

Promenthas felt a rumbling beneath his feet, and he knew that Astafas, God of Darkness, was watching Quar step into a subterranean world of perpetual night. The dazzle must hurt Astafas's eyes, thought Promenthas wryly, and he felt a certain sympathy for his ancient enemy.

At least Astafas has not sunk to the level of these wretches. Trailing along behind Quar, their own radiance lost in the shadow of the shining God, were various others of the One and Twenty. Uevin, shrunken and withered, meekly carried the hem of Quar's robes. Mimrim, head bowed, walked behind, holding a sitting cushion in the eventuality that the God should decide he was fatigued and desired rest. Hammah, the horned, helmed God of the Great Steppes, marched in Quar's retinue. Carrying his spear, the warrior God tried to appear dignified; but he kept his gaze from meeting that of Promenthas, and the white-bearded God knew with a heaviness in his immortal being that the rumors he'd heard were true. Hammah's people had allied with the Emperor and would march to battle on Quar's side.

Other Gods and Goddesses Promenthas saw, but now he was most interested in those notable for their absence. The angry rumblings that were shaking the cathedral's foundations gave indication that Astafas would cast himself in the Pit of Sul before serving Quar. Evren and Zhakrin were missing, though Promenthas had heard rumors of their return. And of course Akhran, the Wanderer, was nowhere to be seen.

Quar's almond-eyed gaze sought out Promenthas. Slowly, with great dignity, the white-bearded God rose to his feet and moved to stand directly before his altar. There were no angels flanking him. The war on the plane of the immortals had drawn away all his subalterns. Only one angel remained, and she was hidden safely in the choir loft.

"Why have you called this gathering of the One and Twenty—or perhaps we might better refer to it as the One and Seventeen," said Quar in his delicate voice. Kharmani gave a tittering laugh at the God's joke.

"I have called this meeting of the One and Twenty," said Promenthas, his voice deep and stern, "to discuss the war currently raging on the plane of the immortals."

"War." Quar appeared amused. "Call it bickering, squabbles among spoiled children!"

"I call it war," Promenthas returned angrily. "And you are the cause!"

Quar raised a finely drawn eyebrow. "I? The cause? My

dear Promenthas, it was I who—seeing the danger existent in these undisciplined beings—attempted to bring order and discipline to the world in our care by confining them safely in a place where they could no longer meddle in the affairs of humans. It is due to the meddlings of the wild and uncontrollable djinn of Akhran that this havoc is being wreaked both in heaven and on earth. It is time we take direct control—"

"It is time *you* take direct control, isn't that what you mean?"

"Are you trying to make me angry, Graybeard?" Quar smiled pleasantly. "If so, you will not succeed. I included all my brethren out of politeness, but if you are too weak to deal with the matter, I am not. Someone must bear the burden of humanity's sufferings—"

"If you truly mean what you say," interposed another voice, coming from outside the cathedral, beyond the walls of Quar's pleasure garden, "then banish the 'efreet known as Kaug, in whom you have consolidated much of your power. Prick your swollen ego, Quar, and let out the stinking air of your ambition. Become one of us once more—a facet in the Jewel—so that its beauty may last forever."

Akhran the Wanderer entered the cathedral of Promenthas, strode into Quar's pleasure garden. Akhran's boots were covered with dust; his flowing robes were frayed and tattered and stained with blood. The Wandering God seemed small and shabby, compared to Quar. Kharmani cast Akhran a glance of imperious disgust, and Benario, yawning, did not bother to leave his place among the shadows.

Quar lifted an orange studded with cloves to his nose to obviate the smell of horse and leather and sweat that entered with the Wanderer and kept his eyes on Promenthas.

"This is the thanks I receive for trying to bring order to chaos." Quar's tone was sad, his manner that of one who has been pierced to the heart. "What am I to expect of two who were instrumental in bringing the foul God of blackest evil, Zhakrin, back to power? But you will regret it. You think those humans who do your bidding have escaped Zhakrin's clutches, but his shadow is long and the darkness once again draws near them. You trust him—a God who drinks the blood of innocents—"

A muffled sound, like a despairing cry, came from the choir loft of the cathedral. Promenthas made a swift gesture with his hand, but Quar glanced up at the dust-covered carved wooden railings, and his smile deepened.

"Sul designed the Jewel so that all facets gleam with equal light—the good and the evil—" began Akhran angrily, removing the *haik* from his face and glowering at Quar.

"Ah, now you know the mind of Sul, do you, Wanderer?" interrupted Quar coolly, flicking a glance at Akhran, then flicking it away as though the sight might soil his eyes. "It is my belief, after much deep consideration, that Sul meant there to be One God, not One and Twenty. Thus his light will shine purely and brightly, beaming directly upon the humans, instead of being refracted, split, diffused."

"Do this, and the Jewel will shatter!" warned Akhran.

"Then I will pick up the pieces." With a graceful bow, Quar, his garden, and his retinue of followers disappeared.

"Beware, lest those pieces cut you," cried Akhran after him. There was no response. Akhran and Promenthas were left standing alone in the cathedral.

"Do not look so glum," said the Wandering God, clouting Promenthas on the back. "Quar has made a serious mistake—he has given too much of his power to the 'efreet. In order to win the war on the plane of the immortals, we have only to defeat Kaug." Akhran's booming voice rattled the panes of stained glass. "When that is done, Quar will fall."

"When that is done, the stars will fall." Promenthas sighed, though the stern face eased slightly at this offer of hope.

"Bah!" Akhran started to spit, recalled where he was, and wiped his mouth with the back of his hand. The sound of a horse whinnying in impatience drifted through the cool darkness. Wrapping the *haik* about his face, the Wandering God turned and walked down the aisle toward the cathedral's doors. Promenthas noted, for the first time, that the God was limping.

"You are injured!"

"It is nothing!" Akhran shrugged.

"What Quar said about Zhakrin, your followers and mine—the young wizard who travels with them. Are they in danger?"

Akhran turned, regarding Promenthas with narrowed black eyes. "My people have faith in me. I have faith in them."

"As Zhakrin's followers have faith in him. He seeks what Quar seeks and always has. He has no mercy, no compassion. Perhaps it was a mistake, helping him return. Admittedly Evren came with him, but she is weakened, her followers far distant, while Zhakrin is near. Very near." Promenthas sighed and shook his head. "We are too few, and we are divided among ourselves. I fear it is hopeless, my friend."

Akhran flung wide the cathedral doors and drew in a deep breath of fresh air. Mounting his horse, he leaned down to clasp reassuringly Promenthas's stooped and bent shoulder. "Only the dead are without hope!"

Raising himself up, he kicked his horse's flanks; the animal galloped off among the stars.

"And without pain," murmured Promenthas. Looking back down the aisle where Akhran had walked, he saw a trail of blood.

THE BOOK
OF ZHAKRIN

Chapter 1

Mathew sat upon a slag heap of shining obsidian. Scattered about the stark white of the salt desert floor, the black rock seemed the embodiment of the dark elements that stirred just below the crust of the world, just below the skin of man. Staring down at the gaping cracks in the surface of the heat-baked earth, Mathew fancied he could see the black rock escaping from the tormented depths, oozing out of the dead land, gangrenous liquid streaming from a putrefied wound.

The young wizard closed his eyes to blot out the horrid vision. Though it was early morning, only a few hours since the sun had risen, the heat was already intense. The Sun's Anvil. It was like the people of this godforsaken land to name it thus—terse, laconic, to the point. Sweating profusely beneath the heavy velvet robes, half-stunned by the heat and exhaustion, Mathew pictured a sinewy arm of pure fire wielding a hammer, slamming it down upon the ground that split and cracked beneath it but did not yield, the sparks flying, waves of heat rolling from the blast. . . .

"Mat-hew!" A hand was shaking him.

Mathew lifted bleary, dreamy eyes. A form shimmered before him—Zohra, clad in the outlandish glass-beaded dress of sacrifice. Each bead caught the sun's light, the slightest movement set them gleaming and glinting and clicking together. Dazzled by the radiance, Mathew blinked at her.

"I'm thirsty," he said. Licking his tongue across his lips, he could taste, feel the salt that rimed them.

"The djinn have brought water," Zohra said, helping him to his feet. "Come, we must talk."

A night, a day, and another night they had sailed the Kurdin Sea. It had taken them this long to cross, where before they crossed in a matter of hours. The winds generated by the perpetual storm around Castle Zhakrin took delight in toying with them, blowing them furiously for miles in the wrong direction, then dying completely and leaving them becalmed, then hitting them from the front when least expected. Without their djinn, the humans on board would have soon lost all sense of direction, for the clouds swirling above them hid sun and stars and made navigation impossible.

Clinging to the side of the boat, sick and drenched and shivering with cold, lacking both food and water—not that they could have kept it down—the miserable occupants gave themselves up for dead. The boat's owner, Meelusk, howled in terror until at last his voice gave out. When the craft finally scraped against the shoreline, two of the djinn, Sond and Pukah, carried their bedraggled passengers ashore. The third djinn, Usti, whose rotund body had been pressed into service as a sail, was as sickly and forlorn as his mortal masters. Stricken with terror by the storms and a panicked fear that they were being chased by ghuls, Usti had kept his eyes squinched tightly shut the entire voyage. At its end, the djinn refused to let go of the mast or open his eyes. Sond poked and prodded and mentioned every luscious dish the djinn could think of, to no avail. Moaning, Usti refused to budge. Pukah finally had to pry the fat djinn's fingers off the mast and his feet from under the boom. Once freed, Usti collapsed like a deflated pig's bladder and lay gasping and moaning in the shallow water.

The Sun's Anvil. It was Pukah who had told them where they were. By night the desert's flames were quenched, the fires were out, the Anvil was cold steel. Clad in his wet robes, Mathew had shivered with the chill that seemed to enter his bones. Khardan and Pukah and Sond had debated the creation of a fire, and Mathew had heard with aching disappointment the three decide that it would be unwise. Something about attracting the attention of an evil 'efreet who apparently lived in that accursed sea.

When dawn came Mathew had reveled in the warmth and managed to sleep fitfully. On awakening, he felt the heat strike him a physical blow. Dragging himself to his feet, he had huddled in the meager shade cast by the outcropping of obsidian and wondered what they would do.

Apparently, according to Zohra, some sort of decision had now been reached. Mathew cast aside the hood of the robes he wore, hoping to catch the faint breeze that wafted occasionally from the surface of the Kurdin Sea. The water was flat and still now, its winds having been sucked up by the savage sun. The youth's long red hair was wringing wet with sweat, and he lifted it off the back of his neck. Noticing what he was doing, Zohra caught hold of the hood and dragged it over Mathew's head.

"The sun will burn your fair skin like meat on a skewer. Its heat will curdle your wits."

That, Mathew could readily believe, and he suffered the hood to remain in place, even drawing it lower over his forehead. Surely we will leave this dreadful place soon, he thought drowsily. The djinn will carry us in their strong arms, or perhaps we will fly upon a cloud.

The sight of Khardan's face jolted Mathew to reality. It was dark with anger; the black eyes burned hotter than the sand beneath their feet. The djinn stood before him, sullen, ashamed, but grim and resolute.

"What do you know of this?" Khardan flared, whirling on Mathew.

"What do I know of what?" Mathew asked dazedly.

"This war in heaven! The news, so Pukah tells me, was brought to them by your djinn!"

"My djinn?" Mathew stared, amazed. "I don't have a djinn!"

"Not djinn, angel," Pukah corrected, keeping his eyes lowered before his master's—former master's—fury. "A guardian angel, in the service of Promenthas."

"There are no such bei.   as angels," Mathew said, wiping the sweat from his brow. Every breath hurt; it was like breathing in pure flame. "At least," he added, shaking his head, thinking dreamily how unreal all this was, "no beings who would have anything to do with me. I'm not a priest—"

"No such beings!" Pukah cried, raising his head and angrily confronting a startled Mathew. "Your angel is the most loyal being in the heavens! For every tear you have shed, she has shed two! Every hurt you suffer, she takes upon herself. She loves you dearly, and you—unworthy dog—dare malign the best, the most beautiful— No, Asrial, I will say it! He must learn—"

"Pukah! Pukah!" Khardan shouted repeatedly, and at last managed to stem the tirade.

"Since when, djinn, do you speak to a mortal in this disrespectful manner?" Zohra demanded.

"I will handle this, wife," Khardan snapped.

"Better than you have handled all else previously, I presume, husband?" Zohra responded with a sneer, tossing the mane of black hair over her shoulder.

"It was not my actions that brought us here, if you will remember, wife!" Khardan drew a seething breath. "If you had left me on the field of battle—"

"You would be dead by now," Zohra said coolly. "Believe me, husband, no one regrets my action to save you more than I!"

"Stop it!" Mathew cried. "Haven't we been through enough? In that dark castle, you were each prepared to offer your life for the other. Now you—"

Mathew hushed. Khardan was staring out to the sea, his face stern and hard. The muscles in the jaw twitched, the tendons in the neck were drawn taut and strained.

My words have done nothing more than send him back to that dread place, Mathew realized sadly. He suffers it all again!

Swiftly Mathew glanced at Zohra. Her face had softened; she was recalling her own torment. If she could see the shared anguish in her husband's eyes . . . But she could not.

From where she stood, she saw only the broad back, the head held high, the neck stiff and unbending. Her lips compressed. Zohra crossed her arms forbiddingly across her chest, the glass beads of her dress clashing together jarringly.

Mathew's own hand reached out to the Calif, the fingers trembling. Khardan turned at the moment, and Mathew snatched the hand back and hid it within the loose, flowing sleeves of his wizard's robes. The Calif took one look at the impassive face of his wife, and his own expression grew harder.

"I humbly beg your apology, *sidi*, and that of the madman—I mean, Mat-hew," said Pukah humbly, anxious to keep clear of domestic disputes. "I have been reminded that the madman—Mat-hew—had no way of knowing anything about his angel, since such contact between mortal and immortal is prohibited by his God, Promenthas, who is if I may say it, a most dour type of God and one who doesn't have a great deal of fun. Still, it seems to me that the madman should be thankful he is at least alive—"

"Thankful! Of course, he's thankful!" Khardan said impatiently. "And you tell me that he doesn't know anything about this . . . this—"

"Angel," contributed Pukah helpfully.

"Yes." Khardan avoided pronouncing the strange-sounding word. "So he knows nothing about this war?"

"No, *sidi*." Pukah was more subdued but, on exchanging glances with Sond, appeared determined to continue on in the face of the Calif's mounting displeasure. "Asrial—that is the angel's name, master—attended a meeting of the One and Twenty. It was there she learned of the war raging on the plane of the immortals. Akhran himself was present, master, and he said that Quar has placed much of his strength in the 'efreet, Kaug, who now seeks to banish the immortals back to our ancient prison, the Realm of the Dead."

"One 'efreet!" Khardan snorted. "Surely Akhran can deal with one 'efreet!"

"The gods are forbidden by Sul to act on the plane of their servants, *sidi*. Not that I think this would stop *Hazrat* Akhran, if he was so inclined. But Asrial tells us that Akhran"—the djinn hesitated, glanced at his fellow djinn, sighed, and imparted the bad news—"Akhran bears many wounds on his body, and though he does his best to hide them, Promenthas fears our God cannot last much longer."

"Akhran . . . dying!" Khardan said in disbelief. "Has our God truly grown so weak?"

"Say rather, the faith of his people has weakened," interposed Sond quietly.

Khardan flushed. His hand moved, unconsciously it seemed, to his breast. Mathew remembered vividly the wounds the Calif had borne, wounds gone now without a scar except for those that would remain forever on the man's soul. Wounds healed by the hand of the God.

Or wounds suffered by the God in his place?

"Our people." The flaring pride and anger faded from Zohra's eyes, leaving them shadowed with fear and concern. "So much has happened . . . we have forgotten our people."

"All the more reason you must help us return to them," Khardan said angrily to Pukah.

"All the more reason we must fight Kaug, Calif." Sond spoke with the sincerest respect, the firmest resolution. "If Kaug wins this battle, all immortals will disappear from the world. Quar, being the strongest of the Gods, will be able to increase his direct influence over the people. He will grow stronger, the other Gods weaker, and eventually the One and Twenty will be the One."

"We will be gone only a few hours, *sidi*," Pukah said confidently. "This Kaug may have the strength of a mountain, but he has the brains to match. We will defeat him and return to you before you can begin to miss us."

"Rest during the heat of the day, *sidi*, in the tent we have prepared for you. We shall be back to serve you dinner," added Sond.

The two djinn began to fade away. Mathew felt something brush against his cheek, something soft and light and delicate as a feather, and he raised his hand swiftly to grasp it, but there was nothing there.

"Khardan!" Zohra cried, clutching at him. "They mean to abandon us out here! You cannot let them go!"

"I cannot stop them!" Khardan shouted irritably, shaking off her hands. "What would you have me do? I am no longer their master!"

"But I am!" shrieked a shrill voice.

Chapter 2

Everyone turned, startled, having forgotten during the ensuing argument all about the scrawny little man. Truth to tell, no one had paid much attention to Meelusk at all during the entire trip. The beady-eyed, leering-faced fisherman had spent the journey huddled in a heap at the bottom of the boat. Whenever anyone—particularly the muscular Khardan—had looked at him directly, Meelusk would give a fawning, servile grin that twisted into a vicious snarl when he thought no one was watching.

Now he came stumping across the sand, clutching Sond's lamp to his chest and dragging Pukah's waterlogged snake charmer's basket (which was as big as the little man) behind him.

"I don't trust you, you black-bearded demon," Meelusk shouted, his gleaming eyes fixed on Khardan. "The woman with you is a she-devil, and I don't know what you are, red-haired freak!" The eyes darted to Mathew. "But be you she-devil or he-demon, I'll soon be rid of you! I'll soon be rid of the lot of you!"

These were fine-sounding words, but the djinn, Sond and Pukah, continued to fade from view, and it suddenly occurred to Meelusk to wonder who was getting rid of whom.

"Come back here!" the little man yelled, waving Sond's

lamp in the air. "I'm your master! I rescued you from the sea! You have to obey me and I say come back here!"

The images of the djinn wavered, then slowly rematerialized.

"He is right, after all," Pukah said to Sond. "He is our master."

"You bet I am!" said Meelusk smugly, casting Khardan a triumphant glance.

"He did rescue us from the sea. We owe him our fealty and loyalty," Sond agreed.

Turbaned heads bowed; the djinn came to prostrate themselves before the scrawny human.

"Damn right you do!" Meelusk cackled. "Now get up and listen to me." He pointed at Khardan and his companions. "Leave the nomads here on the beach to rot. Take away their water and that tent." Protected by the djinn, Meelusk felt safe enough to shake a bony fist at the nomads. "You murderin', black-hearted devils! I've seen you look at me, thirsting for my blood! Ha! Ha! That's not all you'll thirst for." Meelusk turned back to the djinn at his feet. "Now you're going to dress me like a Sultan, then bring me beautiful women, then fix me up a palace that's made of silver and marble, with great high walls so's that no one can get to me. Then you're going to my village. The people there don't respect me enough. But they'll learn to! Yes they will, the curs. When we get there, you're going to kick over their houses, one by one. And stomp 'em into the dirt! And then set 'em on fire. After that, you're going to bring me all the gold and jewels in the world— Hey! What's the matter with you?"

Pukah had put a hand to his forehead and rolled his eyes. "Too many commands, master."

"Ah, slow-witted, are you?" said Meelusk, grinning craftily.

"Yes," said Sond gravely, "he is."

"Beautiful new clothes for my master!" commanded Pukah, clapping his hands.

Instantly Meelusk's skinny, dirt-encrusted body was swathed from head to toe in a cocoon of costly silks. "Hey!" cried a muffled voice, coming from the midst of the cocoon. "I can't breathe!"

"Jewels for my master!" commanded Sond, clapping his hands.

Ropes of pearls, chains of gold, and jewels of every color and description fell from heaven around Meelusk's neck, their weight bending him nearly to his knees.

"Women for my master!"

Nubile, willowy bodies surrounded Meelusk, their soft voices whispering into what little of his ears could be seen under the huge, jewel-encrusted turban that balanced precariously on the man's bulbous head. The women cuddled against him seductively. Gaping and drooling, Meelusk dropped both Sond's lamp and Pukah's basket in order to free up his eager hands.

"A new lamp and a new basket for my master!" shouted Pukah, carried away with enthusiasm.

"Yes! Yes!" Meelusk panted, ogling the women and clutching the soft bodies with grasping fingers. "New everything! More gold! More jewels! While you're at it, more of these beauties."

Pukah cast Khardan a significant look. Slipping up quietly and stealthily, the Calif snatched up Sond's lamp and Pukah's basket and, holding onto them tightly, took a swift step backward.

Instantly, the women, the jewels, the pearls and the gold, the turban, the wool and the silks, all disappeared.

"Ah, Master Meelusk, what have you done?" cried Pukah in dismay.

"Eh? What?" Meelusk glanced around wildly, his hands, which had encircled a slender waist, clasped firmly around empty air. Furious, he accosted the two djinn, who were gazing at him sadly. "Bring 'em back, do you hear me? Bring 'em back!" he howled, jumping up and down in the sand.

"Alas, you are no longer our master, master," said Pukah, with a helpless spreading of the hands.

"You gave away, of your own free will, our dwelling places," said Sond, heaving a sigh.

Raving, gnashing his teeth, Meelusk whirled and made a lunge for Khardan, but before he could take even two steps, the huge Sond had caught hold of the scrawny little man by the arms. Lifting him like a child, the djinn carried Meelusk, kicking and screaming and calling down foul imprecations on the heads of everyone present, to his boat. Sond tossed Meelusk inside and gave the boat a mighty shove that sent it flying over the water.

"Best not shout so, former master!" Pukah called after the rapidly vanishing boat. "The ghuls have excellent hearing!"

Meelusk's curses ended abruptly, and all was quiet once more. When the boat was out of sight, Sond and Pukah came walking slowly across the sand to stand before Khardan. Sond's lamp, dented and scratched and somewhat the worse for wear, lay at the Calif's feet. Pukah's basket, waterlogged and unraveling in places, stood near the battered lamp. Khardan stared down at the objects that bound the djinn to the mortal world, his gaze dark and thoughtful.

The djinn bowed and waited in tense silence.

"Go do what you must, then!" Khardan growled abruptly, impatiently, refusing to look at them. "The sooner you're gone, the sooner you'll return."

Sond glanced at Pukah. Pukah nodded.

"Farewell, Princess, Calif, Madman!" The fox-faced djinn waved. "Look for us to return with the setting of the sun!"

The djinn disappeared.

"A wise decision, husband!" sneered Zohra. "Now we are alone in this accursed place."

"It was my decision to make, wife, not yours!" Khardan returned shortly.

A heavy silence fell upon the three, broken only by the gentle sound of water lapping upon the shore and the snores of Usti, who lay sprawled on the beach like a giant, flabby fish.

"At least my djinn has not deserted us—" Zohra began.

Sond's huge hand reached suddenly out of the air. Gripping hold of Usti by the sash around the djinn's broad middle, the hand jerked him upward. There was a startled cry, a wail of protest, then Usti, too, was gone.

The three humans were alone upon the hostile shore. The sun pounded its hammer upon the cracked earth. Noxious pools of foul-smelling water bubbled and boiled. Behind them stood a tent, its open flap giving a glimpse of the cool, inviting darkness inside. Skins of water hung from the center pole, bowls of fruit and rice stood on rugs spread before cushions. There were even robes for the desert. The djinn had thought of and provided everything.

"Go inside, wife. Change your clothing," Khardan ordered Zohra. "We will wait for you out here."

"You cannot command your own djinn! You certainly do not command me, husband!" Zohra bristled. Her black eyes flicked over Khardan. Clad only in the remnants of the armor of a Black Paladin, his brown skin was beginning to redden. "You are the one who needs the protection. *I* will wait for *you*."

Khardan's face flushed in anger. "Why do you insist on opposing me, woman—"

"Please!" Mathew took a step between them. "Don't—" he began, staggered, and swayed on his feet. "Don't . . ." he tried to speak again, but he couldn't breathe. He couldn't swim against the burning tide. Closing his eyes, he let himself sink beneath it, drowning in sweltering waves of heat.

Chapter 3

Zohra and Khardan carried Mathew inside the shelter of the tent. They stripped off the heavy black robes he wore—Zohra keeping her eyes lowered modestly as was proper when nursing the sick, pretending not to see the young man's frail nakedness—and bathed his face and chest in the tepid salt water of the Kurdin Sea. Working together over the suffering young man, each was very much aware of the other's nearness. When hands touched, by accident, both started and drew quickly apart as though they had brushed against hot coals.

"What is wrong with him?" Khardan asked gruffly. Seeing there was nothing more he could do, he rose to his feet and moved over to stand beside the open tent flap.

"The heat, I think," Zohra replied. Dipping a strip of cloth in water, she laid it upon the hot forehead.

"Can your magic heal him? If the djinn do not return—"

Zohra glanced swiftly at Khardan.

Averting his eyes from the accusation in hers, the Calif stared outside. "—we will have to travel this night," he finished coldly.

"We could stay here." It was a statement of fact, not a suggestion.

Khardan shook his head. "We have water for two days, at most. When that runs out . . ." He did not finish.

When that runs out they would die. Though unspoken, the words echoed through the tent.

Khardan stood tense, waiting his wife's attack. It did not come, and he wondered why. Perhaps she thought it well enough that her barb, once cast, rankled in her enemy's flesh. Or perhaps she had come to regret words spoken before she thought, the interval giving her time to reflect, time to see that Khardan had made the only decision he could. Whatever the reason, she kept quiet. Neither spoke for long moments. Khardan stared moodily across the *kavir*, watching the ripples of heat wash over the land—a mockery of the water for which it thirsted. Zohra made Mathew a crude blanket of his own cast-off black robes, modestly covering the fair-skinned body.

"I cannot use my magic," she said at last. "I have neither charm nor amulet. Where will we go?"

"Back to our people. West. Pukah said something about a city, Serinda—"

"A city of death!" Zohra realized that could have a double, sinister meaning, and bit her lip. "All know the story," she added lamely.

"There may be life for us within its water wells."

Both man and woman added silently, *There had better be*.

"I am going out to look around before the heat of afternoon sets in." Starting to thrust aside the tent flap, he halted. With the toe of his boot Khardan gingerly touched an object lying on the ground—Mathew's belt and a leather pouch. "The boy does possess the magic," he said wonderingly. "I saw him work it."

"He is a very skilled and powerful wizard," said Zohra proudly, as though Mathew were her own personal creation. "He has been teaching me. It was by his magic I saw the vision—"

She was not looking at Khardan; she did not hear him speak or make a sound. But so sensitive was she to his physical presence, she felt rather than saw the tensing of his body, the slight, swift intake of breath.

The vision, the reason—so she claimed—that she had dragged Khardan unconscious from the field of the battle, hiding him from the Amir's forces by dressing him in women's clothing.

"Since you are so skilled in his magic, wife"—the sarcasm flicked like a whip across her raw nerves—"is there nothing of *his* you can use to aid him?"

"I never said I was skilled in his arts," she retorted in a low, passionate voice, not looking at him, her eyes staring down at Mathew's still form. "I said he was teaching me. And I swear to Akhran," she continued, her voice trembling with her fervor, "that I will never use such magic again!"

Reaching out, she started to smooth the damp red hair back from the young man's forehead, but her fingers shook visibly, and she hurriedly hid her hands in her lap. For no reason at all, it seemed, tears sprang to her eyes and slid down her cheeks before she could stop them. She could not raise a hand to brush them away; that would have revealed her weakness to him. Swiftly she lowered her head, the black hair falling forward, veiling her face.

But not before Khardan had seen the drops glistening on the dusky cheeks, sliding down to lose themselves in the curving, trembling lips. The frightful ordeal through which she had been, the long and perilous journey they faced if the djinn did not return—it was enough to daunt the strongest. Khardan took a step near her, his hand reaching out. . . .

Zohra flinched and hastily drew away. "You must leave the tent, husband." She spoke harshly to mask the tears. Rising to her feet, she kept her back to Khardan. "Mat-hew rests comfortably. I will change my clothes."

She stood stiff and straight-shouldered, unyielding. Blinded by the shadows after staring into the glaring sunlight, Khardan could not see his wife's fingers clench and drive into her flesh. He did not notice the long black hair that fell sleek and shining past her waist shiver with the intensity of her suppressed emotion. To him, she was cold and distant. The piles of obsidian, scattered over the desert floor, gave off more warmth than this flesh-and-blood woman.

Words crowded to Khardan's lips, but in such a tangle of fury and outrage that he could utter nothing coherent. Whirling, he stalked out of the tent, yanking down the flap after him, nearly bringing down the tent itself in his anger.

It was impossible, he knew it, for it had been months since Zohra had access to her perfumes. He could have sworn he smelled jasmine.

Fuming, Khardan stalked across the desert sand. The woman was maddening! A she-devil—that bandy-legged fisherman had been right! Khardan wanted to take her in his arms and . . . and . . . choke the life out of her!

The sun was hot, but not hotter than his blood. A high dune rose some distance from him, promising a view of the land. Grimly, he made his way across the cracked earth.

Inside the tent, safely hidden, Zohra fell to her knees and wept.

Mathew slept through the heat of afternoon and awoke, rested and alert, near sunset.

"The djinn, are they back?" he asked.

No one replied. His words fell into a well of silence so deep and dark he could almost hear them bounce off the walls. Something's happened. Hurriedly, he sat up and looked around. Khardan was stretched out full length on one side of the tent. Propped up on an elbow, he stared moodily out into the empty air. On the opposite side of the tent Zohra was deftly packing the food the djinn had provided and apparently making preparations to travel. The immortals were nowhere to be seen.

Mathew felt his throat tighten. The *girba* lay near him. He picked it up and started to drink, caught Khardan's sharp, swift glance, and took only a mouthful, though he was parched. Holding the water in his mouth as long as he could, hoping this would help ease his thirst, he swallowed tiny gulps of the precious liquid, making it last as long as possible. Gently he laid the waterskin back down, and Khardan's dark gaze turned from him.

"It is only just sunset, after all," Mathew said uneasily, waving away the small portion of food Zohra offered him. It was too hot to eat. "They'll be here soon."

Khardan stirred. "We cannot wait," he said, his voice deep and cold as the well that had drowned Mathew's words. "The moment the sun is gone, we must start walking. We have to reach Serinda before day dawns tomorrow." Looking at Mathew, he let his stern face relax somewhat. "Do not look so worried. It is not far. We should make it easily." He gestured. "You can see the city walls from the dunes."

Stiffly, as though he had been lying in one position for a long time, Khardan rose to his feet. He had changed his clothes, putting on the full pants, the tunic that tied around the waist with a sash, and the long, flowing robes of the desert. The *haik*, held in place with the *agal*, covered his head, the facecloth dangling down across his chest. Soft slippers, designed for walking in the shifting sand, covered his feet. Zohra was attired in a woman's loose robes, long-sleeved bodice, and pants that fit snugly around the ankle. A veil covered her head and face. With a sidelong glance at Mathew, her eyes studiously avoiding Khardan, she slipped out of the tent, carrying the food with her.

"Get dressed," Khardan ordered, pointing to two piles of clothing lying in the center of the tent. Mathew recognized the silken folds of a woman's *chador* in one, the other appeared to be robes similar to those worn by the Calif. Not knowing what sex the strange madman might choose to be today, Pukah had thoughtfully left attire for either. Mathew stretched his hand toward the men's clothes, then stopped. Flushing, he looked at Khardan.

"Am I permitted?" he asked.

A fleeting smile touched the Calif's lips and warmed the dark eyes. "For the present, Mat-hew. When we return to the Tel, you may have to resume your role as"—a hint of bitterness—"my wife."

"I will not mind," Mathew said quickly, thinking only to ease Khardan's obvious pain. Realizing too late how his words and tone might be misconstrued, Mathew flushed more deeply still and sought to clarify his statement. But before he could do more than stammer, Khardan had left the tent, courteously giving Mathew privacy.

"Fool!" Mathew cursed himself, fumbling with the yards and yards of material. "Why not just shout your feelings to the four winds and be done with it!"

When he was finally dressed, he went outside to find the other two standing far apart, backs turned slightly, each staring intently into the west where the sun had vanished over the horizon. The air was cooling already, though the collected heat of day radiated up from the ground and made Mathew feel as though he had stepped into a baker's oven.

"I'm ready," he said, and was startled to hear his voice sound small and tight.

Khardan turned and without a word reentered the tent. He came back with the *girba* slung over his shoulder and began walking westward, never glancing behind him. Zohra followed after Khardan, careful, however, to keep clear of his footprints, cutting her own path in the sand. By this and the set of her shoulders, she made it plain that though she traveled the same direction, it was by her choosing, not his.

Sighing, Mathew trudged along behind, his own footsteps, clumsy in the shifting sand, often stumbling across, overprinting, interconnecting, the two separate tracks that marched along on either side of him.

Chapter 4

From the top of the sand dune, staring into the western sky that was a cloudless, oppressive, ocherous hue, Mathew saw the city of Serinda. He knew its history, legends of the dead city being popular among the nomads.

A hundred years before or maybe longer, Serinda had been a thriving metropolis with a population numbering in the several thousands. And then, suddenly, according to legend, all life in Serinda had come to an end. No one knew the cause. Raiders from the north? The plague? The poisonous fumes of the volcano Galos? Gazing at the city walls—a gray-white, lacy border of mosque and minaret against the yellow sky—Mathew felt the stirrings of curiosity and looked forward eagerly to entering the gates that now were never closed. Perhaps he could solve this mystery. Surely there must be clues.

The city looked to be near them, Mathew thought, his spirits lifting. Khardan was right. A walk of a few hours should have them across this desert. They would be in Serinda before morning.

Night's deep blue-blackness washed over the land. Mathew reveled in the coolness. Invigorated, his journey's end in sight, he moved ahead so swiftly that Khardan was forced to remind him curtly that they had hours of walking before them.

Meekly slowing his pace, Mathew looked around him instead of ahead, and once again marveled at the strange, savage beauty of this land. No moon shone, but they could see their way clearly by the lambent light shining from the myriad stars that sparkled in the black heavens. Though Mathew knew it was the stars that cast the eerie, whitish glow upon the sand, it seemed to him as if the land itself radiated its own light, as it radiated the heat it had stored up during the day.

He gazed up, fascinated, at the stars. There were so many more of them, visible in this clear sky, than he could have ever imagined in his land. Having become accustomed already to the shifted positions of the constellations in this hemisphere, Mathew soon located the Guide Star that gleamed in the north sky and pointed it out to Zohra.

"They teach the children of my land that an angel of Promenthas stands there with his lantern to guide travelers through the night."

Zohra glanced at him skeptically. "Your people follow this—what was it?"

"Lantern, like a lamp or a torch. A light in the sky."

"Your people pick out a light and follow it and it leads them where they wish to go?" Zohra regarded him with narrowed eyes. "And the people of your land actually succeed in getting from one place to another?"

"Not just any light, Zohra," Mathew said, seeing her mistake. "That one particular star that always shines in the north."

"Ah! The people all travel north in your land!"

"No, no. When you know the star is in the north, you can tell if you're going east or west or south. Just as in the day you can tell which way you're going by the position of the sun. Don't your people do this?"

"Does *Hazrat* Akhran keep a *chirak* in the sky to guide him? And let his enemies know where he sleeps?" Zohra was scandalized. "Our God is not such a fool, Mat-hew. He knows his way around heaven. We know our way around earth. We follow not only that which we can see, but what we hear and smell. What do your people do when the clouds hide the sun and''—she gestured vaguely skyward—''that star?''

What would she say if I told her that the star was a sun? Or that our sun was a star? Mathew smiled to himself, picturing giving Zohra an astronomy lesson. Instead, he began to explain another marvel to her. ''Our people have a . . . a''—he fumbled for a word in the desert language—''device with a needle inside it that always points toward the north.''

''A gift of Sul,'' she said wisely.

''No, not magic. Well, in a way, but it is not Sul's magic. It is the magic of the world itself. You see, the world is round, like an orange, and it spins, like a top, and when it spins, a powerful force is created that draws iron toward it. The needle in the device is made of iron and it— What are you doing?''

''Drink some water, Mat-hew.''

''But Khardan said not to—''

''I said drink!'' Zohra glowered at him above the veil, her eyes glittering more brightly than Promenthas's Guiding Lantern.

Mathew obediently swallowed a mouthful of the warm water that tasted faintly of goat and seemed as sweet as the clearest, purest snow water that bubbled among the rocks of the stream behind his home.

''Now, Mat-hew, relax,'' said Zohra earnestly, patting his cheek with a gentle hand. ''You do not need to act crazy around us. We will not harm you. Khardan and I *know* you are mad.''

Smiling at him reassuringly, Zohra turned to follow the Calif, who was keeping to their path unerringly, without a glance at the stars.

They stopped to rest only briefly, Khardan pushing them forward at an exhausting pace that Mathew could not understand. Serinda was so near. Why couldn't they take an hour to rest aching legs and burning feet? But Khardan was adamant. The Calif spoke little during the journey; he kept his face covered by the *haik,* and it was impossible to tell what he was thinking. But if his expression matched his voice during those times when he did speak, Mathew knew it must be grim and dour.

Eventually Mathew ceased to wonder why they couldn't stop. He ceased to wonder anything but whether he would take that next step or collapse. His early energy had drained from him. Reaching the point of exhaustion, he had pushed past it. The chill air dried the sweat on his body, and he shivered from the cold. His feet had blistered, and walking was agony. The muscles of his legs ached and twitched from the effort of attempting to keep his footing in the shifting sands of the dunes that crossed their path.

Once, at the top of one, he slipped, and had neither the strength nor the will to catch himself. Down the steep side he rolled, sand scraping the skin off any parts of his body not protected by the folds of enveloping cloth. At the bottom, where he came to a slithering halt, the youth lay still, enjoying the cessation of movement, not caring much whether he ever moved again. Khardan caught hold of him by the arm, hauled him to his feet, and gave him a shove, all without speaking a word. Mathew limped forward.

Where was Serinda? What had happened to it? Had Khardan got them lost? Mathew glanced heavenward, searching dizzily for the Guide Star. No, there it was, on his right hand. They were traveling westward. Promenthas was guiding them.

But my angel is gone, Mathew thought dazedly, reeling as he walked.

My angel. My guardian angel. A year ago I would have scoffed at such a childish notion. But a year ago I did not believe in djinn. A year ago I trusted myself. I had my magic. A year ago I did not need heaven. . . .

"Now I need it," he muttered to himself. "My angel has left me, and I am alone. Magic!" He gave a bitter laugh, staggered, nearly fell, and stumbled on ahead. "I know how to make water out of sand. It is a simple spell." He had taught it to Zohra and nearly frightened the wits out of her.

"I could make this place an ocean!" Mathew gazed about dreamily and imagined himself swimming, floating upon cool water, splashing it over head and body, drinking, drinking all he wanted. His hand fumbled at the scrolls of parchment curled up neatly in the pouch at his belt. "Yes, I could make this place an ocean, *if* I had a quill to pen the words, and ink to write them, and a voice left in this raw and parched throat to speak them.

"A boon to the traveler," he imitated the Archmagus's droning voice. "No need to worry about fresh water. No need to drink at a stream that might be impure."

Hah! In his land, water was never more than a few steps away. In his land, they cursed it for flooding their crops, washing away the foundations of their houses.

"In such a place, I can conjure water!"

Some irritating person was laughing uproariously. Only when Mathew saw Khardan stop and turn to stare at him and Zohra come to stand beside him, her eyes shadowed by weariness and concern, did Mathew realize that the irritating person was himself.

He blinked and looked around. It was dawn. He could see the sweep of the dunes beginning to take on color, the light of Promenthas's Lantern start to fade. Raising his eyes, hope flooding his body with strength, Mathew looked eagerly to the west.

The white city walls, catching the sun's first, slanting rays, glistened against the dark background of waning night. Glistened far away . . . far, far away . . .

"Serinda! What's happened to it?" Mathew cried irrationally, clutching frantically at Khardan's robes. "Have we been walking in circles? Standing still? Why isn't it closer?"

"A trick of the desert," said Khardan softly, with a sigh that no one heard. "I was afraid of this." Suddenly angry, he pried Mathew's hand loose and shoved the young man away from him. He started off down the side of the dune on which they had been standing. "We can walk another two hours, before the heat sets in."

"Khardan."

Refusing to look around, the Calif kept walking, his own legs stumbling tiredly in the sand.

"Khardan!"

Glancing around, he saw Zohra standing unmoving behind him. Silhouetted against the burning ball of the rising sun, she had one arm around Mathew's shoulders. The youth sagged against her strong body, his head bowed, shoulders slumped. His breath came in ragged gasps.

"He can't go any farther," Zohra said. "None of us can."

Khardan looked grimly at her. She stared just as grimly back at him. Both of them knew what this meant. Without more water, stranded out here in the open, they would never live through the scorching heat of coming day.

Tossing the nearly empty waterskin onto the sand, Khardan flexed his aching shoulders. "We will wait for the djinn," he said evenly. "They will meet us here."

Now was the time for Zohra's triumph, bitter though it may be. She eased Mathew down onto the desert floor, then lifted her head to look upon the face of her husband, a face she could not see for the cloth that swathed it.

But she could see the eyes.

"Yes, husband," she said softly. "we will wait for the djinn."

Chapter 5

A blink of an eye took the three djinn and the angel from the desert to the realm of the immortals. Sond led them, and it was at his insistence that they found themselves materializing in a pleasure garden—the very garden, in fact, where Sond had sneaked in to meet Nedjma that fateful night when he'd clasped what he'd supposed was his beautiful djinniyeh to his arms, only to find his face pressed firmly against the hairy chest of the 'efreet, Kaug. The garden belonged to one of the elderly immortals of Akhran, a djinn who claimed to remember when time began. Too old and far too wise to have anything at all to do with humans anymore, the ancient djinn had established himself in a mansion whose bulbous-shaped towers and graceful minarets could ordinarily barely be seen through the lush, flowering trees and bushes of his garden.

The garden had changed, however. The wall that Sond had been accustomed to climb over with such agility was topped with wicked-looking iron spikes. Horses trampled the delicate orchids and gardenias, camels were hobbled on the tiled paths or noisily drank water from the marble fountains. Powerful djinn of all sizes and description surged about in frantic activity—tearing down the delicate latticework and using it to bolster defenses at the garden gate, shouting out to each other in graphic detail what they would do to Kaug and his various anatomical parts when they had him in their grasp.

Huddled in a window at the top of one of the towers, guarded by gigantic eunuchs, the djinniyeh peeped over the balcony, giggling and whispering whenever one of the djinn— who knew well the women were there—was bold enough to brave the baleful glare of the eunuchs and bestow a wink upon a veiled head that had caught his fancy.

Sond's gaze went instantly and eagerly to the balcony. Usti took one look at the strenuous activity going on all around him, groaned, and vanished precipitously behind an ornamental hedge. No one heard the fat djinn, however, or saw him disappear. The other djinn had spotted Sond and, crying out gladly, surged forward.

"Thank Akhran! Sond, where've you been? We can use that sword arm of yours!"

Flushed with pleasure by the welcome, Sond embraced his fellows—many of whom he had not seen in centuries.

"Where is that goat-thieving master of yours living now, Pejm?" Sond questioned one. "Down by Merkerish? Ah, I had not heard. I am sorry for his death. But we will be avenged. Deju! You were freed? You must tell me—"

"Pejm! *Bilhana!*" A loud voice interrupted Sond. "It's me! Pukah! I rescued you from Serinda! Uh, Pukah. The name is . . . well, doesn't matter. See you later." Pukah spoke to the back of another djinn. "Deju, it's me, Pukah! Here's *my* sword arm! Firmly attached to my shoulder. The one that rescued you from the city of Serinda. I— Uh . . . Serinda . . ."

"Serinda? Did you say Serinda?" A djinn rushed up to Pukah. The foxish face beamed in pleasure and cast a sidelong glance at Asrial to see if she was watching.

"Why, yes." Pukah performed the *salaam* with charming grace. "I am Pukah the hero of Serinda."

"Salaam aleikum, Serinda," said the djinn hurriedly. "Did I hear Sond had arrived? Oh, there he is! If you could just step aside, Serinda—"

"My name's not Serinda!" Pukah said irritably to the djinn's back. "I'm Pukah! The *hero* of Serin— Oh, never mind."

Elbowed firmly out of the way by one djinn then another as they crowded around Sond, Pukah was shoved off the path and found himself in a small grove of orange and lemon trees. Near him, huddled among the climbing roses, stood a forlorn-looking Asrial, staring with wide blue eyes at her surroundings.

The noise and confusion, the half-naked bodies—skin gleaming in the bright sunshine—the shouts and oaths, the obvious preparations for a battle, unnerved the angel. She had known, for she had heard her God, Promenthas, speak of a war in heaven. But it had never occurred to her that it would be like this—so much like a war on earth. She shrank back against a wall, hiding herself among the clinging tendrils of a morning glory.

What were the angels of Promenthas doing now? Had war come to them, too? Undoubtedly. An image came to her of the seraphim ripping the heavy wooden pews from the floor of the cathedral and stacking them against the doors; of archangels breaking out the lovely stained-glass windows, standing armed with bow and arrow; of cherubim clasping fiery swords, ready to defend the altar, to defend Promenthas.

It was too horrible to imagine. Asrial turned her face against the wall to blot out the dreadful sights and sounds. She had seen wars upon earth, but those happened among humans. She had never imagined that the peace and tranquillity of her eternal home could be so violated.

"*Bilhana. Bilshifa.* My name is Pukah." Standing alone at the edge of a path, the djinn bowed and shouted and was completely and soundly ignored. "Fedj! Raja! Over here!" Pukah waved his arms, jumping up and down to make himself seen above the heads and shoulders of the larger djinn.

Fedj and Raja, however, were staring warily at Sond, who was returning the favor arms folded across his massive chest. Old enemies, were they to meet as friend or foe? Then Raja's face split into a smile. With one hand he greeted Sond with a blow on the back that sent the djinn headlong into a hibiscus bush, while with the other he proffered a jewel-encrusted dagger.

"Accept this gift, my dear friend!" said Raja.

"My dear friend, with pleasure!" cried Sond, making his way out of the foliage.

"Dear friend," mimicked Pukah in disgust. "Not two weeks ago they would have ripped out each other's eyes."

"Brother!" Fedj threw his huge arms around Sond and clasped him close. "Words cannot tell how I have missed you!" It was undoubtedly fond regard that caused Fedj to nearly squeeze the breath out of his "brother."

Sliding his muscular arms around Fedj's waist, Sond locked a hand over his wrist.

"Words fail me as well, brother!" Sond grunted, returning the embrace with such affection that the sound of cracking bones was distinctly audible.

"I think I'm going to vomit!" Pukah muttered. "And never paying any attention to me—the hero of Serinda! Well, let them! Say"—he paused and hastily looked around—"I've got something that will make their bulging biceps twitch. Asrial, my enchanter! Where are you, my angel?" He peered through a tangle of hanging orchids. "Asrial?" A note of panic tinged his voice. "Asrial! I— Oh, there you are!" He sighed in relief. "I couldn't find you! My shy one!" Pukah gazed at her adoringly. "Hiding yourself away! Come." He took hold of her hand. "I want you to meet my friends—"

"No! Pukah, please!" Asrial hung back, her eyes wide with fright. "Let me go! I must return to my people!"

"Nonsense," said Pukah crisply, tugging at her. "Your people are my people. We're all immortal, and we're all in this together. Come on, there's a sweet child. Come on."

Reluctantly, hoping to avoid attention and still resolute on leaving, Asrial crept forward out of her hiding place.

"Look!" shouted Pukah proudly. "Look here! This is *my* angel!"

Asrial's pale cheeks flushed a delicate pink. "Pukah, don't say such things!" she begged. "I'm not your an—" Her words died away, sucked up and swallowed by a dreadful silence that fell over the djinn assembled in the garden, the eunuchs standing guard on the balcony, the djinniyeh gazing down at her over their veils.

Breathing heavily, one hand feeling his ribs to see if all were intact, Fedj used his other hand to point to Asrial.

"What's this?" he demanded.

"An angel," explained Pukah loftily, his foxish nose in the air.

"I can see it's an angel," Fedj snapped. "What's it doing here!"

"It's not an it, it's a she, as any but a blind beggar could plainly see! And she's with me! She's come to help—"

"Come to spy you mean!" roared Raja.

"A spy of Promenthas's!" shouted the djinn angrily, waving their swords and advancing on the two.

Asrial shrank back against Pukah, who shoved the angel behind him and faced the mob, his chin jutting out so far that any sword slice must have taken that portion of his face off first.

"Spy? If you muscle-bound apes had brains in your heads instead of your pectorals, you'd know that Promenthas is an ally of *Hazrat* Akhran—"

"Wrong! We heard Promenthas fights with Quar!" returned many furious voices.

"That is not true!" Stung to courage, Asrial sprang forward before Pukah could stop her. "I have just come from a meeting with the two of them. Your God and mine pledged to help each other!"

There were unconvinced looks and mutterings.

"A trick! The angel lies. All angels are liars, you know that!"

"Now wait, my friends. I can vouch for the angel—" Sond began.

"Ah, ha! So you're in this, too. I might have known, you thieving eater of horseflesh!" Fedj blocked Sond's path.

"This from one who beds with sheep!" Sond retorted scornfully. "Get out of my way, coward."

"Coward! All know it was the son of your master who fled a battle dressed as a woman!"

Steel flashed in the hands of the djinn.

"Take my advice, Pukah, and get her out of here!" came a yawning voice from somewhere down at their feet. Usti lay flat on his back, hands folded over his fat belly, peering up at them.

"Perhaps you're right," said Pukah, somewhat daunted

and dismayed at the glittering eyes and glinting blades closing in on him.

"I'm not going!" Asrial retorted. Her white wings fanned back and forth in her agitation, her golden hair—stirred by the wind she created—floated in a cloud about her face. "Stop it!" Running forward, she hurled herself between Fedj and Sond, blocking their swords with her small white hands. "Don't you see? This is Kaug's doing! He wants to divide us, split us up. Then he can devour us piece by piece!"

Roughly shoving the angel aside, Fedj lunged at Sond. Asrial fell to the ground, in imminent danger of being trampled by the combatants, and Pukah, with a frantic cry, leaped to drag her out of the way. Before he could reach her, another figure sprang up from the flowers that were being torn to shreds by brawling, stamping feet.

The lithe, supple figure of a djinniyeh clothed in flowing silken pantalons and diaphanous veils stood in front of the fallen Asrial, guarding the angel's body with her own.

"Nedjma!" Sond gasped, falling backward, trembling from head to foot.

Dropping his sword, the enraptured djinn held out his arms and took a step forward, only to find himself suddenly blocked by the massive girth of a gigantic, scimitar-wielding eunuch who reared up from the earth like a mountain and stood rocklike and immovable between Sond and the djinniyeh.

Nedjma did not quite come up to Sond's shoulder. She barely came up to Raja's waist. But the enraged glance she flashed the djinn lopped off heads, cut brawny torsos in two, and reduced towering mounds of muscle and brawn to quivering lumps of immortal flesh. Gently and tenderly, without speaking a word, Nedjma bent down and helped Asrial to her feet. Putting her arm protectively around the angel's shoulder, she drew the white-robed body close to her own. With a last, flaring glance at Sond, Nedjma disappeared, taking the eunuch and Asrial with her.

His face burning with shame, his body shaking with thwarted passion, Sond bent over and retrieved his sword. Straightening, he avoided Fedj's eyes. Fedj, for his part, sheathed his sword and slouched out of the circle, muttering something about women minding their own affairs and staying out of those of men, but not saying it loudly enough that it could be overheard by those veiled and perfumed figures whispering indignantly together on the balcony.

Pukah watched anxiously until he saw white wings and golden hair being soothed and comforted above.

"Well, now that that's settled," began the young djinn brightly, stepping into the center of the garden, "let me introduce myself. I am Pukah, the hero of Serinda. You don't remember me, but I saved your lives, at great risk to my own. It was like this—"

At that moment, Kaug struck.

Chapter 6

A blast of wind from the 'efreet's cavernous mouth swept through the pleasure garden. Tall palms bent double, torn leaves and petals filled the air like rain, water sloshed over the tiled rims of the ornamental pools. Usti, rudely awakened, dove for cover beneath a flower bed. On the balcony above, the djinniyeh screamed and caught hold of their fluttering veils, striving to see what was going on while the eunuchs pushed them toward the safety of the palace. Below, the djinn grimly drew their swords and braced themselves against the buffeting wind.

Fed by his God, the 'efreet's power had grown immense, and so had his size. Many times taller than the tallest minaret that graced the palace, many times wider than the walls surrounding it, Kaug lumbered across the immortal plane. The ground that existed only in the minds of those who stood upon it shook with the footfalls of the giant 'efreet. His breath was a gale, his hands could have picked up the huge Raja and tossed him lightly from the heavens. All the djinn in the garden, standing each upon the others' shoulders, could not have achieved Kaug's height.

Yet they faced him. They would not give up meekly, as they had heard rumors of other immortals doing. Akhran himself—his flesh wounded and bleeding, absorbing the hurts

86

inflicted on his people as he suffered at the same time from their dwindling faith—continued to fight. So would his immortals, until their power was drained, the strength of the mind that created their bodies depleted, and the bodies themselves vanquished, lying broken and bloody on the field of battle.

Kaug stopped just outside the walls of the garden and stared down with mocking triumph at the djinn within.

Sond took a step forward and raised his sword defiantly. Nedjma's perfume was in the djinn's nostrils; the memory of that scathing look she had cast him burned his mind. "Be gone, Kaug, while you still have a chance to save your worthless hide. If you leave now, we will not harm you."

Kaug's ugly face twisted into a grotesque smile. Taking a step forward, he calmly flattened one entire section of wall with a stamp of his foot.

"Sond!" said Kaug pleasantly, moving his other foot and crushing another section of wall. "So you are here? I am pleased, astonished but pleased. I thought you would have returned to the Tel, for I heard that former master of yours—poor old Majiid—has given up and is courting Death. Now there's a woman who will bring peace to his harem!"

Sond's face paled visibly. He cast a swift glance at Fedj, who averted his face from his brother djinn's alarmed, questioning eyes.

"And little Pukah," continued the 'efreet, his rumbling voice cracking the foundation stones of the palace, "here you are while your master sizzles like a lump of hot lead upon the Sun's Anvil. He, too, courts Death, and I fancy he will like her better than the wife he has!" Kaug chuckled and swung his hand, and a tower was swept from the castle walls. The djinn scrambled to avoid the debris that crashed into the garden around them, but remained standing in the ruins, grim and determined.

"You must be sorry you left my service, little Pukah!" The 'efreet continued taunting them, but Pukah was only half listening, most of his attention being concentrated on a conversation taking place within his brain between himself and himself.

"We cannot win this, you know, Pukah," he stated.

"You, Pukah, are wise as always," his alter ego agreed with a sigh.

"And I am smarter than this heap of fish flesh," argued Pukah.

"Of course!" answered Pukah stoutly, knowing what was expected.

"Here's my plan." Pukah presented it, not without some pride. "What do you think of it?" he demanded when his alter ego remained silent for a rather prolonged period of time.

"There are . . . a certain number of flaws," suggested Pukah timidly.

"Of course, I haven't had time to work out all the details." Pukah glowered at himself, who considered that it might be time to keep quiet but couldn't forbear bringing up one more problem.

"What about Asrial?"

"Ah!" Pukah sighed. "You're right. I had forgotten." Then he said in a softer, sadder voice, "I don't think it will matter, friend. I don't believe there is any hope."

"But you should talk to her!" Pukah urged.

"I will," Pukah conceded hastily, "but I must start this to working immediately, so please shut up."

The inner Pukah was instantly silent, and the outer Pukah—all this having taken only flashing moments in his quicksilver brain—bowed gracefully to the 'efreet.

"Truly, Kaug the Magnificent, seeing you now in your glory and majesty, I do deeply regret that I gave in to the vile threats of the brutish Sond and allowed him to force me to leave your side."

Astounded and enraged, the djinn turned and glared at Pukah. Sond made a furious lunge at him, only to be stopped by the 'efreet's commanding voice.

"Halt! No one touch him. I find him . . . amusing." Squatting down, his hulking form casting a shadow black as night over the garden, his breath flattening trees, Kaug confronted Pukah. "So you want to be back in my service, do you, Little Pukah? Better that than the Realm of the Dead, eh?"

The 'efreet cast a significant glance around at all the djinn and the djinniyeh, peering through the windows above, and had the pleasure of seeing them all blench and cringe. Kaug grinned. "Yes, the Realm of the Dead. You remember that, don't you? No more human bodies, no more human pleasures and feelings, no more romps on earth, no more battles and wars, no more human food and drink"—a muffled moan could be heard, coming from beneath one of the flower beds—"no more djinn and djinniyeh. Nameless, shapeless servants of Death, that's what you'll become once I'm finished with you. When you no longer answer their prayers, the humans you serve will think they have been abandoned by their God. They will turn to Quar, to a God who listens to them, and to me—a servant who knows how to provide for their every need and desire as—"

"—as a good master provides for his slaves," supplemented Pukah.

Kaug glowered, this not being the most flattering of metaphors. But Pukah's face was bland and innocent, his tone admiring as he continued. "It appears to me that this will mean a tremendous amount of work for you, O Kaug, and though I have no doubt that your shoulders are big enough to bear the burden, it cannot help but reduce your time for . . . uh . . . whatever pleasures you like to pursue." Momentarily flustered, Pukah had no idea what pleasures these might be, and he certainly didn't care to think on it a great deal.

"My pleasure is serving Quar!" Kaug roared, straightening to his full height, his head punching a hole in the starry sky.

"Oh, yes, it must be, of course!" stammered Pukah, the resultant gale knocking him off his feet. "But," he continued cunningly, picking himself back up, "you won't be serving Quar, will you? You'll be serving humans! Answering to their every whim. 'See that my twelve daughters are married to rich husbands!' 'Bring me a chest of gold and two caskets of jewels!' 'Cure this ailment from which my goat suffers!' 'Convince my son that he wants a job selling iron pots in the marketplace!' 'Make my dwelling as large as my neighbor's!' 'Deliver—"

"Enough!" Kaug muttered. It was plain from the angry

expression on the 'efreet's face that Pukah's shot had hit a vital spot. Endeavoring to fight a war in heaven, attempting to foment distrust and hatred among the various factions of immortals, Kaug was continually being forced to leave his important work to perform those very degrading tasks that Pukah had mentioned. Just a few days ago, in fact, he'd had to leave a pitched battle with the imps and demons of Astafas and return to earth to carry the houri, Meryem, to an audience with the Imam.

"What a waste it will be," added Pukah sadly, "to set us all to guarding the dead, who, after all, aren't in that much need of guarding. Not to mention serving Death. She doesn't have half the responsibility that *you* carry, O Kaug the Overburdened."

Pukah allowed his voice to trail off, seeing a thoughtful look crinkle the 'efreet's eyes. "Perhaps this intense mental process will rupture something," the djinn muttered hopefully. A frown formed in the beetling brows, and he hastened to forestall what he guessed would be the 'efreet's next argument. "I am certain that Quar, having depleted his own supply of immortals—in a most worthy cause, I grant you, but leaving you, unfortunately, short of help—Quar will be most pleased at your resourcefulness and ingenuity in being able to furnish your Great God with additional help to run the world."

Kaug absently uprooted a tree or two as he considered this latest proposition. Sond, taking advantage of the 'efreet's preoccupation, sidled nearer Pukah and hissed out of the side of his mouth, "Have you gone mad?"

"Can you win a fight against him?" Pukah demanded in a piercing whisper.

"No," Sond conceded grudgingly.

"Do you want to guard the Realm of the Dead?"

"No!"

"Then be silent and let me—"

Kaug fixed Pukah with a steely-eyed gaze, and the djinn was immediately all polite and respectful attention.

"You are saying, Little Pukah, that you and your brethren should come work for me instead of Death?"

Pukah bowed, hands pressed together prayerfully. "We will be honored—"

"We will be damned!" Sond started to shout, but Pukah's elbow in Sond's solar plexus deprived the djinn of breath, voice, and defiance all at one blow. There is no doubt the other djinn would have shouted their own resistance but that the baleful eye of the 'efreet swiveled round and gazed fiercely at each of them.

Gracefully Pukah glided in front of the gasping Sond and faced the 'efreet.

"Most Generous Kaug, my brethren are, as you can see, overwhelmed by the opportunity. They are stupefied and cannot express their thanks in a fitting manner."

"Thanks for what? I've made no offer yet!"

"Ah," said Pukah, looking at Kaug out of the corner of his eye, "you dare do nothing without consulting Quar. I understand."

"I do what I please!" thundered the 'efreet, the blast smashing every pane of glass on the djinn's immortal plane.

"Still, we wouldn't want to rush things. Give my brethren and me seventy-two hours human time to consider your terms and decide whether or not we accept."

Kaug's great eyes blinked. The 'efreet was somewhat confused. It was an unusual feeling for the generally sharp-witted Kaug, but then he'd had much on his mind lately. He did not recall offering terms. Or had he? The 'efreet knew that somewhere he'd lost control of the situation, and this angered him. He considered flattening castle, garden, and these irritating djinn at a breath, then snatching their immortal spirits from the shells of their bodies and sending them forthwith to Death. But at that moment, Kaug heard a gong ring three times.

Quar was summoning him. Undoubtedly some human needed his donkey scrubbed.

"You can always return and squash us later, if that is what you decide," suggested Pukah in the most respectful tones. "We're not likely to go anywhere." Except to rescue our master from the Sun's Anvil, the djinn added to himself, exulting in his own cleverness.

Seventy-two hours. Kaug considered. Yes, he could always return and squash them later. And in the meantime, seventy-two hours would be long enough to pluck a thorn from Quar's flesh.

"Smart Little Pukah," said Kaug to himself, "you shall have your seventy-two hours to hatch whatever plan is picking its way out of the shell of your mind. Seventy-two hours that will be the death of the Calif and soon be the death—or enslavement—of all of you."

"Seventy-two hours," Kaug stated out loud and—at the insistent clanging of the gong—the 'efreet started to leave. Seeming, at the last moment, to remember something, Kaug returned. "Oh, and you're quite right, Little Pukah," he said, grinning as he dropped a huge iron cage over the palace and gardens of the ancient djinn. "You're *not* going anywhere!"

Chapter 7

Khardan started up out of an exhausted sleep he never meant to take. He was wide-awake, alert. Unconscious, his mind had warned him of danger, and now, crouching in the meager shade offered by a tall sand dune, he stared around to discover what had quickened his heartbeat and pricked his skin.

He did not have to look long or far. The distant, ominous grinding sound came to him instantly. Turning his head to the west, the direction they were traveling, he saw a thick cloud on the horizon. It was a strange cloud, for it came from the land, not the sky. Its color was peculiar—a pale gray tinged with ocher.

In the top of the cloud, two huge, glistening eyes stared down at Khardan.

"An 'efreet," the Calif said aloud, though no one heard him. Beside him, huddled in the sand, Zohra slept, and next to her Mathew either slept or was dead, Khardan didn't know which. The boy had pitched forward on his face, unconscious, and nothing would rouse him.

Khardan looked away. If the boy was dead, he was lucky. If he wasn't, he would be soon.

Serinda was no longer visible on the horizon. The 'efreet might have swallowed it up, for all Khardan knew.

Glaring at the 'efreet and the sandstorm it generated,

Khardan clenched his hand over the hilt of the dagger he wore in his sash. His djinn had provided the dagger, just as they had provided clothes and water. They had thought of everything.

Everything except defeat.

Khardan wondered where Pukah was. Enslaved? Guarding the Realm of the Dead?

"If so," Khardan muttered, "you are liable to see your master very shortly!"

The death of the desert is a terrible one. It is a death of swollen tongue and cracked lips, a death of pain and suffering and eventual, tortured madness. Drawing his dagger, Khardan stared at the sharp, curved blade. He turned it in his hand. The sun, not yet obscured by the deadly, yellowish cloud, blazed on the steel, half blinding him.

Zohra slept the sleep of exhaustion and did not waken when he gently rolled her over onto her back. Khardan sat for long moments, staring at her face. He was dazed by the heat, and though the storm was still far away, there was a gritty taste in the air that was already making it difficult to breathe.

How long her eyelashes were. Long and thick and black, the lashes cast shadows over her smooth skin. He brushed his finger across them, and then, reaching out, he gently if clumsily unclasped the veil and removed it from her face.

Her mouth was parted, her tongue ran across it as though she drank in her sleep. Lifting the *girba*, he poured the water—the last of the water—onto the curved lips. He spilled most of it; the sand drank it greedily and seemed thirsty for more.

Soon it would have a richer, warmer liquid.

Zohra smiled, sighed, and drew a deep, easy breath. The expression of fierce pride was gone, softened and smoothed by weariness and suffering. Khardan found that he missed it. A burning hot wind rose from in front of the Calif, whipping his robes around him. He glanced up. As the wind blew stronger, the cloud grew larger, the grinding sound louder, the evil eyes in the cloud nearer. Resolutely, Khardan turned the peaceful, serene face away from him.

"Farewell, wife," he said softly. It seemed there should be more to say between them, but he couldn't think of anything. He was too tired, too dazed by the heat. When they met again beyond, then perhaps he could explain, could tell her everything that had been in his heart.

The Calif placed the point of the dagger on the skin right below Zohra's left ear.

A sound—a ringing sound, the tinkling sound of bells that accompanies a camel's plodding, splayfooted steps over the sand—arrested the killing stroke. Khardan paused, raising his head, wondering if the desert madness had overtaken him already.

"Pukah! Sond!" He meant it to be a shout, but the words came from his throat no more than a painful croak. There was no answer, but he heard the ringing clearly. If it was madness, then it had a smell as well. The odor of camel was unmistakable.

Sheathing the dagger, Khardan rose hastily to his feet and scrambled and crawled up to the top of the dune.

Crouched on the ridge, his arms braced against the blasting wind, the Calif looked below and saw camels—four of them tethered together—plodding through the sand. But there were no djinn hovering triumphantly in the air above them. There was only a single rider. Swathed from head to toe in the black, flowing robes of the nomad, he kept his face covered against the sandstorm. Only his eyes were visible, and as he drew near, these stared straight at Khardan.

In the next instant, Khardan saw the stranger's hand dart into his robes.

Realizing suddenly that he was an excellent target poised on the ridge of the dune, the Calif cursed and, hand on his own dagger, slipped swiftly back behind the dune's rim. Peering cautiously over the edge, he kept the stranger within sight.

The man in black made a swift, deft throwing motion. Sun flared on steel. Flinching, Khardan instinctively flattened himself. The knife thudded into the sand, hilt up, inches in front of the nomad's nose.

Khardan barely glanced at the knife. He stared warily at the stranger, waiting for the attack. The man relaxed in the camel saddle. Leaning one arm easily upon the leg that was crossed in front to help him maintain his balance, he gestured toward the thrown dagger. Squinting his eyes against the blowing sand, the Calif diverted his gaze from the stranger to the weapon.

The hilt was made of gold, inlaid with silver, and it was fashioned in a design he himself had worn on a suit of black armor. Two ruby eyes winked at Khardan from the head of a severed snake.

Chapter 8

Lowering his facecloth, Auda ibn Jad shouted over the rising storm. "Greetings, brother!"

Khardan scrambled and slid halfway down the side of the dune and halted some distance from the Black Paladin. Eyes narrowed against the stinging sand, the Calif stood, unmoving. Ibn Jad urged the grumbling camels forward.

"For a man who was expecting Death, you don't look glad to see me," he yelled.

"Perhaps that is because it is Death I see," returned Khardan.

Snagging a waterskin from his saddle, Auda offered it to the nomad.

"I need nothing," said the Calif, not glancing at the water, his gaze fixed on the Black Paladin.

"Ah, of course. You have drunk your fill from the vast rivers that run through this land." Auda lifted the *girba* to his lips and drank deeply. Water trickled down the corners of his mouth, flowing into the short, neatly trimmed black beard that graced his strong jawline. Replacing the stopper, he wiped his mustached lips with the back of his hand, then cast a glance at the approaching sandstorm. "And, on a cool day like today, a man does not thirst as he does when it is—"

"Why are you here?" Khardan demanded. "How did you leave the castle?"

Auda glanced up at the rapidly darkening sky. "First I suggest we make what shelter we can before the enemy strikes."

"Tell me now or we will both die where we stand!"

Auda regarded him silently, then shrugged and leaned close to be heard. "I left as you did, nomad. I placed my life in the hands of my God, and he gave it back to me!" The thin lips smiled. "The Black Sorceress called for my execution. I was accused of aiding prisoners to escape and asked if I had anything to say in my defense. I said you and I had shared blood. Closer than brothers born, our lives were pledged to each other. I had vowed this, before the God, before Zhakrin."

"They believed you?"

"They had no choice. The God himself, Zhakrin, appeared before them. He is weak, his form indistinct and constantly shifting. But he has returned to us," Auda said with quiet pride, "and the strength of our faith increases his power daily!"

These evil people had never wavered in their faith, even when it seemed their God had left them forever. Now he was increasing in strength. Our God, Akhran . . . wounded . . . dying. Khardan flushed uncomfortably and, reaching out his hand, took the waterskin from the Black Paladin. He drank sparingly, but Auda waved a hand at his camels. "Take your fill. There is more."

"There are others in my care," Khardan said.

A spark flickered deep in Auda's dark, hooded eyes.

"So they survived, the two who were with you? The beautiful, black-haired wildcat, your wife, and the gentle Blossom? Where are they?"

"They lie on the other side." Covering his mouth and nose with the cloth against the blowing sand, Khardan turned and began to clamor up the side of the dune, wondering why it was like setting a spark to dry tinder to hear the Black Paladin praise Zohra.

Tugging hard on the camel's lead, shouting imperative

commands, Auda dragged the recalcitrant animals to their knees at the bottom of the dune where they might find some protection from the fury of the storm.

Zohra was awake. Hearing their voices, she had climbed partway up the dune to meet them.

"Mat-hew!" Khardan shouted, pointing and indicating with a wave of his hand that Zohra was to bring the boy with her.

She understood and slid back down to get him. Hand on his shoulder, she shook him hard. There was no response, and she glanced up helplessly at Khardan.

The 'efreet howled furiously, sand swirled around them, making it nearly impossible to see. Sliding down the side of the dune, Khardan reached Zohra. Between them, they pummeled and screamed and managed at last to wake the young man and indicate to him that he must climb the dune to escape the storm.

Dazed and uncomprehending, Mathew did what he was told, responding to the hands that dragged him along and the voices that yelled in his ear. Once over the top, he collapsed and slithered down the side. Auda caught him and carried him to where the camels crouched, heads hunched down. Propping the boy up against the flanks of the animals, sheltered from the blasting wind, Auda flung a blanket over him and returned to assist Zohra.

Black eyes blazing, she drew away from Auda as he would have taken her hand, and stumbled through the sand to make her own shelter near Mathew. She would not even accept water until Khardan took it from the Paladin's hand and gave it to her.

Shrugging, Auda leaned back against the flanks of the camel he had been riding. Khardan sank down next to him.

"This is useless," he yelled. "We cannot fight an 'efreet!"

"Ah, but we do not fight alone," Auda replied calmly.

Looking up into the sky, startled, Khardan saw that the eyes in the storm cloud were no longer gazing at him but at something on their own level, something he could not see. A strong breeze, cool and damp and smelling faintly of salt spray, rose up from the opposite direction, blowing against the 'efreet. Caught in the crosscurrents of opposing winds, the sand swept about them in blinding, whirling clouds. The camels faced out the storm stolidly. The humans ducked beneath blankets. Despite that, sand clogged their mouths and noses, sending them coughing and choking, making each breath a struggle.

Abruptly the 'efreet drew back. The winds ceased to howl, the sand quit its eerie wailing. Stirring, displacing a mound of sand that covered him, Khardan raised his head.

"Either the 'efreet believes we are dead, or he has decided to leave and let the sun finish us off," he stated, spitting grit from his mouth. "The creature is gone."

Auda did not respond. The Paladin's eyes were closed, and the Calif heard a faint murmuring coming from behind the folds of the *haik*.

He is praying, Khardan realized. "So it *was* your God who let you go," he said gruffly when ibn Jad opened his eyes and reached for the *girba*.

"I am honor bound to keep my vow," Auda replied, swishing water in his mouth and spitting it out. "Zhakrin commanded that I be set free. Free . . . to keep another vow—a vow made by another brother."

"I think I know of this vow." Khardan accepted the *girba* and, out of habit, drank sparingly.

"They told you of it that night. . . ."

The first night at Castle Zhakrin. The Calif had been present—a prisoner—at a meeting of the Black Paladins and had heard the story Auda was now repeating.

"Dying at the feet of the accursed priest of Quar, dying of wounds inflicted by his own hand so that the *kafir* could not claim his life nor their God his soul, Catalus, my brother in Zhakrin, laid the blood curse of our God upon the Imam. I have been chosen to redeem that curse."

Khardan's gaze shifted from the man's impassive face to the silver-and-gold hilt that could be seen protruding from his sash. "An assassin's dagger?"

"Yes. Benario, God of the Stealthy, has blessed it."

Grunting, Khardan shook his head. "You are a fool." With this pronouncement, he settled himself more comfortably back against the camel and closed his eyes.

Auda grinned. "Then I travel with a party of fools. How do you think I found you here? How do you think I came to be carrying water enough for three, or that I have brought three riding camels with me?"

Khardan shrugged. "That is easy. You followed our tracks through the sand. As for bringing along the camels, perhaps you like their company!"

Auda laughed—a sound like rocks splitting apart. From his smooth face and cruel, cold eyes, it seemed he did not laugh often. His mirth ended quickly—rocks tumbling down the side of a cliff and vanishing into a chasm of darkness. Leaning near, Auda grasped hold of the Calif's arm, his strong fingers digging deeply into the flesh.

"Zhakrin guided me!" he hissed, and Khardan felt hot breath upon his cheek. "Zhakrin sent me to follow you, and it was Zhakrin who drove off Quar's 'efreet! Once again I have saved your life, nomad. I have kept my vow to you.

"Now you will keep yours to me!"

Chapter 9

They slept fitfully through the day, sheltered from the searing heat in a small tent carried by the *djemel*, Auda's baggage camel. With the setting of the sun they woke, ate tasteless unleavened bread also provided by the Black Paladin, drank his water, then prepared to leave. Few words were spoken.

Though intensely curious about Auda and his arrival that had saved their lives, Zohra could not ask Khardan about him, and the Calif—grim and stern-faced and silent—volunteered no information. It was unseemly for a woman to question her husband, and though Zohra normally cared little about proprieties, she felt a strange reluctance to flout them before the Black Paladin. She kept her eyes lowered, as was proper, when she went about the small duties involved in preparing and serving their meager meal, but glancing at him from beneath the fringe of her lashes, she never failed to notice ibn Jad watching her.

Had there been lust or desire in the black eyes, or even exasperated fury as she was accustomed to seeing in Khardan's, Zohra would have discounted and scorned it. But the Paladin's flat gaze, expressive of no emotion whatsoever, unnerved her. She found herself stealing furtive glances at him more often than she intended, hoping to catch some glimmer of inner light in the eyes, gain some idea of his thoughts and intentions. Whenever she did, she was disconcerted to find her glances returned.

She could have whispered her doubts and fears to Mathew, except that the young man was behaving most oddly. Slow to waken, he moved sluggishly and stared about him in a dazed manner that took in the presence of Auda ibn Jad without surprise or comment. He drank as much as they allowed him but refused food and lay down again while the rest of them ate. Only when ibn Jad shook his shoulder to rouse him when it was time to leave did Mathew react to the man as though he remembered him, flinching away from his touch and staring at him with wild, glistening eyes.

But he meekly followed ibn Jad when bidden to rise and leave the tent. Obediently and without question, he mounted the camel and allowed the two men to position him comfortably in the saddle.

Zohra watched Mathew's strange behavior with concern and again, had they been alone, would have called it to Khardan's attention. Once or twice she endeavored to catch the Calif's attention. Khardan avoided her pointedly, and—with ibn Jad's eyes always on her, even when he was looking at something else—Zohra kept silent.

"We will reach Serinda before morning," Auda announced as they rode out into the rapidly cooling air of the night. "It is well that I came along, brother. For had you made it across the Sun's Anvil to Serinda alive, there—in the city of death—you would surely have died. There is no water in Serinda."

"How could that happen?" asked Khardan disbelievingly, the first words other than commands or instructions concerning their leaving he had uttered. "They must have dug their wells deep, to provide water for so many. How could Serinda's wells ever run dry?"

"Dug?" Twisting in his saddle, Auda glanced at Khardan, riding beside him, with amusement. "They dug no wells, nomad. The people of Serinda used machines to suck the water out of the Kurdin Sea. The water flowed along great canals that stood high in the air and emptied into *hauz* for the city's use. I have heard it said that these canals could sometimes be made to take the water directly into a man's dwelling."

"It is too bad we have no children traveling with us,"

Khardan remarked. "They would be fascinated by such lies. I suppose you will tell me next that these people of Serinda were fish people, who drank salt water."

Auda did not seem offended at this reaction to his tales. "The Kurdin Sea was not always salty, or so I have heard the wise men in the court of Khandar teach. Be that true or not, I repeat we will find no water at Serinda. There will be shelter from the sun there, however. We can spend tomorrow safely within its walls, then travel the next night. We have water enough to last that long, but no longer. The following day when we reach your camp around the Tel, we can lead your people to war against Quar. I presume"—Auda turned his flat, glittering eyes upon Khardan—"that your own wells have not run completely dry?"

It was obvious he was not speaking of water.

"The wells of my people run deep and pure!" Khardan retorted, resenting the insinuation but not daring to say more, since the Paladin's remarks hit closely near the center of his target. Flicking the camel stick across the beast's shoulder, he kicked at the camel's flanks with his heels, driving the animal forward to take the lead.

Riding behind the men, her attention divided between listening to the conversation and worriedly watching a swaying, groggy Mathew, Zohra knew by the hunch of the man's shoulders that Auda was regarding Khardan speculatively.

Her fingers curled over the reins, unconsciously twisting and pleating the leather. She had never—until now—heard true fear in her husband's voice.

Chapter 10

It was in the dark shadows of the walls of Serinda, just as the eastern sky was beginning to brighten with the coming of day, that Mathew tumbled from his saddle and lay like one dead in the sand.

More than once on the long journey, Zohra had seen the young man's head nod listlessly, his shoulders slump, and his body begin to slant sideways. Riding up beside him, she lashed out with the camel stick, striking him a blow across his shoulders. The thin, flexible stick bit through cloth and into flesh like a whip—a painful but effective means of wakening a drifting rider. Mathew jerked upright. In the starlit darkness she could see him staring at her in puzzled hurt. Dropping back behind him, she put her hand to her veiled lips, enjoining him to silence. Khardan would have little patience with a man who could not sit a camel.

Zohra saw Mathew start to sway when they reached Serinda, but she could not urge her camel forward fast enough to catch him. She knelt beside him. One touch of her hand upon his hot, dry forehead told her what she had long begun to suspect.

"The fever," she said to Khardan.

Lifting the young man in his arms—the youth's frail body was as light as that of a woman's—Khardan carried him through the gates of Serinda. Half-buried in the sand, the gates that had once kept out formidable enemies now stood open to the one enemy that could never be defeated—time.

Pukah would not have recognized this city as the one in which he had performed his heroics. Quar's spell had made it appear to the immortals as they wanted to see it—a rollicking city of teeming life and sudden death. Streets choked with sand were streets choked with brawling mobs. Doors falling from their rusted hinges were doors broken in fights. The wind that whispered desolately through empty, dust covered rooms was the whispering laughter of immortal lovers. The spell broken, Death once more walked the world, and Serinda was a city even She had abandoned long ago.

Auda led them through the empty, windswept streets to a building that he said was once the home of a wealthy, powerful family. Zohra, interested only in finding shelter for Mathew, paid scant attention to private bathing pools of colorful inlaid tile or the remains of statuary; except perhaps to note in shock that the bodies of the humans portrayed were completely naked. Though broken and defiled by centuries of looters, it was easy to see that their sculptors had given careful consideration to every detail.

Zohra was too concerned about Mathew to pay attention to carved rock. When Khardan had lifted him in his arms, Mathew had looked straight up at him and had not known him. The young man spoke in a language none of them understood and it was obvious from his rambling tone and occasional shouts and yells that what he was saying probably made little sense anyway.

Searching through the many-roomed dwelling, they finally found one chamber whose walls were still intact. Located in the interior of the large house, it seemed likely to offer relief from the midday heat.

"This will do," said Zohra, kicking aside some of the larger fragments of broken rock that littered the floor. "But he cannot lay on the hard stone."

"I will look for bedding," offered Auda ibn Jad. Silently as a shadow, he slipped from the room.

Sunlight streamed through a crack in the ceiling, its slanting rays visible in the haze of dust and fine sand that their arrival had raised up from the stone floor. The light glistened in Mathew's flaming red hair, touched the pallid face, glinted in the fever-glazed eyes that stared at sights only he could see. Khardan held him easily, securely. The young man's head lolled against the nomad's strong chest, a feebly twitching hand dangled over the Calif's arm.

Moving near to brush a lock of hair from Mathew's burning forehead, Zohra asked in a low, tense tone, "Why has that man come?"

"Thank Akhran he did," Khardan replied without looking at her.

"I was not afraid to die," Zohra answered steadily, "not even when I felt the point of your dagger touch my skin."

Khardan's gaze turned on her in astonishment. She had not been asleep! She had realized what he meant to do and why he had to do it, and she had chosen not to make it difficult for him. Lying completely still, shamming sleep, she would have met her death at his hand unflinchingly, unprotesting. Akhran himself knew what courage that must have taken!

Awed, Khardan could only stare at her wordlessly. In his arms Mathew stirred and moaned. Zohra moved her hand to caress the boy's cheek. Her dark eyes raised to look in Khardan's.

"That man?" she persisted softly. "He is evil! Why—"

"An oath," Khardan growled. "I swore an oath—"

A scraping sound warned them of the Black Paladin's return. He backed in through the chamber door, dragging a wool-stuffed pallet with him.

"It is filthy. Others have used it before us for a variety of purposes," said Auda. "But it is all I could find. I shook it out in the street and dislodged several inhabitants who were none too pleased at finding themselves homeless once more. But at least Blossom will not add scorpion stings to his other troubles. Where do you want it?"

Keeping her eyes lowered, Zohra pointed wordlessly to the coolest corner of the room. Auda threw the mattress down and kicked it into place with his foot. Zohra spread a felt camel blanket on top, then motioned for Khardan to put Mathew down. With clumsy gentleness, the Calif eased the suffering young man onto the pallet. The young man's wide-open eyes stared at them wildly; he spoke and tried weakly to sit up but could barely lift his head.

"Will he be well by morning?" asked ibn Jad.

Kneeling beside her patient, Zohra shook her head.

"Then, more to the point," continued the Black Paladin, "will he be dead by morning?"

Zohra turned her head; the dark eyes looked directly at Auda ibn Jad for the first time since he had joined them. For long moments she gazed at him in silence; then her eyes shifted to Khardan. "Bring water," she ordered—it was a woman's right to command when fighting sickness—and turned back to Mathew.

The two men left the building, walking through Serinda's silent streets to fetch the camels that had been left hobbled just within the gates.

Pulling down his facecloth, Auda smoothed his beard, ruefully shaking his head. "I swear by Zhakrin, nomad, I felt the fire in that look of hers scorch my flesh! I shall bear the scar the rest of my life."

Khardan walked without reply, the *haik* covering his own face, any glimmer of his thoughts lost in the cloth's shadow. Raising an eyebrow, Auda smiled, a smile that was absorbed and hidden by the black beard. Growing graver, the pale face smooth and impassive once more, he laid a slender, long-fingered hand upon Khardan's arm and brought the man to a halt.

"Draw her away, on some pretext or other. It need not be long."

"No." Khardan resumed his walk, his face averted from ibn Jad's, his eye staring straight ahead.

"There are ways that leave no mark. The boy succumbed to the fever. She will never know. My friend"—Auda pitched his voice louder to reach Khardan, who continued to walk away from him—"either Blossom dies now or we all die in a few days when the water runs out."

Khardan made a swift, angry, negating gesture with his hand, slicing it knifelike through the heat-shimmering air.

"My God will not allow the staying of my quest!" called ibn Jad.

Khardan reached the gates where the camels waited with the grumbling patience of their kind.

Auda remained standing, his arms folded across his chest.

"Unless you want to find that *two* have died by morning, nomad, you will take your woman out of that room and keep her out."

Khardan stopped, his hand resting on the splintered wood of the sand-mired gate. The fingers clenched. He did not turn around. "How long," he asked abruptly, "do you need?"

"The count of a thousand heartbeats," answered Auda ibn Jad.

Chapter 11

Soft-footed, Khardan entered the house they had taken over in Serinda, moving silently in the shadows that slanted across the corridors of the long-abandoned dwelling. Always uncomfortable within walls, the nomad felt doubly ill at ease walking the halls of another man's home without his permission or knowledge. No matter whether it was a Sultan's palace or the most tattered tent of the lowest tribe member, a home was a sacred place, inviolate—entered with ceremony, left with ceremony. And though this dwelling had been looted and stripped of its valuable possessions hundreds of years before, the mundane, everyday objects of those unknown people had been preserved in the dry air of the desert so that it seemed to Khardan as though the owners must return any moment—the women bewailing the destruction, the men angered and demanding revenge.

The nomad has little sense of time. Change means nothing to him, since his life changes daily. The nomad is the center of his own universe; he *is* his own universe. He must be, in order to survive his harsh world. The deaths of thousands in a nearby city will mean nothing to him. The stealing of a sheep from his fold will send him to war. Standing within these walls, Khardan had a sudden glimpse of time, the universe, and his own part in it. No longer was he the center, the man the sun rose for daily, the man for whom the stars shone, the man the winds buffeted and challenged to battle in personal contest. He was a grain of sand like millions of others. The stars never knew him. The sun would rise without him some day, the winds toss him heedlessly aside to pick up some other speck.

The man who walked this colored tile long ago once thought himself the center of the universe. The people who built this city knew themselves to be the apex of civilization. They had known their God to be the One, True God.

And now that God was nameless, unremembered, as were the men who worshipped him.

All that remained was of the earth, Sul, the elements. The stones on which Khardan trod were in the world before man came. Used by man, tooled by man, set in place by man, they would be here when man was gone.

The thought was humbling, frightening. The Calif's fingers moved over the smooth surface of the hewn rock, feeling the texture, the coolness within the stone despite the rapidly growing heat of the day outside, the slight depressions here and there where a hand wielding a chisel had slipped.

Sighing, his face grave, he moved on through the house, where the shadows seemed more welcome than he was, and quietly entered the room where Mathew lay.

Kneeling beside the pallet, her back to the door, Zohra glanced at Khardan as he entered, and glanced away. Intent on her patient, she wiped the boy's feverish face with a damp cloth.

"You should not be wasting the water," Khardan said in a harsher tone than he had meant to use. Let her offer what comfort she can. After all, what does it matter? He rebuked himself, but it was too late.

He knew by the set of her shoulders, the sudden twist of her hands, the wrenching of the cloth as she squeezed the liquid back into a cracked bowl, that he had made her angry.

"You are tired, Zohra. Why don't you go to sleep?" he said evenly. "I will tend to the young man."

He saw her flinch, the shoulders jerk, then straighten. She turned to confront him, and he braced himself to meet with impassive expression the black eyes that looked straight into his soul. Patiently, he waited for the storm of her rage to break over him. But her head drooped, her shoulders slumped, her hands dropped the cloth listlessly into the water. Sitting back upon her heels, Zohra raised her face to look into the heavens, not to pray, but to force the tears back down her throat.

"He means to kill him, doesn't he?"

"Yes." Khardan could say no more.

"And you will let him!" It was an accusation, a curse.

"Yes," Khardan answered steadily. "Would you leave him alone with this sickness on him, to let the fever burn him up, or let him do himself an injury in his ravings or be preyed upon by some animal—"

"No!" Zohra glared at him, scorching him with the scorn and fury in her eyes.

"Will you die with him?" Khardan persisted. "Abandon our people when we are within two days' ride of them? Let all we have gone through be for nothing? Let all *he* has accomplished be for nothing?"

"I—" The seething words died on trembling lips. The tears fell then, sliding down her cheeks, leaving tracks in the dust on her skin, dust that sifted in through every chink in the rock wall.

Khardan knelt beside her. He wanted to take her in his arms and share his own grief, his own anger, and the fear, which had overwhelmed him in the empty, silent halls of the dead house, of being that grain of sand. His hand moved to touch her, but at that moment her chin jutted forward proudly, she swiftly wiped her eyes.

"You will kill ibn Jad," she said resolutely.

"I may not. I have taken an oath," Khardan replied. "Even if I hadn't, I could not kill one who has twice saved my life."

"Then I will kill him. Give me your dagger." The black eyes looked at him fiercely, an odd contrast to the tears still glistening on her face.

Khardan lowered his face to hide a smile that came despite the burning in his heart. "That would not solve matters," he said quietly. "Mathew would still be sick and unable to travel. We would still have water enough for only three days and no way of finding any when that is gone. And it will take us two days to reach the Tel."

She could not answer but glared at him with the irrational rage men hold against one who speaks an unpleasant truth.

Mathew twisted and moaned. The fever made the bones ache, joints stiffen, and cramped the belly. Slowly, with a gentleness few ever saw, Khardan reached out and laid a hand upon the boy's forehead.

"Rest easy," he murmured, and whether it was the touch or the sound of the loved and admired voice that penetrated the horrors of delirium, Mathew grew calmer. The tortured limbs relaxed. But it would be only for the moment.

Khardan continued stroking the pale skin that was dry and hot as a sand snake's to the touch.

"He will slip from this life quickly and painlessly. His sufferings will finally be at an end. We do him no disservice, Zohra. You and I both know he is not happy living among us."

"And if he is not, whose fault is that?" Zohra demanded in a low, trembling voice. "We looked down on him and sneered at him and reviled him for his weakness, for disguising himself as a woman in order to survive. But now we know what it is to be alone and afraid and helpless in a strange and alien place! Did we acquit ourselves any better? Did we even do as well? That evil knight may have helped us to escape, but it was Mat-hew who saved you—"

"Stop it, woman!" Khardan shouted, twisting to his feet. "Every word you speak is a knife in my heart, and you do not inflict wounds that I have not already felt myself! But I have no choice! I have made the best decision I can, and it is a decision I must live with the rest of my life! Unless a miracle occurs and water falls from the hands of Akhran"— Khardan pointed at Mathew—"the boy must die. If you are here, and if you try to stop him, ibn Jad will have no compunction over killing you, too." Khardan held out his hand to her. "I saved the boy's life in the desert. He and I are even. Will you come and rest before this night's travel?"

Zohra stared at the hand poised above her, the violent struggle within herself apparent in the flush that made her face nearly as fevered as Mathew's. She gave Khardan one final, piercing glance from her black eyes, a glance tainted with hatred and anger and, amazingly, disappointment—amazingly to Khardan because we feel disappointment in another only when we expect better than we receive, and Khardan found it difficult to believe his wife thought even that well of him. Certainly she did not now. Wringing water from the cloth, she laid it gently on Mathew's brow; then, spurning her husband's outstretched hand, Zohra rose to her feet.

"I will sleep," she said in an emotionless tone, and brushed past Khardan without another look.

Sighing, he saw her wend her way through the corridors of the house, then stood gazing for long moments down at Mathew.

"What she said is true," he told the unhearing boy softly. "I understand your unhappiness now, and I am sorry."

He started to say something more, sighed, and abruptly turned away.

"I am sorry!"

Chapter 12

Zohra chose deliberately one of the many chambers located near Mathew's and hid within the shadows that played upon the stone walls. Holding her breath, she watched as the Calif emerged from the doorway. He paused and, lifting his hands to his eyes, rubbed them and continued down the hallway, shaking his head, toward the door that led outside.

He passed quite near her. Zohra saw his face was lined with fatigue and care, his brow furrowed with an anger that she knew turned in upon himself.

"This is not his fault," she whispered remorsefully, remembering the look with which she had favored him when she left. "If anything, the fault is mine, for without my meddling he would now be riding the heavens in honor with *Hazrat* Akhran. But it will be all right," she promised him silently as he passed by her. Her heart ached for his sorrow, and she wavered in her determination. "Perhaps I should tell him. What would it hurt? But no, he would try to stop me—"

She had unconsciously taken a step toward him, toward the door. She did not hear the sound of stealthy movement behind her nor realize that another person besides herself had chosen that particular room for a hiding place, until a hard-muscled body slammed into hers, pressing her into a corner, and a firm hand covered her mouth and nose.

Khardan stopped, listening, his head slightly turned.

The hand clasped her more firmly, the cool, glittering eyes informed her that the slightest movement was death.

Zohra held very still, and Khardan, shrugging tiredly, went dejectedly on his way.

The hand did not release its hold until they both heard the nomad's footsteps fade in the distance.

"He will sleep outside, where he can breathe the free air. I know him, you see." The hand loosened its grip, moving from her mouth down to close gently around her neck. Zohra stared, terrified yet fascinated, into the expressionless eyes so close to hers. "He is not far. You could bring him with a scream. But it would do you no good." The hand gently touched two points upon her throat. "My fingers here . . . and here . . . and you are dead. I told him I would be forced to kill you if you interfered, and he warned you. I heard him. He will be cleansed of your death."

There was no doubting those eyes.

"I will not scream," Zohra whispered, not so much because she feared being overheard but because her voice had failed her.

"Good."

The hands left her throat, the pressure against her body melted away. Closing her eyes, Zohra drew a deep breath and felt herself begin to tremble.

"Wait here and be silent, then, as you have promised," said ibn Jad, taking a step toward the door that led to the sick chamber. Inside, Mathew could be heard, tossing in his feverish throes. "He will not suffer, I promise you. Indeed, with this, his sufferings will end. Our God waits to award him for his valor, as does his own God. Do not move. I will be back. I have something to discuss with you—"

"No!" Zohra could not believe it was her voice that spoke, her hand that darted out—seemingly of its own accord— and caught hold of the strong, sinewy arm of the Black Paladin. She held on firmly, despite the narrowing of the black eyes that was the only sign of emotion she had yet seen in the man. "Please." Zohra tried to summon moisture enough in her dry mouth to form her words. "Don't kill him! Not yet! I . . . want to pray to Akhran—my God—for a miracle!"

How had she known this plea—and only this—would touch Auda ibn Jad? She wasn't certain. Perhaps it was what she had seen and heard of his people in his dark castle. Perhaps it was the way he always spoke of the Gods—all Gods—with grave reverence and respect. A plea for pity, for mercy, for compassion, for the sanctity of human life—he would only stare at her coldly, walk into that room, and kill Mathew with ruthless efficiency. But to tell him she wanted time to place the matter in the hands of her God—that he understood. That he could respect.

He pondered, looking at her thoughtfully, and she held her breath until it became painful, her chest burned, sparks danced in her vision; and then—finally—he briefly nodded his head.

Zohra relaxed, sighing. Tears came unbidden and un-wanted to her eyes.

"If your God has not responded by nightfall," said ibn Jad gravely, "then I carry out my fiat."

She could not reply; she could only lower her head in what was part acquiescence and part a desire to look no longer into those disturbing eyes. Drawing her veil across her face with a hand that shook so she could barely lift it, Zohra sidled toward the doorway. An arm shot across, blocking her exit.

"I would go to my prayers," she murmured, not daring to lift her head, not daring to look at him.

"You and he are man and wife in name only. The Black Sorceress told me that no man has known you!"

Resolutely, her jaw clenched tightly, Zohra tried to push past the arm.

"Let me go," she said haughtily, in the imperious tone that had often served her so well.

It did not serve her now. Auda snatched the veil from her hand, uncovering her face. "He has forfeited his rights as husband. You are free to come to any man! Come to me, Zohra!"

His hands closed over her upper arms. Shuddering, Zohra shrank back against the wall, averting her face.

Lips brushed against her neck, and she struggled to free herself. His grip tightened painfully. Suddenly angry, she ceased to fight him and stared at him intently. "What do you want from me?'' she demanded breathlessly. ''There is no love in you! There is not even desire! What do you want?''

He smiled; the dark eyes remained flat, without passion. ''I have appetites as do other men. But I have learned to control them since they are sand in the eyes of rational thought. I could find pleasure with you. Of that I have no doubt. But it would be fleeting, of the moment and then gone. What do I want of you, Zohra?'' He drew her nearer, and she was tense and taut. ''I want a son!'' Now there was emotion in the eyes, and she was startled by its intensity. ''My life nears its close. I know this, and I accept it. It is the will of Zhakrin. But I want to leave behind me a son with that strong, wild blood of yours flowing in his veins!''

Auda's lips came near hers, and nearly suffocated with fear and his nearness, she averted her face, pressing her head and her body back against the wall, her eyes closed. No man had ever dared touch her like this, no man had been this close. The drug-induced dreams of passion inflicted on her in Castle Zhakrin came back to her, tinged now with horror that weakened and debilitated.

She felt his breath upon her, fire against her skin; then, slowly, he released his hold on her. Leaning weakly back against the wall, Zohra glanced up at him hesitantly, warily. Auda had backed away several steps, his hands raised in the ageless gesture that means no harm.

The emotion in him had died. The face was pale, impassive, the eyes dark and flat. ''I will not take you by force, Zohra. A woman such as you would never forgive that. I neither want nor expect your love. I will pray to Zhakrin and ask that he give you to me. One night, if he answers my prayer, you will come to me and say, 'I will bear your son and he will be a mighty warrior, and in him you will live again!' ''

With that Auda bowed gracefully, and before Zohra could move or speak, he was gone, silently, from the room.

Zohra began to shake. Her knees would not support her, and she sank, shivering, to the floor and buried her face in her hands. She had seen the Black Paladin do magic that wasn't magic, or so Mathew had told her. It was not the magic of Sul but the magic of the Paladin's God. Auda's faith gave him power, and he was going to use it on her.

I will pray to Zhakrin and ask that he give you to me.

Against all reason, against her will and her inclination, Zohra nonetheless felt herself drawn to Auda ibn Jad.

Chapter 13

Bereft of coherent thought and reason, Zohra remained crouched in a shivering stupor upon the floor until a wild cry from Mathew changed her fear for herself to fear for another. Hastening to her feet, she ran into his room, terrified that ibn Jad had forsaken his promise.

There was no one in the room except the suffering boy; the only thing attacking him was the fever. He needed water, lots of water, to break its grip. It was time for Akhran to perform his miracle.

Reassuring herself with one last look that Mathew was in no immediate danger, either from his sickness or the Black Paladin—who was nowhere to be seen—Zohra left the sick-room and wound her way among the labyrinthine corridors of the house to the outside door.

Camels and men slept in the cool shade of a nearby building. Zohra halted when she saw that ibn Jad had laid himself down on a blanket beside Khardan. Zohra hesitated, loathe to go near the man. Glancing about, she searched for something else that might suit her purpose but knew she searched in vain. Her gaze went to the sash around Khardan's waist, to the hilt she could see glinting in the sun.

She had to have the dagger.

"Since when have you been afraid of any man?" she

asked herself scornfully, and not stopping to think that some men are worthy of fear, Zohra boldly and quietly stole across the sun-drenched street.

The camels raised their heads and gazed at her with stupid, suspicious malevolence, thinking she might try to rouse them from their rest. Thankful it was camels she was facing and not Khardan's horse, who would never have allowed anyone to steal up on his slumbering master, Zohra hissed at the camels, and they lowered their heads. Khardan slept sprawled upon his back; his breathing was deep and regular, and Zohra, after watching for a moment, knew that he slept the sleep of exhaustion and would not easily waken. Drawing near him, she stole a glance at Auda. The man's eyes were closed fast; his breathing, too, was even. But whether he slept or shammed, Zohra could not tell.

It didn't matter, she told herself. Whatever she did, he would not stop her. He had given her until sundown, and she was beginning to know him well enough to understand that he would keep his vow.

Carefully, cautiously, she leaned over Khardan and with a light, delicate touch slowly began to ease the dagger from his sash. He sighed and stirred, and she went motionless, the dagger only halfway hers. He sighed again and lapsed back into unconsciousness.

Sighing herself, in relief, Zohra slipped the weapon out and clutched it thankfully. Turning, she was starting to move back across the street toward the house when her gaze fell upon ibn Jad. The dagger, warm from Khardan's body, was in her hand. One thrust, and it would all be over. No God could ever lure her to a dead man. She stared at him, sleeping soundly to all appearances. Her fingers curled tightly around the knife's hilt.

She took a step toward him, then turned and fled across the street as though he had leaped up and was chasing her. Pausing inside the doorway to catch her breath, Zohra looked back and saw that neither man had moved.

Khardan woke with a start, thinking that someone was sneaking up on him, intending to slit his throat. So real was the impression that he reached out defending hands before he had a chance to focus his eyes, and only when his hands closed on nothing but air did he realize it had been a dream. Wearily he started to lie back down again and try to recapture sleep, patting the sash with the unthinking, instinctive gesture of the veteran warrior reassuring himself his weapon is by his side.

It wasn't.

It didn't need the lingering fragrance of jasmine to bring one person to his mind. "Zohra!" he muttered, and sat upright, looking in every direction.

His first thought was that the headstrong woman was following through on her intention to kill Auda ibn Jad. But a glance showed him the Black Paladin lying beside him, peacefully asleep. Apparently he had gone through with his plan. Mathew must be dead, Khardan thought, a swift, stabbing pain wrenching his heart. But if so, what was Zohra doing with her husband's dagger? Revenge?

He could almost see her, standing in some shadowy recess, the weapon in her hand, dealing vengeance with a swift thrust into an unsuspecting back.

Khardan did not like the evil Paladin. Despite the fact that Auda had saved their lives, rescuing them from the other Paladins of Zhakrin who demanded their blood and their souls, Khardan remembered vividly that this was the same man who, without a second thought, had cast a chained and manacled group of wretched slaves to ghuls. As long as he lived, nothing would ever blot from his eyes the sight of that horrid feast, from his ears the dreadful screams. And Auda had committed, in the name of Zhakrin, other crimes as heinous. Khardan knew this well, having heard the recitation of these deeds from the Black Paladin's own lips.

A dagger in the back was undoubtedly an easier death than he deserved. Had it been six months before, Khardan himself would have wielded the weapon and thought little of it. But it was a changed Khardan who rose wearily to his feet and set off in search of his wife.

Before the enforced marriage to Zohra—a marriage commanded by the God—Khardan had paid lip service to *Hazrat* Akhran but never went much further than that. Twenty-five years old, handsome, bold, courageous, the Calif had fixed thoughts on the world, not upon heaven. After the marriage to Zohra, the only thoughts Khardan entertained about Akhran were bitter ones.

Then had come the moment the Calif stood before his God in the torture chamber of Castle Zhakrin. Khardan—broken in body and spirit—came face-to-face with Akhran.

The Akar believe that the insane have seen the face of the God and that it is the sight of this glory that drives them mad. If that was so, thought Khardan, then I must be touched with madness.

Khardan had seen the God. Khardan had given Akhran his life, and Akhran had given it back to him.

In those few brief seconds Khardan had seen not only the God's face, but his mind as well. It was unclear, indistinct, but dimly he came to realize, thinking about all this now, that perhaps he had been mistaken in those feelings of emptiness he had experienced inside the house. He was not a meaningless grain of sand. He was part of a vast plan. These things were not happening to him by chance.

It seemed to Khardan, as he darted swift glances up and down the street, that if this was true, *Hazrat* Akhran might have handled matters more efficiently, improved on some things. But it occurred to the Calif that in certain areas the God might be as dependent upon his human followers as they were upon him.

"Perhaps if I had acted more wisely from the beginning, my path would have been easier," Khardan reflected, entering the dwelling place and making his way to Mathew's room. "Much of what has happened may be Akhran's attempts to mend the clay pot that I heedlessly smashed."

He and his companions had been taken to Castle Zhakrin for a reason—the freeing of the two Gods Quar was holding captive. That much was apparent to Khardan now. The Gods would presumably join Akhran in heaven's war.

And Akhran had need of his followers still, apparently. He had led them safely from the castle to the Kurdin Sea. There, however, things had begun to go wrong. The djinn had departed and not returned. Khardan remembered Pukah's description of Akhran—weak, bleeding, wounded.

The battle was not going well, then. Akhran had nearly

lost his grasp on them. It was Zhakrin who picked them up, sending ibn Jad to find and save them. For some reason, the Gods had decided that the Paladin's path lay with his.

The Calif entered the boy's room reluctantly, fearful of what he must find.

Apparently the Gods had willed that Mathew should fall sick and die. . . .

No, not die.

Khardan stared at the boy in amazement. Mathew lay upon the pallet, quiet now, having fallen into the unhealthful, dream-ravaged sleep of high fever. But he was asleep, he was not dead. Khardan saw the body twitch, heard the labored breathing. Moving nearer, leaning down to look at the boy closely, the Calif saw that the rag lying on the hot head was cool and moist. It had recently been changed.

But Zohra was not around.

Puzzled by this mystery, Khardan glanced about the room in search of something that might provide him with answers. Perhaps weariness had overcome ibn Jad, and the Paladin had decided to rest before he killed the boy. This seemed unlikely to Khardan, who guessed that the Black Paladin would not let death itself prevent him from carrying out any intention, much less a human weakness such as a need for sleep. It also did not explain his wife and his dagger.

But if so, where was she?

Poking among the few objects in the room, more out of frustration than in real hope of finding anything worthwhile, Khardan noted that the magical pouch Mathew wore on his belt, the pouch the Calif had carefully and gingerly removed when they stripped the boy of his heavy robes, had been upended, its contents recklessly dumped in a corner.

Khardan took a step near it, then stopped. He would have no idea what, if anything, was missing, and there was no sense in touching or handling items that sent shivers through him just to gaze upon them. And at that moment the thought occurred to him that Zohra was trying to work some of Mathew's magic.

Khardan was chilled to the bone. Mathew had been teaching her what he knew. The young man had tried to tell the

Calif about it, but Khardan had refused to listen, not wanting to know. Women's magic. Or worse still, magic of a *kafir* from a faraway land.

He heard a voice. Zohra's voice. It sounded peculiar. . . . She was singing!

If a dozen scimitar-wielding soldiers of the Amir had crashed through the door and attacked him where he stood, Khardan would have fought them with his bare hands and never known fear. This eerie singing unnerved him, left him weak and shaking all over like a horse sensing the coming of an earthquake.

Her voice was quite near, rising from another part of the house. The center, Khardan judged, recalling having seen an open-air courtyard, its floor made of tilted, broken stone. He could easily find her now, if he could force his feet to carry him past the doorstoop. At length came the dim idea that he might be able to stop her before she did anything rash and impetuous. Just what that might be, Khardan wasn't certain, but he saw once again that horrible creature—a demon of some sort—Mathew had summoned forth from Sul.

Moving swiftly, careless of the noise he made, Khardan hurried through the corridors and discovered, as he had guessed, that the singing sound came from the courtyard in the center of the dwelling.

He halted beneath a stone arch. In the center of the courtyard was a large, round pool, full ten feet in circumference, with rock walls that stood about three feet off the ground. Long ago this *hauz* had held water for household use, water carried to the house, perhaps, by those canals of which ibn Jad had told them. That had been long ago. Now the pool was choked with sand blown into the courtyard in the desert's effort to reclaim what man had stolen from it. A vast mound of sand spilled over the edge of the pool, forming a small dune that covered a portion of the courtyard.

At the edge of the dried-up *hauz* stood Zohra. Her back was toward Khardan. She did not see him and, from her unnaturally rigid posture, might not have noticed him had he stepped in front of her. The Calif moved softly near her, hoping to see what she was doing and gain an idea of how to bring it to an end.

Coming around to where he could see her face, he noted that her attention was fixed upon a piece of parchment she held firmly in both hands. The glint of sunlight on a metal blade showed him his dagger. It lay on the edge of the *hauz*, and there was a pool of something dark—red—near it.

Eyes widening, Khardan saw blood dripping from a deep cut in Zohra's left arm. She paid no heed to it, however. Her gaze was fixed upon the parchment, and she was singing the song that wasn't a song in a voice that raised the hair on Khardan's head. Moving to get a look at the parchment, the Calif saw that it was covered with marks, marks drawn in blood!

Awed, shaken, yet determined to stop her, Khardan crept forward and reached out a hand. At that moment Zohra's voice ceased. Khardan stilled his movement, though it did not seem that she was aware of his presence. Her eyes and her entire being were focused upon the parchment to such an extent that he doubted if a thunderclap would rouse her.

His hand stretched forth, shaking, and then fell limp at his side. The bloody marks upon the parchment had begun to move—wriggling and writhing as though in agony! Khardan caught his breath, nearly strangling. His teeth bit through his tongue as he watched the marks crawl off the paper and drop, one by one, into the pool.

And suddenly the Calif was ankle-deep in water.

Water swirled around his feet, flooded the courtyard, flowed into the house. Water—trapped within the strong stone walls of the pool—glistened and sparkled in the noonday sun.

Hesitantly, Zohra dipped her fingertips into the water, as though she could not believe it herself. Her hand came out wet, dripping, and she laughed exultantly.

Hearing the sound of Khardan's breath sucking between his teeth, Zohra knew he was there. Turning, she faced him, and he had never seen her look so beautiful. Her cheeks glowed with a radiance of pride and accomplishment, her eyes sparkled more brilliantly than the water.

"Your miracle!" she said to him proudly. "And it is from my hands!" She held them out to him, and he saw the bloody gash on her arm. "*Not* Akhran's!"

Chapter 14

"Your God has provided his miracle. It is obvious he wants this boy to live. Far be it from me to thwart his will. I do not kill for pleasure, Princess," continued Auda ibn Jad gravely, "but out of necessity."

It seemed to Zohra that Akhran's "miracle" might have been in vain. Water she had now, in plenty; but lacking the herbs and healing stones with which the nomad women usually treat illness, Zohra could do little except to bathe Mathew's burning skin and trickle water into the parched, cracked lips. The fever raged unabated. Mathew ceased even his incoherent babbling and lay in a stupor, panting for breath. The only sound he made was low moanings of pain.

Zohra fought her battle against Death alone, or assumed she did. Tending the sick was woman's work, and she was not surprised when ibn Jad and Khardan left the room that smelled of sickness and of death. Because she was not listening for it, she did not hear Khardan's return, nor did she see him sink down onto the floor of a shadowed alcove outside the open door of Mathew's room, where he could watch unobserved.

The afternoon wore away slowly, time being measured by the panting breaths drawn into the fever-ridden body. Each breath was a victory, a sword thrust at the unseen foe who fought to claim Mathew as prize. Rarely sick himself, Khardan had never been around sickness, had never given much thought to the fight women waged against an enemy ancient and strong as Sul.

It was an encounter grim and wearying as any he had ever fought with steel, and considerably more frustrating. The enemy could not be met with yells and clash of sword, grappled and wrestled to the ground. This dread foe must be combated with patience, with endless changing of dry cloths for wet ones, with refusal to allow heavy eyelids to shut and snatch even a few moments of blessed rest.

The most dangerous time came at *aseur,* sunset. For it is this time between day and night when the body's spirits are at their lowest ebb and the most vulnerable. The sinking of the sun cast the dwelling in shadows long before twilight had faded outside. There was no lamp to light, and Zohra fought her battle in a dim, dusty darkness.

Mathew had ceased even to moan. He made no sound at all, and Khardan thought several times the boy had quit breathing. But then the Calif would hear a dry, rasping gasp or see through the gloom a white hand twitch feebly, and he knew Mathew lived still.

"His spirit is strong, if his body isn't. But it's gone on too long," Khardan said to himself. "He can't take this. It cannot last much longer."

And it seemed as if Zohra realized the same truth, for he saw her head bow, her hands cover her face in a sob that was all the more heartrending in that it was silent, unheard. Khardan rose to go to her, to lend her his strength, if need be, to face the final moments that he had no doubt would be difficult to watch. But the Calif's movement was arrested. Halting, half-risen on one knee, he stared in awe.

A figure had entered the room, a woman with long hair that shimmered with a pale glow in the fading light. Her skin was white, she was clothed in white, and Khardan had the impression—though he could not see her face—that she was very beautiful. The face was turned toward Mathew, and the Calif wondered if this was the immortal guardian, the "angel" of which Pukah had spoken. If so, then why the chill running through his body, congealing his blood, freezing his

breath? Why the fear that shook him until he was near
whimpering like a child?

The woman stretched out white, delicate hands to the
boy, and Khardan knew suddenly that she mustn't touch him.
He wanted to call to Zohra, whose eyes were covered, who
wasn't looking, but his tongue could not form the words. He
made a sound, a kind of croak, and the woman—distracted—
turned toward him.

She had no eyes. The sockets were hollow and dark and
deep as eternal night.

This was no guardian! The boy's guardian was gone and
he was alone and it was Death who leaned over him! The
woman stared at Khardan until certain he would make no
trouble, then turned back to claim her victory. The white
hands touched the boy, and Mathew screamed, his body
convulsed. Zohra raised her head. Crying out defiantly, she
flung her body across Mathew's.

Startled, Death drew back. The hollow eyes darkened in
thwarted anger. The hands reached out again and this time
would have clutched at both, for Zohra held Mathew in her
arms. His head on her breast, she rocked and soothed him.
Her back was to her foe; she did not see her enemy approach.

Khardan moved. Drawing his dagger, he interposed himself between the two and Death. The woman's blond hair
flicked across his skin, and he felt a searing pain. The hollow
eyes stared at him malevolently, the white hand reached for
him, and then, suddenly, she was gone.

Blinking, dagger in hand, Khardan stared around in fearful astonishment.

"Whatever are you doing?" came Zohra's voice.

Khardan turned. Zohra had laid Mathew back down upon
the pallet and was staring at her husband with a narrow-eyed,
suspicious gaze.

"The woman! Did you see her?" Khardan gasped.

"Woman?" Zohra's eyes opened wide. "What woman?"

It was Death! Khardan started to shout in exasperation.
Death was here! She wanted the boy, and you wouldn't let
her, and then she was going to take you both. Didn't you
see her? . . . No, he realized suddenly. Zohra hadn't seen

her. He put his hand to his head, wondering if the heat had touched him. Yet she had been so real, so horrifyingly real!

Zohra was still staring at him suspiciously.

"It . . . must have been a dream," Khardan said lamely, thrusting the dagger back in his belt.

"A dream you chase with a dagger?" Zohra scoffed. Giving Khardan a puzzled look, she shrugged, shook her head, and turned back to her patient.

"How is the boy?" Khardan asked gruffly.

"He will live," Zohra said with quiet pride. "Only a few moments ago I nearly lost him. But then the fever broke. Listen! His breathing is regular. He sleeps peacefully."

Khardan could barely see the boy in the gloom, but he could hear the soft, even breathing.

A dream?

He wondered, and would probably keep on wondering the rest of his life.

Zohra started to rise to her feet, stumbled wearily, and would have fallen had not Khardan caught hold of her arm. Gently he assisted her to stand. Her face was a glimmer of white in the darkness. The only light in the room seemed to come from the flame in her eyes. Exhausted as she was, that inner fire burned brightly.

"Let me go." She tried to withdraw her arm from his grip. "I must fetch more water—"

"You must sleep," said Khardan firmly. "I will bring water."

"No!" Brushing back a straggling lock of black hair from her face, she attempted once more to slip out of Khardan's hold, but the Calif's hand tightened. "Mat-hew is better, but I should not leave—"

"I will watch him."

Khardan steered her toward the room next door.

"But you know nothing of nursing!" she protested. "I—"

"—will tell me all I must do," Khardan interrupted.

Weary, Zohra let herself be persuaded. Khardan led her to a small chamber. Stepping inside, he spread his own outer robe out on the floor and turned to find her pressed back against a wall, staring around the room with fearful eyes. Zohra—seeing him watching her in amazement—suddenly behaved as if nothing were amiss, though she rubbed her arms as with a chill.

"Mathew will need you in the morning when he wakens," Khardan continued, mystified by her strange reaction. But then, it had been a day of mystery. Gently but firmly he eased his wife to the crude bed he had prepared for her.

Feeling exhaustion overcome her, Zohra lay down with a thankful sigh upon the stones. "If he wakes, give him water," she murmured sleepily. "Not too much at first . . ."

That, Khardan knew. Assuring her he could manage, he was almost out the door when she started up, crying out, "Where is ibn Jad?"

Khardan paused and turned. "I don't know. He mentioned something about hunting, trying to find meat—"

"Don't let him come in here!" Zohra said, and he was surprised at the harshness in her voice.

"I won't. But he wouldn't anyway." Where a woman rests is *harem*, forbidden to men.

"Swear, by *Hazrat* Akhran!" Zohra urged.

"Have you so little faith in me?" Khardan demanded impatiently. "Go to sleep, woman. I told you I would keep watch!"

Stalking into the sickroom, which was now almost completely dark, Khardan threw himself down beside the pallet. Fuming, he propped an elbow on a corner of the straw mattress. That she should require of him an oath! When he had protected her from the most feared of all beings! Reaching out, he felt Mathew's forehead. The skin was moist and damp. The young man's breathing was shallow and fast, but the terrible raspy, rattling sound was gone. He would be well and hungry by morning.

"In all of this, the only thing that doesn't surprise me is that Death is a female!" muttered Khardan angrily into his beard.

Chapter 15

Escaping from the fever-world, where dreams are more real than reality, Mathew woke to darkness and terror. Khardan's reassuring voice and strong hands, a sip of cool water, and the knowledge, dimly realized, that he was being watched over and protected led the young man to close his eyes and slip back into a healing sleep.

When he awoke the following morning, about midday, and saw the walls around him, he thought he was back in Castle Zhakrin, where it seemed he had wandered most in his delirious ramblings.

"Khardan!" he gasped, struggling to sit.

Zohra knelt swiftly by his side. Placing her hands on his shoulders, she forced him to lie back down; not a difficult task—his body seemed a limp, wet rag that had been twisted and wrung dry.

"You don't understand," he whispered hoarsely, "Khardan is . . . near death. They're . . . torture! I must—"

"Khardan sleeps soundly," said Zohra, smoothing back the hair from his forehead. "The only torture he suffers is a stiff neck from having slept on a paved street yesterday. Where do you think you are? Back in the castle?"

Mathew looked at his surroundings, his expression puzzled. "I thought . . . But no, we escaped. There was the desert and we walked and then Serinda was still far away and there was the storm.'' He stopped, frowning in an effort to carry his memories further.

"You don't remember what happened next?"

He shook his head. Sliding her arm beneath his shoulders, Zohra lifted his head and held a bowl of water to his lips. "The man called ibn Jad found us," she said. Mathew's wasted body flinched at the mention of the Paladin. He would have turned wondering eyes to Zohra, for there was a tenseness in her voice when she spoke the name, but she kept the water to his lips, and he dared not move his head for fear of spilling it. "He brought camels, and we rode through the night to Serinda. It was then the fever took you.''

Mathew shivered. He had a recollection of a journey by night, but it was accompanied by vague terrors, and he quickly banished it. Having drunk the water, he lay back down.

"Where is ibn Jad? Did he ride on?"

"He is here," said Zohra shortly. "Are you hungry? Can you eat? I made some broth. Drink it, then you should rest."

More weary than he thought, Mathew dutifully drank the steaming liquid that had a faint poultry flavor and then drifted again into sleep. When he woke, it was early evening.

"Have you been here all this time?" he asked Zohra, who held out the bowl of water. "No, you do not need to help me. I can sit myself.'' The thought of what other services she must have helped him to perform during his sickness made him flush in embarrassment. "I have been so much trouble," he mumbled. "And now I'm delaying you. I'm keeping you from returning to your home.''

Home. He spoke the word with a sigh. He had been dreaming again, pleasant dreams, dreams of his own land. Waking this time had not been a terrifying experience, only a very painful one.

Zohra sat down beside him. Awkwardly, as though she were unused to such gentle gestures, she patted his hand with her own. "You must miss your home very much."

Mathew turned his face in an effort to hide the tears that pain and suffering and his weakness wrung from him. The effort was a failure, for the tears became sobs that shook his body. He gulped them down, trying to stop crying, waiting for the gibe or the sneer with which Zohra always met his lapses. To his amazement she said nothing, and he was further astounded when her hand squeezed his tightly.

"I know now what it is, to miss one's home. I am truly sorry for you, Mat-hew." Her voice was soft and filled with a pity that did not offend, but eased, his heart. "Perhaps, when all this is over, we can find a way to send you back."

She rose to her feet and left him, saying something about bringing food if he thought he could keep it down. Grateful for his time alone, Mathew managed to get up from the bed, and though his legs wobbled and his head spun, he was able to wash himself and was sitting up on the pallet, combing out the tangled red hair as best he could with his fingers, when he heard footsteps.

It was not Zohra who came to him, however, but Khardan.

"Your strength is returning," the Calif said, smiling. "I brought you this." He carried a bowl of rice in his hand. "You are to eat as much as you can, according to . . . my wife." He always spoke those two words with a certain grim irony. "Can you manage yourself?" Khardan asked in some embarrassment.

"Yes! Thank Promenthas," Mathew answered fervently, his skin burning. The thought of the Calif feeding him! Taking the dish, glad to have something to occupy his hands and his eyes, Mathew hungrily scooped the rice into his mouth with his fingers.

Seeming relieved himself, Khardan sat down, his back against the wall, and rubbed his neck with a groan.

"I am sorry to . . . have delayed your journey," Mathew mumbled, his mouth full of rice.

"To be honest, I am not that eager to return to my people," said Khardan heavily. For long moments he leaned against the wall in silence, his eyes closed. Opening them a crack, he peered at Mathew from beneath his lids. "I need to talk to you, Mat-hew. Do you feel able?"

"Yes! Assuredly!" Mathew placed the empty rice bowl on the floor and straightened his back and shoulders to appear attentive.

"You will tell me, Mat-hew, if you grow tired?"

"Yes, Khardan. I promise."

The Calif nodded and then frowned, trying to decide how to begin or perhaps *if* to begin. Mathew waited patiently.

"This vision . . . my wife . . . had," he said abruptly. "Tell me about it."

"It would be more fitting if you asked her," suggested Mathew, surprised by the question.

Khardan waved his hand, irritably brushing the notion away from him. "I can't talk to her. When we come together, it is like setting a flaming brand to dry tinder. Rational discussion goes up in smoke! I'm asking you to tell me of the vision that started all of this."

Wondering at the change in the Calif, who had previously scorned the idea that a vision—women's magic—could have prompted Zohra to act as she did in removing him bodily from the battle around the Tel, Mathew related the story.

"I was teaching Zohra a magical spell my people know that allows us to see into the future. It is called scrying. You take a bowl of water and place it before you. Then you clear your mind of all thoughts and outside influences, chant the arcane words, and if you are fortunate, Sul will give you a picture in the water that can foretell the future."

Mathew paused, half expecting to be met with a laugh or a snort of derision. But Khardan was silent. Looking at him intently, Mathew tried to discover if the Calif was simply too polite to make the rude comments that were in his heart, or if he was truly struggling to believe and understand what he was being told. Khardan's face was hidden by the gathering shades of evening, however, and Mathew was forced to continue on without any idea of what the nomad was thinking.

"Zohra performed the magic perfectly. Your wife is very strong in magic," Mathew took a moment to add. "Sul has blessed her with his favor."

This occasioned a reaction, but not quite what he'd expected. Instead of scathing denial, Mathew heard Khardan stir uncomfortably and make a warning sound deep in his throat as if to indicate Mathew was to keep to the main path and avoid any side journeys. Knowing nothing about Zohra's creation of water from sand—a spell Mathew himself had

taught her, but which she had always been terrified to perform—
the young wizard shrugged to himself and continued.

"Looking into the water, she saw two visions." He closed
his eyes, concentrating hard to remember every detail. "In the
first it is sunset. A band of hawks, led by a falcon, fly out to
hunt. But they end up fighting among themselves, and so
their prey escapes. Distracted by their own quarreling, they
are set upon by eagles. The hawks and the falcon fight the
eagles, but they are defeated. The falcon is wounded and falls
to the ground and does not rise again. Night falls. Now, in
the second vision—"

Seeing the scene again in his mind, caught up in the
fascination magic always held for him, Mathew had forgotten
his listener. He was suddenly jolted back to reality.

"*Birds!*" The word fell like a thunderbolt. Springing to
his feet, Khardan glared down at the young man, who was
staring up at him with wide eyes. "She did this to me
because of *birds*?"

"No! Yes! That is—" Mathew stammered. "The pictures
are . . . are symbols that the magus interprets in his heart and
his mind!" He groped frantically for an image he could use to
help the man understand. No good relating symbology to
letters and words, as had been taught Mathew in school. The
nomad could neither read nor write. Many of the legends of
Khardan's people were parables or allegories, but—while the
nomads understood them in their hearts—Mathew wasn't at
all certain that they thought them over in their minds. In any
event, he could not now try to explain that the beggar in the
tale actually represented Akhran and that the selfish Sultan
was mankind. How could he make Khardan understand?

"I can explain it like this," Mathew said, suddenly in-
spired by the symbols themselves. "It is the same as teaching
your falcon to hunt gazelle."

"Bah!" Khardan turned and seemed prepared to walk out
of the room.

"Listen to me!" Mathew pleaded desperately. "You don't
send the falcon after the gazelle without training. You put
hunks of meat in the eye sockets of a sheep's skull and teach
the bird to attack the gazelle by first attacking the meat in the
skull! That skull represents—it symbolizes—the gazelle! Sul

does the same with us. He uses these pictures we see as you use the sheep's skull.''

Interested in spite of himself, the Calif had paused in the doorway. He was no more than a large shadow, shapeless in his flowing robes in the darkness. ''Why does Sul do this? Why not just say what he means?''

''Why not send the falcon after the gazelle without training?''

''The bird would not know what to do!''

''And so it is with us. Sul does not want us to accept his vision too glibly, without 'training.' He wants us to look into our hearts and ponder the meaning of what we see. The hawks are your people. They are led by the falcon—that is you.''

Khardan nodded solemnly, not out of pride, but merely an acceptance of his own worth. ''That makes sense. Go on.''

Mathew began to breathe easier. Although the Calif remained standing, at least he was listening and seemed to be comprehending what the young wizard was trying to teach. ''The hawks—your people—are fighting among themselves, and thus their prey escapes them.''

Khardan muttered irritably, not liking this that was, after all, nothing more than the truth. Hiding a smile, Mathew hurried on. ''The eagles attack—those are the Amir's troops. You are wounded and fall out of the sky and do not rise again. Night settles over the land.''

''And this means?''

''Your people are defeated and vanish into darkness.''

''You are saying that if I had died, my people would have been vanquished. But I did not die!'' Khardan stated triumphantly. ''The vision is wrong!''

''It's what I tried to tell you at the beginning,'' said Mathew patiently. ''There were two visions! In the second, the falcon is hit by the eagles and he falls to the ground, but he manages to rise again, even though . . .'' Mathew hesitated, uncertain how to phrase this, uncertain how the Calif would react. ''Even though—''

''Even though what?''

Mathew drew a deep breath. ''The falcon's wings are

covered with filth," he said slowly. "He has to struggle to fly."

Silence, brooding and heavy, followed. Khardan stood very still; not a rustle of cloth broke the profound quiet. Mathew held his breath, as if that small noise could be a distraction.

"I return . . . in disgrace," Khardan said finally.

"Yes." Mathew let his breath out with the word.

"Is that all? The only difference in the two visions?"

"No. In the second vision there is no night. When you return, the sun rises."

Chapter 16

"It was not an easy decision for Zohra to make, Khardan," Mathew argued earnestly. "You know her! You know her courage! She herself would have preferred to die fighting the enemy rather than run away! But that would have meant the end of your people. That was what mattered to her most. That was why we rescued you from Meryem—"

"Meryem!"

Mathew had known this would surprise the Calif. "Yes," continued the young man, trying to keep all emotion from his voice, knowing that Khardan must come to realize his own truth about the woman. "She was carrying you away on horseback—"

"She, too—trying to save me." Khardan spoke fondly, and Mathew grit his teeth to keep the sarcastic words locked behind them.

"She had given you a charm to wear around your neck—"

"Yes, I remember!" Khardan put his hand to his throat. "A silly thing, women's magic. . . ."

"That 'silly thing' rendered you unconscious," Mathew said grimly. "Do you also remember fighting, then feeling a strange lethargy come over you? Your sword suddenly becomes so heavy you cannot lift it. Ground and sky are mixed up in your vision. The enemy attacks, but you are so weak

139

you cannot defend yourself. The blow falls but bounces off harmlessly.''

"Yes!" Though Mathew could not see him, he knew Khardan was staring at him in amazement. "Is this more scrying? How did you know?"

"I know the charm she used," Mathew said. "I know its effects. She wanted you safe and unharmed and unable to fight. With help, she carried you out of the battle—"

"Help? Do you mean Zohra's?"

"No. When we found you with that woman, Meryem was riding one of the Amir's magic horses. How else could she have escaped that battle except with the help of the Amir's soldiers?"

"There are many ways," Khardan said. "What she did, she did out of love. Misguided, perhaps, but she is a woman and does not understand such things as pride and honor."

Oh, don't women? thought Mathew, but he said nothing. This was no time to argue.

"At least you cannot say my wife acted from the same motive," the Calif stated.

"What Zohra did, she did for your people," Mathew said with more heat than he intended. "Dressing you as a woman was the only way to get you past the soldiers. She didn't do it on purpose to disgrace you! And it wasn't her fault that our plans didn't work out. It was mine. Ibn Jad came searching for me. Blame me, if you must."

There was a long silence, then Khardan said, "It wasn't anybody's fault. It was the God's choosing."

Astonished, Mathew stared intently at Khardan, wishing he could see the man's face through the darkness. He heard the Calif, who had remained standing all this time, settle himself back down on the floor and lean against the wall.

"I have been thinking, Mat-hew. Thinking of what you said to me the night . . . the night that they were torturing me." The words were laden with remembered pain. "You said, 'Maybe your death isn't what your God wants! Maybe you're of no use to him dead! Maybe he's brought you here for a reason, a purpose, and it's up to you to live long enough to try to find out why!' I didn't understand then. But when I came to Akhran, when I saw his face, then I knew. He gave my life back to me to help him fight and win this war. I can do nothing to aid him in heaven, but I can do something on earth.

"The question is"—Khardan continued, sighing—"what? What can we do against the might of the Amir? Even if we had all our people banded together—which we don't. Even if they accept me on my return . . ." He paused, obviously expecting a response.

Mathew could not give him the reassurance he wanted, and so kept silent. His silence answered louder than words, however, and Khardan stirred restlessly. "The falcon rising from the filth. Very well, I return in disgrace. A coward who has obviously been hiding for months, if nothing worse is spoken of me. You are wise for your years, Mat-hew. It was this wisdom that helped you survive the slave caravan, this wisdom that freed us from that evil castle. I am smart, courageous," Khardan spoke simply, a statement of fact, "but I begin to realize that I am not wise. I came tonight to ask your advice. What should I do?"

A warmth flooded over Mathew. He thought at first it might be the fever returning, but this was a wonderful sensation, and he did not respond at once but let himself savor it and bask in it—though he did not feel at all that he deserved it.

"I—I don't know . . . what to say," Mathew stammered, thankful for the darkness that concealed his embarrassed pleasure. "You underestimate yourself . . . overestimate me. I don't—"

"You need time to think about things," Khardan said, rising to his feet. "It is late. I have kept you talking too long. If you sicken again, it will be my fault. Zohra will claw out my eyes."

"No, she wouldn't," Mathew said, believing the Calif spoke in earnest. "You don't know her, Khardan! She is proud and fierce, but she uses her pride like a ring of fire to protect herself! Within she is gentle and loving, and she imagines this to be a weakness instead of a very great strength—"

He spoke fervently, forgetting himself and to whom he

talked until Khardan drew closer to him and, kneeling beside him, fixed him with an intense look. Lambent light from stars and desert glittered in the Calif's dark eyes.

"You admire her, don't you?"

What could Mathew say? He could only look deep into his heart and pluck out the truth. It was not the whole truth, but now was not the time—if that time ever came—for speaking the whole truth.

"Yes," Mathew answered, lowering his head before those piercing eyes. "I am sorry if that displeases you." He looked up again quickly. "And I would never touch her, never think of her in any way that was not proper—"

"I know."

Mathew was trembling in his earnestness, and Khardan rested his hand soothingly upon the boy's shoulder. "And I cannot blame you. She is beautiful, isn't she? Beautiful—not like the gazelle—but like my falcon is beautiful. Courageous, proud. The fire you speak of flares in her eyes. That fire could burn a man's soul to ashes or—"

"—warm him for the rest of his life?" Mathew suggested softly when Khardan did not finish his sentence.

"Perhaps." The Calif shrugged. He rose to his feet. "Right now, in her sight, I am a smoldering cinder. It may be too late to save either of us. She speaks the truth, however, when she says it is our people who matter. Rest easily, Mat-hew. I go to stretch my legs, then I will return and guard your sleep. You must get your strength back. In two days' time, we will begin the journey to the Tel."

The journey to our doom, be it good or evil, thought Mathew. He was weary. The mixed emotions that had assailed him throughout the conversation had drained him of energy. Lying down, he heard Khardan's footsteps echo through the corridors and his voice raised in conversation with another.

Auda ibn Jad.

Maybe He's brought you here for a reason. A purpose.

Or maybe not. What if I'm wrong?

Chapter 17

By next morning Mathew was able to walk with Zohra around the house. His interest in the dead city of Serinda revived as he viewed the wonders of the dwelling and marveled again at what terrible tragedy could have occurred that would destroy a people while leaving their city intact. When he attempted to expound on the mystery to Zohra, she evinced little interest, however, and Mathew realized after a few moments that she was leading him somewhere. There was an air of shy, quiet pride about her, much different from her usual fierce arrogance, and he found his curiosity growing.

They came into a central courtyard that once must have been a cool and charming haven from the bustle of city and household. Now it was choked with sand, littered with broken columns and fragments of statuary. In the midst of such desolation and destruction, Mathew was astonished to see a pool of crystal-clear water—deep and blue and cool from the night's chill.

"So this is why there has been no lack of water!"

The young man drank his fill, then opened his robes and splashed the water on his breast and neck and laved his face. Zohra, smiling, found a fragment of pottery in the shape of a scoop and helped Mathew wash his long red hair. Wringing

143

the wet tresses out with his hands, he stared at the pool and shook his head.

"Isn't it marvelous, Zohra, what mankind can do? Marvelous and sad. The people disappear, Sul slowly takes over their city, and yet here, in this house, somehow the machines kept this working—"

"Not machines, Mathew," said Zohra softly, proudly. "Magic."

Mathew stared at her a moment, uncomprehending. Then suddenly, joyfully, he threw his arms around her and hugged her close. "Magic! Your magic! You made the water! I knew you could do it! And you weren't frightened—"

"I was more frightened of that than of almost anything, except that horrible castle," Zohra said bluntly. She raised her dark eyes to Mathew's blue ones. He felt her shiver and tightened his grasp on her. "But I had no choice. That man, ibn Jad, would have killed you otherwise."

"Ah!" Now it was Mathew's turn to shudder, and Zohra who soothed him with her touch. "I wondered," he murmured. "That is why Khardan has been watching in the night."

"Ibn Jad swore he would not harm you. But I don't trust him." Her breath caught, her voice quavered.

"What is it, Zohra?" Mathew had never seen her frightened. "It's ibn Jad! What's he done to you?" Anger beat in his heart with a violence that startled him. "By Promenthas! If he's harmed you, I'll—"

You'll what? Attack ibn Jad? So might the lamb offer to fight the lion!

It seemed that Zohra might be thinking the same thing, for Mathew saw the corner of her lips twitch as if amused, despite her distress. Then a thought struck her, and she looked up at him in earnest, no laughter in her eyes.

"Mat-hew! Perhaps you can help me! It is possible to break a spell that one is under, isn't it?"

"Sometimes," said Mathew cautiously. He had the impression that there were murky waters ahead and wanted to wade into them slowly and carefully. "It depends—"

"On what?"

"On many things. What type of spell, how it was cast,

what was used in the casting. It is more difficult than perhaps you imagine." Mathew's concern was growing as he guessed where her words were leading. "But how can ibn Jad cast a spell, Zohra? He is not a magus." Memory of the Black Sorceress returned to Mathew forcibly and unpleasantly. Perhaps there *was* a way. "Did he have a charm, a wand—some magical object someone could have given him?"

"It was not Sul's magic," Zohra answered, shaking her head. "It was his God."

"Go on." Mathew didn't know whether to be relieved or even more worried. "Tell me everything."

"I cannot," Zohra said stiffly. "It . . . is not proper for women to discuss such things with men who . . . are not our husbands."

"But I am another wife," Mathew said with a wry smile. "And I must know everything, Zohra, if I am to help."

"I . . . suppose so," Zohra admitted. Reluctantly, refusing to look at him and sometimes speaking so low Mathew had to bend his head to hear her, Zohra told him of her encounter with ibn Jad.

"He said he would pray to his evil God, Mat-hew! To give me to him!" Zohra looked up fearfully; her body trembled. "And . . . Mat-hew . . . when I was in that . . . that place. The woman gave me something to drink that made me dream . . ." She couldn't go on; deep rose red flushed her cheeks, and she hid her face in her hands.

"Of course," Mathew muttered. Some sort of love potion—no, *lust* potion might be a better term. That explained why the female captives were so cooperative and pliable, soft clay in the hands of the Sorceress. "Did you dream of him, of Auda?" the young man asked hesitatingly. Zohra's embarrassment was catching. The blood burned in his skin.

"No, others," Zohra mumbled, her voice muffled by her hands.

Khardan? Mathew longed to ask but did not. A flicker of jealousy flared in him. He recognized it for what it was, but—confusedly—not precisely for whom it was intended. Was he jealous of Zohra for dreaming of Khardan or jealous of Khardan for being in Zohra's dreams? That was something

he would have to work out later. Now, whether he understood himself or not, at least he understood what ibn Jad was
doing—or trying to do. Very clever, Mathew thought. To use
the dreams to insinuate himself into this woman's mind, use
her own faith in Gods and their power to weaken the natural
barriers she had established against him.

Unfortunately this was no time to enter on a discussion of
free will.

"Zohra," said Mathew, shaking her gently so that she
was forced to look up at him through a curtain of shining
black hair, "half the time you don't obey the commands of
your own God. Will you give in to a stranger?"

Zohra's eyes narrowed in thought over this argument.
Coming to understand it and appreciate the irony, she even
smiled slightly. "No, I will not!" Reaching out with her
hand, her fingers lightly brushed Mathew's soft, beardless
cheek. "You are very wise, Mat-hew."

So Khardan had said. But it wasn't wisdom, really. It was
simply the ability to look at something from several different
sides, to see a problem from the top and the bottom and
around the corner instead of staring at it straight on. Like
seeing all the facets of the glittering jewel, instead of concentrating on just one. . . .

"Why do you look at me like that?" Zohra asked.

"Because Khardan was right," Mathew said shyly. "You
are very beautiful."

The roses bloomed in her cheeks, the fire Khardan spoke
of flamed in her eyes.

How those two loved each other! Hiding within walls of
pride. Each nursed wounds. Each knew the other had seen
him vulnerable, her weak. Fearful that he would use this
against her or she would use it against him, both daily added
more stones to the wall they were constructing between them.
Khardan recognized this, but the tasks and the problems
facing both of them were so overwhelming it might be that
they would never be able to tear down the wall, no matter
how much they longed to.

Their people—that was what mattered to both of them—
and their God, their *Hazrat* Akhran.

A cold wind blew through Mathew's soul. For a time he

had forgotten he was a stranger in a strange land. The knowledge returned to him forcibly. He had no people, he had no one to love or to love him—at least a love he could admit to himself without writhing in shame. He had a God, but Promenthas was very far away.

"Mat-hew! You are so pale! Is the fever—" Her hand went to his forehead. Gently he pushed it away and pushed her away from him at the same time.

"No, I am fine. I understand that we are riding tonight?"

"If you feel like it—"

"I am fine," he repeated tonelessly. "Just a little tired. I think I will go lie down and sleep."

"I will come—"

"No, you must have things to do to prepare for the journey. I am not sick now. I no longer need your care."

Turning from her, he walked away.

Confused, hurt by his words, Zohra stared after the young man. The thin shoulders were hunched, the head bowed. She was reminded forcibly of someone trying to protect his body from a blow.

Too late, the blow had fallen. And would continue to fall, repeatedly, cudgeling him into despair.

"Ah, Mat-hew," murmured Zohra, beginning to see, beginning to understand. "I am sorry." Unconsciously she echoed her husband's words.

"I am sorry."

That night they left Serinda, none of them ever to return. The dead city was left to its dead.

THE BOOK
OF THE
IMMORTALS

Chapter 1

Throughout the seventy-two hours' grace period Kaug had granted them, the djinn worked diligently, if not very effectively, to fortify their position. Each djinn decided he knew all there was to know about warfare, and between erecting fantastic battlements (that soared to incredible heights and would probably confound Kaug for the span of a brief chuckle) and arguing strategy and tactics recalled from battles fought forty centuries earlier, nothing much to any purpose was accomplished. Fortifications were jealously torn down as quickly as they were put up. Fights erupted constantly, there was one prolonged battle that lasted two days between one faction of djinn—who claimed that the notorious *batir* Durzi ibn Dughmi, who had mounted ten thousand horses and five thousand camels in an attack on Sultan Muffaddhi el Shimt five hundred and sixty-three years earlier, had defeated the said Sultan—and another faction of djinn who claimed he hadn't.

Hidden from view by the climbing rosebush outside her window, Asrial gazed down upon the pandemonium with mingled feelings of shock, exasperation, and despair. By contrast she pictured to herself the strict, well-ordered discipline of the angels, drawn up for battle in rigid formation. Why can't the djinn see that they are defeating themselves? Why can't they be organized?

Frustrated, she stared out the window, her face flushed with anger, her small fist clenched. Apparently she wasn't alone in her thinking, for she heard—with a start—a voice coming from the room next to hers asking those very questions out loud.

"What is wrong with these fools? Why do they fight each other instead of preparing to fight Kaug?" The voice—for all its fury—was sweet and musical, and Asrial recognized the speaker as Nedjma. Which left no doubt as to the identity of the male who answered her.

"You know as well as I why they do this, my bird," Sond said quietly.

I don't know! thought Asrial. Hurrying over to the wall, she pressed her ear against a velvet tapestry that depicted in glowing colors the magnificent wedding of Muffaddhi el Shimt's daughter Fatima to Durzi ibn Dughmi. But the palace walls were thick, and the angel would not have been able to hear the rest of the conversation had not Sond and Nedjma walked over to stand beside the window in Nedjma's room.

It occurred to Asrial that Sond—being present in the *seraglio*—must be in considerable danger, and she wondered that the couple dared risk being observed from the garden below. Then the angel realized that she had not seen the eunuchs since yesterday, the day she'd been brought here by Nedjma. Perhaps they were working on the fortifications or, more likely, had been pressed into service guarding the body (though at his age there was not a great deal of his body left to guard) of the ancient djinn.

"No, I don't know the reason," said Nedjma petulantly, and Asrial blessed her. The djinniyeh added something else that the angel didn't catch. Returning to her window, Asrial saw the couple had walked out onto a small balcony attached to Nedjma's chambers. The angel could see and hear them quite well, she herself remaining unseen, her white robes and wings mingling with the white roses.

Nedjma stood with her back to Sond, her delicate chin high in the air. She did not wear her veil; in fact, Asrial saw, Nedjma wore very little, and what clothing she did have on seemed artfully designed to reveal more than it concealed. She was all blue silk and golden glints, emerald sparkles and pure white skin. Sond, coming up behind the djinniyeh, laid his hands upon the slender shoulders.

"It doesn't matter, Nedjma, my flower," he said softly. "No matter what we do, it won't stop Kaug. Do you think we would act like this if there was a chance? We do this out of our own anger and frustration and out of the knowledge that tomorrow it will all be over."

As he spoke, Nedjma's chin dropped slowly, the golden hair falling forward around her in a gleaming shower.

"Don't cry, beloved," Sond said gently. He caught hold of a mass of golden hair and, moving it from her cheek, bent to kiss away a shining tear. Putting her hands over her face, Nedjma's sobs became more hysterical. "I should not have told you." Sond straightened and drew back. "I didn't mean to make you unhappy. I only wanted you to know how little time"—he paused, a choke in his own voice—"how little time—" he repeated huskily.

Nedjma whirled to face him, the blue silk shimmering about her like a gilt-edged cloud. Hastily she dried her eyes and, coming to him, rested her hands upon his chest. "My own," she whispered. "I am not crying over what you told me. It was not news. I have known it in my heart. I was weeping because it is the end." Her arms stole around him, and she nestled her head against his chest.

"It may be the end," Sond answered. "But, my darling, we will make it a glorious one!"

Their heads bent, their lips met in a passionate kiss. The blue silk fell to the floor of the balcony, and Asrial, her face scarlet, her eyes wide, withdrew hurriedly from the window. Leaning her burning cheeks against the cool marble wall, she heard Sond's words echo over and over in her head.

"It doesn't matter . . . how little time . . . the end."

He was right. It didn't matter. It wouldn't matter for the angels of Promenthas. It wouldn't matter for the imps and demons of Astafas. It wouldn't matter for the djinn and djinniyeh of Akhran. Kaug had grown too powerful. No weapon was mighty enough to fell him, no wall was tall enough or thick enough to stop him. They could as well try to bring down a mountain with an arrow, stop a tidal wave with a castle of sand.

And like Nedjma, Asrial had known this in her heart.

"The end . . . a glorious one."

Lilting, breathless laughter came floating in the window with the perfume of the roses. Asrial slammed shut the casement. Blinking back the tears in her eyes, she was just about to leave when there came a knock at the ornately painted door to her room.

Asrial hesitated, uncertain whether or not to respond. Before she had a chance, the door opened and Pukah entered.

Seeing her standing in the center of the room, her wings spread, the djinn's cheerful expression melted like goat cheese in the sun.

"You were leaving!"

"Yes!" she said, her fingers nervously plucking at the feathers of her wings. "I'm going back to my . . . my people, Pukah! I want to be with . . . them at the . . . at the . . ." She looked down at her hands.

"I see," Pukah said calmly. "And you were going without saying good-bye?"

"Oh, Pukah!" Asrial clasped her hands together, holding onto them as though she feared they might do something she didn't want them to do, reach out to someone she knew she couldn't hold. "I can't be what you want me to be! I can't be a woman to you as Nedjma is to Sond. I'm—I'm an angel." The hands released themselves long enough to lift the white robes. "Beneath this there isn't flesh. There is my essence, my being, but it isn't flesh and blood and bone. I tried to pretend it was, for my sake as well as yours. I wanted," she hesitated, swallowing, "part of me still wants that . . . that kind of love. But it can never be. So . . . I wasn't going to say good-bye—"

"It was kind of you to spare me the hurt," said Pukah bitterly.

"Pukah, it wasn't you! It was myself I was sparing! Can't you understand?" Asrial turned away from him. Her wings wrapped around her, enclosing her in a feathery shell.

Pukah's face suddenly became illuminated with an inner radiance. The proud, self-satisfied facade crumbled. Hurrying to the angel, he gently parted the white wings that surrounded her and tenderly took hold of her clasped hands.

"Asrial, do you mean to say that you love me?" he whispered, fearful of speaking such joyous words aloud.

The angel raised her head. Tears glistened in her blue eyes, but when she answered, her voice was firm and steady. "I do love you, Pukah. I will always love you." She entwined her fingers in his and held him fast. "I think that even in the Realm of the Dead, once more without form or shape, I will still have that love, and it will make me blessed!"

Pukah fell to his knees as she spoke, bowing his head as though receiving a benediction. Then, when her words had ceased, he slowly raised his head. "I know what I am," he said in sad and wistful tones. "I am conceited and irresponsible. I care too much for myself and not enough for others, even my own master. I've caused all sorts of trouble—without really meaning to," he added remorsefully, "but it was all for my own self-indulgence. Oh, you don't know!" He raised a hand to her lips as she was about to interrupt. "You don't know the harm I've done! It was because of me that the Amir thought my poor master was a spy and tried to arrest him. It was because of me that Sheykh Zeid went to war against us instead of becoming our ally. It was because of me that Kaug stole away Nedjma and imprisoned her in Serinda. And speaking of Serinda," the djinn continued, sparing himself no pain, "*you* were the hero, Asrial. Not I."

The djinn looked very woeful and wretched.

Her heart aching, Asrial sank down on her knees beside him. "No, my dear Pukah, don't berate yourself. As you say, you meant well—"

"But I didn't mean it for others. I meant it for myself," Pukah said resolutely. Standing up, he raised Asrial to her feet and gazed down at her with an unusually earnest and grave expression on his face. "But I'm going to make up for it all. Not only that"—for an instant, the old foxish glimmer appeared in the djinn's eyes—"*I'm* going to be the hero! A hero whose name and sacrifice will last throughout time!"

"Pukah!" Asrial stared at him, alarmed. "Sacrifice? What do you mean?"

"Farewell, my angel, my beautiful, enchanting angel!" Pukah kissed her hands. "Your love will be the shining light in my eternal darkness!"

"Pukah, wait!" Asrial cried, but the djinn was gone.

Chapter 2

"Usti?"

The rotund djinn gave a violent start that began at his broad back and rippled over his flab in undulating waves. Dropping whatever it was he was holding, sending it crashing to the tiled floor, Usti pivoted as swiftly as possible for one so large to face the door.

"The reason I am down here in the storage room is that I am reckoning up the amount of food we have on hand in case we are placed under siege," the djinn stated glibly, hastily wiping vestiges of rice from his chins. Endeavoring to see who it was who had accosted him, he squinted and peered into the thick shadows wavering outside the circle of light cast by a lamp hanging—along with a quantity of smoked meats, dried herbs, and several large cheeses—from the ceiling. "There are . . . uh . . . twenty-seven jars of wine," he pronounced, still trying to see, "six large bags of rice, two of flour, thirty—"

"Oh, Usti! I don't care about any of that! Have you seen Pukah? Is he down here?"

"Pukah?" Usti's eyes opened wide, then narrowed in disgust as the figure stepped into the light of his lamp. "Oh, it's you," he muttered. "The madman's angel."

Any other time Asrial would have bristled angrily over

the aspersion cast upon her protégé. Now she was too worried. Flinging herself at the djinn, she caught hold of his arm, this being markedly similar to thrusting one's hand into a bowl of bread dough. "Tell me he's here, Usti! Pukah, I know you are here!" She let loose of the djinn, who was glaring at her in high dudgeon, and looked intently into the dancing shadows. "Pukah, please come out and we'll talk—"

"Madam," said Usti, in glacial tones, "Pukah is not here. And you have interrupted my repast." He glanced disconsolately at the mess at his feet. "Ruined my repast is nearer the mark." He heaved a gloomy sigh and, squatting down with many grunts and groans, began a vain attempt to salvage something from the wreckage.

"A fine dinner of *fatta,* the vegetables crisp, the rice somewhat gummy, but then this is war, after all. One must make sacrifices. But now! Now!" Shaking his head and all six of his chins, he covered his eyes with his hands in an effort to blot out the terrible sight. "I know I will see it forever," he murmured in hollow tones. "The rice covered with dirt. The vegetables mixed up with bits of crockery. And soon, rats coming to devour—"

"Usti, he's gone!" Asrial slumped down on a cask of olive oil, her white wings drooping. "He's been gone all day and all night, too. Now it is nearly time for Kaug to return—"

"Ahhh!" Blowing like a whale rising to the surface, Usti heaved himself to his feet. "Kaug, did you say, angel of the madman?"

"Mathew isn't mad." Asrial answered automatically, her thoughts on something—someone—else. "He was acting so strangely when he left me. . . ."

"Often a symptom of madness," said Usti knowingly.

"Not Mathew! Pukah!"

"Has he gone mad, too?" Usti readjusted the turban that had slipped over one eye in his feasting. "I am not surprised. Pardon me if I offend you, madam, but it would have been much better for all concerned if you and your madman had not inflicted yourselves upon us—"

"Inflicted ourselves on *you*? *We* didn't want to come to this dreadful place!" Asrial cried. "We never meant to fall in love—'' She stopped, with a gulp. "What is that?" she whispered fearfully, staring up above them.

The earth was shaking and quivering more than Usti's chins. The cheeses swayed alarmingly, the carcass of a smoked goat tumbled to the floor. The lamp swung back and forth on its chain, the shadows in the underground storage chamber leapt and darted about the room like imps of Astafas, themselves gone mad.

"Kaug!" gasped Usti, his face the color of the blue cheese hanging over his head. "Back to the Realm of the Dead for us!" Catching hold of the dangling end of the cloth from his turban, he mopped his sweat-beaded forehead. "No more *couscous*!" He began to whimper. "No more sugared almonds. No more crispy bits of gazelle meat, nicely done, just slightly pink in the center—"

The rumbling increased, the shaking of the ground made it impossible to stand. Clinging to the wall, the cheeses tumbling down to roll around his feet, Usti had his eyes squinched tightly shut and was reciting feverishly, "No more *qumiz*. No more *shishlick*. No more—"

A jar of wine tipped over and broke, flooding the storage chamber and staining the hem of Asrial's white robes crimson. She paid no attention. She was listening.

There it was, rising faintly over the rumbling and cracking and the sound of Usti's lamenting.

"Djinn of Akhran! Attend to me! Quickly! We haven't much time!"

"Pukah!" cried Asrial, and disappeared.

Clutching a cheese to his breast, Usti bowed his head and wept.

Though the immortal plane shook with the terror of the 'efreet's approach, Kaug himself was just barely visible, his bulk darkening the horizon like a bank of storm clouds, lightning flickering from his eyes, thunder pounding the ground at his feet.

The djinn stood beneath their fortifications, weapons of every type and variety in their hands. On the balconies of the castle above the garden, the djinniyeh waited quietly, arms around each other for comfort. Hidden by silken robes, more than one sash wrapped around a slender waist concealed a sharp and shining blade. When their djinn had fallen, the djinniyeh were prepared to take up the fight.

The ancient djinn himself appeared. A tiny, dried-up husk of an immortal dressed in voluminous brocade robes that nearly swallowed him up and banished him from sight, he was carried in a sedan chair by two giant eunuchs onto his own private balcony. Shining scimitars hung at the sides of the eunuchs. The djinn had in his possession, resting across his brocade-covered knees, a saber that might have been the first weapon ever forged. So ancient was its design and so rusted was its blade, it is doubtful if the sword could have sliced through one of Usti's cheeses. Not that it mattered. Kaug's head could be seen rearing up over the edge of the plane, and he was massive—more gigantic than anything the immortals could possibly imagine. A stomp of his foot would crush their castle, his little finger could smash them into oblivion.

Sond stood at the head of the djinn's army. Sword in hand, he tried to keep his balance on the undulating ground. Fedj was at his right hand, Raja at his left. Behind them the other djinn waited, intending to make the price of their banishment as high as possible. Stone cracked, trees toppled. The sky darkened. Kaug's hulking form obliterated the setting sun. Its last rays illuminated something white that drifted through the air and fell at Sond's feet.

Leaning down, the djinn picked it up. It was a rose, and he knew where grew the bush from which the blossom had been plucked. Lifting it to his lips, he turned toward the rose-covered balcony. Though Nedjma's face was veiled, Sond knew she smiled at him, and he smiled bravely back, though he was forced to avert his head hurriedly, the smile twisting into a grimace of despair. Blinking his eyes, he reverently tucked the rose into the sash at his waist and was clearing his throat, preparatory to issuing a command that would have launched the battle, when suddenly Pukah sprang up out of an ornamental fountain right in front of him.

"Where have you been?" Sond snapped irritably. "That angel of yours is driving everyone crazy! Go find her, shut her up, and then see if you can make yourself useful. Where's your sword? Raja, give him your dagger. Pukah, I swear by Akhran—''

But Pukah completely ignored Sond. Climbing up the side of the fountain's central figure—a marble fish spouting water from huge marble lips—Pukah clung to the statue's gills and shouted, ''Djinn of Akhran! Attend to me!''

The djinn began to mutter and grumble; a rustle swept through the djinniyeh like wind through silken curtains.

''Pukah! This is no time for your tricks!'' Sond cried angrily. Reaching up, he grabbed hold of one of Pukah's feet and endeavored to pull the djinn from his perch. Pukah, kicking himself free, shouted loudly, ''Hear me! I have a plan to defeat Kaug!''

The muttering ceased abruptly. Silence—as silent as it could possibly get with the 'efreet drawing ever closer—spread like a pall over the immortals in the garden. Asrial appeared, bursting like a silver star at Sond's side.

''Pukah! I've been so worried! Where—''

The young djinn cast the angel a fond and loving glance. Shaking his head, he did not answer her but continued to speak to the crowd of immortals now gazing at him with full, if dubious, attention.

''I have a plan to defeat Kaug,'' Pukah repeated, speaking so rapidly and with such excitement that they could barely understand him. ''I don't have time to explain it. Just follow my lead and agree with whatever I say.''

The muttering began again.

Sond scowled, his anger mounting, ''I told you, Pukah—''

''The Realm of the Dead!'' said Pukah. His tense voice sliced through the grumblings like a length of taut thread. ''The Realm of the Dead awaits! You haven't got a chance, not a prayer! Where is Akhran? Where is our God?''

The immortals glanced at each other uneasily. It was the one question everyone had in his heart but no one dared bring to his lips.

''I'll tell you where he is,'' continued Pukah in hushed and solemn tones. ''Akhran lies in his tent, weak and injured, bleeding from many wounds. Some of these wounds Quar has inflicted. But others''—he paused a moment to clear his throat—''others have been inflicted on him by his own people.''

The garden grew darker. A foul-smelling wind began to blow, shrieking and howling, stripping leaves from those trees left standing and whipping dust into the air.

"Their faith dwindles!" yelled Pukah above the rising storm, the coming of the 'efreet. "They have lost their immortals! They do not think their God hears their prayers, and so they have quiet praying . . . or worse—they pray to Quar! If we are defeated, it will be the end, not only for us, but for Akhran!"

The wind ripped through the garden, breaking and tearing whatever it could. It clawed at the shining silver hair of the angel, but Asrial paid it no heed. Her eyes were on the young djinn.

"We are with you, Pukah!" she cried.

Sond looked at Fedj, who nodded slowly, and at Raja, who nodded in turn. Glancing behind him, barely able to see through the dust and torn branches and leaves and flower petals and a sudden pelting rain, Sond caught glimpses of the other djinn nodding, and he even heard what he thought was the dried-up rasp of the ancient djinn adding his sanction.

"Very well, Pukah," said Sond reluctantly. "We will go along with your plan."

Heaving a vast sigh, tingling with pride and importance from turbaned head to slippered toe, Pukah turned and prepared to face Kaug.

Chapter 3

The 'efreet stomped up to the outer wall of the garden, and at his approach the storm winds ceased to rage, the thunder to crack, the lightning to flash. When Kaug stood still, the ground no longer shook. A dread and ominous quiet fell over the immortal plane.

"Your time is up," rumbled the 'efreet, and the vibrations of his voice started the plane to quivering again. "Seeing these warlike fortifications and noting that all of you carry weapons, I take it that you choose to fight."

"No, no, Kaug the Merciful," said Pukah from atop the marble fish. "We bring our weapons only to lay humbly at your feet."

Kaug's eyes narrowed suspiciously. "Is that true, Sond?" the 'efreet asked. "Have *you* brought your sword to lay at my feet?"

"Cut off your feet is more like it," muttered Sond, glaring at Pukah.

"Go on! Go on!" Pukah mouthed, making a swift, emphatic gesture with his hand.

His mouth twisting, as though his swallowed rage was poisoning him, Sond stalked up to the 'efreet and, with grim defiance, hurled the weapon point foremost at Kaug's toes. One by one the other djinn followed Sond's example, and soon the astonished 'efreet was standing ankle-deep in a veritable armory.

"And as for fortifications"—Pukah glanced around him, somewhat at a loss to explain the new battlements and turrets and walls that had sprung up—"these . . . uh . . . were just erected to give"—inspiration struck him with such force he nearly fell from his fish—"to give you a hint of the surprise to come!"

"I don't like surprises, Little Pukah," the 'efreet growled, grinding the swords and scimitars and spears to metallic powder beneath his huge foot.

"Ah, but you will like this one, O Kaug the Mighty and Powerful!" said Pukah with an earnest solemnity that made the other djinn gaze at him in wonder. "The world has treated you badly, Kaug. You have grown suspicious and untrusting. We knew, therefore, that we must do something to convince you that we were truly sincere in our desire to serve you. And so"—Pukah paused, savoring the suspenseful hush, the breathless anticipation that awaited his words—"we have built you a house."

Silence. Dead silence. The garden might have been filled with corpses instead of living beings.

"What trick is this, Little Pukah?" Kaug finally spoke, his words grating with suspicion, trembling with anger. "You know that, centuries ago, the wrath of the foul God Zhakrin banished me to the Kurdin Sea. There my house is, and there I must remain until Quar succeeds to his rightful place as the One, True God—"

"Not so, O Much-Put-Upon Kaug." Pukah shook his head. "The God Zhakrin owed me a favor—what for, we will not discuss—but he owed me a favor, and I have asked him, as my gift to you, O Master, that he set you free.

"This is no trick," Pukah added hastily, seeing Kaug's eyes narrow to slits of red flame. "Search within yourself. Do you feel constrained, chained any longer?"

Kaug's ugly face wrinkled, his gaze grew abstracted. Hesitantly he lifted his gigantic arms and flexed his muscles as though testing to see if he was manacled. His arms moved freely and, slowly, gradually, a pleased and gratified expression spread over his face.

"You are right, Little Pukah," Kaug said with a look of wonder. "I am free! Free! Ha! Ha! Ha!" Raising his arms in the air, he shook his fists at heaven. His glee sent seismic waves through the immortal plane. The balcony on which the djinniyeh stood sagged alarmingly, and the women fled in a whirl of silk. Seeing them run, Kaug leered and turned his gaze back to the djinn. "Thank you for this gift, Little Pukah. Indeed, I now truly believe that you mean to serve me, you and these sniveling cowards around you, and you may start doing so right now. You, Sond, fetch me the djinniyeh known as Nedjma. I have a desire to—"

"Don't you want to see your house?" interrupted Pukah.

"What?" Kaug stared at him irritably.

"Don't you want to see your house, Your Magnificence? It has a wondrous bedchamber," the djinn insinuated from his post atop the fish. Seeing that Kaug's attention was on the balcony, Pukah lashed out with a slippered foot at the infuriated Sond, kicking him painfully in the kidneys to remind him to keep quiet. "And while we are viewing your new dwelling, Nedjma can take time to prepare herself so that she may come to you in all her beauty and do you honor, O Kaug, Handsome Charmer."

Kaug was baffled. The 'efreet continued to stare lustfully at the balcony, scraping his hand over his stubbled chin and running his tongue across his lips, but he did this primarily because he knew it was torturing Sond. The 'efreet had a mild interest in Nedjma. When this war was won and the immortals banished, he would undoubtedly keep several of the more comely djinniyeh around for his pleasure, and Nedjma would undoubtedly be one of them.

What was Pukah up to? That was the question tormenting Kaug. His brain was searching for answers, but instead of finding any, his mental process was going round and round like a donkey yoked to a waterwheel. Kaug didn't trust Pukah. The 'efreet didn't trust anyone (his God Quar was no exception), and he knew Pukah was plotting some elaborate scheme.

But he freed me from Zhakrin's curse!

That was the fact that kept the donkey moving in its slow, plodding circle. Kaug simply couldn't believe it. Long, long

ago, when Zhakrin had been a powerful force in the Jewel of
Sul and Quar was but a bootlicking toad—(a toad with ambition but a toad nonetheless)—Quar had secretly ordered Kaug
to wreak havoc upon a fortress of Zhakrin's Black Paladins
located in the Great Steppes. Generally Kaug took little delight in obeying Quar's commands, which—up until the war—
had consisted of raining hail on the heads of recalcitrant
followers or inflicting plagues upon their goat herds. When it
came to battling the Black Paladins, however, Kaug enjoyed
himself thoroughly. The 'efreet was having such a marvelous
time—hurling down fiery rocks on those trapped inside the
castle, plucking their puny spears from his flesh and hurling
them back with such force that they impaled men to the stone
walls—that Kaug stayed longer than he should have. Zhakrin
was able to come to the aid of his beleaguered Paladins.

Descending upon Kaug in his wrath, the God lifted the
'efreet in his mighty arms and slammed Kaug into the Kurdin
Sea. And though it is impossible for one God to completely
control another God's immortal, Zhakrin was able to effect a
curse upon the 'efreet—pronouncing that Kaug must henceforth dwell in the Kurdin Sea so that Zhakrin could always
keep track of the 'efreet's comings and goings.

Quar had meekly swallowed this insult—what else could
he do then? And Kaug had been forced to live in a watery
cave under the baleful eye of the evil God. But Quar and his
'efreet were now joined in mutual hatred of Zhakrin, and it
was shortly after Kaug's banishment that Quar began his
subtle war against the evil God that would end, finally, in the
reduction of Zhakrin himself to a fish.

"And now Pukah has freed me," Kaug reflected. "He
has persuaded Zhakrin to free me. Not that this must have
been so difficult." The 'efreet sneered. "What is Zhakrin
now? A ghost without form or shape. I could have freed
myself had I wanted to, but I've grown accustomed to that
cave of mine. Zhakrin owed Pukah a favor for releasing his
immortals from Serinda, and all know that the Evil God's one
major flaw is his honor. But why would Pukah use this favor
in my behalf unless . . . unless"—the mental donkey came
to a halt—"unless Pukah is like me!

"Of course. I should have realized this before," muttered

Kaug to himself in a low voice that was like the rumblings of a volcano to the djinn watching him warily from below. "Pukah is a self-serving little bastard. I've always known that. His Immortal Master, the Mighty Akhran, lies bleeding, dying. His earthly master, the impudent Khardan, has crossed the Sun's Anvil, but he will soon find himself in greater danger from his own people. Could it be that Pukah is really, in truth, attempting to save his own miserable skin? If this wretched worm has truly been driven to crawling on his belly, I may have an amusing time of it!"

"Very well, Little Pukah," said Kaug aloud, shifting his weight from one foot to the other and crushing three stalwart stone towers in the process, "I will look at this house of yours. You will accompany me, of course, as will Nedjma."

"Nedjma?" A worried frown passed swiftly over Pukah's face. Kaug, watching intently, did not miss it and smiled to himself. "But Nedjma is not ready, O Kaug the Impatient, and you know how long it takes women to fuss over themselves, especially when there is one they truly desire to please."

"Tell her I will take her the way she is," said Kaug with a laugh that split a minaret in two and sent it crashing to the ground. "Run and fetch her, Little Pukah. I am eager to see my new house!"

Climbing down the fish, Pukah was confronted by a darkly scowling Sond. "It will be all right. Trust me," Pukah whispered hurriedly.

"I know it will," Sond said grimly. "I'm coming with you."

"No, you're not!" Pukah snapped. "It would spoil everything."

"Yes, I am. You're not going anywhere with Nedjma! I'll disguise myself as her—"

Pukah gave him a scathing look. "With those legs?"

The two djinn, still arguing, vanished from sight in the garden and materialized within the palace. Intent on his scheming, upset by this sudden, unexpected demand that Nedjma accompany him, Pukah never noticed that Asrial had come with them until she stood blocking his way when he and Sond tried to enter the *seraglio*.

"Asrial, my enchanter!" Pukah put his hands on the angel's arms and endeavored to move her gently out of his path. "At any other time the sight of you would be balm to my sore heart, but right now I have this evil 'efreet on my hands—"

"I know," Asrial said firmly. "I'm coming with you."

"How popular I've become lately," said Pukah, somewhat irritably. "Everyone wants to come with me." Stealing a sidelong glance at Sond, to make certain he was appreciating this, Pukah heaved a long-suffering sigh. "I know that I am irresistible, my angel, and that you cannot bear to be parted from me for the tiniest second, but—"

Pukah's tongue stuttered to a halt. It was no longer Asrial he held in his arms, but Nedjma!

"Here, what is this?" growled Sond, lunging forward to separate the two, when suddenly Nedjma—the real Nedjma—was standing by his side.

Her face pale, the djinniyeh laid a trembling hand restrainingly on Asrial. "No. It's wonderful of you to offer to sacrifice yourself, but I'll go with"—she gulped slightly, then bravely brought the word out—"Kaug. I know what you did for us in Serinda and I . . . we"—she took hold of Sond's hand—"we can't ask you to—"

"You're not asking me," Asrial interrupted. She did not even glance at the djinniyeh, her eyes looked up into Pukah's. "I've decided this myself."

"It's dangerous, my angel," Pukah said softly. "You don't know what I must do, and if anything goes wrong, he'll carry out his threat!"

"I'm not afraid. You'll take care of me," Asrial answered, smiling.

"Like I took care of you in Serinda?" Pukah said wistfully, stroking the golden hair. He glanced at Nedjma, who—though she was trying very hard to be brave—was shivering with terror. "Nedjma will be no help at all," Pukah muttered to his alter ego. "She looks on the verge of passing out as it is. Asrial is courageous, strong. I know—none better—her resourcefulness."

"But what about—you know?" questioned the other Pukah solemnly.

"I'll take care of that," Pukah answered. "Very well," he said aloud. "You may go, but you must promise me one thing, Asrial—you must promise to do exactly as I tell you, without question."

Asrial frowned. "Why, what do you mean—"

"Little Pukah!" The 'efreet's gigantic eyeball appeared in the window of the harem, sending the djinniyeh fleeing in panic. Nedjma, hurriedly drawing the veil across her face, shrank back into the shadows. Sond leapt forward to hide her from Kaug's sight. "Hurry up!" Kaug roared, cracking the window glass. His eye rolled and winked lasciviously. "I must take my pleasure quickly, then return to my master."

Seeing the 'efreet this near, understanding the terrible portent of his words, Asrial could not forbear a shudder that Pukah felt.

"What are you doing with my woman, Little Pukah?" Kaug growled.

"I am just inspecting her to make certain she is worthy of your attention, O Kaug," shouted Pukah. In a hurried undertone he hissed, "Swear to me by Mathew's life that you will obey me!"

Frightened by Pukah's unwonted seriousness, alarmed at the enormity of the oath she was being asked to take, Asrial stared up at him wordlessly.

"Swear!" Pukah said sternly, shaking her slightly. "Or I will be forced to take Sond disguised as Nedjma, and then none of us will survive!"

"I swear."

"By Mathew's life," Pukah urged. "Say it."

"Pukah!" Kaug raged.

"Say it!"

"I swear . . . by Mathew's life . . . to obey you!" The angel's words fell from pale and trembling lips.

Sighing in relief, Pukah kissed Asrial soundly on the forehead, then clasped her hand in his.

"Sond," he said in a low voice, turning to the djinn, "when I leave, you and Fedj and that good-for-nothing Usti must hurry back to Khardan and Zohra. As Kaug said, they will be in terrible danger! Farewell! Oh, and Sond," Pukah added anxiously, "you'll be certain to tell *Hazrat* Akhran that this was all entirely *my* idea, won't you?"

"Yes, but—"

"*My* idea. You won't forget?"

"No, but I don't—"

"You will tell him?"

"Yes, if that's what you want," said Sond impatiently. "But why don't you just tell him yoursel—"

His voice died. The djinn, the angel, and the 'efreet were gone.

Chapter 4

"I will provide transportation, *Bashi*—you don't mind my calling you 'boss' do you, Boss?" Pukah asked humbly.

"Not at all," said Kaug, grinning and leering horribly at Asrial. "You might as well begin getting used to it, Little Pukah."

"Exactly what I thought myself," said Pukah, with a graceful *salaam*, managing—at the same time—to keep his body between Asrial and the 'efreet. "As I was saying, *Bashi*, I will provide transportation if you will but reduce yourself to a more suitable size."

Suddenly suspicious, Kaug glared narrowly at Pukah.

"You will find it difficult to fit into your new bed, *Bashi*," remarked Pukah with lowered eyes, a faint flush on his cheeks.

Kaug's suspicion wasn't the only part of him being aroused. Pukah's cunning reference to the bed inflamed him. The 'efreet had forgotten until seeing her again how beautiful the djinniyeh really was. Vivid memories of his struggles with Nedjma in the garden when he had kidnapped her—the feel of her soft skin, the surpassing loveliness of her body—made his blood tingle, his thick thighs ache with desire.

Still, Kaug was cautious. The hotter the fire in the loins, the colder the ice in the mind. He examined this gem Pukah

THE PROPHET OF AKHRAN

was handing him with the precise, calculating eye a worshipper of Kharmani uses to examine the jewels of his bride's dowry.

He could not find a flaw.

A hundred times more powerful than the scrawny young djinn, Kaug could roll Pukah up into a ball, and toss him out into the eternal void of Sul, to languish forever amid nothingness, and all in less time than it would take the djinn to draw in a lungful of air for his final scream.

"You are right, Little Pukah," said Kaug, shrinking in size until he was only two heads and a shoulder larger than the djinn. "I would not want to be too big for the . . . ahem . . . bed." Laughing, he put his arm around Asrial and dragged the angel roughly to his side.

Pukah, smiling wanly, clapped his hands, and the three began their journey.

Behind them, on the immortal plane, the djinn looked at each other in worried puzzlement and then began to reconstruct their battlements.

"Where are we?" demanded Kaug, staring about, glowering darkly.

"On an insignificant mountain in a range unworthy of your notice, *Bashi*," answered Pukah humbly.

The three stood at about the midpoint of a mountain whose height was so vast that the clouds played about its knees and it seemed that the sun would have to leap to scale the topmost peak. A hoary frost perpetually covered the craggy head; summer's heat never reached the summit. Nothing and no one lived on the mountain. The bitter cold froze blood and sucked air from the lungs. The entire world had once been as desolate as this mountain, before Sul blessed it, according to the legend of those who lived in the mountain's shadow; and, therefore, the mountain was called Sul's Curse.

Kaug did not know this, nor did he care. He could feel the supposed djinniyeh trembling in his grip, and he was impatient, now that he did not have a war with the djinn to occupy him, to satisfy his lust.

"The doors to your abode, *Bashi*," said Pukah, bowing.

As the djinn spoke, two massive doors of solid gold,

studded with glittering jewels and standing sixty feet high, took shape and form within the mountain's rock. By Pukah's command—''Akhran wills it!''—the doors swung slowly inward on silent hinges. Leaving the barren, windswept landscape of the mountainside, Kaug, dragging Asrial with him, entered the golden doors.

The 'efreet drew in a long breath. His grasp on the angel weakened. Kaug could not help himself. He was overawed.

Golden walls, covered with tapestries of the most delicate design done in every color of the rainbow, soared to such heights that it seemed the ceiling must be lit with stars instead of crystal lamps. Objects rare and lovely from every facet of the Jewel of Sul stood on the silver-tiled floor or hung from the gilt walls or adorned tables carved of rare *saksaul*. And as the 'efreet traversed this magnificent hallway, his mouth gaping wide in wonder, Pukah threw open door after door, displaying room after room and chamber after chamber, all filled with the most beautifully crafted furniture made of the rarest and most valuable materials.

"Quar himself has no such dwelling as this!" murmured Kaug.

"Bedroom," said Pukah, opening a door. "Second bedroom, third bedroom, fourth bedroom, and so on for several miles into the heart of the mountain. Then there is the divan for holding audience with those you want to impress"—Pukah threw open double doors—"and the divan for holding audience with those you don't want to impress"—more doors—"and the divan for holding audience with yourself, if you so desire, and then"—continued opening of doors—"here are your summer chambers and here are your winter chambers and here are your spring chambers and here are your in-between winter and spring chambers and—"

"Enough!" shouted Kaug, beginning to tire of the seemingly endless display of riches. "I admit, I am truly impressed, Little Pukah"—the djinn bowed again—"and I apologize for thinking you were trying to trick me."

Pukah's eyes widened, his face crumpled with pain. "*Bashi,* how could you?" he cried, stricken.

Kaug waved a hand. "I apologize. And now"—the 'efreet gave Asrial a vicious tug—"we will retire to one of the bedrooms, if you can tell me where they are?'' The 'efreet stared back down the hall. Every door—and all were closed— looked exactly like every other door.

"Ah, but first," said Pukah, taking advantage of the 'efreet's preoccupation to neatly slide Asrial's hand out of his grasp. "First the unworthy woman must bathe herself and put on her perfume and her finest clothing and rouge her small feet and darken her eyelids with kohl—"

"I care nothing for that!" the 'efreet raged, his thwarted passions rising red into his ugly face. Kaug began to grow in height and swell in breadth. "So this was a trick, after all, Little Pukah? It will be your last one!" The towering 'efreet reached out huge hands toward the djinn.

Ignoring Kaug, Pukah looked straight into Asrial's terrified eyes. "Run," he told her. "Run and shut the mountain's doors behind you."

Catching hold of the angel, Pukah shoved her to one side and then dashed in a direction opposite the doors, down the glittering hallway. The 'efreet's grasping hands caught hold of nothing but the breeze left by the djinn's flight.

"I won't leave you!" Asrial cried frantically, though just what she could do if she stayed was open to question.

"Your oath!" Pukah's triumphant voice came floating back to her. The golden walls picked it up, the words reverberated from the starlit ceiling and bounced off the silver-tiled floor.

Your oath! Oath! Oath!

By Mathew's life . . .

Clenching her fists in frustration, Asrial did as Pukah commanded. Turning, she ran the opposite direction from the one the djinn had taken. The 'efreet made a lunge for her, but the angel had shed the silken pantalons and veil. White wings sprouted from her back. She flew gracefully out of Kaug's grasp and sped toward the golden doors at the end of the hall.

Seeing his prey escaping him in two different directions, Kaug was momentarily at a loss over which to pursue. The answer, once he thought about it, was simple. He would catch Pukah first, rip that glib tongue from the djinn's foxish head, tie his feet into knots, and impale him on a hook in the ceiling above the bed. Then, at his leisure, Kaug would retrieve the angel, who, he calculated, would be glad to do anything she could to free her lover.

The 'efreet set off in pursuit of Pukah, who was running with the speed of a hundred frightened gazelles down the long hallway that led, twisting and spiraling, deeper and deeper into the heart of the mountain.

Run! Run and shut the mountain's doors behind you.

Standing on the mountainside, Asrial grasped the huge golden door rings with both hands, and pulled at them with all her might. The doors, set solidly into the rock, refused to budge.

Asrial prayed to Promenthas for strength and slowly, slowly the mighty doors began to revolve on their hinges. The angel heard Kaug's shouted threats from inside the mountain; his rage shook the ground on which she stood. She hesitated. . . .

By Mathew's life!

Asrial gave a final tug. The huge doors closed with a dull, hollow boom that pierced the angel's heart like cold iron.

Inside the mountain Kaug heard the great doors slam shut, but he didn't give it a thought . . . until, suddenly, everything around him went completely and absolutely pitch dark.

Cold iron.

Asrial, pressing her hands against her heart, understood.

"Oh, Pukah, no!" she moaned.

Running back to the doors, the angel beat on them frantically with her fists, but there was no answer. She shouted over and over—in every language she knew—"Akhran wills it!"—the words of command she had heard Pukah use to open them, but there was no response.

"Akhran wills it!" she said a final time, but this was a whisper, almost a prayer.

The angel, watching in helpless anguish, saw the golden doors begin to fade, the light of the gleaming jewels dwindle and darken.

The entrance vanished, and Asrial was left standing alone on the windswept, cold, and barren mountainside.

Chapter 5

Pukah sat, comfortably ensconced, in a tiny cavern—more a crevice than a cavern, actually—in the bowels of the mountain known as Sul's Curse. Lounging back on several silken cushions, smoking a hubble-bubble pipe, the young djinn listened to the soothing sound of the gurgling water—a sound punctuated now and then by fierce shouts and yells from the trapped 'efreet.

"The one thing I am sorry for, my friend," said Pukah exultantly to his favorite cohort—himself, "is that we missed seeing the expression on his ugly face when Kaug discovered the mountain was made of iron. That would have been worth all the rubies in the Sultan's girdle, the one that was stolen by Saad, the notorious follower of Benario. Have I ever told you that story?"

Pukah's alter ego emitted a tiny sigh at this point, for he had heard the story countless times and knew it as well or better than the teller. He also knew that he was destined to hear this story and many, many others in the days and nights to follow—long days and longer nights that would flow into still longer years, interminable decades, and everlasting centuries. But the other Pukah, after that one tiny sigh, responded stoutly and bravely that he had never heard the story of Saad and the Sultan's Ruby-Studded Girdle and awaited it eagerly.

"Then I will tell it," said Pukah, highly gratified. He began relating the harrowing tale and had just come to the part where the thief, to avoid being captured by the Sultan's guards, swallows one hundred and seventy-four rubies when a particularly ferocious shout from the 'efreet shook the mountain to the core, interrupting him. The young djinn frowned in irritation and righted the hubble-bubble pipe that had been overturned in the resulting tremor.

"How long do you suppose it will be before Kaug finds us?" Pukah asked himself in somewhat worried tones.

"Oh, several centuries I should think," remarked Pukah confidently.

"That is what I think, too," Pukah stated, reassured.

A most tremendous roar rattled the crockery and set the wooden bowls to dancing about the floor.

"And by the time he does find us," Pukah continued, "I am certain that, since I am by far the cleverer of the two of us—the cleverest of all immortals I know, now that I come to think of it—I will have discovered a way out of this iron trap. And then I will be reunited with my angel—my sweetest, most beautiful of angels—and *Hazrat* Akhran will reward me with the most wonderful of palaces. It will have a thousand rooms. Yes, a thousand rooms." Leaning back among the cushions, letting smoke curl lazily from his lips, Pukah smiled and closed his eyes. "I think I will begin planning them right now. . . ."

The alter ego—having always found the end of Saad to be particularly gut wrenching—heaved a sigh of relief and went to sleep.

Above the djinn, beneath him, and all around him, the mountain known as Sul's Curse rumbled and quaked with the 'efreet's rage. Those few hardy nomadic tribes of the Great Steppes, who raised long-haired goats at the mountain's feet, fled with their flocks in terror, convinced that the mountain was going to split wide open.

The mountain remained intact, however. Encased in iron, Kaug had lost his power to do anything except to rage and storm. There was no possible way he could escape.

From that time on it became a joke among the Gods to refer to the mountain as Kaug's Curse.

But to Sond and Fedj and the immortals of Akhran and one loving angel of Promenthas, the mountain was henceforth known as Pukah's Peak.

THE BOOK OF
PROMENTHAS

Chapter 1

Reluctantly Achmed rolled off his pallet. A soft arm twined about his neck, urging him to come back. Warm lips brushed against his throat, whispering promises of yet untasted pleasures. Succumbing, Achmed buried his head in the shower of golden hair that fell over the pillows at his side and let himself be enticed by the lips and the flesh for several breathless moments. Then, groaning as he felt the desire surge up within him again, he rose hurriedly from his bed and went to dress himself.

Propping herself up on one arm, languishing among the cushions, her nakedness covered with only a thin blanket, Meryem gazed at Achmed through the tousled hair that shone like burnished gold in the lamplight.

"Must you go?" she asked, pouting.

"I am officer in charge of night watch," Achmed said shortly, trying to keep from looking at her but unable to resist gazing hungrily at the smooth, white skin.

Buckling on his armor, his hands fumbled and slipped, and he muttered a brief curse. Rising from the bed, the blanket sliding to the tent floor, Meryem came to him.

"Let me do that," she said, pushing aside his shaking hands.

"Cover yourself! Someone will see!" Achmed said, scandalized, hurriedly blowing out the flame of the lamp.

"What does it matter?" Meryem asked, shrugging and deftly fastening the buckles. "Everyone knows you keep a woman."

"Ah, but they don't know *what* a woman!" Achmed replied, clasping her close and kissing her. "Even Qannadi said—"

"Qannadi?" Shoving him back, Meryem stared up at him in fear. "Qannadi knows about me?"

"Of course." Achmed shrugged. "Word spreads. He is my commander. Don't worry, my beloved." His hands ran over the body that was trembling with what he thought was passion. "I told him that I found you in the Grove. He shook his head and said only that it was all right to lose my heart, just not to lose my head."

"So he doesn't know who I am?"

"He knows nothing about your true identity, gazelle-eyes," said Achmed fondly. "How could he? You keep your face veiled. Anyway, why should he recognize you as the Sultan's daughter? He must have seen you for only a few moments at most when his troops captured your father."

"Qannadi has seen as much of me as you, fool," Meryem muttered beneath her breath. Aloud she murmured coyly, "And have you lost your heart?" Her arms twined around his waist.

"You know I have!" Achmed breathed passionately. "Meryem, why won't you marry me?"

"I am not worthy—" Meryem began, drooping her head.

"It is I who am not worthy to slipper your foot!" Achmed said earnestly. "I love you with all my heart! I will never love another!"

"Perhaps, then, someday I will let you make me your wife," Meryem said, seeming to relent beneath his caresses. "When Qannadi is dead and you are Amir—"

"Don't talk like that!" Achmed said abruptly, his face darkening.

"It is true! You will be Amir! I know, I have foreseen it!"

"Nonsense, my dove." Achmed shrugged. "He has sons."

"There are ways to handle sons," Meryem whispered, reaching her arms up to his neck.

Achmed pushed her from him. "I said not to talk like that," he responded, his voice grown suddenly cool. Turning his back on her, he reached for his sword that hung from the tent post.

Though she saw she had gone too far, Meryem smiled—a cunning, unpleasant smile that was hidden by the darkness. "No, you are not ready yet," she said to herself. "But you will be. You are getting closer every day."

Putting her head in her hands, Meryem began to weep softly. "You do not love me!"

There could be only one answer to this, and Achmed, his anger melting beneath her tears, gave it—with the result that he was about half an hour late relieving the officer on watch and was summarily and sternly reprimanded, the only thing saving him from a more severe punishment being the common knowledge that he was the Amir's favorite.

When Achmed was finally gone, Meryem sighed in relief. Washing off the sweat of passion, she dressed herself, looking with disfavor on the poor caftan of green cotton she was forced to wear, dreaming longingly of the silks and jewels she had been wont to wear in the palace.

"Someday," she said resolutely, talking to Achmed's robes that lay in a heap in a corner. "Someday I will have all that and more, when I am head wife in your *seraglio*. And yes, you will be Amir! If Qannadi does not die in this war, which seems unlikely now that it is won, then perhaps he will meet with a fatal accident back in Kich. And then, one by one, his sons, too, will fall ill and die." Reaching her hand into her pillow, she slid forth a bag containing many scrolls, rolled tight and tied with various-colored ribbons. Caressing these and smiling, she pictured in her mind the various deaths of Qannadi's sons. She pictured Achmed receiving the news as he rose higher and higher in the Emperor's favor. She saw him glance at her and bite his lower lip but remain silent, knowing that by this time—though he might rule millions—he himself was ruled by one.

Meryem smiled sweetly and dressed herself in the green caftan. It had been a gift from Achmed and therefore—poor as it was, though it had cost Achmed more than he could afford—she was forced to wear it. Then she drew forth her scrying bowl and filled it with water. Clearing her mind of all disturbing thoughts, she began the arcane chant, and soon an image formed in the bowl. Staring at it, Meryem muttered most unwomanly words. Hastily twisting to her feet, she wrapped a veil of green and gold spangled silk around her head and face—another gift from the besotted youth—and slipped out of Achmed's tent.

Chapter 2

"I tell you I must see the Imam!" Meryem insisted. "It is a matter of greatest urgency."

"But madam, it is the middle of the night!" remonstrated one of the soldier-priests who now served Feisal in place of slaves, ordinary men being considered unworthy of attending to the Imam's personal needs. "The Imam must rest—"

"I never rest," came a gentle voice from the depths of night's shadows that crowded thick behind the candlelit ram's-head altar. "Quar watches in heaven. I watch on earth. Who is it that needs me in the dark hours of the night?"

"One who calls herself Meryem, My Lord," answered the priest, hurling himself to the floor and prostrating his body as he would have if the Emperor himself had entered the room. Or perhaps he might not have groveled this low for the Emperor, who, after all—Feisal was now teaching—was only mortal.

"Meryem!" The gentle voice underwent a subtle change. Nose to the floor, the soldier-priest did not hear it. Meryem did, and from her place on the floor, whither she had thought it politic to drop herself, she grinned in triumph. "Let the woman come forward," Feisal said with dignity. "And you may leave us."

The soldier-priest sprang to his feet and bowed himself

185

out. Meryem remained on the floor until he had gone; then, hearing the rustle of Feisal's robes near her, she raised her head and peered into the shadows.

"I have seen him!" Meryem hissed through her veil.

She heard a swift intake of breath. Stepping into the light cast by the altar candles, Feisal made a motion for the woman to rise and face him.

The priest's face appeared cadaverous in the altar light— the cheeks hollow, the skin waxen and tightly drawn over fragile bones. The robes hung from his wasted body, his neck thrust up out of them like the scrawny neck of a new-hatched bustard, his arms seemed nothing but bone covered by brittle parchment. No wonder his followers believed him to be immortal—he looked as if Death had claimed him long ago.

"Whom have you seen?" the priest asked indifferently, but Meryem was not fooled.

"You know well who I mean!" she muttered to herself, but said smoothly, "Khardan, Imam. He is alive! And he has returned to his tribe!"

"That is not possible!" Feisal clenched his fist, the bones of his fingers gleamed white in the altar light. "No man could survive crossing the Sun's Anvil! Are you certain?"

"I do not make mistakes!" Meryem snapped, then caught herself. "Forgive me, My Lord, but I have as much or more at stake here as you."

"I sincerely doubt that," Feisal said dryly. "But I will not argue." He raised a thin hand to prevent Meryem from speaking. Thoughtfully he began to pace back and forth before the altar, glancing at it occasionally as if—had the woman not been here—he would have found consolation in discussing the matter over with his God. The answer he sought apparently came to him without need for prayer, however, because he suddenly halted directly in front of Meryem and said, "I want him dead, this time for good."

Meryem started and glanced at him from beneath her long lashes. "Why should you bother, Holy One?" she said diffidently. "He is, after all, only one man, leader of a ragtag rabble—"

"Let us say I mistrust anyone who rises from the dead," Feisal remarked coolly. "We will leave it at that, Meryem, unless you think this is the time for both of us to share our little secrets?''

Meryem evidently did not, for she did not respond.

''Then we are both agreed that Khardan should die, are we not, Meryem, my child? After all, it would be a pity if Achmed should find out that his brother lives. There is no telling what he might do when he discovers you to be the lying little whore who deceived him. At the least he will kill you himself. At the worst he will turn you over to Qannadi—''

''What do you want of me?'' Meryem demanded in a tight voice, barely able to speak for the smothering sensation that was choking her.

''It will take a very special person to get close enough to Khardan now to accomplish his death,'' said Feisal, coming close himself to Meryem and staring at her with his burning eyes. She felt his breath hot upon her skin, and she involuntarily shrank from the disturbing presence. He grasped her wrist painfully. ''This close!'' he said. ''Or closer still!'' He jerked her forward; her body touched his, and she shuddered at the awful sensation.

''There is someone who can get this close to him?'' the Imam demanded.

''Yes!'' Meryem gasped. ''Oh, yes!''

''Good.'' Feisal released the woman suddenly. Unnerved, Meryem sank to the floor and remained there, on her knees, her eyes lowered. ''You are skilled in your craft. I need not tell you how to proceed. You must start your journey tonight. You will have to go on horseback—''

Meryem looked up, startled. ''Why not Kaug?''

''The 'efreet is . . . busy upon matters of Quar, important matters,'' said Feisal.

The priest appeared uneasy, and Meryem wondered for the first time if the rumors that had been whispered in the dark and dead of night were true. Rumors that Kaug had disappeared, vanished. Rumors that he had not been seen nor his power felt in days. Delicately, Meryem probed.

''Surely you do not want me to waste time, Imam! It will take me weeks—''

''I said you will go by horseback!'' the Imam interrupted sharply, his eyes flaring in anger.

Meryem prostrated herself humbly in response, more from a need to keep her flurried thoughts concealed than out of reverence. Where was Kaug? What was all this about? Something was wrong. She could smell Feisal's fear, and she reveled in it. Undoubtedly she could turn this to her advantage.

"I will leave tonight, as you wish, Imam," she said, rising to her feet. "I will need money."

Going to a huge strongbox that stood behind the altar, Feisal opened it and returned presently with a sackful of coins.

"I can give you escort as far as Kich, but no farther. Once you are in the desert, you are on your own. That should be no problem for you, however, my child," the Imam added sardonically, handing Meryem the money. "Even snakes must flee *your* path."

Not deigning to answer, Meryem took the sack, her own cool gaze meeting Feisal's burning one. Much was said, though nothing was spoken. These were two people who knew each other deeply, distrusted each other intensely, and were willing to use each other mercilessly to gain their heart's desire.

Without a word Meryem bowed and left Feisal's presence.

"Quar's blessing be with you, my child," he murmured after her.

Late, late that night, a soft knocking—several distinct taps repeated in a peculiar manner—resounded on the door of the dwelling of one Muzaffahr, a poor dealer in iron pots, cauldrons, and spikes whose stall was the shabbiest in the *souk*. His goods, unskillfully made, were purchased only by those as poor as himself who could not afford better. Servile and humble, Muzaffahr never raised his eyes above the level of a person's knees when he spoke.

But it was a very sharp eye, not a servile one, that peeped through the slats of the wooden door of the ironmonger's hovel, and it was not his usual whining voice that queried softly. "What's the word?"

"Benario, Lord of Snatching Hands and Swift-Running Feet," came the answer.

The door opened, and a woman, shrouded in a green

caftan and heavily veiled, glided over the doorstep. The ironmonger shut the door softly and—finger to his lips—took the woman's hand and led her through a curtained-off partition into a back room. Lighting an oil lamp that gave only a feeble glow from its trimmed wick, Muzaffahr—still enjoining silence—threw aside a threadbare rug on the floor, opened a trapdoor that appeared beneath it, and revealed a ladder leading down into total darkness.

He motioned at the stair. The woman shook her head and drew back, but the ironmonger motioned again, peremptorily, and the woman, casting him a threatening glance from her blue eyes, made her way slowly and cumbersomely, entangled in her robes, down the ladder.

Muzaffahr followed swiftly, sliding the trapdoor shut above them. Once below he lit another lamp, and light filled the room. The woman glanced around in amazed appreciation, to judge by the widening of the eyes that were barely visible above her veil. The ironmonger, rubbing his hands, smiled proudly and bowed several times.

"You will find no greater stock, madam, between here and Khandar. And there are very few in Khandar," he added modestly, "who carry such an extensive line as do I."

"I can believe that," the woman murmured, and Muzaffahr grinned in pleasure at the compliment.

"And now, for what is madam in the market? Daggers, knives? I have many of my own make and design. This one"—he lifted proudly a wicked-looking knife with a serrated blade and a handle made of human bone—"has been blessed by the God himself. Or perhaps poison—the favorite of genteel ladies?" He gestured to several shelves built into the cavernlike walls of the hole in the ground. Jars of all shapes and sizes stood in neat rows, each with a label attached. "I have poisons that will kill within seconds and leave no trace upon the victim's body."

Gliding closer, Meryem read the inscriptions on each jar with the air of one who knows her wares. Her eyes lighted on a heavy stone crock, and the ironmonger nodded. "I see you are an expert. That is an excellent choice. Takes thirty days to work. The victim suffers the most excruciating agonies the entire time. Ideal for a rival for your man's love." He started to lift the lid, but the woman shook her head and turned away.

"Ah, my rings. So it is not a rival then, but a lover? I know, you see. I know how the needs of women and how they prefer to work. I am a sensitive man, madam, very sensitive. Let me see your hand. Slender fingers. I do not know whether I have any that small. Here is one—a chryso-beryl in a silver setting. It works thus."

Turning the stone a half-twist, Muzaffahr caused a tiny needle to spring out of the ring's setting. The sharp point gleamed in the lamp light.

"When you curl your finger under, like this, the point extends beyond the knuckle and is easily inserted into the flesh." The ironmonger gave the stone another half-turn and the needle disappeared. "And, once again, an innocent ring. I can treat the needle for you or perhaps Madam would prefer to purchase the where-with-all and do that herself?"

"Myself," said the woman in a low voice, muffled by her heavy veil.

"Very well. Shall you wear it?"

The shrouded head nodded. Holding out her hand, the woman allowed the ironmonger to slip the ring upon her finger.

"How much and what kind? Fast acting or slow?"

"Fast," she said, and pointed to one of the jars upon the shelf.

"Excellent choice!" Muzaffahr murmured. "I bow before an expert."

"Never mind that. Hurry!" the woman spoke imperi-ously, and the ironmonger hastened to obey.

A small perfume vial was filled with the selected poison. The woman concealed it in the folds of her robe. Money exchanged hands. The lamp was extinguished, the ladder climbed, the trapdoor raised. Soon both stood in the ironmon-ger's hovel that was a hovel once more, the tools of the assassin's trade well hidden beneath the trapdoor.

"May Benario guide your hand and blind your victim's eyes." Muzaffahr repeated the Thieves' Blessing solemnly.

"May he indeed!" the woman whispered to herself and glided into the night.

*   *   *

That morning, when Achmed returned to his tent, he found the following message scrawled upon a piece of parchment.

My beloved. I overheard something this night which leads me to believe that your mother and the other followers of our Holy Akhran being held prisoner in Kich are in terrible danger. I have gone to warn them of their peril and do what I can to save them. As you value my life and those of the ones you love, say nothing of this to anyone! Trust in me. There is nothing you can do except remain here and perform your duty as the brave soldier that you are. To do anything else might bring suspicion down upon me. Pray to Akhran for us all. I love you more than life itself.

—Meryem

Achmed had learned to read in the Amir's service. Now he wished his eyes had been torn from his head rather than bring him such news. Rushing from his tent, missive in hand, the young man searched the camp. He dared not risk asking anyone if they had seen her, and hours later, dejected, he was forced to return to his tent alone.

She was gone. There was no doubt. She had fled in the night.

Achmed pondered. His overwhelming desire was to rush after her, but that would mean abandoning his post without leave—a treasonous offense. Not even Qannadi could shield the young soldier from the death penalty attached to desertion. He considered going to the Amir and explaining everything and requesting leave to return to Kich.

As you value my life and those of the ones you love, say nothing of this to anyone!

The words leapt off the paper and burned into his heart. No, there was nothing he could do. He must trust to her, to her nobility, her courage. Tears in his eyes, he pressed the letter passionately to his lips and sank down on the bed, gently caressing the blankets where her fragrance lingered still.

Chapter 3

Khardan and his companions left Serinda in the early hours of evening, intending to cross the Pagrah desert during the cool hours of night. The journey was accomplished in silence, each person's thoughts wrapping around him or her as closely as their face masks. Lulled by the rhythmic swaying of the camels, cooled by the night air, Mathew stared moodily at the myriad stars above that seemed to be trying to outdo the myriad grains of sand below and wondered what lay ahead for them.

To judge by Khardan's grim expression and Zohra's darkly flashing eyes whenever Mathew broached the subject, it would not be pleasant.

"Surely no one saw us," Mathew repeated comfortingly over and over until the words plodded along in his mind in time to the camel's footsteps. "We have been gone months, but that can be explained. Surely no one saw us. . . ."

But even as he repeated the litany, willing it to come true, he felt someone watching him and, twisting in the saddle, saw the cruel eyes of the Black Paladin glitter in the moonlight. Auda's hand patted the hilt of the dagger at his waist. Shuddering, Mathew turned his back on the Paladin and hunched over in the saddle, determined to put a closer guard upon his thoughts.

They rode far into the morning. Mathew had discovered

that he could sink into a half doze that permitted part of his mind to sleep while another part kept awake and made certain he did not "drift." He knew Zohra was watching him from the corner of her dark eyes, and he had no desire to feel the sting of her camel stick across his back.

They slept through the heat of the day, and Khardan allowed them to rest in the early evening, then they set off again. The Calif figured to arrive in the camp at the Tel at dawn.

Their first glimpse of the nomad's campsite was not auspicious. The four stood atop a large sand dune, highly visible against the morning sun that was rising at their backs. Thus, though no one in the camp below could possibly recognize them—seeing only black silhouettes—Khardan declared by his willingness to be seen that he had no hostile intentions.

It took long minutes before anyone noticed them, however. A bad sign, apparently, thought Mathew, watching Khardan's face grow grimmer as he surveyed the scene below. In the center of the landscape was the Tel, the lone hill that jutted up inexplicably from the flat desert floor. A few patches of brownish green dotted its red surface—the cacti known as the Rose of the Prophet. Khardan's frowning gaze lingered on the Rose, flicked sideways to Zohra, and back again before any but the young man noticed.

Mathew knew the history of the Rose. Zohra had related to him how their God, Akhran, had brought about her detested marriage to Khardan by pronouncing that the two must wed and their warring tribes dwell together in peace until the ugly-looking cacti bloomed. Perhaps Khardan was surprised to note that the plant was still alive. Certainly Mathew was surprised. It seemed remarkable to him that anything—humans included—could live in such bleak and forbidding surroundings.

The oasis was nearly dry. Where before Mathew remembered a body of cool water surrounded by lush, green growth, there was now only a large, muddy puddle, a few straggling palms, and the tall desert grass clinging to life on its shore. A herd of scroungy-looking camels and a smaller herd of horses were tethered near the water.

The camp itself was divided into three separate and distinct groups. Mathew knew the colors of Khardan's tribe, the Akar, and he recognized the colors of Zohra's tribe, the Hrana. But he did not know the third until Khardan murmured, "Zeid's people," and he saw Zohra nod silently in response. The tents themselves were poor, makeshift affairs straggling across the sand without order or care. And though it was early morning and the camp should have been bustling with activity before the heat of the late summer's afternoon drove them to rest in their tents, there was no one about.

No women met to walk to the well together. No children scampered across the sand, rounding up the goats to be milked, leading the horses to be watered. At length the four saw one man leave his tent and make his way, shoulders sagging, to tend to the animals. He glanced around at his surroundings, more out of despairing boredom, it seemed, than out of care. His surprise when he saw them standing on the dune above him was evident, and he ran off, shouting, toward the tent of his Sheykh.

Khardan dismounted and led his camel down the dune, the others following. Auda moved to walk beside the Calif and would have displayed his sword openly, but Khardan put his hand upon the Paladin's arm.

"No," he said. "These are my people. They will do you no harm. You are a guest in their tents."

"It is not myself I fear for, brother," returned Auda, and Mathew shivered.

Men came running, and as Khardan approached the camp he slowly and purposefully removed the *haik* that covered his face. Mathew heard a collective sucking in of breaths. Another man broke and ran back through the silently staring throng.

Khardan came to the edge of the campsite. The men stood before him in a row, blocking his path. No one spoke. The only sound was the wind singing its eerie duet with the dunes.

Mathew's hands, clutching the camel's reins, were wet with sweat. The hope in his heart died, pierced by the hatred and anger clearly visible in the eyes of the Calif's people. The four stood facing the crowd that was growing larger every minute as the word spread. Khardan and Auda were in front, Zohra slightly behind and to their right, Mathew to their left. Glancing at Khardan, Mathew saw the man's jaws tighten. A trickle of sweat ran down his temple, glistened on the smooth, brown skin of his face, and disappeared into the black beard. Grimly, without speaking a word, Khardan took a step forward, then another and another until he was almost touching the first man in the crowd.

The man stood with arms folded across his chest, dark eyes burning. Khardan took another step. His intention to either walk through the man or over him was obvious. Shrugging, the man stepped back and to one side. The rest of the crowd followed his lead, backing up, clearing a path. Slowly, his head high, Khardan continued on into the campsite, leading his camel. Auda, beside him, kept one hand thrust into his robes. Mathew and Zohra followed.

Unable to bear the stare of the eyes, the enmity that beat on them with the heat of the sun, Mathew kept his gaze fixed on his feet and tried to control a tremor in his legs. Once he sneaked a quick glance at Zohra and saw her walking majestically, chin in the air, her eyes fixed on the sky as if there were nothing worthy of her notice any lower.

Envying her the courage and pride that refused to give way to fear, Mathew shivered and sweat beneath his robes and kept his eyes on the ground, nearly walking into the rear end of Khardan's camel when the group suddenly came to a halt.

There had been a spoken command; Mathew remembered hearing it through the blood pounding in his ears, and now someone took the camel's reins from his nerveless hand and was leading the beast away. With some vague thought of covering Khardan's back, Mathew moved forward, only to bump into Auda, who was doing the same thing with far more speed and adeptness.

"Keep out of the way, Blossom," Auda ordered harshly, beneath his breath.

Flushing, feeling frightened and clumsy and useless, Mathew backed up and felt Zohra's hand catch hold of his and thrust him behind her. Reluctantly, lifting his eyes, Mathew saw the reason for their halt.

Three men stood before them. One—a scrawny, bandy-legged man with a perpetually gloomy expression—Mathew recognized easily as Sheykh Jaafar, Zohra's father. The other was a short, fat man with an oily-looking face and neatly trimmed black beard. This, Mathew assumed, must be the Zeid that Khardan had mentioned on the dune. The other man seemed familiar, but Mathew could not place him until Khardan, his voice tight, his breathing heavy, said softly, "Father."

Mathew gasped audibly and felt Zohra's nails dig rebukingly through the folds of cloth and into his flesh. This was Majiid! But what dreadful change had come over the man? The giant frame had collapsed. The man who had once towered over the short Jaafar now stood even with him. The shoulders that had once squared in defiance were stooped and rounded in defeat. The hands that wielded steel in battle hung limply at his side, the feet that had proudly trod the desert shuffled through the sand. Only the eyes shone fierce and proud as the eyes of a hawk; the large, fleshless nose jutting forward from the outthrust head might have been the tearing beak of a predatory bird.

"Do not call me father," said the old man in a voice shaking with suppressed fury. "I am no one's father! I have no sons!"

"I am your eldest son, Father," said Khardan evenly. "Calif of my people. I have come back."

"My eldest son is dead!" retorted Majiid, froth forming on his lips. "Or if not, he should be!"

Khardan flinched; his face grew pale.

"You were seen!" cried Jaafar's shrill voice. "The djinn, Fedj, saw you fleeing the battle dressed as a woman, in company with that wildcat I once called daughter and the madman! The djinn swore it with the Oath of Sul! Deny it, if you can!"

"I do not deny it," said Khardan, and a low muttering rippled through the crowd of men. Auda's dark eyes darted here and there, his hand came out of his robes, and Mathew saw steel flash in the sun.

"I do not deny that I fled the battle!" Khardan raised his voice for all to hear. "Nor do I deny that I was dressed as . . ." he faltered a moment, then continued strongly, "as a woman. But I deny that I fled a coward!"

"Slay him!" Majiid pointed. "Slay them all!" His words bubbled on his tongue in his fury. "Slay the coward and his witch-wife!" The Sheykh himself reached for his scimitar, but his hand closed over nothing. He had long ago ceased to wear his weapon. "My sword!" he howled, turning on a cringing servant. "Bring me my sword! Never mind! Give me yours!" Rounding on one of his men, he grabbed the sword from the man's hand and, swinging it ferociously, turned on Khardan.

Auda slid in front of the Calif with practiced grace and ease, bringing his sword up to meet Majiid's wild blow. The Black Paladin's next stroke would have sliced Majiid's head from his shoulders had not Khardan and Sheykh Zeid each restrained the two.

"Cursed for eternity is the father who slays his son!" gasped Zeid, grappling with Majiid for the weapon.

"These are my people! I forbid you to harm them!" Khardan caught hold of Auda.

"The Calif must be fairly judged and have a chance to speak in his own defense," Jaafar cried.

Majiid struggled briefly, impotently. Then, seeing it was useless in his weakened condition to try to break free, he hurled the sword aside. "Pah!" Glaring at Khardan, he spit on the ground at his son's feet and, turning, shambled back to his dwelling.

"Take the Calif under guard to my tent," ordered Zeid hastily, hearing the low rumbling of the crowd. Several of the Sheykh's men closed in on Khardan. Divesting him of sword and dagger, they started to lead him away, but Auda stepped in front of them.

"What of this man?" demanded Jaafar, pointing a trembling finger at Auda.

"I go with Khardan," said the Black Paladin.

"He is a guest," Khardan stated, "and shall be treated as such for the honor of our tribes."

"He drew steel," muttered Zeid, regarding the formidable Auda warily.

"In my defense. He is sworn to protect me."

There was some awed murmuring over this. Clearly it went against Zeid's heart to offer the black-clad Auda his hospitality, but as Khardan had said, their tribal honor hung in the balance. "Very well," said Zeid reluctantly. "He shall be granted the guest period of three days, so long as he does nothing to violate it. You take him to your tent," he instructed Jaafar.

The Sheykh opened his mouth to protest, caught Zeid's glare, and snapped it shut. With an ungracious *salaam*, Jaafar bowed and indicated that his home was Auda's home and showed the way with a sweep of his bony hand.

Nodding reassuringly to the Black Paladin, Khardan suffered himself to be led away by his captors. Auda followed them, watching until the tent flap closed behind the Calif; then, with a black-eyed stare at Jaafar that made the little man fall back a pace, he bowed sardonically and walked over to the tent that the Sheykh had indicated as his.

"And what of your daughter?" Zeid shouted after Jaafar.

"I don't want the witch near me!" screeched the Sheykh. "Send her with her accursed husband!"

Though Zohra's face was veiled, Mathew saw the scorn in her eyes.

Sheykh Zeid al Saban was clearly at a loss. He could not take the woman into his dwelling. Such a thing would not be seemly. "There are no women's tents," he said to her apologetically. "Since there are no women." The Sheykh dithered. "You"—he finally pointed at one of his tribesmen—"vacate your dwelling. Take her there and keep her under guard."

The man nodded, and he and another hurried forward to lead Zohra away. They would have taken her by the arms, but the look she flashed them warned them back as effectively as if she had wielded a blade. Tossing her head, she walked where they led. She had not spoken one word the entire time.

The only one who remained behind was Mathew, standing alone, his face burning beneath a hundred glowering gazes.

"What of the madman?" said someone at last.

Mathew closed his eyes against the baleful stares, his fists clenched as though he held his courage in his hands.

"We may not touch him," said Zeid at last. "He has seen the face of Akhran. He is free to go. Besides," said the Sheykh, turning away and shrugging, "he is harmless."

The rest of the men—eager to put their heads together and discuss this development and speculate on what the Sheykhs would decide and how soon the execution of the coward and his witch-wife would take place—agreed without question and hurried off to their gossip.

Opening his eyes, Mathew found himself standing alone.

Chapter 4

On the evening of the day they had arrived in the camp at the Tel, Mathew walked toward the tent where Zohra was being held prisoner. It was near Khardan's tent, he noted, as he approached. Standing at the entrance to both were guards, who appeared uncomfortable and ill-at-ease, their hands constantly straying to touch their swords reassuringly. The reason for their discomfiture was readily apparent. In the shadow of a nearby tent Auda squatted on the desert floor, the dark, flat eyes never leaving Khardan's dwelling. The Black Paladin had posted himself at noontime. He had not moved all day, and it did not seem likely, from his watchful manner, that he intended to move ever again.

Avoiding the gaze of those eyes that he knew all too well, not envying the guards their being forced to endure that malevolent stare for hours on end, Mathew quickened his pace to Zohra's tent.

Both guards bowed with the officious politeness the no-mads always exhibited to the madman. Mathew had, after all, seen the face of the God. It would never do to insult him, lest he take it out on them after death when they themselves would come face-to-face with Akhran. This gave Mathew a certain power over them, albeit a negative one. He intended to use it, and he had even changed back into women's clothing that he had begged of Jaafar in order to enhance his appearance of being mentally infirm.

"I want to see Zohra," he said to the guard. He indicated a bundle he held in his hands. "I have some things for her."

"What things?" demanded the guard, reaching for the bundle.

"Women's things," Mathew said, holding onto it firmly.

The guard hesitated—certain private belongings of women were not considered suitable to the sight of men. "At least let me feel to make certain you do not carry a weapon," the guard said after a moment's pause.

Willingly Mathew held out the bundle, and the guard grasped it and prodded it and poked at it and, satisfied at last, let Mathew pass into the tent without comment.

No man would have been permitted to enter this tent, Mathew thought bitterly, closing the flap behind him. But a madman—a man who chose to hide himself in the clothes of a woman rather than face an honorable death, a man they shun, a man they consider harmless—*me* they will allow inside.

An honorable death. The words caused his heart to constrict painfully. Khardan would die before he let his people brand their Calif a coward. That must not happen.

We will see how "harmless" I am, Mathew resolved.

Zohra sat cross-legged on the bare tent floor. There were cushions in the tent, but after one look and a wrinkling of his nose, Mathew understood why she had tossed them into a corner rather than use them for her comfort. She glanced up at him without welcome or hope.

"What do you want?" she asked dully.

"I came to bring you a change of clothing," said Mathew for the guard's benefit.

Zohra made a disdainful movement with her hand, started to speak, then stopped as Mathew swiftly put his finger to his lips.

"Shhh," he warned. Kneeling down beside her, he unfolded the garments.

"A knife?" Zohra whispered eagerly, but the fire in her eyes faded when she saw what the bundle contained. "Goatskin?'' she said in disgust, lifting the limp pieces of cured skin with a thumb and forefinger.

"Shhh!" Mathew hissed urgently. Kohl, used to outline the eyes, and several falcon feathers tumbled out onto the floor. Seeing them, Zohra understood. The dark eyes flared.

"Scrolls!"

"Yes," said Mathew, breathing his words into her ear. "I have a plan."

"Good!" Zohra smiled and lifted a feather whose quill had been sharpened to a fine point. "Teach me the scrolls of death!"

"No, no!" Mathew checked an exasperated sigh. He should have known this would happen. He considered telling Zohra that he could not take a human life, that the ways of his people were peaceful. He considered the notion briefly and, sighing, dismissed it just as fast. He could imagine Zohra's reaction. She already thought him crazy. "You will make scrolls of water," he whispered patiently.

Zohra scowled. "Water! Bah! I will kill them. Kill them all! Beginning with that sniveling swine, my father—"

"Water!" said Mathew sternly. "My plan is this—"

He was about to explain when voices came from outside.

"Let me in," demanded a grating voice at the near-by tent. "I will see the prisoner."

Mathew, drawing aside the tent flap ever so slightly, peeped outside.

It was Majiid, talking to Khardan's guard.

"Leave us," the old man ordered the guards. "I will not be in any danger and he will not run away. Not again."

Swiftly Mathew drew back. He and Zohra heard the guards' footsteps crunch over the sand. There was a moment's pause and Mathew could imagine Majiid glowering at the unmoving Auda, then they hard the tent flap thrown aside and Khardan's voice respectfully—if somewhat ironically—welcoming his father.

Zohra's guards were talking this over in low tones. Exchanging meaningful glances, both Zohra and Mathew crawled quietly to the rear of her tent. It stood close to Khardan's and, holding their breaths, they were able to hear much of the conversation between father and son.

"Have the Sheykhs determined my fate?"

"No," growled Majiid. "We meet tonight. You will be allowed to speak."

"Then why are you here?" Khardan's voice sounded weary, and Mathew wondered if he had been asleep.

There was silence as if the old man was struggling to speak the words. When they finally came out, they blurted forth, forced out past some great obstacle. "Tell them that the witch ensorcelled you. Tell them that it was her scheme to destroy our tribe. The Sheykhs will judge in your favor since you acted under the constraint of magic. Your honor will be restored."

Khardan was silent. Zohra's face was pale, but cool and impassive. Her eyes were liquid night. But she was not as calm as she seemed. Involuntarily she reached out and caught hold of Mathew's hand with her own. He squeezed it tightly, offering what poor comfort he could.

After all, Majiid had asked nothing of Khardan but that he speak the truth.

"What will happen to my wife?"

"What do you care?" Majiid demanded angrily. "She was never wife to you!"

"What will happen?" Khardan's voice had an edge of steel.

"She still be stoned to death—the fate of women who practice evil magic!"

They heard a rustling, as if Khardan rose to his feet.

"No, father. I will not say this to the Sheykhs."

"Then your fate is in the hands of Akhran!" snarled Majiid bitterly, and they heard him storm from the tent, yelling loudly to the guards to take up their posts again as he left.

Mathew and Zohra started to return to their work when they heard Khardan speaking again—not to a human, but to his God. "My fate is in your hands, *Hazrat* Akhran," said the Calif reverently. "You took my life and gave it back to me for a reason. My people are in danger. Humbly I come before you and I beg you to show me how I may help them! If it means sacrificing my life, I will do so gladly! Help me, Akhran! Help me to help them!"

His voice died. A tear fell hot on Mathew's hand. Looking up, he saw its mate slide down Zohra's pallid cheek.

"I talk of killing them," she murmured. "He talks of saving them. Akhran forgive me."

She did not bother to wipe the tear away but moved swiftly and soundlessly back to the center of the tent. Taking up the quill, she rubbed it in kohl, and bending over the goatskin, keeping it hidden from view in case anyone entered the tent, she began to laboriously trace out the arcane words that would bring water out of sand.

Chapter 5

The council convened shortly after Majiid left Khardan's tent, or at least Mathew assumed that this was the reason for a loud burst of raised voices and vehement arguing that carried clearly in the still night air. When he had first begun working on his scroll, he feared they might not have enough time to complete the work. But gradually, as the hours passed and the haranguing continued, Mathew relaxed. From the occasional shout, he gathered that the Sheykhs were fighting over whose side of the camp should hold the judgment and which Sheykh and whose *akasul* should preside.

Zeid claimed that since he was not near kin to any of the parties involved, he should be the one who sat in judgment. This precipitated an hour's shouting match over whether a father's mother's sister's seventh son's brother's son related to Majiid on the father's side was considered near kin. By the time this dispute was resolved (Mathew never did find out how), the argument over the site began again with an entirely new set of issues involved.

But though the bickering bought them time, Mathew found his feeling of ease seeping away. The yelling and the clamoring rasped on his nerves like a wood mason's file going across the grain. He found it increasingly hard to concentrate, and when he had ruined his second scroll by misspelling a word he had known how to spell since the age of six, he tossed down the quill in exasperation.

"After all, why should be hurry?" he said abruptly, startling Zohra. "They're not going to decide anything for a week! They couldn't agree on the number of suns in the sky! Jaafar would say it was one, Majiid would swear it was two and one was invisible, and Zeid would claim them both wrong and state that there were no suns in the sky and he would slit the throat of anyone who accused him of lying!"

"All will be determined by morning," returned Zohra softly. She knelt upon the floor, bent nearly double to trace the letters upon the goatskin. Her lips slowly and deliberately formed the sound of each letter she drew, as though this would somehow aid her hand in executing the symbol.

Executing. The word made Mathew's hand tremble, and he hastily clasped one over the other. "How do you know?" he asked irritably.

"Because they have it all decided in their minds already," Zohra returned, shrugging. She glanced up at Mathew, her eyes dark pools in the lamplight. "This is a serious matter. How would it look to the people if they made a decision in only a few hours?"

A sudden clashing of steel made Mathew jump and almost spring to his feet, thinking that they were coming for them. Zohra went on writing, however, and Mathew—realizing the sound was confined to the council tent—supposed bitterly that this matter of putting to death their Calif and his wife was so serious that the Sheykhs needed to shed some of their own blood first.

Maybe they'll all kill each other, he thought. Savages! Why do I bother? What do these barbarians matter to me? They think I'm mad! They are kind to me only out of superstition. I will always be some sort of strange and rare creature to them, never accepted. I will always be alone!

Mathew did not know his despairing thoughts were stamped plainly upon his face until an arm stole around his shoulders.

"Do not fear, Mat-hew," said Zohra gently. "Your plan is a good one! All will be well!"

Mathew clung to her, letting her touch comfort him until he became aware that her caressing fingers were no longer soothing but arousing. Hastily, gulping, he sat back and looked at her with a wild hope beating in his chest. There was caring in the dark eyes, but not the kind for which he longed. The smooth face was expressive of worry, concern, nothing more.

But what more did he want? How could one be in love with two people at the same time?

Two people one could never have . . .

A groaned escaped Mathew's lips.

"Are you sick again?" Zohra drew near, and Mathew, cringing, repelled her with an upraised hand.

"A slight pain. It will pass," he gasped.

"Where?" Zohra persisted.

"Here." Mathew sighed, and pressed his hand over his heart. "I've had it before. There is nothing you can do. Nothing anyone can do." That, at least, was truth enough. "We had better finish the magic if we are to be ready by morning," he added.

She still seemed inclined to speak, then checked herself and, after gazing intently at the young man, returned silently to her work.

She knows, he realized forlornly. She knows but does not know what to say. Perhaps she loved me once, or rather wanted me, but that was when I first came and she and I were both frightened and weak and lost. But now she has found what she sought; she is sure of herself, strong in her love for Khardan. She doesn't know it yet, she won't admit it. But it is there, like a rod of iron in her soul, and it is giving her strength.

And Khardan loves her, though he has armored himself against that love and fights it at every turn.

What can I do, who love them both?

"You can give them each other," came a voice soft and sad, echoing his heartbreak, yet with a kind of deep joy in it that he didn't understand.

"What did you say?" he asked Zohra.

"Nothing!" She glanced at him worriedly. "I said nothing. Are you sure you are all right, Mat-hew?"

He nodded, rubbing the back of his neck, trying to rid himself of a tickling sensation, as of feathers brushing against his skin.

Chapter 6

The following dawn the sun's first rays skimmed across the desert, crept through the holes in Majiid's tent, bringing silence with them. The arguing ceased. Zohra and Mathew glanced at each other. Her eyes were shadowed and red-rimmed from lack of sleep and the concentration she had devoted to her work. Mathew knew his must look the same or perhaps worse.

The silence of the morning was suddenly broken by the sound of feet crunching over sand. They heard the guards outside scramble to their feet, the sound of footsteps draw nearer. Both Mathew and Zohra were ready, each had been ready for over an hour now, ever since first light. Zohra was clad in the women's clothes Mathew had brought for her. They were not the fine silk she was accustomed to wearing, only a simple *chador* of white cotton that had been worn by the second wife in a poor man's household. Its simplicity became her, enhancing the newfound gravity of bearing. A plain white mantle covered her head and face, shoulders and hands. Held tightly in her hands, hidden by the folds of her veil, were several pieces of carefully rolled-up goatskin.

Mathew was dressed in the black robes he had acquired in Castle Zhakrin. Since he was able to come and go freely, he had left the tent in the middle of the night and searched the camp in the moonlit darkness until he found the camels they had ridden. Their baggage had been removed from the beasts, thrown down, and left to lie in the sand as though cursed. Mathew could have wished the robes—retrieved by Auda from their campsite on the shores of the Kurdin Sea—cleaner and less worse for wear, but he hoped that even stained and wrinkled they must still look impressive to these people who had never seen sorcerer's garb before.

Stealing back to the tent once he had changed his clothes, Mathew noted the figure of the Black Paladin sitting unmoving before Khardan's tent. The slender white hand, shining in the moonlight as if it had some kind of light of its own, beckoned to him. Mathew hesitated, casting a worried glance at the watchful guards. Auda beckoned again, more insistently, and Mathew reluctantly approached him.

"Do not worry, Blossom," the man said easily, "they will not prevent us from speaking. After all, I am a guest and you are insane."

"What do you want?" Mathew whispered, squirming beneath the scrutiny of the flat, dispassionate eyes.

Auda's hand caught hold of the hem of Mathew's black robes, rubbing the velvet between his fingers. "You are planning something."

"Yes," said Mathew uncomfortably, with another glance at the guards.

"That is good, Blossom," said Auda softly, slowly twisting the black cloth. "You are an ingenious and resourceful young man. Your life was obviously spared for a purpose. I will be watching and waiting. You may count upon me."

He released the cloth from his grasp, smiled, and settled back comfortably. Mathew left, returning to Zohra's tent, uncertain whether to feel relieved or more worried.

The eyes of the guards opened wide when Mathew, clad in his black robes, emerged from the tent into the first light of day. The young wizard had brushed and combed his long red hair until it blazed like flame in the sunshine. The cabalistic marks, etched into the velvet in such a way that they could not be seen except in direct light, caught the sun's rays and appeared to leap out suddenly from the black cloth, astonishing all viewers.

Mathew's hands—gripping his own scrolls—were concealed in the long, flowing sleeves. He walked forward without saying a word or looking at anyone, keeping his eyes staring straight ahead. He saw, without seeming to, Khardan leave his tent, saw the puzzled look the man cast him. Mathew dared not respond or risk breaking the show of mystery he was wrapping around himself.

What the Archmagus would have said had he seen his pupil now came to Mathew's mind, and a wan smile nearly destroyed the illusion. "Cheap theatrics! Worthy of those who use magic to trap the gullible!" He could hear his old teacher rage on, as he had once a year at the beginning of First Quarter. "The true magus needs no black robes or conical hat! He could practice magic naked in the wilderness" —since no one dared laugh in the presence of the Archmagus, this statement always occasioned sudden coughing fits among the students and was later the source of whispered jokes for many nights to come—"practice magic naked in the wilderness if he has only the knowledge of his craft and Sul in his heart!"

Naked in the wilderness. Mathew sighed. The Archmagus was dead now, slaughtered by Auda's *goums*. The young wizard hoped the old man would understand and forgive what his pupil was about to do.

Looking neither to the right nor the left, Mathew made his way through the camp, past the ranks of staring nomads, and walked straight to the Tel. He seemed to travel blindly (although in reality he was watching where he was going and carefully avoided large obstacles), occasionally stumbling most convincingly over small rocks and other debris in his path.

Behind him he could hear the men following after him, the Sheykhs questioning everyone as to what was going on, the nomads responding with confused answers.

"This is ridiculous!" Zeid said angrily. "Why doesn't someone stop him?"

"He is mad," muttered Majiid sullenly.

"*You* stop him," suggested Jaafar.

"Very well, I will!" humphed Zeid.

The short, pudgy Sheykh—hands raised, mouth open—planted himself in front of Mathew. The wizard, staring straight ahead, kept walking and would have run the Sheykh down had not Zeid—at the last moment—scrambled to get out of his way.

"He didn't even see me!" gasped the Sheykh.

"He is being led by the God!" cried Jaafar in an awed voice.

"He is being led by the God!" The word spread through the crowd like flame cast on oil, and Mathew blessed the man in his heart.

Hoping everyone—including Khardan—was following him, but not daring to look behind, Mathew reached the Tel and begin to climb it, slipping and falling among the rocks and the scraggly-looking Rose of the Prophet. When he was about halfway up, he faced around and spread his arms wide, keeping the goatskin scrolls concealed by turning his palms away from his audience.

"People of the Akar, the Hrana, and the Aran, attend to my words," he shouted in a voice as deep as he could possibly make it.

Standing at the foot of the Tel directly below him was Zohra. Khardan, held by his guards, was staring darkly at Mathew, perhaps convinced that the young man had now truly gone mad. Near him, Auda—face covered by his *haik*—watched with a glint of a smile in his dark eyes and his hand near his dagger. The sight of him made Mathew nervous, and he quickly shifted his gaze.

"Madman, come down!" Majiid sounded impatient. "We have no time for this—"

"No time for the word of Akhran?" Mathew called out sternly.

The crowd muttered. Heads came together.

"Get him down from there, and let's get on with the judgment," ordered Zeid, waving at several of his men.

At first Mathew thought they were going to refuse to obey, and they thought so, too, it seemed, until Zeid grew red in his face, swelling indignantly at this disobedience. Three men began to climb the Tel.

Mathew muttered a swift prayer to Promenthas and another to Sul, then—reciting the words he had written with such deliberation—he hurled one of the scrolls to the ground at his feet.

An explosion sent fragments of rock and dust shooting out in all directions. Purplish green smoke rose up, obscuring the young wizard from sight. Trying to keep from coughing— he'd remembered to hold his breath only at the last minute— Mathew attempted to compose himself so that, when the smoke cleared, the crowd would see a sorceror in command, not a young man, tears running down his cheeks from the smoke in his eyes, gagging at the smell of sulphur.

Cheap theatrics, maybe. But it worked.

The three men who had been climbing up the hill were now scrambling back as if for their lives. Zeid had gone white as his turban, Majiid's eyes bulged, and Jaafar had covered his head with his hands. Even Zohra, who knew what he was going to do, appeared impressed.

"I have not only seen the face of Akhran, I have spoken to him," Mathew shouted. "As you can see, he has lent me his fire! Attend to my words or I will cast it among you!"

"Speak then," growled Majiid in a tone that said plainly, "Let's humor him; then we can get on with our business."

This was rather disconcerting. Mathew had no choice, however, but to plunge ahead.

"I do not intend to deny what the djinn Fedj told you. Zohra and I did carry this man"—he pointed at Khardan, who was shaking his head, making signals that Mathew should keep silent—"away, disguised as a woman!

"But," Mathew shouted over the murmurings of the crowd, "it was not a live body we carried. It was a corpse. Khardan, your Calif, was dead!"

As Mathew expected, this caught their attention. There was a rustling as those who had been talking demanded a repeat of the madman's words from those who had been listening. Silence descended; the air was heavy and charged as a thundercloud.

"You, his father, know it to be true!" Mathew jabbed a finger at Majiid. "You knew in your heart your son was dead. You told them he was dead, didn't you!" The pointing finger encompassed the tribe.

Taken aback, the Sheykh could do nothing but glower, his white eyebrows bristling fiercely, and glare at Mathew. There were nods from his tribesmen and narrowed, suspicious glances from those not of his tribe.

"How many of you have ridden into battle with this man?" Mathew's finger shifted and aimed at Khardan. "How many of you have seen his valor with your own eyes? How many owe your very lives to his courage?"

Lowered heads, shameful glances. Mathew knew he had them now.

"And yet this is the man you charge with cowardice? I say to you that Khardan was dead before any of the rest of you ever found your way to the battlefield!" Mathew quickly followed up his advantage. "Princess Zohra and I, having fought off the Amir's troops who would have taken us prisoner as they took the rest of the women, saw the Calif fall, mortally wounded. We took him from the field so that the foul *kafir* would not defile his body.

"And we dressed him in women's clothing."

The hush was breathless; not a man so much as moved lest he miss Mathew's next words.

"We did that—not to hide him from the troops," said Mathew in a quiet voice that he knew all must strain to hear. "We did that to hide him from Death!"

Now they breathed, all at once, in a rush of air that was like a night breeze. Mathew risked a swift glance at Khardan. No longer scowling, the Calif was attempting to keep his face as expressionless as possible. Either he had some glimpse of where Mathew was headed, or he now trusted the young man to lead him there blindfolded.

"Death was searching the field for victims of the battle, and since we knew she must be looking for warriors, we clad Khardan in women's clothes. Thus Death did not find him. Your God, *Hazrat* Akhran, found him.

"We fled Death, escaping into the desert. And there Akhran appeared to us and told us that Khardan should live, but that in return for his life he must offer his aid to the first stranger who came by. The Calif drew breath and opened his eyes, and it was then that this man"—Mathew pointed at Auda, who was standing alone amidst the crowd, no one wanting to come too near him—"came to us and asked for our aid. His God, Zhakrin, was being held prisoner by Quar. He needed us to help free him.

"Mindful of the bargain he had made with Akhran, Khardan agreed, and we went with the stranger and freed his God. The stranger is a knight in his land, a man sworn to honor. I ask you, Auda ibn Jad, is this the truth I speak?"

"It is," replied ibn Jad in his cool, deep voice. Removing the snake dagger from his belt, he lifted it high in the air. "I call upon my God, Zhakrin, to witness my oath. May he plunge this knife into my breast if I am lying!"

Auda let go the knife. It did not fall but remained poised in the air, hovering above his chest. The crowd gasped in astonishment and awe. Mathew recovered his voice—he had not been expecting that—and continued, somewhat shakily.

"We left the homeland of ibn Jad and traveled back to the desert, for Akhran had come to us once again to tell us that his people were in danger and needed their Calif. We crossed the Sun's Anvil—"

"No! Impossible!"

The nomads, who could swallow to a man a child's tale about Khardan fleeing Death in a disguise, scoffed at the thought of anyone crossing the *kavir*.

"We did!" Mathew cried them down. "And this is how. Your Calif is not the only one to receive a gift from Akhran. He bestowed a gift upon your Princess, as well."

Their lives now depended on Zohra. The tribesmen turned wary, suspicious eyes upon her. Mathew nearly closed his, afraid to watch, afraid that the spell wouldn't work, that in her agitation she had written the wrong words or written them the wrong way or a hundred other things that could go wrong with the gift of Sul.

Taking the goatskin from the folds of her robes, Zohra held it up and read the words in a clear voice. The letters began to wriggle and writhe and one by one fell off the skin onto the sand at her feet. Those near her began to shout and exclaim and stumbled over themselves to fall back, while those who could not see shouted and questioned and pushed forward. Mathew could not see the pool of blue water at the woman's feet—her white robes blowing in the wind obscured the view. But he knew it must be there, from the reaction of those around her and from the look of pride that swept over Khardan's face as he gazed at her.

"Khardan has returned to you—a Prophet of Akhran. Zohra has returned to you—a Prophetess of Akhran. They have returned to lead you to war! Will you follow them?"

This was where Mathew expected the rousing cheer. It was not forthcoming, and the young man stared at the crowd beneath him in rising apprehension.

"That is all very well," said Sheykh Zeid smoothly, stepping forward. "And we have seen some fine tricks, tricks worthy of the *souk* of Khandar, I might add. But what about the djinn?"

"Yes! The djinn!" came the cry from the crowd.

"I say to you"—Zeid faced the people, raising his stubby arms for silence—"I say that I will name Khardan Prophet and I will follow him to battle or to Sul's Hell if the Calif chooses *provided* he can return to us our djinn! Surely," Zeid continued, spreading his hands, "Akhran will do no less for his Prophet!"

The crowd cheered. Majiid shot his son a dark glance that said, "I warned you." Jaafar eyed Zohra fearfully, seemingly expecting her to turn the entire desert to an ocean that would drown them all and Zohra was glaring at the people as if this idea was not far from her mind. Khardan cast Mathew a grateful, resigned glance, thanking the young man for the vain attempt.

No! It wouldn't be in vain!

Mathew took a step forward. "He will bring back the djinn!" he announced. "In a week's time—"

"Tonight!" countered Zeid.

"Tonight!" clamored the crowd.

"By tonight," Mathew agreed, his heart in his throat. "The djinn will return by tonight."

"If not, then he dies," said Zeid calmly. "And the witch with him."

There was nothing more to say, and Mathew could not have been heard in the uproar had he wanted to say it. Head bowed, wondering how he'd managed to lose control of things so rapidly, the young wizard made his way dejectedly down the Tel. When he reached the bottom, Zohra put her arm consolingly around him.

"I'm sorry," he said to her, when a voice interrupted him.

Khardan, surrounded by guards, stood before him.

"Thank you, Mat-hew," said the Calif quietly. "You did what you could."

Mathew had the sudden strange sensation of being wrapped in a blanket of feathers.

"The djinn will be back!" he said, and suddenly, for some reason, he believed his own words. "They will be back!"

Khardan sighed and shook his head. "The djinn are gone, Mat-hew. As for Akhran, he may be defeated himself now, for all we—"

"No, look!" Reaching down, Mathew touched one of the ugly cacti. "Tell me how this remains alive, when all around is dead and withered! It is because Akhran is alive—just barely, perhaps, but he lives! You must continue to have faith, Khardan! You must!"

"I agree with Blossom, brother," said Auda unexpectedly, coming up behind them. "Faith in our Gods and in each other is all we have left now. Faith alone stands between us and doom."

Chapter 7

"Faith. I must have faith," Mathew repeated to himself over and over during the day that lasted far too long and seemed likely to end all too rapidly.

Minute after minute slid past, precious as drops of water from a punctured *girba*. Mathew tasted each minute; he touched it, heard it fall away from him and vanish in the vast pool of time. Every noise—be it the barking of one of the mangy camp dogs or the shifting of a guard outside Zohra's tent—brought him to his feet, peering eagerly out the tent flap.

But it was nothing, always nothing.

Noon came and went and the camp quieted, everyone resting in the blazing heat. Mathew gazed enviously at Zohra. Exhausted by her night's work and the tension of the morning, she had fallen asleep. He wondered if Khardan was sleeping, too. Or was he lying in shadowed darkness, thinking that if he'd done the talking—as, by rights, he should have—all would have gone well?

Sighing heavily, Mathew let his aching head sink into his hands. "I should have kept out of this," he reprimanded himself. "These aren't my people. I don't understand them! Khardan could have handled it. I should have trusted him—"

Someone was in the tent!

218

Mathew saw a shadow from the corner of his eye but had no time to draw a breath before a hand clapped firmly over his mouth.

"Do not make a sound, Blossom," breathed a voice in his ear. "You will alert the guards!"

His heart pounding so that he saw starbursts before his eyes, Mathew nodded. Auda released his grip and, motioning to Mathew to wake Zohra, melted back into the darker shadows of the tent.

It seemed a shame to disturb her. Let her have her few last moments of peace before—

Auda gestured peremptorily, the cruel eyes narrowed.

"Zohra!" Mathew shook her gently. "Zohra, wake up."

She was awake and alert instantly, sitting up among the cushions and staring at Mathew. "What? Have they—"

"Shh, no." He pointed toward Auda, barely visible in the dim light at the back of the tent. The Paladin had removed the facecloth and now pressed his finger against his lips, commanding silence.

Zohra shrank away from him in fright; then seeming to recollect herself, she stiffened and glared at him fiercely.

Moving softly, Auda crept over to them and, beckoning them near, said in a barely heard undertone, "Blossom, what killing magic can you have ready?"

Deadly cold swept over Mathew, despite the sweltering heat. His fingers went numb, his heart ceased to function, he could not draw in air. Slowly, unable to speak, he shook his head.

"What? You don't know any?" Auda said, his dark eyes glinting.

Mathew hesitated. That was what he would answer. He didn't know any. The Black Paladin must accept this. The words were on his lips, but he saw then that he had waited too long. The lie must be plain in his eyes. He shook as with a chill and said tightly, "I will not kill."

"Mat-hew!" Zohra's fingers dug into his arm. "Can you do this . . . killing magic?"

"He can do it," Auda said calmly. "He won't, that's all. He will let you and Khardan die first."

Mathew flushed. "I thought you were the one who coun-seled faith!"

"Faith in one hand." Auda held forth his left hand, closed in a fist. "This in the other." His right hand reached into his robes and brought forth the snake dagger. "So my people have survived."

"We returned to the Tel to save your people!" Mathew looked to Zohra. "And now you want to slaughter them?"

Zohra ran her tongue over her lips; her face was pale, her eyes wide and burning with a fierce, inner fire of hope that was slowly being quenched. "I—I don't know," she whis-pered distractedly.

"We do what we must do! These"—the Paladin mo-tioned outside the tent—"are not all of your people." Auda's voice was soft and lethal. It might have been the serpent-headed dagger speaking. "The women and children and young men are being held prisoner in Kich. We can save them, but only if you and Khardan are alive! If you die—" He shrugged.

"He is right, Mat-hew."

"My God forbids the taking of life—" Mathew began.

"There is no war in your land?" Auda questioned coolly. "The magi do not fight?"

"I do not fight!" Mathew cried, forgetting himself. The guards stirred outside. Auda's eyes flashed dangerously. He twisted to his feet. A ray of the burning sun that filtered through the tent flap glinted off the blade of the knife in his hand.

Mathew tensed, sweat running down his body. The guards did not enter, and it occurred to Mathew that they must be half-stupified with the heat.

Settling himself beside Mathew, Auda took hold of the young man's arm and squeezed it painfully. His breath burned Mathew's skin. "You've seen a man beheaded before, haven't you, Blossom? Swift and fast, a single stroke of the blade across the back of the neck."

Mathew cringed, going limp in the man's cruel grasp. Once again he saw John kneeling in the sand, saw the *goum* raise his sword, saw the steel flash in the sun's dying light. . . .

Auda's grip tightened; he drew Mathew closer.

"This is how Khardan will die. Not a bad death. A flash

of pain and then nothing. But not Zohra. Have you ever watched anyone being stoned to death, Blossom? A rock strikes the head. The victim, bleeding and dazed and in pain, tries desperately to avoid the next. It hits the arm with a crunching sound. Her bones break. Again she turns, trying to flee, but there is nowhere to run. Another rock thuds into her back. She falls. Blood runs in her eyes. She cannot see, and the terror grows, the pain mounts. . . ."

"No!" Mathew clenched his fists in agony behind his head, covering his ears with shaking arms.

Auda released him. The Paladin, sitting back, gazed on him with satisfaction.

"You will help us, then."

"Yes," said Mathew through trembling lips. He could not look at Zohra. He had seen her in his mind's eye, lying limp and lifeless on the bloodsplattered sand, crimson staining the white robe, the black hair clotted with red. "The spell I cast this morning." He swallowed, trying to maintain his voice. "More powerful . . . much more powerful . . ."

"You will use the magic of Sul. I will call down the wrath of my God," said Auda. "Those we do not stop will be too terrified to chase after us. I will have the camels ready. We can make our way to Kich. What components do you need for this spell of yours, Blossom? I assume this one cannot be cast using the skin of a goat."

"Saltpeter," Mathew mumbled. "It's a chemical. Perhaps, the residue from the urine of horses—"

"I refuse!" cried a long-suffering voice. "It is bad enough that I must clean up the tent after madam's cushion-ripping tantrums. Bad enough that I never have a moment's peace in which to eat a quiet bite. Bad enough that I am ordered to go here, fetch this, do that! But I refuse"—a curl of smoke flowed out of one of Zohra's rings and began to take shape and form in the center of the tent—"I absolutely refuse," said a fat djinn with great dignity, "to fetch horse piss."

No one spoke or moved. All stared at the djinn dazedly.

Then Zohra leaped forward. "Usti!" she cried.

"No, madam! Don't!" The djinn flung his flabby arms protectively over his head. "Don't! I beg of you! Where are the horses? Hand me a bucket! Just don't hurt me—I . . . madam! Really! You are a married woman!''

Flushing bright red, the scandalized djinn fended off Zohra, who was hugging and kissing him and laughing hysterically.

''What is going on in there?'' demanded a guard.

Auda slipped out of the tent, disappearing as swiftly and silently as if he were a djinn himself.

''Where are Sond and Fedj and Pukah?'' Zohra asked suddenly. ''Answer me!'' she insisted, shaking the fat djinn until his teeth rattled in his head.

''Ah! T-t-this is m-more like it-t-t,'' stuttered Usti. ''If m-m-madam will re-l-lease m-me, I will—''

''The djinn!'' A guard, thrusting his way into the tent, stared at Usti in awe. ''The djinn are back! Sheykh Jaafar!'' He turned and fled, and Mathew could hear him shouting as he ran. ''Jaafar, *sidi*! The djinn are back! The madman spoke truly! Khardan is a Prophet! He will lead us to defeat the *kafir*! Our people are saved!''

Relief thawed Mathew, melting his anguish. Hurrying outside, he saw Khardan emerge from his tent in company with Sond, Fedj, and a huge, black-skinned djinn that the young wizard did not recognize.

But where, Mathew wondered, is Khardan's djinn? Where is Pukah?

The Sheykhs came running. Zeid's round face was red with pleasure and delight. He declared to anyone who would listen that he had always known Khardan was a Prophet and he—Zeid al Saban—was responsible for proving it. Jaafar's mouth gaped wide in astonishment. He started to speak, inhaled a large quantity of dust kicked up by the gathering crowd of cheering tribesmen, and would have choked to death had not Fedj solicitously pounded his master on the back.

Majiid said nothing. The old man ran straight to his son and, flinging his arms around him, cried the first tears he had shed in over fifty years. Khardan embraced his father, tears streaming down his own cheeks, and the men from all the tribes united to cheer wildly.

When Zohra stepped from her tent, they cheered her, too. Jaafar darted over to press his daughter to his bosom but, daunted by the fire in her eye and recollecting certain unfortunate statements he had made concerning her, decided to give her a gingerly pat on the arm. The Sheykh then ducked hurriedly behind the muscular Fedj.

Standing tall and upright, his arm around his son's shoulder, Majiid faced the dancing, singing crowd and was about to call—somewhat belatedly—for a celebration. Zohra was walking over to stand next to her husband when a disturbance at the rear of the crowd caused those in front to turn around, their yells dying on their lips.

A rider was approaching. Coming from the east, the figure on horseback was muffled to the eyes, and there was no telling who or what it was. It was alone, and so no weapons were drawn.

The horse, covered with lather, foam dripping from its mouth, dashed into camp. Men scrambled out of its way. The rider checked it in its headlong course, pausing to scan the faces as though searching for someone.

Finding the person sought, the rider guided the weary animal straight to Khardan.

The rider drew aside a veil covering the head, revealing a quantity of golden hair that shone brightly in the sun. Holding out her hands to Khardan, Meryem cried out his name and then fell, fainting, from her horse into his arms.

Chapter 8

"And so," Sond finished his tale solemnly, "Pukah sacrificed himself, luring Kaug to the mountain of iron and tricking the 'efreet inside while the immortal, Asrial, guardian angel of the madman—I beg your pardon, *Effendi*." Sond bowed to Mathew. "Asrial, guardian angel of a great and powerful sorcerer, slammed shut the doors of the mountain, and now both Kaug and Pukah are sealed forever inside. Since the 'efreet is no longer stirring up strife among the immortals, many of us have banded together and now almost all on the heavenly plane have united to fight Quar."

The men who crowded in and around the tent nodded gravely and murmured among themselves, rattling swords and intimating by their actions that it was time they, too, went to battle.

"May I speak, My Lord?" said Meryem timidly from her seat next to the Calif.

"Certainly, lady," replied Khardan, looking at her fondly.

Next to Mathew, Zohra growled deep in her throat, like a hungry lioness. Mathew closed his hand over hers, wanting to hear what Meryem had to say.

"It is very noble of the Calif to have sacrificed his djinn for the sake of his people, and it is a wonderful thing that the evil Kaug has been finally rendered harmless, but I fear that this—instead of helping our people in Kich—has only put them in the most terrible danger.''

"What do you mean, woman?" Sheykh Zeid demanded.

Aware that all eyes were on her, Meryem became suitably pale and more timid than before. Khardan, taking hold of her hand in his, urged her to courage. Flushing, Meryem cast him a grateful glance and continued. "The Imam returns to Kich in two weeks' time. He has proclaimed that if your people being held prisoner in Kich have not converted to Quar by then, he will put them—every one—to the sword.''

"Is this possible?" Khardan demanded, shocked.

"I fear so, Calif," said Zeid. "He has done it before, in Meda and Bastine and other cities. I, myself, heard this same threat. If, as the djinn say, Quar is truly desperate now—" he shrugged his fat shoulders despairingly.

"We must rescue them, then," said Khardan firmly. "But we cannot attack Kich—"

"I know a secret way into the city," said Meryem eagerly, her eyes shining. "I can lead you!"

Rising to her feet, Zohra stalked out of the tent. Khardan saw her leave, and it seemed he started to say something, then shook his head slightly and turned back to the conversation around him. Mathew, casting the Calif an exasperated look, hurried to catch up with Zohra.

"We must tell him!" he said urgently.

"No!" Zohra said, angrily shaking off Mathew's hand from her arm. "Let him make a fool of himself over the houri!"

"But if he knew she tried to murder you—"

"You told him about the spell she cast over him!" Zohra whirled and faced Mathew. "Did he listen? Did he believe? Bah!" She turned, continued walking, and stormed into her tent.

Mathew took a step after her, then stopped. He took a step back to the Calif's tent and stopped again. Confused, upset, and uncertain what to do, the young wizard turned his footsteps toward the open desert, the coolness of the oasis. Though night had fallen, the sand radiated so much heat from the day that it would be some time before the temperature became bearable.

"I told him about Meryem casting the spell on him. I told him about her trying to capture him and take him to the Amir. Obviously he didn't believe me, or maybe it flattered him to think she cared so much for him. Why can't he see?" Mathew fumed. "The man is intelligent about everything else! Why, in this one instance, is he such a blind fool?"

Had Mathew been more experienced in the sweet torment of love, he would never have asked the question, let alone been unable to find the answer. But he wasn't, and he fretted and swore and paced back and forth until he worked himself into a fevered sweat that dried on his body and set him to shivering as night's chill grew.

When he became aware, finally, that the babble of voices had ceased, he realized it was late, very late at night. The meeting had broken up, the tribesmen wending their ways to their tents. Weariness overwhelmed the young man. Returning to the camp that was empty and silent, he discovered that by night all tents look alike. Mathew stumbled sleepily and irritably first this direction, then that, hoping to find some late roamer who could guide him. Catching sight of movement, he headed toward the person, a plea for aid on his lips. The words died unspoken, and Mathew—wide awake— darted back into the shadow of a tent, out of the light cast by stars and a half-moon.

A lithe figure glided through the camp. She was wrapped in silken veils, but Mathew had no trouble recognizing the delicate, diminutive stature, the graceful walk. Stealthily the young man followed Meryem and was not surprised to see her creep up to the closed flap of a tent Mathew guessed must be Khardan's.

"Who is it? Who is there?" called the Calif, alert, it seemed, to the slightest sound.

"It is Meryem, My Lord," responded the woman in a half-smothered whisper.

Keeping to the deepest shadows, Mathew saw the tent flap open. Khardan appeared, silhouetted against golden lamp light. "What are you doing here? It is not proper—"

"I don't care!" Meryem cried, clasping her hands, her voice quivering. "I have been so miserable! You don't know what it was like! The Amir's troops captured me during the battle and carried me back to Kich! I was terrified that they would recognize me as the Sultan's daughter and drag me before the Amir. But, thank Akhran, they didn't!'' She began to weep. ''Your mother, Badia, cared for me as if I were her own daughter. She never believed you were dead, and neither did I!''

Khardan put his hands on the girl's heaving shoulders. ''There, there. It is all right now.'' The Calif paused, his fingers twining themselves in the silken veil. ''If my mother is imprisoned, how is it that you are not there also?''

The question was carelessly put. Mathew caught the slight tenseness in the voice, however, and hope surged through him.

''I managed to escape,'' said Meryem, swallowing her tears and gazing up at the Calif adoringly. ''I came to you as fast as I could.''

The answer seemed to satisfy Khardan, to judge by his fond smile. Mathew grit his teeth. Can't you see she's lying? It was all he could do to keep from rushing from his hiding place and shaking some sense into the man.

''Let us be happy, my love!'' Meryem continued, drawing near and putting her hands caressingly on his chest. ''I don't want to wait for us to be married. Danger is so near.'' She nestled into his arms. ''Who knows how long we may have together?''

Smiling at her, Khardan drew Meryem into his tent.

A fury gripped Mathew by the throat, a fury such as he had never experienced.

''By Promenthas, I'll confront her with the attempt on Zohra's life! Let her deny it before Khardan, if she can! And I'll remind him of that little silver charm she hung around his neck while I'm at it!''

Not stopping to think what he might be interrupting, Mathew ran over to the tent. The flap had been left open; Khardan was so taken by passion, apparently he forgot to close it.

Mathew entered the tent silently. Blinking in the bright lamplight, he waited impatiently for them to acknowledge his presence. Neither did. Khardan's back was to Mathew, the Calif appeared intent on kissing soft flesh. Meryem's arms

were around Khardan's neck. Her eyes were closed and she
moaned in ecstasy. Wrapped up in their pleasure, neither
noticed the young man.

Suddenly the realization of what he was doing and how
Khardan would react to this violation of his privacy struck
Mathew. His face burning with shame, he started to quietly
edge his way out, intending to slink off into the desert and
spend the night fuming in what he recognized was the rage of
jealousy.

As he moved, his attention was caught by Meryem's
hands; the skin glimmering white in the lamplight. Instead of
caressing the Calif, the hands were doing something very
strange. Dainty fingers closed over the stone of a ring she
wore and gave it a deft twist. A needle shot out, gleamed for
an instant, then vanished in shadow as Meryem slowly and
deliberately moved the ring toward Khardan's bare neck.

Mathew had seen assassin's rings. He knew how they
worked. He knew that Khardan would be dead or dying
within moments. The Calif's weapons lay on a wooden chest
at the foot of his bed. Springing forward, Mathew grabbed
the dagger, and in the same moment, never noticing that
Khardan's hand was closing over Meryem's wrist, the young
wizard plunged the knife into the woman's back.

A wailing scream deafened him. He felt Meryem's body
stiffen. Warm blood drizzled over his hand. The body jerked
horribly in its death throes; a heavy weight sagged against
him. Appalled, Mathew sprang back, and Meryem dropped to
the floor. She lay on her back, her legs twisted at an awkward
angle. Blue, glassy eyes stared up at him.

"My god!" whispered Mathew. The bloodstained knife
fell from his fingers, which had gone limp and numb.

A shadow entered the tent. Pausing, it looked from Mathew
to the corpse. Khardan bent over Meryem, perhaps searching
desperately for life.

"Ah, well done, Blossom," commented Auda.

"Khardan!" Mathew licked his tongue across his dry
lips. He felt a hot sickness welling up inside him. The ground
canted away beneath his feet. "I—I . . . She was . . ."

To his amazement, Khardan looked up coolly at Auda.

"You were right," he said heavily. "This is a tool of

Benario's.'' Lifting the flaccid hand, the Calif gingerly exhibited the ring with its deadly needle.

Mathew's weakness abated momentarily, lost in his shock. "You knew?" he gasped.

Khardan gave him a rebuking glance. "Of course. I thought long about what you told me. I remembered certain things she said to me, and finally I began to understand. She failed in her attempt to capture me for the Amir, and so she returned to do the only thing left—murder me.''

Mathew swayed on his feet. Khardan, rising swiftly, caught the young man in his arms. Easing Mathew onto the bed, the Calif gestured to the Black Paladin to bring water.

"I'm all right!" Mathew gasped, shaking his head in refusal, fearing if he drank anything he would gag.

"Auda recognized her. He had seen her at Khandar,'' Khardan continued. Putting his arm around Mathew's shoulders, he forced the young man to sip at least a small mouthful of the tepid liquid. "Meryem was not a Sultan's daughter, but the Emperor's daughter by one of his concubines. She was given to Qannadi as a gift and was acting in his service.''

"I killed her!" Mathew said hollowly. "I felt her . . . the knife going in . . . that scream . . .'' Gazing at his hand, the blood, moist and sticky, shining black in the moonlight, he shuddered and doubled up, retching.

"Her life was forfeit,'' said Auda calmly, standing over the bed and looking down at Mathew with amusement in the dark eyes. "She has murdered before, not a doubt of it. Benario's followers must, you know. They call it 'blooding.' Only one who was high in the God's favor and knowledgeable in his ways could have secured a ring like this.''

"Khardan! Are you safe? I heard a scream!" Voices were clamoring outside the tent.

Motioning for the Calif to remain where he was, Auda lifted Meryem's body in his arms and carried her out. "An assassin,'' he shouted to the gathering, murmuring crowd, "sent by Quar to murder your Calif. Fortunately I was able to stop her in time!''

Mathew looked up at Khardan. "Ibn Jad is right, Khardan. She tried to kill Zohra,'' he said in a croaking whisper, his throat raw. In broken sentences he related the incident to the Calif, who listened gravely, his face serious.

"You should have told me."

"Would you have believed us?" Mathew asked softly.

"No." Khardan sat back on his heels. "No, you are right. I was then—as you thought me now—a blind fool."

Mathew flushed, hearing his innermost thoughts spoken aloud. "I didn't—" he began confusedly.

Khardan rested his hands on the young man's shoulders. "Once again, Mat-hew, you have saved my life."

"No," said Mathew miserably. "You knew about her. You knew what she would do. You were ready for her."

"Perhaps not. All she had to do was prick the flesh once and . . ." Khardan shrugged. His eyes left the young man and stared out into the night, seeing—perhaps—the lithe figure entering once again. "Believe this, Mat-hew," he said softly. "I have faced death in many forms, but when I saw that ring on her finger, when I felt her hands touch my skin, a horror came over me that changed my bowels to water and stole the strength from my body!" He shivered and shook his head, looking back at Mathew. "It was well you came. Akhran guided you."

"I've taken a human life!" Mathew cried in a low voice, clenching his crimson-stained hand.

"We do what we must do," Khardan said offhandedly. "Come, young man," he added somewhat impatiently when Mathew shook his head, refusing to be comforted, "would you rather have let her kill me?"

"No, oh no!" Mathew looked up swiftly. "It's just—" How could he explain to this warrior the teachings of his parents that even in time of war their people refused to fight, insisting that all life was sacred. And yet, thought Mathew confusedly, there had never come a time to them when the sanctity of their home had been rent asunder, their children torn screaming from their mothers' arms.

"You are tired," said Khardan, clapping him on the shoulder and helping him rise from the cushions. "Sleep, and you will feel better in the morning. We have much to talk about tomorrow."

I am tired, Mathew said to himself. But will I sleep? Will

I ever sleep again? Or will I feel the blood, hear always that horrible, dying scream?

At least, he noted thankfully when he left the tent, he wouldn't have to talk to anyone. He could make his stumbling way back in secret and alone. The tribesmen who had gathered in the initial excitement paid no attention to him. There was an amazed reaction as Auda told his story, Mathew inwardly blessing the Paladin for taking credit for the killing and leaving him out of it. The tribesmen talked volubly, a few Hrana stated that they had mistrusted the woman the first time they saw her. Since this implied criticism of the Calif— now Prophet—those few making such claims were shouted down. The Akar were speaking loudly of how all had been duped by Meryem's beauty, innocence, and charm.

"Throw her to the jackals!" cried someone.

Auda, with a procession of nomads accompanying him, carried the corpse to the outskirts of camp. The body hung limp in the Paladin's grasp. A white arm—entangled in a silken scarf—dropped suddenly down, to dangle and sway in a mockery of seduction as though she were trying, one last time, to avoid her fate. But the jackals, looking at that nubile body, would see only meat.

Shuddering, suddenly dizzy and sick, Mathew turned away.

He felt eyes upon him and, glancing around, saw Zohra standing in the entrance of her tent. She said nothing, and he could not read her eyes. She made no sign, and Mathew did not go to her. She had heard Auda talking, of course. Mathew guessed she knew the truth.

He walked blindly on. Reaching his tent, more by accident than design, he started to go inside, but the thought of stepping into the smothering darkness—the darkness that no matter what he did to alleviate it always smelled strongly of goat—made him gag. Mathew drew his hand back from the flap.

He breathed in the cool night air and looked at the tents scattered around him. Many nights before he had done this same thing—stepped outside to gaze despairingly at the moon and stars, imagining them shining down upon his homeland, glinting off the water of countless streams, rivers, lakes, and pools.

Tonight he saw a new moon—a tiny wisp of a moon—balance on its tip on the horizon as if it were testing itself before rising farther. For the first time Mathew saw the moon shine—not on the castle walls of his homesickness—but on the desert. The stark and barren beauty pierced the young man's heart.

The desert is lonely, but then so are we all, wrapped in our frail husks of flesh. It is silent, vast, and empty, and it brushes away man's marks in its sand with an uncaring hand. It is eternal, everlasting, yet constantly changing—the dunes shift with the wind, sudden rain brings forth life where there was nothing but death, the sun burns it all away once more.

The past few months, I have been living only because I was afraid to die. He saw himself suddenly as the sickly brown cacti, the Rose of the Prophet, clinging to a meaningless existence among the rocks. Auda had said to him, *Your life was obviously spared for a purpose*. And all he could do with that life, apparently, was mope about whining and crying that it wasn't what he wanted. *Blossom*, Auda called him. He could either decay and rot away or blossom and give meaning not only to his life, but to his death.

Suddenly, humbly and joyfully, Mathew reveled in being alive.

He looked down at his bloodstained hand. He had taken a life. Promenthas would call him to account for it. But he had done it to save a life.

And he was no longer afraid.

Chapter 9

"I do not trust that woman—Meryem's—story of the Imam's return to Kich," growled Majiid.

"I never trusted her," piped up Jaafar. "I didn't believe a word she said. It was you took her into your dwelling, Sheykh al Fakhar—an insult to my daughter, a woman whose virtues number as the stars in heaven."

Majiid's eyes bulged; he bristled like a cornered tiger.

"Come, come," interposed Zeid smugly. "There were three who were victims of the Emperor's whore—two of them old goats who should have known better."

"Old goats!" Jaafar shrieked, rounding on Zeid.

Khardan, rubbing his aching temples, bit back the hot words of anger and frustration that rose to his lips. Forcing himself to remain calm, his voice slid swiftly and smoothly between the combatants.

"I have sent the djinn to Kich to verify Meryem's story. They should return at any moment with word."

"Not my djinn?" Zeid glared at Khardan.

"All the djinn."

"How dare you? Raja is my personal djinn! You have no right—"

"If it hadn't been for my son, you would have no personal djinn!" laughed Majiid raucously, stabbing a bony finger into Zeid's shrunken, flabby middle. "If my son wants to use your djinn—"

"Where's Fedj?" Jaafar was on his feet. "Have you taken Fedj?"

"Silence!" Khardan roared.

The tent quieted, the Sheykhs staring at the Calif with varying looks—Zeid sly and furtive, Jaafar offended, and Majiid indignant.

"A son does not say such things to his father!" Majiid stated angrily, rising to his feet with help from a servant. "I will not sit in my son's tent and—"

"You will sit, Father," said Khardan coldly. "You will sit in patience and wait for the return of the djinn. You will sit because if you do not, our people are finished, and we might as well all go and throw ourselves at the feet of the Imam and beg for Quar's mercy." Saying thus, he cast a stern glance around at the other two Sheykhs.

"Mmmm." Zeid smoothed his beard and gazed at Khardan speculatively. Jaafar began to moan that he was cursed, mumbling that they might as well give themselves up to Quar anyway. Majiid glared at his son fiercely, then abruptly threw himself back down upon the tent floor.

Khardan sighed and wished the djinn would hurry.

It was night. The Sheykhs were meeting in Khardan's tent, holding council about their future plan of action. Crowded around the tent were the men of all three tribes, glaring suspiciously at each other but maintaining an uneasy peace.

The council had not begun auspiciously. Zeid had opened it by announcing, "We have now a Prophet. So what?"

So what? Khardan repeated to himself. He knew his predicament all too well. With the capture of the southern lands of Bas, the Amir had grown more powerful than he had been when he raided the nomad's camps. Qannadi's army numbered in the tens of thousands. His cavalry was mounted on magical horses, and Zeid had heard reports from his spies that—due to Achmed's training—the soldiers of the Amir rode and fought on horseback as well any *spahi*. Facing this army was a handful of ragged, half-starved tribesmen who could not agree on which way the wind blew.

A cloud materialized in the tent, and Khardan looked up

in relief, glad to turn his gloomy thoughts to something else for the time being. Although, he told himself, this news was liable to make his problems just that much more difficult.

Four djinn appeared before him—the handsome Sond, the muscular Fedj, the giant Raja, and the rotund Usti. Each djinn bowed with the utmost respect to Khardan, hands folded over their hearts. It was an impressive sight, and Majiid cast a triumphant glance at his two cousins to make certain they did not miss it.

"What news?" Khardan asked sternly.

"Alas, master," said Sond, who was apparently spokesman since he now served Khardan. "The woman, Meryem, spoke truly. The Imam is even now on his way back to Kich, accompanied by the Amir and his troops. And he has decreed that when he reaches the city, all its inhabitants are to welcome him in the name of Quar. Any who do not will be put to death. This spear is aimed directly at our people, *sidi*, for they are the only unbelievers in the city."

"Have they been imprisoned?"

"Yes, *sidi*. Women and children and the young men—all are being held in the Zindan."

"Without food!" put in Usti. Panting from his unaccustomed exertion, fanning himself with a palm frond, the djinn was livid at the thought. The other three djinn turned on him, glaring. Usti shrank back, waving a pudgy hand. "I thought the master should know!"

"They are starving them?" Majiid shouted.

"Hush!" ordered Khardan, but it was too late.

"What? Dogs! They will die!"

An uproar started outside the tent, Majiid's voice having carried clearly to the tribesmen.

"We had not meant to tell you quite so suddenly, *sidi*," said Sond, casting Usti a vicious glance. "And that is not quite the truth. They are getting some food, but only enough to keep them barely alive."

"I don't believe it," Khardan said firmly. "I met the Amir. He is a soldier! He would not make war on women and children."

"Begging your pardon, *sidi*," said Fedj, "but it is not the

Amir who issues this order. It is Feisal, the Imam and—many now say—the true ruler of Kich.''

"Quar is desperate," added Raja, his rumbling voice shaking the tent poles. "The war in heaven has turned against him, and now he dares not allow any *kafir* in his midst on earth. The people of the captured southern cities are restless, and there is talk of revolt. Feisal will make of our people a bloody example that will quiet the rebels and keep them in line.''

"Then there is no help for it," Khardan said harshly. "We must attack Kich!''

"The first to die will be our people in the prison, *sidi*," wailed Usti. "So the Imam has threatened!''

Glaring at the fat djinn, Sond sucked in an impatient breath, his fists clenched.

Looking vastly injured and much put upon, Usti pouted: "You can threaten me all you like, Sond! But it's the truth. I went to the prison, you recall! Not you! And I saw them, master!'' The djinn continued, thrusting his way forward to Khardan. "Our people are held in the prison compound, *sidi*, ringed round by the Imam's fanatic soldier-priests, who stand—day and night—with their swords drawn.''

"These same soldier-priests are the ones who committed the slaughter of the *kafir* in Bastine, *sidi*," added Sond reluctantly. "There is no doubt that they would carry through the Imam's order to murder our people. In fact, they await it eagerly.''

"Our people would be dead before we got inside the city walls," Raja growled.

"And we will never get inside the walls," Sheykh Zeid pointed out gloomily. He waved a hand toward the camp, where the crowd had fallen ominously silent. "A few hundred against the might of the Amir! Bah! All we could do for our people is die with them!''

"If that is all we can do, then that is what we must do!'' Khardan said in bitter anger and frustration. "Can we acquire more djinn, perhaps, or 'efreets?''

"The immortals do battle on their own plane, *sidi*," said Fedj, shaking his turbaned head. "Though Kaug is gone, the war rages still. Quar freed the immortals that he had kept bottled up, and though they are weak, they are numerous and are defending their God valiantly. *Hazrat* Akhran can spare none of his.''

"At least we should be thankful that no immortals will be defending Kich," said Sond, anxious to say something hopeful.

"With a hundred thousand men, who needs immortals?" commented Usti, shrugging his fat shoulders.

Sond ground his teeth ominously. "I think I heard your mistress calling you."

"No!" Usti paled and glanced around in fear. "You didn't, did you?"

"My cousins in Akhran," said Sheykh Zeid, leaning forward and beckoning those in the tent to bring their heads nearer his. "It is true, as the djinn have reported, that the Amir despises the idea of senseless slaughter. Facing us in battle, man to man, he would kill us all without hesitation, but not the innocent, the helpless—"

"He murdered the Sultan of Kich and his family," interrupted Jaafar.

Zeid shrugged complacently. "So a wise man not only kills the scorpion in his boot but searches well for its mate, knowing that the sting of one is as painful as the other. But did he then go ahead and murder the followers of Mimrim and the other Gods whose temples—however small—were in Kich? No. It was only when this Feisal took control that we began hearing of Quar in the heart or steel in the gut. If something should happen to this Feisal . . ." Zeid made a graceful hand motion, his eyes narrowed to slits.

"No!" said Khardan abruptly, standing up and drawing his robes aside as if to remove even his clothing from the presence of such defilement. "Akhran curses the taking of a life in cold blood!"

"Perhaps now, in modern days," said Zeid. "But there was a time, when our grandfathers were young—"

"And would you go backward instead of forward?" demanded Khardan. "What honor to stab a man—a priest, at that—in the back? I will not be an assassin like a follower of Benario or of—"

"Zhakrin?" suggested a soft voice.

No one had heard Auda enter. No one knew how long he had been there. Starting, frowning, the Sheykhs glared at him. Moving with his catlike grace, the Paladin rose to his feet to stand before Khardan.

"I remind you of your oath, brother."

"My oath was to protect your life, avenge your death! Not to commit murder!"

"I do not ask you to. I will do what must be done," said Auda coolly. "Indeed, no hand but mine may strike Feisal if I am to fulfill the oath made to my dead brother. But I would not leave my back undefended. I call upon you, therefore, to ride with me to Kich and help me win my way through gate and Temple door and—"

"—turn my head while you thrust your accursed dagger in the man? Avert my eyes like a woman?" Khardan's hand slashed through the air. "No! I say again, no!"

"A squeamish Prophet," murmured Zeid, stroking his beard.

Khardan whirled to face them. "The Imam has taken our families, our wives, our sisters, our children, our brothers, our cousins. He has destroyed our dwellings, stolen our food, left us with nothing but our honor. Now it seems that you want to hand him that as well. Then, truly, no matter what happens, we would be slaves to Quar." The Calif stood tall, his voice shook in proud anger. "I will not surrender my honor, nor the honor of my people!"

One by one the eyes of the Sheykhs dropped beneath Khardan's. Majiid's fierce stare was the last to lower before his son's, but at last even his gaze sought the carpet beneath his legs, his face flushed in chagrin, frustration, and fury.

"Then in the name of Akhran, what are we to do!" he cried suddenly, smiting his thigh with his gnarled hand.

"I will do what I would do with any other enemy who has offered me this affront," said Khardan. "I will do what I would do if this Feisal were not Feisal but were Zeid al Saban"—he gestured—"or Jaafar al Widjar. I will travel to Kich and challenge the Amir to fight us in fair combat with the understanding that if we win, we will leave his people unharmed, and that if we lose, he will do the same for us.

"Thus I will fulfill my oath to you, Auda ibn Jad," added Khardan, glancing at the Paladin, who stood listening with a lip curled in disdain. "I will myself go and present our challenge to the Amir. You shall enter the gate with me, and we will face its perils together. But first you must give me your word that if the Amir agrees to our bargain, you will do nothing to the Imam until my people are safely in the desert."

"The Amir will not go along with this plan, brother! If you are lucky, he will lop off your head as you stand before him. If you are not, he will take you to the Zindan and let his executioners teach you of honor! And I will have two deaths to avenge instead of one!" Auda said in disgust.

"Most likely," replied Khardan gravely, nodding his head.

The Black Paladin eyed Khardan. "I could leave you now and go forth and do this deed without you. You know that. Your sword arm is strong, but I can find those just as strong and far more willing. Why do I stay? Why do I endure this? Why did the gods mingle our blood and hear our oaths knowing them to be mismatched, spoken in mistaken belief?"

Auda ibn Jad shook his head slowly, his eyes dark with mystification. "I do not know the answer. I can only have faith. This I will promise, Khardan, Prophet of a Strange God. Should by some wild chance you prevail, I will not harm so much as a thread of the Imam's robes until the sun has risen and set upon your people three times after they leave the city. Satisfied?"

Khardan nodded. "I am satisfied."

"Then let it be also noted that your death cry absolves me from this vow," said Auda wryly.

"That, of course," agreed Khardan with a faint smile.

"So we ride to Kich," said Majiid grimly, rising to his feet.

"We ride to Death," muttered Jaafar.

"Without hope," added Zeid.

"Not so!" came a clear, confident voice.

Chapter 10

Zohra parted the tent flap and entered, Mathew following behind her.

The Sheykhs glowered. "Begone, woman," commanded Majiid. "We have important matters to discuss."

"Don't you speak like that to my daughter!" Jaafar shook his fist. "She can make water from sand!"

"Then I wish she would make of this desert an ocean and drown you!" roared Majiid.

Worried and preoccupied, exasperated by the arguing, Khardan waved his hand at his wife. "My father is right," he began peremptorily. "This is no place for women—"

"Husband!" Zohra did not speak loudly. The clarity and firmness of her tone, however, brought the haranguing to a halt. "I ask to be heard." Politely, her eyes on Khardan alone, Zohra moved to stand before her husband. Her veiled head was held proudly; she was dressed in the plain white caftan. Mathew, clad in black, came behind her. There was a newly acquired dignity about the young man that was impressive, a calm and sureness about the woman that caused even the djinn to bow and give way to them both.

"Very well," said Khardan gruffly, trying to appear stern. "What is it you want to say, wife?" The word was tinged with its customary bitter irony. "Speak, we don't have much time."

"If you fail to persuade the Amir to fight, it is obvious to me that we must rescue our people from the prison."

"That is obvious to all of us, wife," snapped Khardan, rapidly losing patience. "We are planning—"

"Planning to die," Zohra remarked. Ignoring the Calif's scowl, she continued. "And our people will die. This is not a battle that can be won by men and their swords." She looked at Mathew, who nodded. Zohra turned her gaze back to her husband. "This is a battle that can be won by women and their magic."

"Bah!" Majiid shouted impatiently. "She wastes our time, my son. Tell her to go back to her milking of goats—"

"Two with magic can free our people where hundreds with swords cannot!" Zohra said, overriding Majiid, a glittering in her dark eyes like stars in the night sky. "Mat-hew and I have a plan."

"We will hear your plan," said Khardan, wearily.

"No." Mathew spoke up, stepping forward. He had seen the exchange of glances between the Calif and the others, the preparations made to humor the woman and then send her on her way. He knew that the Sheykhs, that Khardan himself, would never understand; that to describe his idea would bring incredulity and scoffing, and Mathew would be left behind while Khardan rode to certain death. "No, this is of Sul and therefore forbidden to be spoken. You must trust us—"

"A woman who thinks she is a man and a man who thinks he is a woman? Hah!" Majiid laughed.

"All we ask," said Mathew, ignoring the Sheykh, "is that you take us with you into Kich—"

Khardan was shaking his head, his face stern and dark. "It is too dangerous—"

Zohra thrust Mathew aside. "Akhran sent us to that terrible castle together, husband, and together he brought us forth! It was by his will we two were married, by his will we were brought *together* to save our people! Take us with you to the Amir. If he slays us as we stand before him, then that is the will of Akhran, and we die together. If he sends us to the Zindan to die with our people, then—with our magic—we

will have a chance to save them!'' She lifted her chin, her
eyes flaring with a pride that matched the pride in the eyes
intently watching her. ''Or has Akhran given you the right to
risk your life for our people, husband, and denied that right
to me because I am a woman?''

Khardan gazed at his wife in thoughtful silence. Majiid
snorted in disgust. The djinn exchanged speculative glances
and raised their eyebrows. Zeid and Jaafar stirred uncomfortably, but neither said anything. There was nothing anyone
could say that hadn't been said before. The Calif's face grew
darker, his frown more pronounced. His gaze turned on
Mathew.

''These are not your people. It is not your land, nor your
God. The danger for us in Kich will be great, but the danger
for you will be greater. If they capture you, they will not rest
until they have discovered where you are from and what
secrets you hold in your heart.''

''I know this, Calif,'' said Mathew steadily.

''And do you also know that they will rip these secrets
from you using cold iron and hot needles. They will gouge
out your eyes and hack off your limbs—''

''Yes, Calif,'' answered Mathew softly

''We fight to save those we love. Why do you risk this
peril?''

Mathew raised his eyes and looked directly into Khardan's.
Silently he said, I could make the same reply, but you would
not understand. Aloud he responded, ''In the sight of my
God, all life is sacred. I am commanded in his name and with
the help of Sul to do all I can to protect the innocent and
helpless.''

''His danger will not be greater than ours. He can disguise himself as a woman, my husband,'' suggested Zohra.
''The baggage of the she-devil, Meryem, is still in her tent.
Mat-hew can wear her robes. It would be better so, anyway,
for the guards will keep us together and put us both in with
the women when we enter the prison.''

Khardan was about to refuse. Mathew could see it in the
man's tired eyes. The young wizard knew Zohra saw it as
well, for he felt her body stiffen and heard the deep intake of
breath with which to launch arguments, shout vituperation, or

perhaps both, that would do nothing but cause further troubles. He was just thinking about how he could get her out of the tent, take her someplace where he could discuss this with her rationally, when suddenly Auda leaned near Khardan and whispered something to the Calif.

Khardan listened reluctantly, his eyes on his wife and on Mathew. He cut Auda off with an impatient gesture. The Paladin ceased speaking and withdrew. Khardan was silent long moments; then, "I had thought to leave you with the sick and elderly in the camp. They are in need of your skills. But very well, wife," he said dourly. "You will come, and Mat-hew as well."

Majiid, staring at his son in amazement, opened his mouth, but a swift gesture from Khardan caused him to snap it shut in seething silence.

"Thank you, husband," Zohra said. If the sun had suddenly chosen to drop from the sky and burst into flame in the center of the tent, it could not have flared more brilliantly or shone with such dazzling radiance. She bowed respectfully, her eyes lowered; but as she did so, she cast a swift, triumphant glance at her husband and a warm, thankful glance at Auda.

Khardan's brow grew darker, but he said nothing. Mathew, seeing Auda's eyes on Zohra and a slight smile on the man's lips, did not like this change of heart on Khardan's part and the sudden interest in Zohra on Auda's. He mistrusted what was behind it and would have very much liked to stay and hear what was said next, but Khardan dismissed both of them, and the young wizard had no choice but to follow the elated Zohra from the tent.

Mathew lingered outside, hoping to overhear the conversation, but Sond appeared in the tent flap, staring at him sternly. There was only silence from within, and Mathew knew that conversation would be resumed only when he and Zohra were gone.

Sighing, he trailed behind a Zohra thrilled with her victory, and the young man wondered soberly and somberly who had really won.

*   *   *

"Are they gone?"

Sond, standing at the tent entrance, nodded.

"Auda ibn Jad is right," said the Calif, cutting off his father's argument before Majiid could speak. "As headstrong as"—he swallowed—"my wife is, if we left her here alone, she would undoubtedly try some foolish plan of her own. Better to keep them both with us, where we may watch them."

Those had not been Auda's words. He had reminded Khardan of what the Calif already knew—Mathew was a skilled sorcerer, Zohra an apt pupil. In this desperate situation they could not turn down any offer of hope, however small. Auda would have gone on to remind Khardan of his wife's courage, but the Calif remembered that well enough, and it was at that point he had stopped the man short. Khardan wondered why it should irritate him to hear Auda praise a wife who was not a wife, but it did; the Paladin's words of praise for her nipping at the Calif like the fiery bite of the red ant.

"Have the men ready to ride by morning," Khardan said abruptly, rising and putting an end to discussion. He wanted, needed, desperately, to be alone. "If all goes well, the Amir will face us in fair battle—"

"Fair? Ten thousand to one?" muttered Jaafar gloomily.

"Fair for the Akar!" Majiid retorted. "If the Hrana are cowards, they can hide behind their sheep!"

"Cowards!" Jaafar bristled. "I never said—"

"If matters go awry," continued Khardan loudly, relentlessly riding over the impending altercation, "and I am taken, I will fight to the end. So will our people in the prison. Though ringed round by swords, they will battle for their lives with their bare hands. And you will attack the city, without hope, perhaps, but send as many of Quar's followers to their God as you can before you fall!"

Majiid—his gray cheeks regaining a measure of color, his faded eyes their old, fierce spark—clapped his son upon the back. "Akhran has chosen his Prophet wisely!" Gripping Khardan with both hands, he kissed the Calif's cheeks, then left the tent, his voice booming across the desert as he called forth his people to war.

Jaafar sidled near the Calif. The face of the small, wizened man, which seemed perpetually sad even in his happiest moments, now appeared ready to crumble into tears. Patting Khardan's arm, glancing furtively around to see that no one heard him, he whispered, "Akhran knows, I am a cursed man. Nothing has ever gone right for me. But I begin to think I have not been cursed in his choice of a son-in-law."

Zeid said nothing, but stared at Khardan shrewdly, as through mistrusting even this and wondering what trick the Calif had in mind to play. The *mehariste* made a respectful *salaam,* then departed, taking Raja with him. Auda, too, had apparently gone, for when Khardan remembered him and turned to speak, the Black Paladin was not in the tent.

Alone, the Calif sank down despondently upon the cushions on the tent floor. He was not meant for this kind of life. He did not enjoy the taste of honey on his tongue—honey used to sweeten bitter words so that others would gulp them down. He preferred direct and honest speech. If words must be spoken, then let his tongue be as sharp and true as his blade. Unfortunately he did not possess, in this dire time, the luxury of speaking his mind.

His shoulders slumped in exhaustion, and he lay down. Tired as he was, he did not have much hope of sleeping, however. Every time he closed his eyes, he saw blond hair, smiling lips, and felt the prick of a poisoned needle. . . .

"I beg your pardon, master," said a quiet voice, causing Khardan to sit up in alarm. "But I have something to say to you in private."

"Yes, Sond, what is it?" Khardan asked reluctantly, seeing in the djinn's grave expression more bad news.

"As you may have surmised, *sidi,* we djinn divided up in our search for information. Usti was sent to the prison—we thought he could cause less trouble there than anywhere else. Raja went among the people of Kich. Fedj spied upon the Imam's priests as best he could without entering the Temple, which we cannot do, of course, since it is the sacred precinct of another deity. I traveled north, *sidi,* and went among the troops of the Amir."

"You have news of Achmed," guessed Khardan.

"Yes, *sidi*." Sond bowed. "I hope I have not done wrong."

"No. I am glad to hear of him. He is my brother still. Nothing—not even my father's disavowal of him—can change that."

"I thought that was how you felt, *sidi*, and so I took the liberty. I overheard some odd things spoken about him and a woman he had taken recently. A woman who has since left him under mysterious circumstances."

Khardan's face grew shadowed. He said nothing but gazed at the djinn intently.

"I waited until the young man left to perform some duty or other, then I entered his tent. I found this, *sidi*." Sond handed to Khardan a small piece of parchment.

"What does it say?" asked the Calif, staring at the strange markings with distrust.

Sond read the message Meryem left for Achmed.

"She was with him many weeks, apparently, *sidi*," said Sond gently. "There is no doubt he was infatuated with her. That was common gossip among all the men. Since she has been gone, all note his sad face and sorrowing aspect."

"What did she mean to do with him?" Khardan asked, crushing the paper in his hand.

"One can only speculate, master. But I heard many more things about your brother while I was among the troops. He is a favorite with Qannadi, whose men, as well, have grown to respect the *Kafir*, as they call him. Achmed has proved himself, both on the field and off. Qannadi has sons, but they are far away in the Emperor's court. There is little doubt that were the Amir to die, Achmed might find himself able to rise to a position of great power and authority. My guess is that the woman, Meryem, knew of this and intended to rise with him. Perhaps even see to it that he moved somewhat faster than expected."

"What can our God mean by this?" Khardan remarked, puzzled. "In killing Meryem, we may have saved the Amir's life." He drew a deep breath, unwilling to ask the next question, unwilling to hear the answer. "Sond, will my brother come to Kich?"

"Yes, *sidi*. He is Captain of the Amir's cavalry."

"Has he— Has he converted to Quar?"

"I do not think so, *sidi*. The men say that your brother worships no God. He claims that men are on their own, responsible only to themselves and to each other."

"What will he do if his people are attacked?"

"I do not know, *sidi*. My sight reaches far, but it cannot see into the human heart."

Khardan sighed. "Thank you, Sond. You may go. You have done well."

"The blessing of Akhran upon you, master," said the djinn, bowing. "May he touch you with wisdom."

"May he indeed," Khardan murmured, and lay down to stare thoughtfully into the darkness that seemed to grow ever deeper around him.

THE BOOK
OF AKHRAN

Chapter 1

Hrana, Akar, Aran: the tribes, united at last—if only in despair—rode for Kich swiftly and in dour silence, each man occupied with his own dark thoughts. No one—not even Khardan himself—believed the Amir would accept their challenge. The Imam had declared the *kafir* would convert or die, and he would not retreat from that stand. This was the last ride of the desert people. This was the end—of life, of future. The hope that grew in almost every heart had the taste of a bitter herb—it consisted only of being able, in death, to stand before Akhran and state, "I died in honor." Khardan was not surprised to see, as the nomads left the camp about the Tel, that the Rose of the Prophet looked nearer death than it ever had before. Still, it clung to life with stubborn persistence.

Two hearts on that grim journey, however, nurtured true hope. Zohra had never heard of this "fog" of which Mathew spoke, and which he said was common in the alien land from which he came. She found it difficult, if not impossible, to imagine clouds coming down from the sky to obey her command, surrounding and protecting and confusing the eyes of her enemies. But she had seen Mathew summon one of these clouds from water in a bowl in her tent. She had felt its cold and clammy touch on her skin, smelled its dank odor, and watched in astonishment as Mathew gradually faded from her sight and familiar objects in the tent either disappeared or looked strange and unreal.

She had thought he was gone—his body turned into the mist—until he had spoken and reached out to her. His hand had clasped hers, and then she had known disappointment.

"What use is a cloud that will not stop a hand, let alone swords or arrows?"

Patiently Mathew had explained that if each woman was taught the magic and summoned her own "fog," it would be as the creation of a gigantic cloud that would cover them all. They could take advantage of the guards' certain confusion and panic to attack and win their way free of the prison walls before anyone caught them.

"Surely there is magic you know that can fight for us as an army!" she said persistently.

Yes, he had answered with patience, but it takes study to use it effectively. Without practice the magic is more dangerous to the spell caster than to the victim.

"The fog spell is relatively simple to cast. We can teach the women to write it easily. All we need," Mathew had added offhandedly, "is a source of water, and surely there must be a well in the prison."

"Have you done this before?" Zohra had asked.

"Of course."

"With many people?"

He had not answered, and Zohra had not pursued the matter further.

At this point, it didn't matter.

Two days hard riding on the *mehara,* and those horses that had been saved in the battle brought the men to the hills of the sheep-herding Hrana. There were few left to greet them, mostly old men and women who had been considered worthless and left behind by the Amir. They welcomed their Sheykh but regarded their Princess and her husband with sullen words and bitter looks. It was only when Fedj appeared and told the tale of Khardan the Prophet that their darting, sidelong glances widened with awe and they began to look upon the Calif with more respect—if not less suspicion.

By the time the tale was concluded, late in the night, it

had been rewoven and embroidered, cut here, mended there, until, as Khardan muttered aside to Auda, he would not have known it for the same suit of clothes. The tale had its intended effect, however—or at least so Khardan supposed. The moment the people of Jaafar's tribe, who had been skulking in the hills with the remnants of their flocks, heard that Khardan was favored of Akhran, they began to pour their woes into his ears until it was a wonder his brain didn't overflow.

Their woes were the same as those of their cousins around the Tel—water was scarce, food was dear, wolves were raiding their flocks, they were worried about their families held prisoner in Kich. When was the Prophet going to make it rain? When would he give them wheat and rice? When was he going to drive off the wolves? When was he going to march on Kich and free their people?

Long after Majiid had gone to his bed, long after Zohra had retired to the empty yurt of one of her half brother's captive wives, long after Mathew had rolled himself up in a blanket on the floor of an empty hut that had been assigned for his use, Khardan remained seated with his father-in-law and the silent, watchful Auda around a sputtering fire. Blinking eyes that burned with fatigue, he stifled yawns and patiently answered either "yes" or "in Akhran's time" to everything. He did not say that "Akhran's time" was "no time," but all heard his unspoken words, saw the despair in the dark eyes and, one by one, they left him. Sond almost carried the bone-weary Calif to his dwelling where he sank into a desolate, gloom-ridden sleep.

The silence of night in the hills is not the silence of night in the desert. The silence of the hills is the weaving of many tiny sounds of tree and bird and beast into a blanket that rests lightly over the sleeper. The silence of the desert is the sibilant whisper of the wind across the sand, the snarl of a prowling lioness that sometimes jolts a sleeper to sudden wakefulness.

The silence of the hills had lulled her to sleep, but when Zohra started up, striving with every sense to determine what had alarmed her, it seemed to her that she was back in the desert. There was no sound; all was too quiet. Her hand slipped beneath her pillow, fingers grasping for the hilt of her dagger, but a crushing grip closed over her wrist.

"It is Auda." His breath touched her skin. He spoke so softly, she felt his words more than heard them.

"There is not much time left to us!" breathed his voice in her ear. "Tomorrow we arrive in Kich, and my life is forfeit to the service of my God, the fulfillment of my oath. Lay with me this night! Give me a son!"

The fear surging in her slowly calmed. Her heart no longer pounded in her breast, her blood ceased to rush in her ears. That had been her initial fright, her reaction to being taken by surprise. Her breath came more easily; she relaxed.

"You do not cry out. I knew you would not." He released his grip on her hand and drew near her.

"No." Zohra shook her head. "There is no need. I am sure of myself."

He could not see her; the darkness was intense, impenetrable. But he could feel the movement of her head, the long, silky hair brushing against his wrist. He moved his hand to part her hair; his lips touched her cheek.

"No one but you and I will ever know."

"One other," she said. "Khardan."

"Yes." Auda considered. "You are right. He will know. But he will not begrudge me this, for I will be dead. And he will be alive. And he will have you."

He ran his hands through her tousled hair. The darkness was soft and warm and smelled of jasmine. Cupping her chin, he guided her lips to his and waited expectantly, confidently, for her answer.

The next morning the nomad army left the Hrana, taking along those old men who insisted they could ride farther and fight better than three young ones. Khardan, riding at their head, noted that Zohra seemed unusually quiet and preoccupied.

He had insisted at the beginning of their journey that she and Mathew accompany him, instead of following in the rear in the accustomed place of women. This was both a concession to his father—who never ceased to suspect Jaafar and his daughter were plotting against him—and to himself. As Zohra had said, they had traveled long and far together, faced many perils together. He came to realize, in the long hours of the ride when he had too much time to think, that he would have found it difficult, leaving her behind. It was somehow a comfort to him to look over and see her sitting her horse with the confidence of a man, a grace all her own.

Yet this day, riding out of the hills, wending their way through the tortuous paths carved into the red rock that thrust up into the blue sky of late summer, Khardan felt again the nip of fiery pincers, the unease of some nameless, nagging irritation. Zohra seemed aloof, distant. She rode by herself, instead of near Mathew, and coldly rebuffed the young man's attempts to draw her into conversation. She would look at no one who rode near—neither Mathew, Khardan, nor the ever-present, ever-watchful Paladin. Zohra kept her eyes lowered, the man's *haik* she wore during the ride drawn closely over her face.

"A fine woman," said Auda, guiding his horse up beside the Calif, his gaze following Khardan's. "She will bear some man many fine sons."

No blade that had ever struck Khardan inflicted pain as did these words. Reining in his horse with such fury that he nearly overset the beast, he stared angrily, questioningly at the Black Paladin. Khardan searched the cruel eyes. Let him see the tiniest spark and—oath or no oath, God or no God—this man would perish.

"Many fine sons," Auda repeated. The eyes were cold, impassive, except for a flicker that was not the gleam of triumph, but of admiration for the victor. "—For the man she loves."

Shrugging, his thin lips parting in a self-deprecating smile, Auda bowed to the Calif, wheeled his horse, and rode farther back to join the main body of men.

Left alone, Khardan drew a deep, shivering breath. The iron had been plucked from his heart, but the wound it had made was fresh and bled freely, flooding his body with a haunting, aching warmth. He looked over at Zohra, proud and fierce, riding by herself—riding beside him, not behind him.

"Fine sons," he said to himself bitterly. "And many fine

daughters, too. But not to be. Not to us. It is too late. For us, the Rose will never bloom.''

After a week's hard journeying, the nomads came within sight of Kich. It was late afternoon. Khardan had sent scouts forward to find a safe resting place; they had returned to report the discovery of a large vineyard planted on a hillside, near enough to the city that they could see its walls and the soldiers manning them, yet far enough to remain hidden from view of those walls. At the foot of the hill, a smooth wide road ran through the plain, leading to the city walls.

Khardan appraised the thick, twisting stems of the grapevines that grew around him. The harvest had apparently been gathered, for there were few of the small, wrinkled grapes left hanging among the leaves that were slowly turning yellow, the plant going dormant following the plucking of its fruit. A tree-lined stream ran down alongside the grapevines. The ground underfoot was damp, the owner having flooded his vineyards after the grapes were gathered. Until harvest the fruit does better without water—the grapes growing sweeter and more sugary when allowed to dry in the sun.

"This will be a good place to camp," announced Khardan, agreeing with his scouts and forestalling the arguments of the Sheykhs that he could see bubbling on their lips by adding swiftly, "The fruit has been harvested. The owner will be tending to his wine, not his plants. We are hidden from sight of the road and the city walls by the vines."

To this the Sheykhs could make no reply, although there was, of course, some grumbling. Unlike many vineyard owners, this man must be a man of enterprise and forethought, for he had caused his vines to grow up stakes. Rather than straggling over the ground, the leaves were twined around a length of string that had been tied from stake to stake above the ground at about shoulder level. The foliage easily hid both man and beast from sight.

Khardan was directing the watering of the horses when Sond materialized at the Calif's stirrup.

"Would you have us go to the gate and see how many men guard it and how carefully they scrutinize those who enter, *sidi*?''

"I know how many men guard it and how carefully they guard it," Khardan answered, jumping down from his horse. "You and the other djinn stay out of the city until it is time. If the immortals of Quar should discover you, the God would be alerted to our presence."

"Yes, *sidi*." Sond bowed and vanished.

Khardan unsaddled his horse and led the animal to drink in the stream. The other men did the same, making certain to keep the animals in the lengthening shadows, settling the beasts for the night. The camels were persuaded to kneel down near the banks of the rushing water. The men crouched on the ground below the grapevines, eating their one daily meal, talking in low voices.

Zohra began to mix flour with water, forming balls of dough that, if they had dared light a fire, could have been baked and made slightly more palatable. As it was, the nomads ate the dough raw, a few lucky ones supplementing their meager dinner with handfuls of overlooked, wrinkled grapes, stripped from the vines that sheltered them. The most that could be said for the repast was that it assuaged their hunger. Somewhere, from out of the air around them, they could hear the djinn Usti groan dismally.

Finishing his food without tasting it or even being consciously aware that he ate, Khardan rose to his feet and walked up to the top of the rise to stare at the city. The sun was setting beyond the walls of Kich, and Khardan gazed into the red sky with such intensity that the minarets and bulbous domes, tall towers and battlements seemed etched into his brain.

At length Auda rose and went to the stream to wash the sticky dough from his fingers. Removing the *haik*, he plunged his head into the water, letting it run down his neck and chest.

"The stream is cold. It must come from the mountains. You should try it," he said, rubbing his shining black hair with the sleeve of his flowing robes.

Khardan did not reply.

"I do not think it will quench the fire of your thoughts," Auda remarked wryly, "but it may cool your fever."

Glancing at him, Khardan smiled ruefully. "Perhaps later, before I sleep."

"I have been thinking long about what you said—your God forbids the taking of life in cold blood. Is that true?" Auda leaned against a tree trunk, his gaze following Khardan's to the soldiers of the city walls.

"Yes," Khardan answered. "Life taken in the hot blood of battle or the hot blood of anger—that the God understands and condones. But murder—life taken by stealth, by night, a knife in the back, poison in a cup . . ." Khardan shook his head.

"A strange man, your God," remarked Auda.

Since there could not be much comment made regarding this statement, Khardan smiled and kept quiet.

Auda stretched, flexing muscles stiff from the long ride. "You are worried about entering the gates, aren't you?"

"You have gone through those gates. You know what the guards are like. And that was in days of peace! Now they are at war!"

"Yes, I have entered Kich, as you well know. You made my last visit a very unpleasant one!" Auda grinned briefly, then sobered. "It was due to their strict vigilance that I was forced to entrust the enchanted fish to Blossom. And yes, you are right. They are at war; their lookout will have increased tenfold."

"And you still go along with our original plan?" Khardan cast a scowling glance at the large bundle lying on the ground—a bundle containing women's heavy robes and thick veils.

"Chances are they will not search females," Auda answered carelessly.

"Chances!" Khardan snorted.

Auda laid a hand on the Calif's arm. "Zhakrin has brought me this far. He will get me through the gate. Will your God not do as much for his Prophet?"

Was the voice mocking, or did it speak truly, from faith? Khardan stared at Auda intently but could not decide. The man's eyes, the only window to his soul, were—as usual—closed and shuttered. What was it about this man that drew Khardan near as it repelled him? Several times the Calif thought he had found the answer, only to have it flit away from him the next instant. Just as it did now.

Khardan bathed in the stream, then spread his blanket beneath the trees near where Zohra and Mathew sat talking in whispers, perhaps going over their own plans, for Mathew was repeating strange words to Zohra, who murmured them over and over to herself before she slept.

Night came and with it a gentle rain that pattered on the leaves of the grapevines. One by one the nomads sank into sleep, secure in the knowledge that their immortals guarded their rest, and leaving their ultimate fate in the hands of Akhran.

Chapter 2

As Sul would have it, it was neither *Hazrat* Akhran nor Zhakrin, God of Evil, who opened the gate of the city of Kich to the nomads.

It was Quar.

"Master, wake up!"

Khardan sat bolt upright, his hand closing over the hilt of his sword.

"No, *sidi,* there is no danger. Look." Sond pointed.

Khardan, blinking the sleep from his eyes, peered through the haze of early morning to where the djinn indicated.

"When did this begin?" he asked, staring.

"Before it was light, *sidi.* We have been watching for over an hour and it grows."

Khardan turned to wake Auda, only to find the Paladin reclining on his arms, watching in relaxed ease. Last night, the road had been empty of all travelers. This morning it was jammed with people, camels, donkeys, horses, carts, and wagons, all coming together, jostling for position, breaking down in the center of the road, and snarling up traffic. But despite the confusion, it was clear that they were all headed in one direction—toward Kich.

Springing to his feet, Khardan shook Zohra's shoulder

roughly and, grabbing Mathew's blanket, pulled it out from beneath him, dumping the young man rudely to the ground. "Hurry! Wake up! Gather your things! No, we won't need those. Only Mat-hew will dress as a woman. Ibn Jad and I won't need a disguise, thank Akhran."

"I do not think we need rush," remarked Auda coolly, his gaze on the road and the winding snake of humanity that crept along it. "This is unending, it seems."

"One of our Gods has seen fit to answer our prayers," remarked Khardan, tossing the saddle over his horse's back. "I will not offend whoever it is by seeming lax in my response."

Auda raised a thoughtful eyebrow and, without more words, prepared to saddle his own animal. By this time the camp was roused.

"What is it?" Majiid hurried over, his grizzled hair standing straight up on all sides of the small, tight-fitting cap he wore beneath his headcloth. Cinching his saddle, Khardan grunted and nodded his head at the road below, but by that time Majiid had seen and was scowling.

"I don't like this . . . this crowd coming to the city."

"Do not question the blessing of the God, father. It gets us into the gate. Surely with this mob the guards will not look too closely at four."

"Then they will not look too closely at four hundred. I'm going with you!" stated Majiid.

"And I!" cried Jaafar, hurrying up. "You'll do nothing without me!"

"Make my camel ready!" Zeid, dashing over, turned and started to dash away.

"No!" Khardan called as loudly as he dared before the entire hillside erupted into confusion. "How will it look to Qannadi if a crowd of armed *spahis* surges into his city? The Amir remembers what happened the last time we went to Kich. He would never agree to listen to me! We follow the plan, father! The only ones who enter the city are Auda, my wife, Mat-hew, Sond, and I. You and the men remain here and wait for the djinn to report back."

Sheykh Jaafar argued that the mob on the road was an ill omen and that no one should enter the city. Sheykh Majiid, suddenly siding with his son, repeated once again that Jaafar was a coward. Zeid glowered at Khardan suspiciously and insisted that the Calif take Raja with him, as well as Sond, and Jaafar shouted that if Raja went, Fedj should not be left behind.

"Very well!" Khardan lifted his hands to the heavens. "I will take all the djinn!"

"I will not be offended, master, if you leave *me* behind," began Usti humbly, but a glimpse at the Calif's dark and exasperated expression caused the flabby immortal to gulp and disappear into the ethers with his companions.

When all were ready, Khardan cast a stern glance at the Sheykhs. "Remember, you are to wait here for word. This you swear to me by *Hazrat* Akhran?"

"I swear," muttered the Sheykhs unwillingly.

Knowing that each of the old men was perfectly capable of deciding that this vow applied to all with the exception of himself, Khardan calculated he had no more than a few days' peace before he could look forward confidently to a chaos equivalent to that of Sul's legions breaking loose out here in the vineyard. Not at all reassured by seeing Majiid brandishing his sword in a salute that nearly decapitated Jaafar, Khardan led his horse from the grove, followed by Auda, Zohra, Mathew, and—he assumed—three invisible djinn. The thought of this procession attempting to sneak into Kich unobserved preyed on his mind. It was probably just as well, therefore, that the Calif did not know an angel of Promenthas was tagging along, as well.

Hurriedly Khardan led the group through the vineyards, bringing them to a halt some distance from the road in the shelter of the trees along the stream.

"Either Auda or I will do the talking. Remember, it is not seemly for our women to speak to strangers."

This was said to Mathew, who was once again disguised as a female in a green caftan and a green and gold spangled veil he had taken from Meryem's tent. But Khardan could not help his glance straying to Zohra. Mathew accepted the instruction gravely and somberly. Zohra glared at Khardan in sudden fury.

"I am not a child!" she snarled, giving a rope wrapped

around a bundle on the back of the horse a vicious jerk that sent the startled animal dancing sideways into the stream with a splash.

Checking an exasperated retort, the Calif turned from Khardan and, leading his horse out of the vineyards, headed for the road. He ignored the low chuckle he heard come from the Paladin, walking beside him.

Very well, he berated himself, he deserved her anger. He shouldn't have said it. Zohra knew their danger. She would do nothing to expose them. But why couldn't she understand? He was worried, nervous, afraid for her, afraid for the boy, afraid for his people. Yes, if truth be told, afraid for himself. A battle in the open air, grappling with Death face-to-face— that he understood and could meet without blenching. But a battle of duplicity and intrigue, a battle fought trapped inside city walls—this unnerved him.

It occurred to him that perhaps it was not quite fair to demand of Zohra that she honor her husband for his strength and pretend not to see his weakness, while at the same time expecting her to make allowances for the very weakness he refused to admit having. But so be it, he decided, sliding and slipping down the terraced slope. Akhran had never said that anyone's life was fair.

Leading their horses by the reins, the four stepped hesitantly, cautiously, into the road, joining the throng of people heading for Kich. They were immediately absorbed into the crowd without question or notice. Everyone appeared to be in a state of anticipatory excitement; and Khardan was wondering which of those pressing around would be safe to question when Auda, touching him gently, gestured in the direction of a rascally looking, sunburnt man clad in a well-worn *burnouse* and a small, greasy, sweat-stained cap that fit tightly over his skull.

The man held, at the end of a lead, a small monkey, who wore a cap similar to its master's and a coat made in imitation of one of the Amir's soldiers that was almost, but not quite, as filthy. The monkey scampered among the crowd, to the delight of the children and Mathew. The young man stared at it wide-eyed, having never seen an animal such as this before. Holding out its tiny hand, the monkey would run up to a person, begging for food or money or anything anyone seemed inclined to hand it. When the monkey had taken the grape or the copper piece, it would perform a head-over-heels flip at the end of its leash, then run back to its master.

Removing from his money pouch one of the last, precious coins of his tribe, Khardan considered a moment. He had no idea how long they might be forced to stay in Kich until the Amir returned. They would need food and a place to sleep. But he had to have information. Slowly Khardan held up the coin between thumb and forefinger. Catching the glint of money, the monkey ran up and hopped about in the dust at Khardan's feet, chittering wildly and beating its tiny hands together to indicate that the nomad was to toss the coin.

"No, no, little one," said Khardan, shaking his head and talking to the monkey, though his eyes were really on its master. "You must come and get it."

The monkey's master spoke a word, and to the Calif's astonishment the monkey leapt onto his robes and crawled up the nomad as deftly as if Khardan had been a species of date palm. Scampering along the Calif's arm, the monkey neatly plucked the coin from Khardan's fingers, then flipped over backwards to land on its feet in the street. Those in the crowd who had witnessed the feat applauded and laughed at the expense of the nomad.

Khardan's face flushed red, and he was of half a mind to make the monkey's master do a few flips himself when he heard an odd sound behind him. Turning, he glowered at Mathew.

"I'm sorry, Khardan," murmured the young man from behind his veil, stifling his giggle, his eyes dancing in merriment. "I couldn't help myself."

"Be quiet, you'll call attention to us!" Khardan said sternly, reminding Mathew of what the Calif himself had nearly forgotten. Khardan's gaze darted to Zohra. She lowered her eyes, but not before he had seen laughter sparkling in their dark depths.

Khardan felt a smile tug at his lips despite himself. I must have looked ridiculous, I'll admit that. And to hear the young man laugh—after all this time. Especially facing such danger. It is a good omen, and I accept it.

"*Salaam aleikum,* my friend," called out Khardan to the monkey's master, who had taken the coin from the animal and, after inspecting it closely, carefully tucked it into a ragged cloth bag he carried slung over his shoulder.

The monkey's master bowed and came over to walk beside the two nomads and their wives, his sharp-eyed gaze going to the place in the Calif's flowing robes from where he had seen the money emerge. "*Aleikum salaam, Effendi,*" he said humbly.

The monkey was not so polite. Riding on its master's shoulder, the creature bared its sharp little teeth at Khardan and hissed. With a deprecating smile the master stroked the creature and admonished it in a strange language. The monkey, shaking its head and making a rude noise, skipped over to the other shoulder.

"I apologize, *Effendi,*" said the man. "Zar does not like to be teased. It is his one failing. Other than that he is a wonderful pet."

"He seems a very useful one," remarked Khardan, eyeing the cloth bag.

The monkey's master clapped his hand over the bag, his gaze suddenly narrowed and scowling. But seeing the nomad walking beside him amiably, his own eyes friendly and innocent of evil intent, the man relaxed.

"Yes, *Effendi,*" he admitted. "I have walked the road with Starvation my only companion for many years before I came across Zar, here. His name means 'gold' and he has been worth his weight in that to me many times over. Of course," he added hastily, making a sign over the animal's head with his hand, "Zar is a foul-tempered little beast, as you have seen. Many is the time he has sunk his tiny teeth into my thumb. See?" The man exhibited a dirty finger.

Khardan expressed condolences, and knowing it would not be wise to discuss the monkey further lest the evil eye seek the animal out and destroy it, the Calif found it easy to change topics.

"You spoke words I did not understand. You are not from around here."

The man nodded. "My home—what home I have—is in Ravenchai. But I have not been back there for many years.

To be quite honest, my friend"—he drew nearer Khardan and gave him a conspiratorial glance from narrowed eyelids—"there is a wife in that home who would greet me with something less than loving devotion if I returned, if you know what I mean."

"Women!" grunted Khardan sympathetically.

"It wasn't her fault," said the rascally man magnanimously. "Work is not fond of me."

"It isn't?" returned Khardan, somewhat at a loss to understand this strange statement.

"No, Work and I do not get along well at all. I take up with him on occasion, but we always end up in a dispute. Work demands that I continue pursuing him, while I am inclined to leave off and get something to eat or to take a small nap or to go around to the *arwat* for a cup of wine. Work ends up leaving me in a fit of anger, and there I am, with nothing to do except sleep, with no money to buy food to eat or wine to quench my thirst." The man shook his head over this and appeared so truly devastated at this ill fortune that Khardan had no difficulty pronouncing Work to be the most unreasonable being in existence.

"When Zar came to me— And that is a very strange story, my friend, for Zar *did* come to me, literally. I was walking the streets of—well, it does not matter to you what streets they were—when the Sultan rode out in his palanquin to take in the air. I was following along at his side, just in case the Sultan happened to drop anything that I might have the honor of restoring to him, when I saw the curtains part, and out from the bottom hopped this little fellow." He patted the monkey, who had fallen asleep on his shoulder, its tail curled tightly about its master's neck.

"He leapt straight into my arms. I was preparing to return him to the Sultan when I noticed that the guards were engaged in beating off several beggars who had crowded around the other side of the palanquin. The Sultan was watching them with interest. No one, it seemed, had noticed the creature's absence. Thinking that the monkey must have been badly treated, or he would never have left his owner, I thrust him beneath my robes and disappeared down an alley. That was several years ago, and we have been together ever since."

And he saves you from being involved with that dread fellow Work, Khardan thought with some amusement. Aloud he merely congratulated the man on his good fortune and then asked, casually, "Why is this great crowd going into Kich?"

The man looked ahead. The city walls were close enough to them now that Khardan could see clearly the heavily armed guards walking the battlements. The morning sun gleamed brightly off a golden dome—a new addition to the temple of Quar, Khardan concluded. Paid for with the wealth and blood of the conquered cities of Bas, no doubt.

The monkey's master turned his gaze to Khardan in some amazement. "Why, you must have been far out in the desert not to have heard the news, nomad. This day the Imam of Quar returns victorious to his city."

Khardan and Auda exchanged swift glances.

"This day? And the Amir?"

"Oh, he comes, too, I suppose," the man added without much interest. "It is the Imam all gather to see. That and the great slaughter of *kafir* that will be held tonight in his honor."

"Tonight!"

"Slaughter of *kafir*?" Auda pushed forward to ask this question, drawing attention away from the white-faced Khardan. "What do you mean, my friend? This sounds like a sight I would feign not miss."

"Why, the *kafir* of the desert who have been imprisoned in Kich for many months and who have refused to convert to Quar." The man looked intently at Khardan and Auda, noting the *haik* and the flowing robes with sudden uneasiness. "These *kafir* wouldn't be relatives—"

"No, no," Khardan said gruffly, having recovered from the jolting shock. "We come from . . . from . . ." He faltered, his brain refusing to function.

"Simdari," inserted Auda, well aware that the nomad's world was encompassed within his sand dunes.

"Ah, Simdari," said the monkey's master. "I have never traveled in that land, but I am planning on journeying there when this festival is concluded. Tell me, what do you know of the *arwats* of Simdari . . ."

Auda and the rascally man who did not get along with Work entered into a discussion of various inns, of which

Khardan heard not one word. So much for good omens! All their plans, running like sand from between his fingers! How could he ever hope to see the Amir, who would be busy with returning to his palace, his city? And the Imam, prepared to destroy his people this night!

It is hopeless, Khardan thought despondently. I can do nothing but stand and watch my people murdered! No, there is one thing I can do. I can die with them as I should have months ago—

A hand touched his. Thinking it was Auda, he turned swiftly only to find Zohra walking at his side. Irrationally, he felt as if this bad luck was somehow his fault and she was going to gloat over him again. He was about to order her to return to her place when she saw and forestalled his intent.

"Do not despair!" she said softly. "Akhran is with us! He brought us here in time, and his enemy opens the gates for us to enter."

The dark eyes above the veil glittered, and her fingers brushed lightly against his hand. Before he could respond or reach out to her, she was gone.

Glancing behind, he saw her talking to Mathew, their heads bent close together, whispering. The young wizard nodded his veiled head several times, emphatically. His delicate hand made gestures, graceful as a woman's. He and Zohra walked side by side, shoulders, bodies touching.

Khardan suffered a twinge of jealousy, looking at the two, seeing their obvious closeness. It wasn't the hurting, shriveling anguish he'd experienced when he'd feared Auda had . . . well, when he'd feared Auda. He couldn't be jealous of the young man in the same way. He was jealous because this gentle wizard was closer to his wife than he, Khardan, could ever come. It was a closeness of shared interests, respect, admiration. And then it occurred to Khardan, startlingly, that just as his wife was closer to Mathew than to him, so he was closer to Mathew than to his wife.

Khardan was genuinely fond of the young man. He knew his courage, for he had seen it in Castle Zhakrin. The fact that he—Khardan—could relate to Mathew as a man and that Zohra could, at the same time, relate to Mathew as a woman was a phenomenon that completely baffled the Calif. He allowed it to occupy his mind, crowd out more dismal and hopeless thoughts. These returned full force, however, when Auda came to walk beside him once more.

"The situation is not quite as desperate as you first thought, if what this fellow says can be trusted. The Imam will make a speech this night in which he will exhort all *kafir* to renounce their old Gods and come to the One, True God, Quar. Those who refuse will be given the night to consider their waywardness. In the morning, at dawn, they will choose to find salvation with Quar or be considered beyond redemption in this life and considerately put to death to find it in the next."

"So we have until dawn," muttered Khardan, not overly comforted.

"Until dawn," Auda repeated with a casual shrug. "And our Enemy opens his gate to us."

The second time I have heard that. Khardan tried to see this as the miracle that everyone else did. Yet he was naggingly reminded of the fable of the lion who told the foolish mouse he knew of a wonderful place where the mouse could find shelter for the winter.

"Right here," said the lion, opening his mouth and pointing down his gullet. "Just walk in. Don't mind the teeth."

Khardan raised his eyes to the city walls, the great wooden gates, the soldiers massed on top of the battlements.

Don't mind the teeth. . . .

Chapter 3

They swept through the gate on a tide of humanity. No guard saw them, let alone attempted to stop and question them. The nomads were in far more danger from the crowds then the soldiers. It was all Auda and Khardan could do to keep hold of their horses. Brave in battle, accustomed to blood and slashing steel, and to being accorded the highest respect by humans, the animals were angered by the rough jostling, the elbows in the flanks, the whines of the beggars, the clamoring cries, pushings, and shovings of the mob.

Just inside the gate was a large, cleared area where wagons used to haul goods to the city were stored. Slaves of every type and description were driving camels and donkeys into, out of, and around the cart-standing area; the fodder sellers were doing a literally roaring business. Khardan glanced askance at the confusion, but a momentary regret that he had chosen to bring the horses passed swiftly. They would need them in their escape . . . Akhran willing.

Catching sight of a tall, thin boy of about eleven or twelve years who was staring at them intently, Khardan motioned him near. The boy's eyes had not been on the nomads themselves, but on the horses, gazing at the magnificent animals of the desert with the hungry love and yearning of one who has grown up in the twisted streets of the city.

The child never knew the freedom of the singing sands, but he could see it and feel it in the beauty and strength of the descendants of the horse of the Wandering God. At Khardan's gesture the boy shot forward as though hurled from a sling.

"What is your bidding, *Effendi*?"

Khardan's gaze scanned the cart-standing area, then turned to the boy. "Can you find food and water and rest for our horses and watch over them while we conduct our business?"

"I would be honored, *Effendi*!" breathed the boy, stretching forth trembling hands to take the reins.

Khardan fished another precious coin from the purse. "Here, this will purchase food and stable space. There will be another for you if you keep your trust."

"I would let myself be split in two by wooden stakes driven through my body, *Effendi*, before I allowed harm to come to these noble beasts!" The boy put a hand upon the neck of Khardan's steed. Feeling the gentle touch, the animal quieted, though he stared around with rolling eyes and pricking ears.

"I trust that will not be necessary," Khardan said gravely. "Watch over them and keep them company. You need not worry about theft. I do not like to think what would happen to any man who tried to ride these horses without our sanction."

The boy's face fell at this. "Yes, *Effendi*," he said wistfully, twisting the mane lovingly in his fingers.

Grinning, Khardan caught hold of the boy around the waist and tossed him up on the horse's back. The boy gasped in delight and astonishment and could barely hold the reins the nomad thrust into his eager, trembling hand.

"You may ride him, my fine *spahi*," said the Calif, handing the boy the leads for the other three animals. A word in his horse's ear and the animal suffered himself to be ridden away by the proud boy who bounced unsteadily in the saddle and wore the look of one who has ridden since birth. The other three horses followed their leader without hesitation.

"Sond," muttered Khardan beneath his breath to the air, "see that all is well with them."

"Yes, *sidi*. Shall I have Usti stand guard?"

"For the time being. We may need him later."

"Yes, *sidi*."

The Calif heard a yelped protest, "I refuse to be left in a horse stall!" that ended in a smacking sound and a blubbering whimper.

Now that the horses were settled, Khardan stared around him confusedly. His chief worry had been getting through the gate. This having been accomplished with an ease and swiftness that left him breathless, the Calif again felt a sense of disquietude about it, as if he had been given a valuable gift that he knew deep within was no gift and feared the dread payment that must be exacted later.

A shout from Auda saved Mathew from being ridden down by two donkey riders and recalled Khardan to the fact that they were standing in the center of the main road of Kich and were in danger of being trampled or separated by the mob. Though it was Zohra's first time to see the city, she was glancing about in a haughty disdain which, Khardan had come to know, masked uneasiness and awe. He knew how she felt; he could feel his own face settling into that very expression. Mathew was calm, but very pale. Above his veil, his green eyes were wide, and he kept darting swift glances at something behind Khardan. The Calif looked back, saw the slave market, and understood.

"What now, brother?" asked Auda.

What now indeed? Khardan continued to gaze around helplessly. The Amir had once referred to the nomads—outside of their hearing, of course—as naive children. If Qannadi had been present to witness Khardan's confusion, the Amir would have been able to acknowledge himself a wise judge of men. Months ago, in the pride of his standing as Prince of the desert, Khardan had walked into the palace and demanded and received an audience with the Amir. He'd had it in mind this time to do the very same thing when—standing once again in the city streets and reliving that audience months before—he suddenly realized that he had been duped. He had been admitted purposefully, attacked purposefully, allowed to escape purposefully. He'd had a glimmer of this; Meryem's assassination attempt revealed as much, but now the light of truth shone glaringly down on him. Just why the Amir had gone to this trouble with him was still vague to Khardan, who did not know—and probably never would—of Pukah's bungling, double-dealing, mischief making.

The Calif swore bitterly, cursing himself for a fool. Would the Amir see him now? A ragged Prince whose people were imprisoned, doomed to death? Qannadi was just returned triumphant from battle. There would be supplicants and well-wishers by the hundreds who had undoubtedly been waiting weeks to see him and might possibly wait weeks longer until the Amir was at leisure to turn his attention to them. Qannadi might not even have arrived in the city.

A blare of trumpets came as answer to Khardan's thoughts. A clattering of many hooves warned him of his peril just moments before the cavalry of the Amir swept through the city gate. Their flags whipping behind them, the soldiers' uniforms were vivid splashes of color among the drab browns and whites, grays and blacks worn by those milling about the streets. Hurrying to the side of the road just moments before they would have been stampeded into the hard-packed earth, Khardan and his companions watched the soldiers ride heedlessly through the crowd, knocking aside those who did not move out of their way, ignoring the curses and shaking fists that heralded their entry.

They were all business, these men. It was their duty to clear the way, and this they did, with ruthless efficiency. An ax through flesh, they cleaved through the masses, the well-trained horses pressing the people back against the walls of the Kasbah on one side, the slave market and the first stalls of the bazaar on the other. Foot soldiers, marching in ranks behind them, were swiftly deployed by their officers to keep the crowd back, taking up positions on either side of the street, holding spears out horizontally before them to form a living barricade. Those who tried to cross or who surged forward were given a swift clout with the butt-end of the weapon.

Khardan searched the faces of the riders intently, looking for Achmed, but there was too much confusion, and the soldiers, in their steel helms, looked all alike to him. He heard Auda shouting, "What is it? What is happening?" and several voices crying at once, "The Imam! The Imam is come!"

The stench, the heat, the excitement, was suffocating. Khardan felt fingers dig into his arm and turned to see Mathew clinging to him desperately so as not to be knocked off his feet by the heavings and surges of the mob. Khardan gripped the young man by the arm, holding him close, and looked to see Auda deal swiftly and silently with an overzealous believer attempting to shove Zohra out of his line of vision. A gasp, a groan, and Quar's faithful sank down into the dust where his unconscious body was immediately set upon and picked clean by the followers of Benario.

A mighty shout rose from the throats of the people, who strained forward with such force that the soldiers holding them back stumbled and fought to keep their footing. Line after line of the Imam's own soldier-priests appeared, walking proudly down the street. Unlike the Amir's men, these soldier-priests wore no armor, believing themselves to be protected from harm by the God. Clad in black silken tunics and long, billowing pantalons, every soldier-priest had a story about how an arrow, shot at his heart, had bounced off, how Quar's hand had turned aside a sword thrust meant for the throat. Such tales were often not far from the truth, for the soldier-priests ran into battle in a shrieking, confused knot, hacking with their naked blades, the light of fanaticism gleaming in their eyes. More than one enemy broke before them in sheer panic. The soldier-priests carried their curved blades in their hands. At the cheers of the crowd, they raised the swords above their heads and shook them in triumph.

After the arrival of the soldier-priests—and Khardan was aghast and amazed at their numbers—the roaring of the crowd reached a din impossible to believe. A hundred mamelukes, clad in gold skirts with white headdresses made of ostrich plumes, followed. In their hands they carried baskets and tossed handfuls of coins into the clamoring crowd. Khardan caught one and Auda another—pure silver. The Calif could not hear, but he knew by the expression on Auda's face the words formed by his grinning lips.

"Our Enemy not only opens the gate but pays us to enter!"

Behind the mamelukes two huge elephants hove into view, the sun gleaming brightly off ruby- and emerald-encrusted headdresses. Slaves rode their backs, guiding them through the streets. Golden, gem-studded bracelets glittered around the elephant's thundering feet. Their long tusks were tipped with gold. Khardan felt Mathew's body, pressed close against him by the crush of the crowd, tremble and sigh in awe. The young wizard from the strange land across the sea had never before seen such giant, wondrous creatures, and he gaped in staring-eyed amazement.

The elephants pulled behind them a gigantic structure built on wheels that, when it came nearer, could be seen to be a representation of a ram's head. Cunningly constructed of wood covered with parchment, the huge ram's head was painted with such skill that one might have mistaken it for a larger version of the real ram's-head altar that wavered and rocked on the swaying wooden base. Standing next to the altar, which had been hauled over the long miles traveled by the Amir's conquering army, was Feisal, the Imam.

At his coming, the cheers rose to a frenetic pitch, then dropped to an eerie hush that resounded in the ears more loudly than the shouts. Many in the crowd sank to their knees, prostrating themselves in the dust. Those that could not move because of the masses pressing around them extended their arms, silently beseeching their priest's blessing. Feisal gave it, turning first one way, then the other, from his perch on the great wheeled wagon. Several high priests stood proudly beside him. A horde of soldier-priests marched around the wagon's wheels, glaring fiercely and suspiciously at the adoring crowd.

Glancing at Auda, Khardan saw the man's usually impassive face thoughtful and grave and guessed the Paladin was imagining how best to penetrate this ring of steel and fanaticism. He did not appear perturbed or daunted by this sight, however; he was simply speculative.

Probably leaving all the mundane details, such as getting round a thousand swords, in the hands of his God, Khardan thought bitterly, and turned his eyes back to the Imam just as the Imam's eyes turned to him.

Khardan shuddered from head to toe. It was not that he had been recognized. That must be impossible with thousands of faces surrounding the Imam. No, the shudder was from the look in the eyes—the look of one possessed body and soul by a devouring passion, the look of one who has sacrificed reason and sanity to the consuming flame of holy fervor. It was the look of an insane man who is all too sane, and it struck terror to Khardan's heart, for he knew now that his people were doomed. This man would pour their blood into his golden chalice and hand it to his God without a qualm, believing firmly that he was doing the slaughtered innocents a favor.

The Imam passed by, and the terror faded from Khardan's thoughts, only to leave despair behind. The crowd turned to follow after the procession, which was apparently meant too wind its way through the city streets before returning to bring the Imam to his Temple. The Amir's soldiers fell back once the priest was safely past, Khardan and his companions were swept along with the masses.

"We've got to get free of this!" Khardan yelled at Auda, who nodded. Linking arms, he and the Calif held firmly to each other's shoulders, forming a shield with their bodies around Zohra and Mathew. They fended off jostlers with blows and kicks and struggled to make their way down a quiet side street or into one of the nooks along the Kasbah's walls.

Gloom descended on Khardan like a huge bird of prey, tearing out his heart, blinding him with its black wings. Though he had repeatedly told himself he came without hope, he knew now that he had in reality been carried this far on the strong wave of that most stubborn of all human emotions. Now hope was draining from him, leaving nothing but emptiness. His arms ached, his head throbbed with the noise, he felt sickened from the stench. The desire in his heart was to sink to the ground and let the trampling feet of the mob beat him into oblivion, and it was only concern for the welfare of those dependent on him, and Auda's firm grip on his shoulder, that kept him going.

Tirelessly the Black Paladin forged a path for them, thrusting, shoving, and constantly tugging and pulling at them to follow him. Khardan marveled at the man's strength, still more at his faith that had apparently not sunk beneath the weight of impossible odds.

"Faith," muttered Khardan, stumbling, falling, feeling Mathew and Zohra clinging to him, pulling himself up again, hearing Auda's shouts driving him on. "Faith—all that is left once hope is gone. *Hazrat* Akhran! Your people are in desperate need! We do not ask you to come fight for us, for you are fighting your own battle if what we hear is true. We have the courage to act, we need a way! Show us, Holy Wanderer, a way!"

The four were swept up against a wall with a suddenness that left them bruised and scraped. A panicked moment when it seemed they must be crushed against the stone passed, and then the worst of the crowd was by them, running after the procession, leaving relative quiet behind.

"Is everyone all right?" Khardan asked. He turned to see Mathew nod breathlessly, his hands fumbling with the veil that had been torn loose from his face.

"Yes," Zohra answered, hurriedly assisting Mathew, for it would not do to let anyone catch sight of that fair skin or glimpse the fiery red hair.

A glance was sufficient to show that Auda ibn Jad was the same as always—cool and unperturbed, his gaze fixed on several soldiers who, now that the excitement had passed, appeared to be taking an undue interest in the robed nomads.

"Haste!" hissed Auda from the side of his mouth, giving elaborate attention to the arrangement of his disarrayed robes. Without seeming to hurry, he moved deftly into the shadows cast by the wall, herding Zohra and Mathew with him. Khardan, seeing this new danger, wheeled to accompany them, tripped, and nearly fell headlong over an object at his feet.

A groan answered him.

"A beggar, trampled by the mob," said Auda indifferently, one eye on the guards who were standing on the opposite side of the street, obviously watching them with interest. "Of no consequence. Keep moving!"

But Zohra was on her knees beside the old man, helping him with gentle hands to sit up. "Thank you, daughter," grunted the beggar.

"Are you injured, father? I have my healing *feisha*—"

"No, daughter, bless you!" The beggar reached a groping, frantic hand. "My basket, my coins— Stolen?"

"Leave him! We must go!" Auda said insistently, and was bending down to drag Zohra away when Khardan stopped him.

"Wait!" The Calif stared at the beggar—the milky white eyes, the basket in the lap . . . Only he wasn't seeing him now, he was seeing the beggar months ago, seeing a white hand fling a bracelet into that basket, seeing a hole in the wall—once gaping open—closed and sealed shut. Khardan looked around him. Yes, there was the milk bazaar where he had stolen the scarf for her head. Glancing up, he could see palm fronds swaying above the wall.

"Praise be to Akhran!" Khardan breathed thankfully. Kneeling beside the old man, pretending to be offering aid, he examined the wall and motioned Auda to kneel down beside him. "Guards of the Amir are pursuing us!" he whispered to the beggar. "I know about the hole in the wall. Can you get us inside?"

The milky white eyes turned their sightless gaze on Khardan, the wrinkled face was suddenly so shrewd and cunning that the Calif could have sworn the blind eyes were studying him intently.

"Are you one of the Brotherhood?" queried the old man.

Khardan stared at him in puzzlement, not understanding. It was Auda who knelt near and, dropping the silver coin into the beggar's basket, said under his breath, "Benario, Lord of Snatching Hands and Swift-Running Feet."

The beggar's toothless mouth parted in a swift leer, and he reached behind him with a dexterous hand. What hidden latch he tripped was kept concealed by his skinny body and the rags that covered it, but suddenly there was a gap in the wall behind him, large enough for a man to slip through.

"The soldiers are coming this way!" said Auda calmly. "Make no move!"

"Damn!" Khardan swore, able to see the pleasure garden of the Amir only inches from him.

"Akhran be with you, *sidi*," whispered a voice from the air. "We know what to do."

The soldiers were walking toward them, evidently wondering what the desert dwellers could find so interesting in a beggar of Kich, when two drunks—one of them a towering, muscular giant of a man with gleaming black skin, the other a well-dressed servant, obviously belonging to the royal household—rounded a corner and slammed right into them.

Startled—Khardan had completely forgotten the presence of the djinn—he stared at the soldiers grappling with the drunks and was jolted to movement only when he felt Auda shove him roughly toward the wall. Mathew and Zohra had already crept inside, Khardan followed, and Auda came hastening after. A grinding sound and the hole was gone, the wall smooth, unblemished. A covering thornbush trundled back into place with such alacrity that the Paladin had to tug his robes free of the flesh-tearing brambles before he could move.

"You realize we are in the harem, the forbidden place!" said Auda coolly, glancing around the garden. "If the eunuchs catch us, our deaths will be prolonged and most unpleasant."

"Our deaths aren't likely to be any other way no matter where we are," said Khardan, stepping cautiously onto a path and motioning for the rest to come after him, "and this at least gives us a chance of talking to the Amir."

"Also a chance of getting into the Temple," continued Auda. "When I served in the Temple at Khandar, I learned that there was, in Kich, a tunnel that ran from the Temple below the ground to the palace of the Amir."

"First we talk to Qannadi!" Khardan started to say harshly, when there came the snapping of a twig underfoot, a rustle in the trees, and a shout of joy and longing.

"Meryem!"

Chapter 4

Obsession sees only the object of its madness. It believes everything it wants to believe, questions nothing. Achmed grabbed hold of the slender figure clad in the well-remembered green and gold spangled veil and whirled it around to face him.

Mathew, startled, let fall his veil.

"You!" Achmed cried, and hurled the young man from him.

Looking around at the others with fevered eyes, he saw his brother, but it did not occur to him to question why Khardan was here, in the Amir's garden. For Achmed there was only one question in his heart.

"Where is she?" Achmed demanded. "Where is Meryem? This . . . man"—he choked on the word, pointing a shaking finger at Mathew—"is wearing her clothes. . . ."

Too late Zohra laid restraining fingers on Khardan's arm. "Meryem's dead," said the Calif harshly, before he thought.

"Dead!" Achmed went white to the lips; he staggered where he stood. Then, in a swift motion, he yanked the sword from its scabbard at his side and jumped at Khardan. "You killed her!"

The young soldier's leap was halted by a strong arm wrapping around his neck, throttling him. A silver blade gleamed; the cruel eyes of the Paladin glittered beside him. Within another second Achmed's blood would have flowed from the slit in his throat.

"Auda, no! He's my brother!" Khardan caught hold of the Paladin's knife hand.

Auda stayed his killing stroke, but he held the young man tightly, his arm crushing the windpipe so that Achmed could neither speak nor yell. His eyes—staring at his brother—blazed with fury. He struggled impotently to escape his captor, and the Paladin tightened his grip.

"I'm sorry, Achmed," Khardan said lamely, mentally reviling himself for his callous bungling. "But she tried to kill me—"

"It was my hand slew her," Mathew said in low tones, "not your brother's. And it is true, she wore a poison ring."

Achmed ceased to struggle; he went limp in Auda's grasp. His eyes closed, and hot tears welled beneath the lids.

"Let him go," Khardan ordered.

"He'll alert the guards!" Auda protested.

"Let him go! He is my blood!"

Auda, with an ill grace, released Achmed. The young man, pale and shivering, opened his eyes and stared into Khardan's. "You had everything! Always!" he cried hoarsely. "Did you have to destroy the one thing that was mine?"

A sob shook him. "I hope they kill you, everyone of you!" Turning, running blindly, the young soldier plunged into the garden's sweet-smelling foliage. They could hear him crashing heedlessly among the plants.

"Don't be a fool, Khardan! You can't let him go!" Auda held his knife poised.

The Calif hesitated, then took a hurried step forward. "Achmed—"

"Leave the boy be," came a stern command.

Abul Qasim Qannadi, Amir of Kich, stepped out from the shadows of an orange tree. The perfume of late morning hung heavy in the garden—roses, gardenia, jasmine, lilies. The palm trees whispered their endless secrets, a fountain gurgled nearby. Somewhere in the darkest shadows a nightingale lifted his voice in his pulsing song—trilling a single, heart-piercing note until it seemed his small chest must burst, and then holding it longer still.

The Amir was alone. He was not dressed in armor but clad in loose-fitting robes, thrown casually over one arm. One shoulder was bare, and from his wet hair and the glistening of oil upon his skin it seemed he had just come from his bath. He looked tired and older than Khardan remembered him, but that may have been because he was not king in a divan but a half-dressed man in a garden. Certainly he had not ridden with his troops this morning, nor—apparently—had he been present to watch the entrance or greet the Imam upon his arrival into the city.

"Assassins?" asked the Amir, looking coolly and unafraid at the sunlit blade of Auda's dagger.

"No," said Khardan, putting his own body between the Paladin and the Amir. "I come as Calif of my people!"

"Does the Calif of his people always sneak through holes in the wall?" Qannadi asked drily.

Khardan flushed. "It was the only way I could think of to get in to see you! I had to talk to you. My people . . . They say they're going to be slaughtered this next dawning!"

Qannadi's brown and weathered face hardened. "If you have come to beg—"

"Not beg, O King!" Khardan said proudly. "Let the women and children, the sick and the elderly, go free. We"—he gestured out past the palace walls toward the desert—"my men and I, will meet you in fair and open battle."

Qannadi's expression softened; he almost smiled. He glanced where Khardan pointed, though there was nothing to be seen but tangled, flowering vines and waxy-leafed trees. "There must be very few of you," the Amir said in a soft voice. He turned his penetrating gaze to Khardan. "And my army numbers in the thousands!"

"Nevertheless, we will fight, O King!"

"Yes, you would," said Qannadi reflectively, "and I would lose many good men before we succeeded in destroying you. But tell me, Calif, since when does the desert nomad come to issue a battle challenge with his women and"—his gaze lingered on Auda—"a Paladin of the Night God.

"Or, perhaps not women plural but woman alone." Qannadi considered Zohra gravely, speaking before Khardan could reply. "Flowers bloom in the desert as beautiful as in a king's garden. And more courageous, it would seem," he added, noting that Zohra's defiant eyes were fixed on him, not lowered in modesty as was proper.

There was no time for propriety, however. A word from Qannadi and the intruders in his garden would face the Lord High Executioner, who would see to it that they left this world in agonized slowness. Why hadn't Qannadi said that word? Khardan wondered. Was he toying with them? Hoping to find out all he could? But why bother? He would soon have everything they knew ripped from their mangled bodies.

"And you." Qannadi had been obliquely studying Mathew ever since the beginning of this strange conversation, and now his eyes finally settled on the object of their curiosity. "What are you?" the Amir asked bluntly.

"I—I am a man," Mathew said, crimson staining the smooth, translucent cheeks.

"I know that . . . now!" Qannadi said with a wry smile. "I mean what manner of man are you? Where are you from?"

"I am from the land of Aranthia on the continent of Tirish Aranth," said Mathew reluctantly, as though certain he would not be believed.

Qannadi simply nodded, however, though he raised an eyebrow.

"You know of it?" Mathew asked in wonder.

"And so does the Emperor," the Amir remarked. "If Our Imperial Majesty has his way, I might soon see this homeland of yours. Even now, Quar's Chosen readies his ships to sail the Hurn Sea. So you are the fish bone that has been sticking in Feisal's gullet."

Mathew blinked in confusion, not understanding. Qannadi smiled, but it was a smile that was not reflected in the eyes, which remained somber and sober. Khardan shifted uneasily. "The Imam received word that one of the followers of your God—I forget the name. It is not important." He waved a hand as Mathew would have spoken. "One of the followers who were presumably all struck down on the shores of Bas still lived and walked our land. And not lost and alone, but with friends, it appears.''

He was quiet, thoughtful. Khardan waited nervously, not daring to speak.

''So Meryem is dead''—Qannadi's voice was smooth—''and it was you who struck her down.''

The blood drained from Mathew's face, leaving it livid, but he faced the Amir bravely and with a quiet dignity. ''I did what I thought right. She was going to murder—''

''I know all about Meryem,'' Qannadi interrupted.

''But it was not you who sent her, was it, O King?'' said Khardan in sudden understanding.

''No, not I. Not that I wouldn't have slept easier nights knowing she had succeeded,'' the Amir admitted with a smile, which this time warmed the eyes embedded in their web of wrinkles. ''You are a danger, nomad. What is worse, you are an innocent danger. You have no conception of the threat you pose. You are not ambitious. You cannot see beyond your dunes. You are honorable, trustworthy, trusting. How does one deal with a man like you in a world like this? A world gone mad.''

The smile faded from the weary eyes. ''I tried to insure that you left it. Oh, not through Meryem. I sent her there the first time, sent her to spy on you. And when she reported that your tribes were allying against me, I did you honor, though you did not know it. I sent you death in the form of Gasim, my best Captain. I sent you death in battle, face-to-face, blade-to-blade. Not death by night, with poison, in the guise of love.''

''The Imam,'' said Khardan.

''Yes.'' Qannadi drew a deep breath. ''The Imam.'' He paused. In the silence they could hear the murmur of the falling water. The nightingale had hushed his song. Beyond the walls, in the distance, could be heard the cheering of the crowd growing nearer. The procession was wending its way to the Temple. ''So you come here to ask for the lives of your people,'' the Amir continued, and his voice chill. ''I refuse your demand for battle. It is senseless. A waste of lives I can ill afford to spare. Let the conquered cities I control get whiff of this, and they would go for my throat.

"And now what do you do, Calif? What do you do with a woman whose eyes are the eyes of the hawk? What do you do with a man of an alien land where, they say, men possess the magical powers of women? What do you do with a Paladin of the Night, who has a blood curse to fulfill?"

Khardan, startled at these words striking so close to home, could not, at first, reply but only stare at Qannadi, trying to fathom the man's intent. He couldn't. Or if he did, it was only dimly, as a man sees through a storm of swirling sand.

"I will go to prison and die with my people, O King," the Calif said calmly.

"Of course you will," said Qannadi.

One corner of the mouth sank deep into the weathered cheeks. Raising his voice to the call that could sound over the pounding of hooves, the rattle and press of battle, the Amir shouted for his guards.

"What about Achmed?" Khardan asked hurriedly, hearing the stamp of booted feet on the garden path. Zohra stood proudly, head high, eyes flashing. Mathew watched Qannadi in silence. Auda ibn Jad thrust his dagger into some secret, hidden place and stood with his arms folded across his chest, a smile as dangerous and dark as Qannadi's on his lips. Khardan kept a wary eye on him, expecting him to fight—uncomfortable when he didn't.

"My brother should know the truth about the girl," the Calif pursued.

"He knows the truth. It festers in his heart, nomad," said Qannadi. "Would you yank out the arrow and let the barbs rip out his life? Or would you let it work its way out slowly, in its own time?"

"You love him, don't you?"

"Yes," Qannadi answered simply.

"So do I." The guards had come and taken hold of Khardan and his companions roughly, not sparing Zohra or Mathew but clasping them with firm hands and bending their arms behind their backs. "Keep him away tomorrow, O King," the Calif pleaded urgently, struggling to face the Amir as the guards tried to drag him off. "Don't let him see his people butchered!"

"Take them to the Zindan," said Qannadi.

"Promise me!"

Qannadi made a gesture. A jab to Khardan's kidney, and the Calif ceased to fight, doubling over with a groan of pain. The guards hustled them, unresisting, out of the garden.

Standing on the path, watching the strange group being led away, Qannadi spoke softly, "Your God be with you, nomad."

Chapter 5

Four prisoners started out for the Zindan, but only two arrived.

Zohra never heard what happened, in the confusion of the streets through which they were led, and neither, apparently, did the lieutenant responsible for delivering the nomads to the Zindan. The look upon his face when he turned around and saw that the number of his charges had been reduced by half was laughable.

Indeed, Zohra did laugh, which did not endear her to her captor. "You will not be laughing in the morning, *kafir*!" the lieutenant snapped. "Where are the men—the nomad and his friend?" he demanded of his soldiers, who were staring, dumbfounded, at each other.

"Perhaps they were stopped by the crowd," suggested the prison commandant complacently, folding his hands over his fat belly and regarding Zohra with appreciative eyes.

"Bah!" the lieutenant said, angered and more than half-frightened. It would be his responsibility to report this loss to the Amir. "We weren't stopped by the crowd. Send some of your men out to search."

Shrugging, the commandant ordered several of his prison guards to retrace the lieutenant's steps from the Zindan back to the palace to see if the Amir's soldiers needed aid in bringing in their prisoners. The lieutenant took exception to the commandant's insinuation but—being in no position to vent his spleen—kept silent and aloof and stared intently out the window of the brick guardhouse into the crowded prison grounds.

"What do we do with these two beauties?" asked the commandant, his fingers twiddling.

"Put them with the others," said the lieutenant offhandedly. "They are not to be mistreated."

"Mmmmm." The commandant ran his tongue over greasy lips. "They won't be, I can assure you. I know exactly how to . . . uh . . . handle them." Rising ponderously to his feet he, glanced out the window. "Ah, here come my men, with news from the looks of it."

Mathew took advantage of the opportunity to creep nearer Zohra.

"What has happened? Where is Khardan? What have they done to him?"

"He is with the Paladin, of course," she whispered back. "There is nothing more we can do for them, Mat-hew, nor they for us. Our roads have separated. We are on our own."

The two prison guards arrived at the commandant's office, red-faced and breathless. "We found two of the Amir's men, sir, in a back alley. Dead. Their throats have been cut."

"Impossible! I heard nothing!" said the stunned lieutenant. "Did anyone see anything?"

The two guards shook their heads.

"I will go take a look for myself before I report to the Amir."

"You do that," said the commandant expansively. "And I'll make a special cell ready for you on your return," he muttered gleefully, watching the lieutenant walk stiffly out into the streets.

The prison chief—remembering regretfully the easy life under the Sultan—had little use for the Amir and none at all for his soldiers, a snooty lot who looked down their noses at him and were constantly interfering with what the commandant felt to be his prerogatives in the treatment of the scum assigned to his care.

"Treat you well! That I will, my flowers!" Gazing hungrily at Zohra, he rubbed his hands together. "I would have enjoyed the company of a few others of your kind if that pompous old ass in the palace hadn't kept his soldiers snooping about. But tonight everyone will be attending the Imam's ceremony. Your men have deserted you." He sidled up to Zohra with a leering grin, reaching out a flabby hand. "The cowards! But you will not miss them. Tonight I will show you *kafir* what it is to enjoy the company of a real man, one who knows how to—"

Zohra drove her foot hard into the crook of the man's knee. His leg collapsed under him, and he was forced to catch hold of a chair to keep from falling. Pain paled the heavy cheeks; his chin quivered in fury. "*Kafir* bitch!" Grabbing her veiled hair, he yanked her head back and started to kiss her. Zohra's nails flashed for his face. Mathew shoved his arm between the man's body and Zohra, endeavoring to break the embrace and drag Zohra away.

"Commandant," came a voice from the door.

"Ugh?" The prison chief, flinging Mathew from him, turned around, one hand still holding Zohra painfully by the hair.

"You are to report to the Amir," said the guard, endeavoring to look anywhere else but at his sweating chief. "Immediately. Word has already reached him about the murdered soldiers, it seems."

"Hunh!" The commandant hurled Zohra to the floor. Straightening his uniform, he mopped his face and, cursing beneath his breath, waddled out toward the palace walls. "Take them to the compound," he ordered, waving his hand.

The guard stood over Zohra and Mathew, waiting for them to rise, not offering assistance but watching them with an unpleasant grin. The prison guards—dregs of humanity, many of whom had once been prisoners themselves—had been chosen by the commandant for their coarse and brutal natures. To be fair to the commandant, few others except men like these could be found who could stomach the work. A man sentenced to prison in this harsh land often had good cause to envy those sentenced to death. It was only through the intervention of the Imam, who never ceased to try to convert the *kafir*, that the nomads taken prisoner at the Tel had received good treatment. The guards had been forced to keep the women under their care for a month, forbidden to touch them. But that would end this night. The Amir's soldiers and the Imam's soldier-priests would be needed to help control the crowd. No one would pay any attention to the prisoners. Rapine, murder—who would know in the morning, when all were to be slaughtered anyway in the name of Quar? Who would care?

Zohra saw the hatred and lust burn in the man's animal eyes and understood clearly the doom that hung over the prisoners once darkness descended. It would be a night of horrors. Mathew's hand, as he helped her to her feet, was chill and clammy, and she knew that he understood as well. The two exchanged glances, exchanged fear.

Khardan was gone, prisoner of Auda or willing helper. He had not foreseen this danger; it had not occurred to him. Did the women in the prison realize their peril? Could they be made to fight it? Knowing her people, Zohra had no doubt that they would fight. She wondered uneasily if she could convince them to fight using this strange magic, taught by a madman.

They must, she said to herself firmly. They would.

With Akhran's help. Or without it.

Khardan saw, from the corner of his eye, the guard marching behind Auda ibn Jad suddenly drop out of sight. The Calif felt a violent wrenching from behind. The hands of the guard holding his arms clenched spasmodically, then fell away from him. He was free. Turning, astonished, he saw the bodies of the two guards lying in the street, a red slit across each neck.

"This way!" hissed a voice.

"Zohra—" began Khardan, starting after the guards who, having heard nothing, were leading Zohra and Mathew away.

"No!" Auda blocked his path. "Would you ruin all?"

It was the most difficult decision the Calif had ever been forced to make, and he was forced to make it within seconds. *Do you deny me the right to die for my people because I am a woman?* Zohra's words echoed in his head.

Auda was right. Khardan might well ruin the only chance they had. He had to let her go—at least for the moment.

The Paladin and the Calif dived into a dark alley. Two shadowy shapes, blacker than night, flowed before them. A door opened suddenly. Hands yanked Khardan inside a building that was cool, lit only by the sunlight that streamed in when the door stood open. The Calif could see nothing when the door was slammed shut.

"Do you need anything else, *Effendi*?" whispered a voice that was vaguely familiar to Khardan.

"Yes, Kiber. Two robes of the soldier-priests'."

"Only two, *Effendi*?" The man sounded disappointed. "Are we not to help you in your task?"

"No, my life is forfeit for this cause. Your lives are not, and our people must not be wasted." There came a rustling sound, as of a hand clasping a shoulder. "You have been a faithful squire, Kiber. You have served both myself and the God well. My last request of my Lord is that you be knighted in the service of Zhakrin and take my place. Say to him, when you return, that this is my will."

"Thank you, *Effendi*." Kiber's voice was reverent. "The robes will be beneath the blackened stones of what used to be our mosque in this city. You will find food and drink on the floor near the center of this room. It has been my privilege to serve you these many years, Auda ibn Jad. You have taught me much. I pray that I will be a credit to you. Zhakrin's blessing!"

The door opened, the light stabbed brilliantly into the room, then the door shut and all was darkness and silence but for the breathing of the two men left behind.

"Zohra and Mat-hew." Khardan turned. "I must go—"

A hand of iron closed over his forearm. "They do what they must, brother, and so will we. I call upon you now, Khardan, Calif of your people, to fulfill the vow you made to me—of your own free will—in the dungeons of Castle Zhakrin."

"And if I do not," said Khardan, "will you strike me down?"

"No," said Auda softly. "Not I. How does your God deal with oath breakers?"

Reluctant, undecided, Khardan waited for his eyes to adjust to the darkness. He could see ibn Jad now, a vague, gray shape moving in the gloom.

"I should be with my wife, wives," he amended ironically, remembering that Mathew belonged to him. "I should be with my people. They are in danger."

"So they are. So are we. Zohra and Mathew understand how to fight it. Knowing no magic, can you help them? No, you might do them great harm. They are one hope for your people, and you are the other. And your way is with me."

"You don't give a damn about my people," said Khardan, angry, frustrated. He knew Auda was right, but he didn't like it, fought against it. "You'd slit their throats tomorrow if that God of yours ordered it."

Reaching down, he grabbed a loaf of flat, unleavened bread and bit off a great hunk, washing it down with warm, stale-tasting water from a goatskin bag.

"You are right, brother," said ibn Jad, the white teeth flashing for an instant in a grin. "But I know what drives you. That is the bond between us. We are both willing to sacrifice our lives for our people. And you see now, do you not, brother, that the only hope for the life of your tribe is the death of this priest?"

Khardan said nothing, but chewed bread.

"Surely you noticed," pursued Auda, "that the Amir himself sent you off with his blessing."

The Calif's eyes narrowed in a disbelieving scowl. Auda burst out with a laugh, then stifled it instantly, his glance darting toward the closed door. "You fool!" he lowered his voice. "Qannadi could have—should have—ordered his guards to slay us on the spot! The Amir is a traveled man. He knows the people of Zhakrin, he knows my goal. And he sends me off to prison under light guard! Nomads!" Auda shook his head. "You have the sword arms of warriors, the courage of lions, and the guileless souls of children.

"Here is this Amir, a soldier, a military man who would like very much to see the emperor's rule spread as far as possible but would appreciate having some subjects left alive to benefit by it. Men will suffer beneath heavy taxes. They will grit their teeth and bear the lash. But touch a man's religion, and you touch his soul, his life in the hereafter, and that is something most men will willingly fight to protect. I suspect from certain words Qannadi let drop that the southern cities are rife with rebellion. He speaks of his army numbering in the thousands, but I have not seen near that many in Kich. He is spread thin to protect his holdings. The Amir was right,'' the Paladin added more thoughtfully. ''You do not yet know how dangerous you are, nomad. When you do, I think the world will tremble.''

He fell silent, eating and drinking. Khardan was quiet, too, thinking. His thoughts got him nowhere except to despair, however, and he changed the subject. ''Where did those men of yours come from?'' he asked irritably. ''How did Kiber know we were in Kich?''

''The Black Sorceress sent them in case I needed aid. She has sent our people to all other cities where I might have gone in search of Feisal.''

''And how did you contact Kiber?'' Khardan pursued insistently. ''I was with you the entire time! I saw no one. You spoke to no one—''

''I summoned him through my prayers, nomad. Our God sent my squire to me when I called. Never mind, you cannot understand.'' Auda finished the bread and stretched out comfortably on the floor, hands behind his head. ''You should get some sleep, brother. The night will be long.''

Khardan lay down upon the hard-packed dirt floor of the squalid hut. The heat was stifling. No hotter than the desert, perhaps, but he felt closed in, trapped, unable to breathe. Restlessly he turned and twisted and tried in vain to make himself relax.

Zohra. He feared for her, but he trusted her. That was why he had let her go. He knew her courage, none better. She had stood up to him more than once and won. He acknowledged her intelligence, though—he smiled wryly—she would never be wise. Always impetuous, with her sharp tongue and flash-fire temper, she acted and spoke before she thought. He only hoped that this fault did not lead her over the edge of the precipice she walked. But Mathew was with her. Mathew has wisdom enough for both of them, for all three of us, if it comes to that, Khardan admitted to himself. Mathew would guide her and, Akhran willing, they would be safe.

Safe . . . and then what?

Sighing bleakly, Khardan closed his eyes.

A long night.

It could be a very long night. One to last an eternity.

Chapter 6

There not being nearly enough cells to accommodate them, the women and children of the nomads had been herded into the central compound of the Zindan. When first captured several months ago, they had been given houses in the city and the freedom to make their livings as best they could in the *souks* of Kich. In return the Imam had hoped that a glimpse of city life—education for their children, food, shelter, safety—would cause them to renounce their wandering ways and convert to Quar. He hoped that their husbands would leave the desert and come join their families, and a few did. But when month after month passed and most did not, when it was reported to Feisal that the nomad women— though seemingly pliable and obedient—nevertheless kept their children out of the *madrasah* and never passed the Temple of Quar without crossing over to the opposite side of the street, the Imam began to lose patience.

Feisal was feeling desperate, driven. It was an irrational feeling, and he couldn't understand it. He was the most powerful priest in the known world. He had been invited to Khandar, to take over leadership of the church. It would be he, Feisal, who would lead the Emperor's troops across the sea to bring the unbelievers of that far-distant land of Tirish Aranth to the knowledge of the One, True God. Yet here

were a handful of ragtag followers of a beaten-down God
openly defying him, openly making him appear foolish in the
eyes of the world. He, Feisal, had been merciful. He had
given them their chance to redeem themselves. He would
show mercy no longer.

Summarily the word had gone forth, and the nomads,
mostly women and children but a few young men, fathers,
and husbands, had been rounded up and sent to the Zindan.
The men were placed in cells, the women given the compound in which to make their beds, cook their meals, tend
their children. The men were beaten, surreptitiously, when
the Amir's soldiers weren't around. The women and young
girls were watched with hatred and lust. The soldier-priests,
naked swords in hand, stood around them. The spectral figure
of Death often passed by the Zindan, her hollow eyes eager,
watchful.

When Zohra and Mathew entered the compound, shoved
through the gate by the grinning guards, everyone was watching them. Yet no one said a word. The play of children was
hushed, mothers clasping them tightly to the skirts of their
robes. Conversation ceased.

Gritting her teeth, her chin held firm and high, Zohra
walked among her people. Mathew—looking and feeling very
uncomfortable—followed a few paces behind.

Glancing around, Zohra saw many she knew, but nowhere did she see any friends. The women of her own tribe,
the Hrana, despised her for her unwomanly ways that told
them plainer than words the contempt their Princess had for
them. The women of the Akar hated Zohra for being a Hrana,
for marrying their darling, their Calif, and then being insensi-
ble of this great honor, for refusing to cook his meals and
keep his tent and weave his rugs. The women of Zeid's tribe
disliked her for being a Hrana and for the gossip they had
heard about her.

As for Mathew, he was crazy—a man who chose to dress
as a woman to escape death. Akhran decreed that the insane
were to be treated with all courtesy, and so he was treated
with courtesy. Respect, friendship? Out of the question.

The women separated to let Zohra and Mathew pass.
Zohra viewed them all at first with her lip curled in scorn, her

own feelings of hatred and derision burning her blood with poison. Turning, she cast a sideways glance at Mathew, prepared to ask why they had bothered. The expression on his face stopped her cruel words. Compassion, mingled with growing anger, had brought a shimmer of tears to the young man's green eyes. Zohra looked at her people a second time—and saw them for the first time.

Conditions for the people were wretched—inadequate, unhealthful food, little water; they lived daily, literally beneath the sword. Each woman had a space in the crowded compound big enough for her to spread her blanket. Children whimpered in hunger or sat staring out at the world with eyes that had seen too much, too early. Here and there a woman lay on a blanket, too weak to move. There was a sound of coughing, a smell of sickness. Without their herbs and *feishas*, the women had been unable to tend the sick. In a quiet corner of the yard a blanket covered those who had died during the night.

Yet these women, like their men, had one thing that their captors could never take from them: their dignity, their honor. Looking at them, looking at the quiet calm that surrounded them, seeing the eyes that were unafraid, the eyes that held the faith in their God and in each other that sustained them, Zohra felt her own pride ooze from her. The wound in her spirit, lanced and drained of its infection, would at last begin to heal. The eyes of these women were a mirror, reflecting her to herself, and Zohra suddenly did not like what she saw.

Longing for the power of men, she had not seen—or refused to see—that women had their own power. It took both forces, acting together, to keep their people alive, to bring children into the world, to protect and shelter and nurture them. Neither was better nor more important than another; both were necessary and equal.

Respect and honor for each other. This was marriage in the eyes of the God.

Zohra could not articulate these confusing thoughts. She couldn't even begin to understand them. She knew only at that moment that she felt ashamed and unworthy of these courageous, quiet women who had fought a daily, grinding, hopeless battle to keep their families together and maintain their faith in their God.

Zohra's head drooped before those eyes. Her steps faltered, and she felt Mathew's arm steal around her.

"Are you sick, hurt?"

Wordlessly she shook her head, unable to speak.

"I know," he said, and his voice burned with an anger she was startled to hear. "This is heinous! I cannot believe men could do this to each other! We must, we will get them out of this place, Zohra!"

Yes! So help her, Akhran, she would! Lifting her head, Zohra blinked back her tears and searched the crowd for the one she sought. There she stood, at the end of the line of silent women, waiting. Badia—Khardan's mother.

Zohra walked up to the woman, who did not quite come to the Princess's chin. Looking at Badia, Zohra saw the wisdom in the dark eyes whose beauty seemed emphasized by the lines of age in the corners. She saw in those eyes the courage that ran in her son's veins. She saw the love for her people that had led Khardan here to give his life for them. Humbled, Zohra sank to her knees before Badia. Extending her hands, she grasped those of her mother-in-law and pressed them to her bowed forehead.

"Mother, forgive me!" she whispered.

If a leopard had come up and laid its head in her lap, Badia could not have been more astonished. Perplexed, a thousand questions in her mind, Badia reacted from her own compassionate nature and from the secret admiration she had always felt for this strong, obstreperous wife of her son. She remembered that the girl's mother was dead, had died too early, before she could impart a woman's wisdom to her daughter. Kneeling, putting her arms around Zohra, Badia drew the veiled head to her breast.

"I understand," she said softly. "Between us, daughter, there is nothing to forgive."

"My son lives!" The joy and gratitude in Badia's eyes was a gift Zohra was pleased and proud to present her mother-in-law.

"Not only lives, but lives with great honor," said Zohra,

saying this more warmly than she had intended, apparently, for she saw a spark of amusement flicker in Badia's dark eyes.

The two, together with Mathew, spoke quietly during the afternoon, the other women surrounding them. Those in front passed along the news to those in the rear who could not hear. The guards glanced at this huddling of chickens—as they viewed it—without interest and without concern. Let them cackle. Small good it would do them when it came time to wring their necks.

"Khardan has been named Prophet of Akhran, for he brought the djinn back from where they had been held imprisoned by Quar." Not quite true, but true enough to speak of in this hurried time.

"And Zohra is a Prophetess of Akhran," added Mathew, "for she can make water of sand."

"Can you truly do this thing, daughter?" asked Badia, awed. A murmur swept through the women, many—not as forgiving as Badia—regarding Zohra with suspicion.

"I can," said Zohra humbly, without the pride that generally accompanied her words. "And I can teach you to do the same. Just as Mat-hew''—she reached behind for the young man's hand and held it fast—"taught me."

Badia appeared dubious at this and hastened to change the subject. "My son, where is he? Is he with his father?"

"Khardan is in the city—"

There was an excited rustle, an indrawn breath of hope among the women.

"He has come to rescue us!" Badia spoke for all.

"No," said Zohra steadily, "he cannot rescue us. Our men cannot rescue us. We must rescue ourselves." Slowly, carefully, she explained the situation, presenting the dilemma of the nomads, who dared not attack the city to free their families, knowing that their families would be put to death before they ever reached the city walls.

"But the Imam has decreed that we will die by morning!"

"And so we must be gone from this place by morning," said Zohra.

"But how?" Badia glanced helplessly at the tall walls. "Do you propose we sprout wings and fly?"

"Or perhaps you can turn the sand to water, and we will swim out," suggested one of Zeid's wives with a sneer.

Mathew's hand tightened on Zohra's, but his warning was not necessary. The Princess's newly found coolheadedness quenched the hot words that would normally have scorched the flesh of her victim.

"We have come here with a plan to save ourselves. Sul gives magic to men in the land across the sea from which Mat-hew comes. Mat-hew is, in his own land, a powerful sorcerer."

The women exchanged glances, frowning, not quite certain how to react. One must, after all, be courteous.

"But my daughter, he is mad," said Badia cautiously, bowing to Mathew to indicate that she intended no offense.

"No, he isn't," said Zohra. "Well, maybe just a little," she was forced to add in honesty, much to Mathew's discomfiture. "But that doesn't matter. He has a magical spell that he can teach all of us, just as he taught me the spell to make water."

"And what will this spell do?" Badia asked. She glanced around sternly to enjoin silence.

"In my land," said Mathew, speaking uneasily, aware of hundreds of pairs of dark eyes turned upon him, "it is very cool, and it rains nearly every day. We have large bodies of water—lakes and streams—and because of this there is a tremendous amount of water in the air. Sometimes, in my land, this water in the air becomes thick enough that it is possible to see it, yet not so thick that one cannot breathe it." He wasn't getting very far. Most appeared more convinced now than ever before that he was crazy as a horse who eats moonweed.

"It is as if the God Akhran sent a cloud down from the skies. This cloud is known as fog in my land"—he plunged recklessly forward. Time was growing short, they still had much to do—"and when this fog covers the earth, people cannot see very clearly through it, and consequently they feel confused and disoriented. Familiar objects, seen through fog, look strange and unreal. People have lost their way walking through a wood that they have known all their lives.

"With Sul's blessing the sorcerer can create his own

version of this fog and use it to protect himself. Through the power of this spell the magus surrounds himself with a magical fog that has the power of instantly creating doubt and confusion in the minds of all who look at him."

"Does he disappear?" questioned Badia, interested in spite of herself.

"No," said Mathew, "but it seems to those looking directly at the magus as if he has disappeared. He can neither be seen nor heard, for the fog deadens the sound of his movements. Thus he can escape his enemies by slipping away."

Just how he would go through locked gates was another matter, but Mathew hoped a solution to that would present itself when the time came. In his land, where people were accustomed to seeing fog, this spell was only partially efficient and was mainly used by those who found themselves set upon by robbers in the woods or dark alleys of the city. It was, as he had said, a simple spell, one of the first taught to novices and often practiced gleefully to escape their tutors at bedtime. Mathew hoped, however, that the creation of fog in this land where it had never before been imagined, let alone actually seen, would unnerve the guards sufficiently that the men could wrest the keys from them and unlock the gates.

There was one tiny, nagging doubt in Mathew's mind, but he chose to ignore it. At the very bottom of the page in the spell book, written with red ink, was the warning that the spell be used by an individual, never by a group, unless warranted by the most dire circumstances. He supposed some instructor had explained to him the reason for this warning, but—if so—Mathew must have slept through class that day, for he could recall nothing of it. It had never seemed important in his own safe, serene country.

But now . . . well, certainly these could be considered dire circumstances!

"The only things we need to perform the spell," he continued, seeing the quickening interest in the women's eyes and feeling himself heartened, "is the parchment upon which each of you must write it. Zohra and I carry these beneath our robes. And we need water."

"Water?" Badia appeared grave. "How much water?"

"Why . . ." Mathew faltered. "A bowlful apiece. Isn't there a well here in the prison?"

"Outside the walls, yes." Badia pointed.

Mathew cursed himself. Would he never come to accept the fact that in this land water was scarce, precious? He thought frantically. "The guards must bring you water. When? How much?"

Badia's face cleared somewhat. "They bring us water in the mornings and evenings. Not much, maybe a cup each, and that must be shared with the children."

Seeing the swollen tongues and cracked lips of the women— forced to stand or work in the hot sun of the prison compound— Mathew guessed how much they drank and how much they gave to the children. His rage startled him. If he'd had the Imam beneath his hands, he would have choked the life out of the man and never felt a qualm. With an effort he mastered himself.

"When the guards bring the water this evening, you must not drink it but keep it hidden, keep it safe. Not a drop must be wasted, for you will need every bit." And pray Promenthas that is enough!

"Will you do it?" asked Zohra eagerly.

All the women looked to Badia. As Majiid's head wife, she had the right to command a leadership role, and she had earned it during this crisis. All respected her, trusted her.

"What about the young men and some of our husbands, locked in the cells?"

"Where are the cells?" Mathew asked, looking around.

"In that building."

"Any guards?"

"Three. They keep the keys with them so that they may enter the cells when they choose to mistreat those within," Badia answered bitterly.

"Before we cast the spell, we will go first to the guard-house, overpower the guards, and free the men." Mathew said this glibly, completely unaware of how this would be done. "The men must stay near you when the spell is cast, and the fog will surround them as well."

"They will want to fight," said a young wife knowingly.

"We must see to it that they do not," countered Badia

crisply, and there was the glint of steel in the eyes that had
been known to bring even the mighty Majiid to his knees on
occasion. The glint faded, however, and she looked at Zohra
with grave earnestness. "If we do not do this thing, daughter,
what chance do we have?"

"None," said Zohra softly. "We will die here, die"
—she faltered, glancing at the leering guards—"most horribly. And our men will die to avenge our deaths."

Badia nodded. "An end to our people."

"Yes." There was nothing more to say, no softer way to
say it.

The women in the compound waited, watching Badia,
whose head was bowed in either solemn thought or perhaps
prayer. At last she raised her eyes to meet those of her
daughter-in-law. "I begin to see Akhran's wisdom in choosing you to marry my son. Surely the God has sent you here
and perhaps sent us the madman"—she appeared none too
ready to credit even Akhran with this—"to aid us."

Badia turned to Mathew. "Show us what we must do."

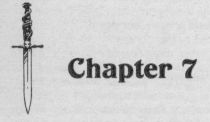

Chapter 7

Night fell over parts of the city of Kich, was held at bay in others. The Temple and the grounds surrounding it shone more brightly than the sun; torches and bonfires hurled back the darkness and kept it outside the barrier that had been erected around the Temple steps from where the Imam was to speak to his people. The great golden ram's-head structure was in readiness. The golden altar having been carried inside the Temple, another altar had been constructed and made holy by the under priests, to prepare for the presentation of the faith of the living and the souls of the dead to Quar.

The Imam and his priests were due to speak to the people at midnight. Feisal intended holding them spellbound and enthralled with his words, whipping them to a fevered pitch of holy frenzy in which they would lose all thought for themselves or for others and exist only for the God. In such a state the smoke of the burning bodies of butchered women and children would not stink with the foulness of murder but would be sweetest perfume and rise like incense to the heavens.

The bright radiance of the lights around the Temple made those parts of the city left to night that much darker by contrast. The streets late in the evening were—for the most part—empty. Except for the occasional merchant who took the very last opportunity to try to wring money out of lingering customers and who was only now shutting up shop and starting to hurry toward the Temple, there were few loiterers. The soldier-priests of Feisal could sometimes be seen, looking for those who might need a little extra persuasion to receive Quar's blessing. Thus it was that two soldier-priests, walking down the street near the Kasbah, attracted little attention.

The street was dark and empty, the stalls across from it shuttered and closed up. The lights of house and *arwat* were extinguished, for none would sleep in their beds this night. At first glance the street seemed too empty, and Khardan cursed.

"He's not here."

"Yes, he is," returned Auda coolly.

Squinting, peering into the deep shadows, Khardan could barely make out, by the reflected light of the flaring flames that lit the sky, a huddled figure squatting next to the wall.

"The followers of Benario will not be worshiping Quar this night, but their own God, to whom these celebrations are meat and drink," said Auda with a grim smile.

True enough. More than one person in that crowd would discover his purse missing, her jewelry stolen. More than one man would return home and find his coffers empty.

Creeping down the streets, keeping a wary eye out for the Amir's soldiers, Khardan caught hold of Auda's arm and pointed.

"Look, not everyone in the palace is attending the celebration."

Far up in a tower shone a single light. There sat—although the two below could not see him—Qannadi. Alone in his room, surrounded by his maps and his dispatches, he was reading each one attentively, concentrating on each, making notes in a firm, steady hand. Yet as he listened to the silence that was breathless, hushed, and tense, the Amir felt himself poised on a dagger's edge. He had set forces in motion over which he had no control, and whether for good or for ill, Sul alone knew.

Auda shrugged. The light was far away and posed no threat. Moving softly, he and Khardan walked over to where the blind beggar sat, his back against the wall of the Kasbah. But though their bare feet had not made a sound that either of them could hear, they had not moved softly enough. The milky eyes flared open, the head turned toward them.

"Soldier-priests," he said, holding out his basket. "In the name of Quar, take pity."

"You smell our clothes, not the men inside," returned Auda softly, dropping several coins in the basket and motioning Khardan to do the same. The Calif handed over his purse, containing every last piece of money of his tribe.

The beggar wrinkled his nose. "You are right. You reek of incense. But I know that voice. What do you want, you who speaks the password of Benario yet is not one of the Brotherhood?"

Auda appeared discomfited by this, and the blind beggar grinned, his toothless mouth a dark, gaping hole in the flame-lit night. Reaching out a groping hand, he took hold of Khardan's arm, clutching him with a grip surprising in one who appeared so feeble and infirm. "Tell me what you will do, man who smells of horse"—the other hand grabbed hold of Auda—"and man who smells of death."

"Death is my mission, old man," said Auda harshly. "And the less you know the better."

"Death is your mission," repeated the beggar, "yet you do not come to kill the Amir, for that you could have done this day. I heard you talking—my ears are very good, you may have noticed. What Benario takes away, he sometimes repays in double measure. I am thinking you might want to know how to find the tunnel that leads beneath the street to the Temple."

"Such information might be of interest," said Auda off-handedly. "If not this night, then another."

The beggar cackled and let loose his grasp of each of them. So hard had he held them, however, that Khardan continued to feel, for long minutes after, the warm pressure of the gnarled fingers on his flesh.

"We have no more money," said the Calif, thinking that this was what the old man was after.

The beggar made a gesture as if to consign money to the nether realms of Sul. "I do not want your coin. But you have something you *can* give me in exchange for my help."

"What is that?" Khardan asked reluctantly, having the

uncanny impression that the unseeing eyes could see through him.

"The name of the woman who stopped to help a poor beggar when her man would have passed him by this day."

Khardan blinked, starting in surprise. "Her name?" he looked dubiously at Auda, who shrugged and indicated impatiently that they needed to make haste.

"Zohra," said Khardan, speaking it slowly and reluctantly, feeling that there was something very special about it and not liking—somehow—to share it.

"Zohra," the blind beggar whispered. "The flower. It suits her. I have it in my heart now"—the empty eyes narrowed—"and it will protect me. When you go through the wall, take four steps forward, and you will come to a flagstone path. Follow this path for a count of forty steps, and you will come to another wall with a wooden door set within. On this door is placed the mark of the golden ram's head. There is no lock, though I'll wager Qannadi has often wished there were," chuckled the old man. "The Imam and his priests have free run of the palace these days. Follow the tunnel, and it will bring you to another door that *does* have a lock. But you, man of death, should have no trouble opening it. The door will bring you out into the altar room itself."

So saying, the beggar slid his hand behind his back. They heard a click and the wall gaped open. Auda darted inside, and Khardan was about to follow when he touched the beggar's bony shoulder. "The blessing of Akhran be on you, father."

"I have the woman's name," the beggar said sharply. "That will be all I need this night."

Puzzled, not understanding, but thinking the beggar was probably touched with madness, Khardan left him and—for the second time that day—sneaked into the forbidden pleasure garden of the Amir's palace.

They had no trouble following the beggar's directions. It was well he gave them in counted steps, for the darkness beneath the trees was thick and impenetrable. They moved as blind men themselves, Khardan forced to grasp Auda's forearm so that they did not become separated. Slipping ahead cautiously, they fended off low-hanging branches, but for the most part found the pathway free of debris and easy to follow. Auda counted the steps under his breath, and they hurried over the flagstone, gliding beneath the perfumed trees, past the dancing fountains. Forty steps brought them to a part of the garden that was less overgrown than the rest. Coming out from under the tree branches, they could see by the red glow in the sky and discovered the door they sought.

The golden ram's head on the wood gleamed eerily. Khardan had the uncomfortable impression that the eyes were watching him with enmity, and he pushed forward to open the door and enter the tunnel but Auda stopped him.

"One moment," said the Paladin.

"What is it? You were the one impatient to get here," Khardan snapped nervously.

"Wait," was all ibn Jad said.

To Khardan's astonishment, the Black Paladin sank down on his knees before the golden ram's head, whose eyes seemed to flare brighter than ever. Removing something from within his robes, Auda held it forth in his right hand. Khardan saw that it was a black medallion, the image of a severed snake worked upon it in glittering silver.

"From this moment," said Auda ibn Jad clearly, "my life is in your hands, Zhakrin. I walk forth to fulfill the blood curse cast by the dying Catalus on this man called Feisal, who has sought to take away not only the lives and freedom of our people, but our immortal souls as well."

Auda reached into his robes and took out an object Khardan recognized easily—the severed-snake dagger. The Paladin held it up in his left hand, level with the medallion. "The hand that holds this dagger is no longer my hand, but yours, Zhakrin. Guide it with unerring swiftness to the heart of our enemy."

Auda's face, turned toward the light, was pale and cold as marble, frozen with an unearthly calm, the cruel eyes dark and more empty than the sightless orbs of the blind man. A chill wind rose and blew through the garden. A wave of evil smote Khardan so that he could barely stand, leaving him weak and shaking and powerless, or he would have turned and fled this place that he knew was accursed.

What am I doing here? the nomad Prince thought in

horror. Was it you who sent me, Akhran, or have I been deceived? Have I been yoked to this evil man by trickery, and will it end with my falling into the dark Pit of Sul and losing my soul forever? What difference is there between Auda and this Feisal? What difference between Quar and Zhakrin? Surely Zhakrin would strive to become the One, True God if he could! What is transpiring in the heavens that has led me to this path on earth?

I would take this wicked priest's life in battle, but I want no part of wrenching it from him in the dark. Yet he will not face me in battle, and how can I save my people other than by striking him down? Help me, Akhran! Help me!

And then Auda spoke, and there was a softness and wry humor in his voice. "One final prayer, Zhakrin. Absolve this man, Khardan, of his vow, as I absolve him of it. When I am dead, he will have no need to avenge my death. If my blood touches him, it will be only in blessing, not a curse. I ask this, Zhakrin, as one who goes forth with the expectation of being with you soon."

Auda bowed his head, raising both dagger and medallion higher to the night.

Khardan leaned back against the wall, shivering, yet feeling somehow that he'd received his answer, if only to understand that he was free to act of his own will. Whatever constraint—if there had truly been one—had been lifted.

Auda, prostrating himself to the ground, rose to his feet. Kissing the dagger, he slipped it into the folds of his stolen priest's tunic. Kissing the medallion, he hung it around his neck.

"It will be seen," said Khardan.

"I want it to be seen," answered the Paladin.

"When they set eyes upon it, they'll know you for what you are and strike you down."

"Very probably. I will live long enough to obtain my objective—my God will see to that—and then it does not matter."

Auda opened the door, but Khardan barred his way.

"I would see and hear this man speak," said the Calif gruffly. "I want to give him one final chance to rescind his order regarding my people. Promise me that before you attack?"

"I am not the only one they will strike down," returned Auda with a fleeting ghost of a smile across the bearded lips.

"Swear, by your God!"

Auda shrugged. "Very well, but only because you could prove a useful diversion. I swear."

Breathing somewhat easier, Khardan moved his arm and entered the tunnel, walking beside Auda.

The door shut without sound behind them.

Chapter 8

"Well, that's tnat," said Sond, staring gloomily at the tunnel door through which his master had just vanished. "We may not enter the holy place of another God."

"We could stay here and guard their way back," suggested Fedj.

"Bah! Who is there to guard against?" retorted Sond sourly. "Everyone is gathering for the ceremony. Only the Amir's bodyguards are about, and there's not many of them. From what I could gather, Qannadi has sent them to reinforce those responsible for controlling the crowd."

"We could go to the Amir's kitchens and see what they have prepared for dinner," suggested Usti, rubbing his fat hands.

"Didn't I hear your mistress calling you?" Sond scowled.

"You have played that trick on me one time too many, Sond," said Usti with lofty dignity. "It is well past dinnertime, lacking only an hour or so of being midnight. There is nothing more we can do here, and I do not think any harm would come of visiting the kit—"

"Usti!"

It was—most definitely—a feminine voice.

"Name of Akhran!" Usti went pale as the belly of dead fish.

"Hush!" ordered Sond, listening carefully. "That is no mortal tongue—"

"Usti! Sond! Fedj! Where are you?" The names were called urgently, yet reluctantly, as if the speaker vied within herself.

"I know! It is that angel of Pukah's!" Sond looked amazed and not entirely pleased. "What can she be doing—"

"You forget the madman," interrupted Fedj. "She is his guardian, after all."

"You are right. It had slipped my mind." The djinn frowned. "She should not be calling like that. It will alert every one of Quar's immortals in the city."

"I will go to her," offered Raja, and disappeared only to return presently with the white-robed, silver-haired angel, looking small and delicate and fragile beside the powerful djinn.

"Thank Promenthas I have found you!" Asrial cried, clasping her hands. "I mean"—she flushed in confusion— "thank Akhran—"

"How may we serve you, lady!" asked Sond impatiently.

"First," interposed Fedj, with a rebuking glance at his fellow, "we want to offer our sympathy for your sorrow."

"My sorrow?" Asrial seemed uneasy, uncertain how to respond.

"Pardon us, but we could not help but notice that our companion, Pukah, had earned—although I'm not certain how—a very special and honored place in your heart."

"It is . . . foolish of me to feel that way, I fear," said Asrial shyly. "It is not right that we immortals should care for each other. . . ."

"Not right!" Touched by her sadness, Sond took her by the hand and squeezed it comfortingly. "How can it not be right, when it was your love for him that brought out the best qualities in Pukah and gave him the strength to sacrifice himself?"

"Do you truly believe that?" Asrial gazed up searchingly into the djinn's eyes.

"I do, lady, with all my heart," said Sond.

"And I, too," rumbled Raja.

"And I. And I," murmured Fedj and Usti, the latter wiping away a tear that was creeping down his fat face.

"But you were calling us," said Sond. "How is it we may serve you?"

Asrial's fears, seemingly forgotten a brief moment, returned, causing the color to leave the ethereal cheeks. "Mathew, and your mistress, Zohra! They are in the most terrible danger, or soon will be! You must come and help them."

"But we may not. We have not been summoned," said Sond, appearing worried, yet not certain what to do.

"That is because they don't know they're going to be in danger!" Asrial wrung her hands. "But Matthew is talking of overpowering guards, and he carries a dagger one of the women managed to sneak into the prison with her. He knows nothing about fighting, and the guards are strong and brutal! You must come with me! You must!"

"We are certainly useless here," prodded Fedj.

"That is true." Sond gnawed his nether lip. "Yet we have not been summoned."

"Yes, we have," said Usti unexpectedly. He pointed a jeweled, chubby finger at Asrial. "*She* summoned us!"

"An angel summoning a djinn?" Sond appeared doubtful.

"Let them argue about it at the next tribunal," said Raja. "I, for one, am going with the lady." He bowed, hand over his heart, to Asrial.

"Are all resolved?" Sond looked at Fedj, who nodded.

"My mistress is so stubborn, she would never summon me," Usti commented. "I will go."

"Not stubborn. Intelligent—knowing well if she summoned what she'd get," returned Sond. "Lady Asrial, we are yours to command. And may Akhran have mercy on us if he ever finds out we worked for an angel!" breathed the djinn, casting a worried glance toward heaven.

Inside the cell block of the Zindan, the prison guard, his face twisted in sadistic pleasure, brought his lash down on the bare back of his victim. The boy writhed in the arms that held him, but he did not cry out, though the effort it cost him drove his teeth deep into his tongue.

"Hit him a couple more times and loosen his voice," said one of the guards, holding the boy by the arms.

"Yes, his screams won't be noticed this night," said the other.

The guard did as he was requested, striking at the back that was already marked with scars from previous "punishment" sessions. The boy flinched and gasped but swallowed his scream and managed to cast a triumphant glance at his captors, though blood ran from his mouth and he knew he would pay for that look with the next blow.

The next blow did not fall, however. The guard stared in astonishment as the whip was plucked from his grasp by a gigantic, disembodied hand and carried up to the ceiling.

The three prison guards stood near the cell block's outer door where they could keep watch and see if any of the Amir's soldiers might be snooping about. This area was their usual location for "punishment," as could be witnessed by the numerous splotches of dried blood upon the stone floor. Surrounded by three walls, it was not a large area and it grew smaller still when it was filled with the massive bodies of four huge djinn (Usti taking up as much room sideways as the others did lengthwise).

"Ah, you seem to have dropped this," said Raja, the huge whip dangling between his thumb and forefinger. "Allow me to return it to you, *sidi*!" He deftly wrapped the whip around the guard's neck.

The guard fought and struggled, but he was no match for the djinn and was soon trussed up like a chicken, as Usti commented, licking his lips.

"Order them to let the boy go," said Raja.

The guard glared balefully at the djinn. "I take no orders from you, *kafir* spawn. And I'm not afraid of you, either. When Quar gets hold of you, he'll make you wish you'd never been born!"

"As intelligent as he is handsome," said Sond gravely. "Let us see if he will reconsider."

Raja, nodding, gave the lash a twist and a tug that sent the man spinning wildly across the floor, smashing headfirst into the far wall. His limp body sagged to the floor. The other two guards suddenly released their hold on the boy, who staggered and fell at their feet.

The boy was up almost at once, moving more hurriedly when he saw Sond coming toward him. The djinn stared at the boy closely. "A Hrana?" he asked.

"Yes, O Djinn," said the boy warily, staring at Sond and recognizing him as an immortal belonging to his enemy. Seeing Sond in company with Fedj—the immortal of his own tribe—the boy did not know quite what to make of it.

"You are brave, Hrana," said Sond approvingly. "What is your name?"

"Zaal." The boy's wan face glowed at the djinn's praise.

"We have need of you, if you can walk."

"There is nothing wrong with me," said the boy, though he grimaced with every move he made.

Sond concealed his smile. "Where do these dogs keep the keys to the cells, Zaal?"

"On their fat bodies, O Djinn," answered Zaal with a glance of bitter hatred.

Sond walked over to investigate. "You do seem to be carrying a monumental load in the area of your gut, *sidi*," the djinn said, speaking to the guard who was slumped against the wall. "I will relieve you of some of that weight, *sidi*, if you will but give me the keys to the cell."

The guard, coming around with a groan, retorted with a foul oath suggesting something physically impossible that Sond might do to himself.

Fedj slammed the man's head against the wall with a swift backhand. "What kind of language is this? How do you expect the boy to learn to respect his elders if you speak in that manner, *sidi*?"

"I grow tired of this," growled Raja impatiently. "Let us kill him and take the keys."

'Oh, ho!'' howled the guard, glaring around them from rapidly swelling eyes. "You don't frighten me! I know that you djinn may not take a human life without the permission of your God. And where is the Wandering Akhran these days? Dead, from what we hear!" The guard spit on the floor. "And good riddance. We'll soon make short work of his followers!"

"He has a point," said Fedj. "We cannot take a human life."

"Ah, but is he human?" Usti inquired complacently. "Is any of this . . . this"—the djinn waved a hand at the guards—"excrement?"

"An interesting technicality," commented Fedj.

The other two guards looked fearfully to their leader, who turned exceedingly red.

"What do you mean? Of course, I'm human!" he blustered. "You just try killing me and see how much trouble you'll be in!"

"Is that a command, *sidi*?" inquired Sond politely. "If so, I hasten to obey—"

"N-no!" stammered the guard, realizing what he'd said. His voice raised to a shrill shriek as the djinn loomed over him. "No!"

"The keys, *sidi,* if you please?" Raja held out a gigantic hand that would have engulfed the guard's neck without any effort at all.

With a vicious snarl the guard lifted the keys from a belt around his waist and hurled them, cursing, to the floor. At Sond's gesture, Zaal leaped to pick them up and brought them to the djinn.

At that moment there came a rattling on the door, and it burst open under the combined strength of Mathew and several nomad women, who flooded into the room, daggers flashing in their hands.

Mathew gasped and stared at the massive djinn. His face was grim. He had obviously prepared himself either to meet death or to mete it out, and this unlooked-for respite literally stole away his breath.

Walking forward, Sond bowed low before the astonished wizard and held out the keys. "These are yours to do with as you will, O Sorcerer. Have you further need of us this night?"

"I . . . I— You don't serve me," Mathew faltered.

"No, Lord Sorcerer. We serve one who serves you." Sond looked to a point above Mathew's shoulder, to the boy's great confusion. "The Lady Asrial."

"Wait!" said Zohra. "Yes, we need you. The gates—"

"Raja, come with me! Hush!" Sond cocked his head, listening. "My master!" he cried in a hollow voice, and vanished.

Raja disappeared. Fedj and Usti remained, staring at each other uncertainly.

Then they heard the sound—a strange and eerie sound that made the hair on the neck rise and sent a shiver over the bodies of all those in the room.

The frenzied yell of a rampaging mob.

And it was coming closer.

Chapter 9

The tunnel ran from the palace, dipping down below the busy central street of Kich, rising up to the newly built and lavishly decorated Temple of Quar. The tunnel's floor was smooth, swept clean, and dry, its condition undoubtedly maintained by the servants of the Imam. Torches stood in wrought-iron sconces affixed to the wall, their flames smoking and wavering in the draft that came with the opening of the door from the garden. Entering the cool, dimly lit tunnel, Khardan marveled at the peace and silence below ground when all above him was noise and chaos.

Moving swiftly, neither speaking—bodies tensed and readied for danger—the Calif and the Paladin of the Night traversed the narrow tunnel. They traveled a long distance. Glancing back, Khardan could no longer see the entrance. The floor they walked began to slope upward, and they knew that they were nearing the Temple. They moved more cautiously and quietly—out of instinct more than necessity. With the praying, swaying, chanting, screaming crowd located almost directly above them, they could have held a game of *baigha* down here, complete with horses, and no one would have heard them.

Soon the two could see, glittering in the torchlight, the eyes of another golden ram's head, and they knew they had reached their destination. Auda carefully studied the door. Carved of a single, massive block of marble, it sealed shut the tunnel entrance like a plug. There were no seams that Khardan could see, no ring embedded in the rock with which to pull it open, and he was just about to suggest—in mingled relief and frustration—that their way was blocked when Auda laid his hands on either side of the golden ram's head, fingers covering the eyes, and pressed.

There was a click and a crunch, and the stone door shivered slightly, then began to turn, revolving around some unseen central post. Stepping back, Auda waited with obvious impatience for the slow-moving stone to swing into an open position. Beyond the door, Khardan could hear a voice speaking, and he tensed, thinking they had been discovered. He soon realized—from the tone and the few words he could catch—that it was the Imam, and he was apparently addressing his priests prior to going out to address the crowd.

No one had noticed them.

"How did you know how to work this?" Khardan whispered, his hand gingerly touching the locking device.

"What, the door opening?" Auda glanced at him, amused at the nomad's awe. "I have operated hundreds more intricate and complicated than this. In the palace at Khandar, one must be a mechanical genius to move from one's bedroom to the bath."

"What about the door on our way out?" Khardan asked uneasily, looking behind him again, though it had long since been lost to sight. "Will it be locked? We may be needing to get through it in a hurry!"

"There was no such device used on entering that door. I doubt if *you* will find one on your return." The Paladin coolly emphasized the singular. "This door is much newer, built more recently than the tunnel itself, which is—I should judge—probably as old as the palace. Who knows where it led before this? Some private playground of the Sultan's, I should imagine."

The stone had almost completed its rotation, moving in oiled silence.

"But why a locking device here and none at the palace?" Khardan argued.

Auda made an impatient gesture. "Undoubtedly the entryway is guarded by the Amir's guards, nomad. Except on this one night, when they were needed to help with the crowd or"—his thin lips tightened in a grim smile—"perhaps Qannadi gave the guards orders to be elsewhere."

Spend the cold winter in here, little mouse, said the lion, pointing to his throat. *It is warm inside and safe, very safe . . .*

Khardan shivered and, suddenly anxious to end this, pushed past Auda and slid through the crack in the stone that was barely wide enough to admit one man turned sideways.

He entered a murmuring, whispering chamber, warm with the heat of many bodies, smelling of perfumed oil and incense and melting candle wax and sweating flesh and holy zeal. It was lit by the light of many, many candles flickering somewhere on the altar at the center of the room. Khardan caught only a glimpse of that altar, his view blocked by the soldier-priests. Their backs turned to the Calif, they were staring straight ahead with rigid intensity at the Imam, who stood in their midst. No one had heard the opening of the stone door, which was not surprising, considering the reverberating voice that held them mesmerized. But they must feel the rush of cool air on their backs, and Khardan realized with a pang that it would be necessary to shut the door. Hurriedly he glanced about the candlelit altar room, trying to find something that would give him a point of recognition for the tunnel door, which—he could see—would become one with the wall once it was shut. But to his astonishment, Auda left it open. Taking the nomad by the arm, the Paladin hustled Khardan well away from the entry. They moved silently, their backs pressing against the wall, until they were almost halfway around the large room.

Of course, Khardan thought to himself, the blood beating in his ears, it doesn't matter if they discover someone has entered their sanctuary. They're going to know in a matter of moments anyhow, and this insures our way out.

"—Sul's Truth seen in Quar," the Imam was saying. "The world united in worship of the One, True God. A world freed of the vagaries and interference of the immortals. A world where all differences are smoothed out, where all think alike and believe alike—"

As long as they think and believe like Quar, added Khardan silently.

"A world where there is peace, where war becomes obsolete because there is no longer anything over which to fight. A world where each man is cared for, and no one will go hungry."

Slaves are cared for, in a manner of speaking, and rarely allowed to go hungry since that would inhibit their usefulness. A chain made of gold is a chain still, no matter how beautiful it looks upon the skin.

Khardan turned to glance at Auda, to see how the Paladin was reacting to this, and saw suddenly that ibn Jad was no longer standing beside him. The Paladin of the Night had been absorbed into the darkness that was his birthright, the darkness that watched over and guided him.

Khardan was alone.

"We will go forth!" continued Feisal, and Khardan could see above the heads of those standing in front of him the priest's thin arms upraised in exhortation. "We will go forth and bring this message to our people!"

Khardan began to move, impelled by fear that ibn Jad might strike before the Calif could speak, impelled by the need to try to bring sight to the blind eyes of these fools, impelled by his own need to make this one last attempt to save his people.

"In the eyes of Quar, all men are brothers!" Feisal lifted his voice to a shout.

"If that be so," answered Khardan, his own cry reverberating off the walls, the candles flickering in the rush of cool air that was flowing in through the open doorway, "if that be so, then prove it by freeing your brothers—my people—who are sentenced to die with the dawn."

Gasps and shouts of alarm rippled through the crowd. The soldier-priests reacted with a speed that astonished Khardan. Before those around him could have comprehended who he was, they turned on him. Rough hands grabbed his arms, steel cut into his back, a sword was at his throat, and he was a prisoner before the last words had been spoken.

"Let us slay him now, Holy One!" One of the soldier-priests pleaded. "He has defiled our Temple!"

"No," said Feisal in a gentle voice. "I know him. We
have spoken before, this man and I. He calls himself Calif o
his people. Calif of barbarous bandits. Yet there is hope fo
his salvation, as there is hope for all, and I would not deny i
to him. Bring him to me."

The order was obeyed with alacrity, and Khardan wa
thrown at the Imam's feet, where he lay on the floor, sur
rounded by a ring of steel.

Slowly, as his eyes raised to meet the liquid-fire eyes o
the priest, Khardan rose to his knees. He would have stoo
face-to-face with this man, but the hands of the soldier-priest
pressed on his shoulders, holding him down.

"Yes, you know me," Khardan said, breathing heavily
"You know me and you fear me. You sent a woman to try t
murder me—"

A roar of outrage met these words. The hilt of a swor
smashed into Khardan's mouth; pain burst in his skull. Grog
gily, tasting blood from a split lip, he spit it on the floor, an
he raised his throbbing head to look into Feisal's eyes. "It i
the truth," he said. "That is how Quar will rule. Swee
words in the daylight and poisoned rings in the night—"

He was prepared for the blow this time and took it as bes
he could, averting his head at the last possible moment t
keep it from breaking his jaw.

"No more!" said Feisal, seeming truly distressed by th
violence. He laid his delicate fingers on Khardan's bleedin
head. The touch was hot and dry, and the fingers quivered o
the nomad's skin like the feet of an insect. The intense
zeal-maddened eyes gazed into Khardan's, and such was th
strength and power of the soul within the priest's frail bod
that the Calif felt himself shrinking and shriveling beneath th
fiery sun blazing above him.

"This man has been sent to us, my brethren, to show u
the overwhelming difficulties we will face when we go ou
into the world. But we will surmount them." The finge
stroked Khardan with hypnotic sensuality. The candleligh
the pain, the noise, the smell of the incense, began to caus
everything in his sight to swirl around him. He found a foca
point only in the eyes of the priest. "Who is the One, Tru

God, *kafir*? Name him, bow to him, and your people are freed!''

The fingers soothed and caressed. Feisal was certain of triumph, certain of his own power and the power of his God. The soldier-priests held their breath in awe, awaiting another miracle. Had they not seen, countless times, the Imam lead one poor benighted soul after another into the light?

Khardan had only to speak Quar's name. He held the life of his God in his hands. The Calif shut his eyes, praying for courage. He knew that—by speaking the next words—he doomed himself, doomed his people. But he would save Akhran.

"I know nothing of One, True God, Imam," he gasped, the words bursting past a barrier erected by Feisal's stroking fingers. "I know only *my* God. The God of *my* people, *Hazrat* Akhran. With our dying breath, we will honor his name!''

The fingers on his face grew cold to the touch. The eyes stared down at him not with fury but with sorrow and disappointment. "Give me a knife!" Feisal said softly, holding out his hand to his priests. "Death will close this man's mortal eyes and open those of his soul. Hold him fast, that I may do this swiftly and cause him no undue suffering." The soldier-priests gripped Khardan's arms. One tilted back his head, exposing his throat.

Khardan did not fight. It was useless. He could only pray, with his last conscious thought, that Zohra would succeed where he had failed. . . .

"Give me a knife," Feisal repeated.

"Here, My Lord," said a voice, and the body of the Imam suddenly jerked and went rigid, the eyes opened wide in astonishment.

Auda yanked his blade free. He raised his hand to strike again, when Feisal wheeled and faced him. An expanding stain of blood was spreading across the back of the priest's robes.

"You would murder me?" he said, staring at Auda, not so much in anger and fear, but in true amazement.

"The first blow I struck was for Catalus," said Auda coolly. "This I strike in the name of Zhakrin." The silver dagger, the hilt decorated with a severed snake, flashed in the light of the candles on the altar of Quar and plunged into the breast of the Imam.

Feisal did not scream or try to dodge the blow. Flinging wide his arms, he received the deadly blade into his body with a kind of ecstasy. The dagger's hilt protruded from his flesh. Clutching at it, the Imam staggered and lifted his eyes to heaven. Prayerfully holding up his hands—crimson with his own blood—Feisal tried desperately to speak.

"Quar!" He choked and pitched forward across the altar, falling in his last prostration to his God.

Paralyzed with shock and horror, the soldier-priests stared at the body of their leader. It seemed impossible that he could die and they waited for him to stand, they waited for a miracle. Yanking the black medallion from around his neck, Auda tossed it upon the corpse—then, darting forward, the Paladin caught hold of Khardan. He managed to drag the nomad from his captors' nerveless grip and propel him, stumbling, toward the door in the wall before the fury hit.

"They have slain the Imam! The Imam is dead!" The wail was terrible to hear, rising to a shriek of insane rage as they realized their miracle was not forthcoming. "Kill them!" came one cry. "No," cried others, "capture them alive! Save them for the torturer!" And still another cry, "Slay the prisoners! The blood of the *kafir* to pay for his! Slay them now! Do not wait for morning!"

A sword flashed in front of Khardan. Smashing its wielder in the face, the Calif grabbed the blade from the man's hand, drove it into the body, and ran past without looking to see his enemy fall. The door stood ajar. The path to it was clear. No one had thought to block it.

"Nomad! Behind you!" came a hollow cry.

Khardan turned, knocked aside a sword-thrust in time to see the Paladin sinking to the floor, one soldier-priest driving a sword into his back, another into his side.

Yelling wildly, Khardan slashed at the priests, killing both of them. Others, undaunted, longing to martyr themselves and die with their Imam, ignored the danger of his flashing blade and hurled themselves at him. Grabbing hold of Auda, hacking to the left and the right, Khardan dragged the wounded man to his feet.

The Calif saw out of the corner of his eye a priest raise a knife. He held it poised to throw, but it was knocked from his hand by another, who howled, "Do not kill them! The executioner must make them pay! A thousand days and nights they will live with their agony! Capture them alive!"

Savage faces loomed near Khardan. He heard blades whistle, saw them flash, and beat them off, thrusting and kicking, clawing and fighting his way inch by inch toward the tunnel door. One hand kept hold of the Paladin, and he did his best to try to protect Auda, but he could not be on all sides at once, and he heard another groan escape the man's lips, felt the body shudder.

"Sond!" cried Khardan desperately, though he knew the djinn could not enter the Temple.

"Sond!" Fire spread along Khardan's upper arm and tore through his shoulder blade. But he was at the tunnel door, and he had made it to safety.

Then it was that he realized, in despair, that he had no idea how to shut the door. Khardan turned at the entrance, intent on forcing them to kill him or be killed, when a huge hand caught hold of him and plucked him through the opening.

Sond flung Khardan into the tunnel. Reaching back inside, the djinn grabbed Auda and dragged him into the tunnel.

"Now?" grunted Raja.

"Now!" yelled Sond.

The gigantic djinn thrust the stone door shut with a shove of his powerful hands. A screech of protest and a grinding, snapping sound indicated that the mechanism had been rendered useless. They could hear heavy blows being rained on the door from the other side.

"How long can you hold it?" Khardan gasped for breath.

"Ten thousand years, if my master desires!" Raja boasted, grinning broadly.

"Ten minutes will be sufficient," breathed Khardan, and groaned in pain.

"You are hurt, *sidi*," said Sond solicitously, bending over the Calif.

"No time for that now!" Khardan shoved the djinn away from him and staggered to his feet. "They're going to murder our people! Did you hear? I must reach them and—" Do what against that raging mob? "I must reach them," he added with the sullenness of despair. "Go to the tunnel entrance and deal with any guards who come!"

"Yes, *sidi*," and Sond vanished.

Khardan turned to Auda, who was sitting where Sond had left him, his back propped up against the tunnel wall. The front of the Paladin's robes was covered with blood. He held his hand over a wound in his side, the fingers glistening wetly in the torchlight. Khardan knelt beside him. "Come, quickly! They'll be sending guards—"

Auda nodded wearily. "Yes, they will be sending guards. You must hurry."

"Come on!" said Khardan stubbornly. "You could have saved yourself. You risked your life to save me. Vow or no vow, I owe you—" Putting his arm around the Paladin's back, the Calif felt blood instantly soak his sleeve.

Understanding, Khardan slowly stood up.

"I can go no farther," Auda said. "Leave me, nomad. You owe me nothing. You must save"—he coughed, a trickle of red ran from his mouth—"your people."

Khardan hesitated.

"Go on!" The Paladin frowned. "Why do you stay? Our oath is dissolved."

"No man should die alone," Khardan said.

Auda ibn Jad looked up at him and smiled. "I am not alone. My God is with me."

His eyes closed, he sank back against the wall—whether dead or fainted, Khardan could not tell. He looked at the Paladin, his thoughts a confusion of grief and loss mixed with the knowledge that, by rights, he was doing wrong to mourn the death of this evil man. This man who had given his life for his.

The Calif turned to Raja, who stood with his back against the door, his arms folded across his chest, as unmovable and implacable as if a mountain had been dropped across the tunnel. "See to it that they do not take him alive," Khardan commanded. "Then come as soon as you judge you can safely leave. I will have need of you."

"Yes, *sidi*," said Raja, his face grim. His hand closed over the hilt of his scimitar.

Turning, with a final puzzled, unhappy glance at the seemingly unconscious Paladin, the Calif ran down the tunnel.

Auda ibn Jad opened his eyes and gazed after the nomad. "Many fine sons . . ." the Paladin said softly, and died.

Chapter 10

The young men of the nomad tribes came from their cells in the Zindan, blinking dazedly at their unexpected freedom. Their eyes then widened in astonishment at seeing their mothers and sisters and wives crowding into the small blockhouse. There was a moment's joy that faded at the sound of the mob—a dread baying at the silver moon, which shone brightly as the sun in the black sky, as if the Gods—unwilling to miss the sight—had turned a watch light upon this grim scene.

"Fedj, go see what has happened," Zohra commanded. The djinn fled in obedience, and the Princess of the Hrana nervously twisted and tugged at the rings upon her fingers as she waited in fear and impatience for his return. Deep within she knew the cause, she knew the reason the voices howled in fury and wailed in grief. But she waited stolidly for the djinn and prayed to Akhran with every heartbeat that she was wrong.

"Princess!" cried the Fedj, appearing with a bang that shook the cell block. "The Imam is dead! Murdered!"

"Dead!" No cheers from those gathered together. Only pale faces and frightened eyes. They knew what this meant for them. Mothers clasped their arms tightly around their babes, brothers caught hold of sisters, husbands grasped their wives.

Fedj spoke their fears aloud. "Feisal was assassinated in

Quar's Temple, and now his soldier-priests come to wreak their vengeance upon our people.''

"Those who did it,'' said Zohra in a thin, tight voice. "What of them?''

"The mob will be here in moments, Princess!'' Fedj said urgently, sweat glistening on his face. "We must prepare to defend—''

"What of those who murdered the Imam?'' Zohra persisted coldly.

Fedj sighed and shook his head. He had not wanted to speak this news. "The priests cry to the mob that the two men responsible were captured and . . . slain.''

"Ah!'' The knife that slew Feisal might have entered Mathew's heart. Clutching his hands together, he stared pleadingly at the djinn as if to beg the immortal to take back his words.

Zohra felt something within her die, something she had not known lived until now, when it was too late. Her first thought was a wish to die, too, rather than face the terror that she knew was coming. So proud of her courage, the Princess of the Hrana was as frightened and lost as the newborn lamb standing, bleating, in the darkness beside the wolf-ravaged body of its protector.

Princess of Hrana.

He is dead, and now I am responsible for the people.

The knowledge rose out of the emptiness within her. Already Zohra could hear pounding footsteps. The prison guard had been alerted to the mob's coming. There would be confusion among the guards, perhaps even panic, for a mob might not take the time to distinguish between jailed and jailer before it tore them to shreds.

"People of Akhran, hear me!'' Zohra raised her voice, and its timbre of courage, darkened with grief, made her people attentive. "The mob comes to murder us in the name of Quar. There is hope, but only if we think and act as one. Men, your women hold your lives in their hands. This is a time for magic, not swords, if indeed you had swords. Listen to your women, follow their instructions. Your lives and the lives of those you hold dear rest on this!''

She caught hold of Mathew and thrust the young man

forward. His veil had come loose from his head; the red hair
blazed like flame in the torchlight. Clad still in women's
clothes, he might have been a ludicrous sight but that his own
bitter loss and sense of responsibility as great as Zohra's gave
him a dignity and power that made many regard him with
awed reverence.

"From this moment on, Mat-hew—a mighty sorcerer in
his land—is your leader. He comes to you in"—she drew a
shaking breath but spoke without faltering—"Khardan's name.
Obey him as you would the Calif. Fedj, Usti." She summoned the djinn. "Go see to the opening of the gate."

The djinn bowed low to her, and this alone impressed
many of the doubtful.

Fearful that she could say no more without breaking down
and revealing how weak and frightened she really was, Zohra
turned and walked rapidly out of the blockhouse into the
compound. She had seen the men frowning with displeasure,
but she had no time to spare for argument and persuasion.
Behind her, she could hear the voices of the women explaining—
or attempting to—in hurried, broken whispers. The men would
go along with them, she hoped and prayed. At this moment
they had no choice They had no weapons except for what a
few had managed to wrest from the cell-block guards. Once
the magic started, Zohra hoped, they would see it work and
so do what was needed.

She heard Mathew speak a few words to the women. Not
many— there wasn't time for many, and they knew already
what they had to do. The screams and yells of the mob were
getting closer. Looking out past the tall gates, Zohra could
see the lights of their torches reflected against the sky. The
commandant was up on the battlements, racing first to one
end, then the other, shouting conflicting orders that sent his
men scurrying about in aimless confusion. Occasionally, re-
gretting the loss of his own private plans of savagery, the
commandant was seen to shake his fist at the approaching
mob. But for all that, Zohra knew he would open the gates to
them.

We will be ready. Pray Akhran, pray Sul, pray that
strange God of Mat-hew's that this works!

The women flowed out of the prison, shapeless forms in

their robes and veils, moving silently on slippered feet. Their
men and boys, those few there were, came after them. Grim,
defiant, doubtful, they obeyed their Princess more because
they were in the habit of following those in command than
because they understood or agreed with her. The nomads had
survived through long centuries by granting obedience to their
Sheykhs. In their Princess the people saw the authority they
were accustomed to obeying.

A touch on Zohra's arm caused her to turn her head.
Mathew had come up unheard to stand beside her. The young
wizard was very pale, and there were smudges of darkness
beneath the eyes, but he appeared calm and quietly confident.
He and Zohra exchanged one eloquent look—a sharing of
inner, wrenching pain, and that was all. There was time for
nothing more. They separated, Zohra going to her place in the
center of the women, who were separating themselves into
rows as Mathew had instructed. The sorcerer took his place at
their head.

Gathering her children and her menfolk around her, each
woman knelt upon the ground of the prison compound. Before each stood a precious cup of water that had been saved
from the evening meal. Hands fumbled here and there, drawing out the parchments each had spent the afternoon laboriously copying, the words written crudely with the only ink
they had—their own blood. The guards had been amused at
this undertaking, not understanding it and making rude jokes
about the *kafir* writing their death testaments.

Each women held the parchment above the cup as Mathew
had taught them. All tried to concentrate, to shut out the
sounds of approaching horrors, but it was difficult, and for
some, impossible. A muffled sob and the soothing murmur of
one woman comforting a sister and bidding her regain her
courage came to Mathew's ears. He, too, heard Death—in
hideous aspect—drawing near and wondered at his own lack
of fear.

He knew the answer. He was sheltered, once again, in the
comforting arms of Sul.

His own cup of water standing before him, Mathew began
to chant the words of the spell. He chanted loudly, so that the
women could hear him and remember the difficult pronuncia-

tion. He chanted loudly, so that his calm voice might help obliterate that of the shrieking soldier-priests bearing down on them.

He heard the women repeat the words after him, slowly and faltering at first, then more loudly as they gained confidence.

Mathew sang the chant three times, and at the third recitation the words on his parchment began to writhe and crawl and tumbled off into the water. He could tell, by the sudden catching in the throats of those who followed him, that the same phenomenon was happening to at least most of the women in the compound. There would be some, to be sure, who would fail; but Mathew was counting upon the likelihood that the numbers who would succeed would be such that the fog would enshroud them all and allow them to slip through their enemies unharmed.

The words tumbled into the cup, the water began to bubble and boil, and then, slowly, a sinuous cloud drifted upward. Mathew looked out across the compound. The sound of cheering and of thudding feet breaking into a run told him that the mob had come within sight of the prison. The young wizard did not turn around but continued to face his people and chant—as much to keep their minds occupied with the soothing flow of words as to continue to work the spell. For now he could see hundreds of tendrils of mist rising into the air. He heard the men's deep-voiced murmurings of awe and dread mingle with the delighted cries of small children who, not comprehending their danger, were enchanted by the magic their mothers were performing.

The fog spiraled up from Mathew's cup and encircled him, beginning at his feet and writhing and twisting about him like a friendly snake.

It was doing the same with the women, surrounding them and those who were near them, drawing them into Sul's protective coils. It muffled sound, flattened out and rendered harmless the terrifying shouts of the mob. The nomads lost their fear and gathered together, and the fog grew thicker and more dense around them.

The misty cloud was swelling and spreading with a rapidity that astonished Mathew. He had thought they would be fortunate if it enveloped each woman and those she kept near her. But the mist—shining an eerie white in the moonlight—was wafting and drifting through the compound with what Mathew could have sworn was some type of intent purpose, as though it sought something and would not be satisfied until it had gained its goal.

A sharp thorn of doubt pricked Mathew's satisfaction. He saw the warning again, printed clearly in red ink in the book. *Large numbers of magi should never resort to the use of this spell except in the most dire circumstances.* And suddenly he remembered words that followed, words that had seemed irrelevant, almost laughable, in his land:

Make certain there is a plenteous source of water.

Mathew understood. He knew what he had created, he knew why the warning had been given. He foresaw clearly and with horror what must happen, but there was no way he could stop it.

The magical mist crept over the ground—delicate white arms with thin, long, curling fingers, guided by a searching, central intelligence. Some of the prison guards had taken to their heels. Others had leapt from the wall and were striving to push open the gates that, for some reason, wouldn't budge (not with the bulk of an invisible Usti planted against them). Their commandant stood on the battlements above them, alternately berating his guards for their slowness and pompously shouting out to the mob that he was in charge here.

The mob, led by the soldier-priests, ignored him. They stormed the walls, those at the front being crushed against the stone by those surging forward in the rear, and began flinging themselves at the wooden gates in an effort to force them open.

The commandant, still shouting, was beginning to get the dim impression that no one was listening to him and that he might want to consider removing himself from this area, when a panicked cry from one of his guards caused him to turn around and stare into the compound with bulging eyes.

His prisoners were gone! Vanished in a cloud that had seemingly fallen from heaven and swallowed them up. The commandant couldn't believe it. He stared into the writhing, shifting mist, but he could neither see nor hear any signs of life. The commandant's fat body shook until his teeth rattled in his head. There was no doubt in his mind that the God of these people had come to their rescue, and all knew Akhran to be a vengeful, wrathful deity. The mob was still hurling itself against the gates; the wooden doors were starting to splinter and crack from the combined weight of hundreds pressed against them.

The guards in the compound gazed fearfully at the mist whose delicate fingers seemed to be reaching for them. Usti and Fedj, nearly as terrified of Sul's magic as the guards, had abandoned their posts and were staring at each other helplessly. Frantically the guards sought to unlatch the gates and push them open—a crowd of humans held no terrors for them compared to this accursed fog. But the pressure on the gates from the mob pushing in the opposite direction held them firmly shut. The guards could not escape and could only watch, in tongue-tied horror, the first tendrils curl about their feet.

Their screams split through the voice of the mob like a whistling sword blade, so awful that even the most fanatical of those clamoring for blood beyond the prison walls hushed and listened.

The commandant, atop the wall, saw the fog curl around the legs and trunks of his screaming men, saw them wrapped in clutching fingers of shimmering white. He saw the mist boil and writhe. The screams ended, dying to dry whispers. The fog lifted and continued on, rising thicker than before.

On the ground in front of the gates lay several piles of dust.

A plenteous source of water!

One wizard casts this spell in a land of deep wells and moist air and travels safely within his cloud, the spell drawing the water from all around it. Many wizards cast the spell together, and the same thing occurs, except that the power is so much greater, the spell so much stronger, that it demands more water to sustain it. A land of lush vegetation, of gigantic trees and green grass and thick foliage, a land of running streams and raging rivers, a land of rain and snow—the spell has all the water it needs.

But cast the spell in an arid land, a land of sand and rock, where water is measured in precious drops, and the spell thirsts and becomes desperate to maintain itself, sucking life from what sources it can find.

Mathew saw the guards fall, he heard their screams. He saw the commandant race back and forth across the wall in a frenzy of terror, trying to avoid the clutching fingers of the mist, falling victim to them at last with a frightful, gurgling wail. Mathew watched the magic drain what small amount of water there was in the wood of the gate, saw the beams wither and wilt. He heard the joyous shouts of the mob change to cries of amazement, and he heard the first wails of those tangled in the mists, the awful screams as they felt their lives being sucked from their bodies.

He, who had agonized over killing one, would now be responsible for the deaths of hundreds!

Zohra was beside him, grabbing hold of him.

"Mat-hew!" Her eyes glistened through the fog. "We have done it! They run before us!"

She didn't know. She had not seen, or if she had, she didn't comprehend. Or maybe she didn't care. After all, Mathew tried to force himself to remember, the mob had intended a death for her people as horrible as that to which they themselves were falling victim. He had to think of that, concentrate on that, or go mad.

Zohra led her people forth. Surrounded by the magic, moving slowly that they might not outrun the mist, the nomads walked calmly through the withered prison gates, trampled the dust of their enemies beneath their feet. The fog, growing stronger as it fed, billowed around them—a silvery, lethal cloud rolling down the streets of the city of Kich.

Chapter 11

Hearing no warning from Sond that the tunnel exit was guarded, Khardan sprang incautiously through the open door into the Amir's pleasure garden. The Calif was brought up short by a soldier clad in helm and armor, a naked sword blade gleaming brightly in the moonlight. Casting a bitter, reproachful glance at the djinn, who was standing nearby, Khardan raised his bloodstained weapon to attack.

"*Sidi*," Sond said quietly, "it is your brother."

Khardan, lowering the sword, stared.

Slowly the young man removed the helm and let it fall to the paving stone, where it clattered and rolled beneath a bush. Without the helm, which had hidden the face, Khardan could recognize the features of his half brother, but that was as far as recognition went. In all other aspects, this tall, battle-scarred young warrior was a stranger to the Calif.

And though Achmed had dropped his helm, he held his sword poised and ready.

"I knew it had to be you," he said in a toneless voice, his eyes dark shadows in the pale face. "I knew when I heard that the Imam had been slain that it was you who did it, and I knew where to find you. The other guards ran to the Temple, but I knew—"

"Achmed," said Khardan, attempting to moisten dry lips

with a tongue nearly as dry, "the priests have gone to murder our people!"

The young soldier nodded. "Yes," he said, and no more.

Khardan could hear angry shouts and the clashing of weapons. He shot a swift glance at Sond, who shrugged his shoulders helplessly as if to beg, "I will gladly obey you, *sidi*, but what would you have me do?"

I could send the djinn against the mob, Khardan thought frantically, but it would take an army of 'efreets to stop those fanatics. He could order Sond to transport him, take him away from this place. But what about his brother? Achmed was one of his people, no less important. Must he lose him forever, completely?

"Come with me!" Khardan held out a hand. "We will fight—"

"No!" Achmed stared at the outstretched hand, and Khardan saw that it was covered with blood. His own, Auda's, the Imam's . . . The young soldier's words echoed hollowly in his throat. "No!" he repeated, and though the night air was cool, Khardan saw sweat glisten on his brother's face. Achmed glanced behind him, toward the prison, though nothing could be seen of it beyond the tall walls of the palace. There was horror in his eyes now, and it was obvious he was seeing not the present, but the past. "There is nothing you can do! Nothing I can do! Nothing!"

"Achmed," Khardan said desperately, "your mother is in that camp!"

"Maybe." The young man tried to shrug, though his face was strained, and as the howls of the mob grew louder and more savage, the sweat trickled down his cheekbones. "Maybe she is dead already. I haven't seen her or heard from her for months."

"Very well, then, brother," Khardan said coldly, "I am leaving. If you want to stop me, you had better be prepared to kill me, for that is the only way—"

The horror-darkened eyes turned to him, and slowly the nightmare vision receded. Once again they were cool and impassive. Achmed fell into a fighting stance. Khardan did the same, pain shooting through the wounded shoulder that was already stiffening. It would not be an even match. The

Calif felt his strength flag. The only thing keeping him going was fear for his people, and that was more an impediment than a goad, for he felt his mind distracted. He could not concentrate. He could not help letting his gaze dart toward the area of the prison, and thus he nearly missed his brother's first lunge. Moonlight flashing on the blade, a timely slip of Achmed's foot on loose rock, and the reaction of the appalled djinn, who leaped between the two, saved Khardan.

"*Sidi*! You are brothers!" gasped Sond, grabbing the bare blades of both scimitar and sword in his crushing hands and holding them apart. "In the name of the God—"

"Don't preach to me of the Gods! I have seen what has been done in the name of the Gods!" Achmed cried furiously, trying to wrench his weapon free. He might as well have tried to pull the raw ore out of the mountain where it was forged. "There are no Gods. They are only an excuse for man's ambition!"

"Then how do you explain Sond? An immortal?" shouted Khardan angrily. He could tell by the sound that the mob had reached the prison.

"Sond deludes himself into believing he is mortal," Achmed returned. "Look, he bleeds!" It was true; blood rolled down the djinn's arms from where the blades bit deep into his ethereal flesh. "Just as we mortals have deluded ourselves that immortal beings exist!"

Khardan was finished. Stepping back, he released the handle of the sword, and it fell from the djinn's bloodied hand. "Sond, take me to—"

An explosion shook the ground; a blast of air whooshed from the tunnel, followed by a rumble and another blast of flying rock and debris. Coughing and choking, both brothers peered through clouds of dust to the tunnel entrance to see Raja emerge from the ruin, covered with dirt and rubbing his hands in satisfaction.

"You need not fear pursuit from that direction, *sidi*," said the djinn, bowing to Khardan. "And," Raja added, more gravely and solemnly, "it is a fitting tomb for the one who lies within. Only Death will be able to find him now."

"May his God be with him," Khardan responded, subdued. He did not look at Achmed, but—turning his back on the young man, making himself a target if his brother chose—he bent down to pick up his sword. "Sond, you and Raja come with me—"

He ceased speaking, lifting his head to hear more clearly. The sound of the mob had changed—no longer threatening, but threatened.

"What is it?" asked Khardan, puzzled.

"Great magic is being worked, *sidi*," said Sond in awe. "It is as if Sul himself had entered this city!"

Hope alive within him, Khardan ran down the pathway through the garden, heading for the opening in the wall. He had not waited for his brother, detected no footsteps behind him for long moments, and then—to his vast but unspoken relief—he heard booted feet pounding after him.

"This way," said Achmed when Khardan, in his excitement and confusion in the moonlit garden, would have taken the wrong path.

Together they reached the place where the thornbush mounted on a sliding platform could be moved aside and the sliding panel in the wall revealed. To Khardan's astonishment and consternation, the hole gaped open. He could have sworn that the blind beggar had closed it behind them when he and Auda had entered. Warily, the Calif slowed his pace. Achmed bounded ahead, however, and was out into the street, motioning Khardan to follow.

"The way is clear, *sidi*," said Sond, growing thirty feet in height and peering over the wall. "The street is empty except for the beggar."

"What of the prison?" Khardan demanded, when he had emerged to stand beside the old man, who sat cross-legged and relaxed, in the street.

"It is covered with . . . with a billowing mist, *sidi*," said Sond, his eyes huge with wonder. "I have never seen anything like this in all my centuries!"

"Nor will you, ever again!" cackled the beggar.

Khardan started off at a run, but a hand caught hold of his tunic and yanked him backward with such force that he nearly lost his footing. Turning in anger, thinking it was Achmed, the Calif found himself staring down into the milk white eyes that glistened with a terrible brilliance in the moonlight. A bony, scrawny hand, reaching upward, clutched a handful of fabric.

"It will be your death if you approach, for though the magic saves those within, it is killing those without. Look! Look! It comes!"

How the blind eyes saw it, Khardan was never to know, but at the end of the street, winding among the shuttered stalls of the bazaars, long white tendrils crept over the paving stone, licking thirstily at whatever they touched. Stalls fell with a crash, the wood sucked dry of what small moisture was within. A man, darting out into the street to see what was happening, was caught in the silvery white hands, the water of his body wrung from him as though he were a piece of clothing on wash day. The fog moved past, leaving behind a heap of dust that only moments before had been living flesh and blood.

Khardan began to back up, his eyes fixed on the approaching, curling mists with awe and horror. "We must run!"

"There is no escape," said the blind beggar with a peculiar satisfaction, "except for those sheltered behind stone walls. And for those whose hearts are one with those wielding the magic. Quick, sit beside me!" The old man tugged peremptorily on Khardan. "Sit beside me and bring to your lips the name of someone in your heart, someone who moves safely through that mist and thinks of you!"

"Sond, is he right?" questioned Khardan, unable to take his eyes from the drifting, deadly fog.

"I think it is your only hope, sidi," sid the djinn. "I can do nothing. This is Sul's work." He glanced uneasily at a wide-eyed Raja, who gulped and nodded. "In fact, we are going to leave you for the moment, sidi. We will return when Sul is gone!"

"Sond!" Khardan cried in fear and exasperation, but the djinn had vanished.

"Quickly!" the old man cried, dragging the nomad down.

The fog was almost upon him. Khardan saw Achmed, squatting beside the old man. His brother's face was livid.

"The name!" the beggar insisted shrilly. "Speak a name,

if one exists in your heart, and pray that she is thinking of you!''

Khardan licked his parched lips. "Zohra," he murmured. The mist, as if catching sight of the moisture-laden bodies, bounded toward him. "Zohra!" he repeated, and involuntarily shut his eyes, unable to watch. He could hear the old man muttering Zohra's name, too, and recalled—with a start— how the beggar had demanded that name in payment for opening the wall. Near him, Achmed was whispering his mother's name with a sob in his throat.

A chill as of a cavern dug deep in the earth clutched the nomad's ankles, freezing the very marrow of his bones. The pain was intense, and it was all he could do to keep from screaming. Feverishly, he repeated the name over and over and with it an image of Zohra came to his eyes, the faint smell of jasmine to his nostrils. He saw her riding her horse through the desert, the wind tearing off the headcloth, blowing the black hair behind her—a proud, triumphant banner. He saw her on their bridal bed, the knife in her hands, her eyes gleaming with triumph, and he felt the touch of her fingers, light and delicate, healing the wound in his flesh she herself had inflicted.

"It is passing," said the beggar, with a deep sigh.

Khardan opened his eyes, stared around to see the mist retreating, being sucked back down the street as if by a massive intake of breath. An ominous quiet settled over the city.

"Your people are safe, man who smells of horse *and* death," said the beggar, his toothless mouth a black slit in his skull-like head. "They have passed through the gate and are out in the plains. And there are none left alive to follow."

Despite his thankfulness, the Calif could not help but shudder. The night wind rose, and he saw with a start a cloud drifting up into the night air. It was not fog. It was a cloud of dust—a dreadful, oily kind of dust. Shivering, Khardan stood up and glanced back down at the beggar.

"I must go to them. Will it be safe?"

"Once they understand that they are free, the magic will begin to dissipate. Yes, it will be safe."

Khardan turned to Achmed. "Will you go with me, brother? Will you come home?''

"This is my home," said Achmed, standing and facing Khardan. "All I love is here."

Khardan's gaze shifted, almost as if drawn, to the solitary light in the palace. He could see the silhouette of a man—arms folded—standing at the window, staring—where? Down at them? Out over his ravaged city?

"This means war, you know that," Achmed continued, following Khardan's gaze. "The Amir can't let you get away with this."

"Yes," Khardan agreed absently, his mind too much occupied with the present to consider the future. "I suppose it does."

"We will meet on the field, then. Farewell, Calif." Achmed's voice was cold and formal. He turned to make his way back through the opening in the wall.

"Farewell, brother. May Akhran be with you," said Khardan quietly. "I will bring news of you to your mother."

The armored back stiffened, the body flinched. For a moment Achmed halted. Then, straightening his shoulders he passed through the wall without another word. The stone wall ground to a close behind him.

"You'd best hurry, nomad," said the beggar. "The soldier-priests are dead, but there are still many alive in this town who, when the shock is past, will be crying for your head."

"First I would ask who you are, father," said Khardan staring intently at the old man.

"A humble beggar, nothing more!" Curling up like a mongrel dog, the old man lay down upon a ragged blanket pressing his back against the stone walls to garner some of the lingering warmth left behind by the heat of the day "Now get you gone, nomad!"

The beggar shut his eyes, wriggled his body into a more comfortable position, and a rasping snore rattled in his lungs.

His fear for his people gone, Khardan felt a great weariness come over him. His shoulder burned with pain, his arm had stiffened beyond use. Every move seemed an effort, and he dragged himself through the moonlit streets, keeping his hand over his mouth to avoid inhaling the horrid dust that stung his eyes and coated his skin with a greasy feel. The city of Kich appeared to have fallen victim to a marauding army—an

rmy that attacked wood and water and plant and humans and
eft stone alone. Sick and wounded, he stared at the devasta-
ion in dazed disbelief, and his brother's words sank home.
Yes, this would mean war.

Reaching the place where he had left the horses, Khardan
aw only large piles of dust. The last of his strength was
draining fast, and he knew he could not go far on foot. Grief
or the gallant animal that had carried him to glory and
gnominious defeat wrung his heart, when he heard a shrill
vhinny that nearly deafened him. Hastening forward, hope
;iving him strength, he found all four horses alive and well
nd dancing with impatience to leave this awful place.

Curled up in one of the stalls, shivering with fear, was the
oung boy the Calif had set to watch them.

"Ah, *sidi*!" He sprang to his feet when he saw Khardan.
'The cloud of death! Did you see it?"

"Yes," said Khardan, letting his horse nuzzle and sniff
nd snort at the strange smells, including that of his own
*lood. "I saw. Did it come here?"

Useless to ask, seeing the mounds of dust beneath camel
*lankets, smaller mounds that had once been donkeys, and
ven mounds that had once been—he didn't like to think.

"It came and they . . . they all died!" The boy spoke
dreamily, in shock. "All but me! It was the horses, *sidi*! I
wear, they saved my life!" The boy buried his head in the
tallion's flank. "Thank you, noble one! Thank you!" he
obbed.

"They know in their hearts those who care for them,"
aid Khardan, rubbing the boy's head fondly. "As do we
ll," he murmured with a smile. "As do we all. Now go
ome to whoever cares for you, young man!"

Jumping onto the animal's back, the Calif guided the
orse from its stall, the others following obediently behind.
And here were the djinn to help him. Together they rode out
f the city of Kich, galloping through the gates that stood
pen, the gigantic wood posts withered and shrunken, the
ron bands that had held them together fallen in a heap on the
ust-covered ground.

Chapter 12

Khardan returned to the Tel to find an army awaiting him. It was not the Amir's.

It was the Calif's own.

The ride from Kich had been wild and joyous on the part of the *spahis,* reunited with their families. Singing songs of praise to Akhran, waving their banners high in the air, extolling the virtues of their Prophet and Prophetess, the horsemen of the Akar, the shepherds of the Hrana, and the *mehariste* of the Aran were united at last in glorious victory over their common foe. The only persons on that uproarious, saber slashing ride who were not drunk with triumph were the Prophet, Prophetess, and the young man whom the nomads now called Marabout, a term Mathew came to understand—with a sigh—meant to them a sort of insane holy man.

Husband and wife met formally and spoke coolly when reunited, then turned and went their separate ways. Wounded and exhausted, supported by the djinn, Khardan missed seeing the flash of joy that illuminated and softened Zohra's hawk eyes. Zohra did not notice the pride and admiration in the eyes of Khardan when he praised her for her courage and her skill in saving the people. A wall stood between them that neither—it seemed—was willing or able to scale. It had been built over months. Every stone was an angry word, a demeaning remark, a bitter moment. The mortar that held the wall intact was both centuries old and newly mixed, compounded of blood, jealousy, and pride. What it would take to shatter the wall, neither knew, though each lay awake during the cool, star-filled nights and pondered the matter long and hard.

That was not all each was being forced to confront within his or her own soul. Going to war with the Amir when death was certain and the nomads had everything to gain and nothing to lose was one thing. But going to war when their families were restored to them, when the nomads had everything to lose and little to gain, was a completely different matter. Yet Khardan knew he had no choice. Qannadi dare not let this affront go unpunished. The Amir must exhibit, to those captive cities of Bas, what happens to those who defy him. The only question in Khardan's mind was whether to gather his forces, take the initiative, and strike the city while it was in confusion, or to wait in the desert, build up his strength, force his enemy to come to him, and fight on his own ground. Both sides of the argument had its advantages and disadvantages and occasioned the gloom and abstraction that hung over the Calif during the ride back to the Tel.

Zohra was having her own problems. The sudden ability to see herself and to take pride in herself as a woman was, at this early stage, uncomfortable and unsuited to her. Thus she kept herself aloof from the other women during the ride, though they made no secret of the fact that they now accepted her as one of themselves and would have welcomed her to their group with pleasure. A few began to remark that their Princess had not changed after all, but their disparaging words were cut short by Badia, who alone thought she understood somewhat of the battle raging in the breast of her daughter-in-law. The fight for self-understanding is like fighting an enemy who never stands in front of you but always attacks from the rear, who is never seen clearly, who continually jabs away at every weakness. Only the most fortunate get the best of him.

As for Mathew, every time he shut his eyes, he saw again the people dying all around him. He asked himself bluntly—as Khardan had asked him when the young wizard had killed

Meryem—if he wanted to reverse the outcome and die at the hands of his enemies. But he knew that the memory of those withering faces seen dimly through the fog would remain with him into the next life, and that there he would be held to account.

One by one, every fine precept in which Mathew had believed had been hacked up, slashed open, and left to die in the sand of this harsh land. Mathew tried to bring his old, comfortable beliefs back to life, but it was impossible even to summon their ghosts. He was so far changed from the boy who had walked the forested, water-rich land of Aranthia that he seemed to have split into another being. But what amazed and truly confounded him during the long nights, when he had nothing to do but think and stare at the stars, was that he looked back on that boy wistfully, sadly, but no longer with regret. Perhaps he wasn't a better person, but he was a wiser, more thoughtful one. He knew himself to be truly one with every other human, no matter how different in manners and appearance, and he found an abiding sense of comfort in this knowledge.

The only question remaining to him was what his future held. Mathew began to see the road he was traveling nearing its end, and he knew in his heart he must soon be called to make a choice. The Amir had mentioned ships sailing to the continent of Tirish Aranth. He could return to Aranthia, the land of his birth, or remain in Tara-kan, the land of his rebirth. Right now he had no idea what that choice would be.

The other members of the three tribes had no such besetting preoccupations. The three Sheykhs rode side by side at the front of their people and were the best of friends, the closest of cousins, the most loving of brothers. Instead of attempting to rival each other in insults, they sought to outdo each other in flattery.

"It was because of the courage of the Hrana that our people escaped the prison," said Majiid expansively, patting Jaafar on the shoulder with a friendly hand.

"But without the fortitude of the Akar, the courage of the Hrana would have been for naught," said Jaafar, leaning out—somewhat nervously—in his saddle to twitch at Majiid's robes, a sign of respect.

"I may safely say," added Zeid from the height of his swift-moving camel, "that without the courage of the Hrana and the fortitude of the Akar, the Aran would, at this moment, be feeding the jackals."

"Ah," cried both the other Sheykhs as one, "without the wisdom of the Aran it is *we* who would be feeding the jackals."

And so on and so forth until the djinn rolled their eyes and Khardan became so disgusted with all of them that he took to riding at the end of the line.

Thus it was that the Sheykhs, and practically everyone else in all three tribes, topped the crest of one of the gigantic dunes overlooking the Tel and came to a halt, staring down in loudly exclaiming wonder, and calling for their Prophet.

Fearing, irrationally, that Qannadi had somehow stolen a march on him and was in the Tel waiting his return, Khardan rode his horse at breakneck speed, driving the animal, foundering and sliding, up to the top of the dune.

Spread out before him in such numbers that the floor of the desert now resembled a vast city were tents of every shape and description and size—ranging from small ones designed for one man to rest through the heat of the day, to others full seven poles long. In addition, there seemed to have fallen an unseasonable and unusual rain during the time they were gone, for the oasis was green and thriving. Women crowded around the well, drawing water in plentiful supply. Children played and splashed in the pools. Horses, camels, donkeys, and goats were tethered and hobbled near the water or roamed the camp. On the Tel itself the cacti known as the Rose of the Prophet was green and thriving, though as yet no blossom appeared.

Their return had evidently been expected—a group of riders were seen detaching themselves from the camp and dashing madly toward the dune. In their hands they carried *bairaq*—tribal flags—not weapons. Khardan, along with the Sheykhs, rode down to meet them on the desert floor, leaving the people on the dune to watch and speculate in tones of wonder.

"We seek one known as the Prophet of Akhran," shouted a man clad in the uniform of a soldier of some unknown army.

"I am called the Prophet of Akhran," said Khardan, riding forward, his face dark and glowering. "Who are you, and who are these who camp around the well of the Akar?"

"Those who come to do you honor, Prophet," said the soldier, dipping his flag to the ground as did those who rode with him. "We come to ride with you into battle against the Amir of Kich!"

"But where are you from?" asked Khardan, so amazed that he wouldn't have been at all surprised if the man had answered modestly that he'd dropped from the moon.

"From Bastine and Meda, from Ravenchai and the Great Steppes—everywhere the Emperor has placed the heel of his boot on a man's neck."

Seeing a familiar face, Khardan gestured to an old man seated on an aged horse—both man and beast had outlived several generations of offspring. "Abdullah, come forward."

The *aksakal*, one of the tribal elders of the Akar, rode his ancient beast up to the line of Sheykhs. Mindful of where it was and who it carried, the horse kept its neck arched proudly and lifted its rheumatic feet as high as possible.

"What is this, Abdullah?" Khardan asked the old man sternly. "You were in charge in our absence. Why have you allowed this?"

"It is as the man says, O Prophet of our God," answered the *aksakal*, speaking with dignity. "They began arriving almost the day you left, and there has been a steady flood of them ever since. I was minded at first to turn them away, but that night a storm struck such as I have never seen this time of year. The water poured from the heavens. It rained four days and four nights, and now the well is filled, the pools are deep and cool, the desert blooms, and here is an army at hand. Should I be so mad as to throw the blessings of *Hazrat* Akhran back in his face?"

"No," said Khardan, troubled and wondering why his heart was heavy when all burdens should be lifting from him. "No, you did right, Old One, and we are grateful."

"Hail, Prophet of Akhran!" shouted the soldier, and the

desert resounded with the cheers that came from the throats of
the multitude.

They assisted Khardan from his horse and bore him on
their shoulders with boisterous ceremony to the largest, most
luxurious tent in the camp. Zohra was no less honored,
though she would have been, if she could have escaped.
Nothing would do but that she must be led on a pure white
donkey to her own tent, hardly less magnificent than Khardan's.
Here she was greeted by women bearing costly silks and
jewels, food and sweetmeats. Usti was in a rapturous state
and refused to be parted from his "dear Prophetess" no
matter what threats she issued under her breath.

Mathew, too, was given a tent, though no one offered to
carry him to it or dared touch him at all but stared at him as
he passed in silent, reverent awe. The Sheykhs were accorded
the same honors as their children, and even Jaafar was observed to look happy for the first time that anyone, including
his own elderly and infirm mother, could remember. Zeid
suddenly recalled that he was uncle to both Prophet and
Prophetess, though how this could be no one knew; but all
were pleased at any excuse to honor anyone, and the rotund
Sheykh was granted his due.

As soon as Khardan was settled in his tent and had
thought wearily of going to his bed, the people began to form
lines outside, demanding an audience with their Prophet.
Khardan could not refuse and, one by one, they brought him
their problems, their needs, their wants, their requests, their
suggestions, their demands, their gifts, their offerings, their
daughters, their good wishes, and their prayers. Meanwhile,
in another tent, the Sheykhs and the djinn were gleefully
planning to go to war.

Chapter 13

The talk and celebration lasted far into the night. The noise of shouting, drunken laughter, and tramping, dancing feet roared into a wild cacophony that drove Mathew to seek the quiet and solitude of his tent. Walking through the crowded camp, his ears battered by noise, he found himself missing the sounds of the night desert—the incessant, eerie song of the wind; the throaty growls of night animals about their business; the restless murmurings among the horses catching scent of a lion; the gentle reassurances of those who guarded the herds; the clicking of the palm fronds.

How many nights, he wondered, had he lain in his tent and listened to those noises in terror and loneliness, and hated them? Now, in place of this hubbub of humanity, he longed for them back.

He passed Zohra's tent on the way to his and decided to enter and talk to her. She had been so silent and preoccupied upon the journey, and he, too, had been taken up with his own thoughts and wonderings. They had not spoken more than a handful of words since that awful, triumphant night in Kich. Peering into the open tent, he saw Zohra surrounded by women—chattering and laughing and exclaiming over the latest gifts that came pouring in—perfume, jewelry, bolts of silk and wool, candied rose petals, slaves, brass lamps enough to light a palace. Usti—his fat face radiating warmth until it seemed them might douse the lamps and rely instead upon the djinn—hovered about the Prophetess, accepting the gifts with unctuous gratitude, casting a critical eye upon them, and then nearly driving his mistress wild by whispering in her ear how much each was really worth.

Mathew lingered, watching, unnoticed. The Princess Zohra that he knew would have fled this perfumed prison, caught her horse, and galloped away among the shifting dunes. The young wizard waited to see if this would happen. His thoughts touching her, Zohra raised her dark eyes and looked into his, and he saw there that very longing. But he saw also resignation, enforced patience, rare self-discipline. His astonishment must have been visible, for a flush deepened the rose in her complexion. She smiled a rueful, twisted smile and shrugged slightly as if to say, "What else can I do? I am Prophetess of Akhran."

Mathew smiled back, bowed to the Prophetess, and left. And just as he missed the wind and the song and the lion's growl, so did he miss the impetuous, unpredictable Princess.

Weary from the long ride, Mathew lay gratefully among his cushions. He was just wondering if it would be worth his while to douse his *chirak* and hope sleep would come to him, when the tent flap opened suddenly. A dark figure, the *haik* covering its face, darted in. Avoiding the lamplight, it sank back swiftly into the shadows. Reminded unreasonably of the Black Paladin, Mathew started up in alarm. But the figure raised an admonishing hand and, drawing aside the facecloth, let his features be seen.

"It is only Khardan," came a tired voice.

"*Only* the Prophet," returned Mathew with a gentle, mocking smile.

Khardan groaned and threw himself down among the cushions. His handsome face was lined and brooding; dark shadows could be seen beneath the eyes, and Mathew's smile gave way to true concern.

"Are you well? Does something pain you? Your wound, perhaps?"

Khardan waved it all away with a gesture. "The wound is

healed. I had it attended to when I first rode into camp. How long ago was that? A week? It seems a year, a thousand years!'' Sighing, he leaned back and closed his eyes. ''My tent is filled with storytellers and tea drinkers, gift bearers and would-be advisers, soldiers and dancing girls—all staring at me hungrily as if I were some sort of stew that each could dip his fingers in and take away a piece! I would have ordered Sond to clear them out, but the djinn have vanished, disappeared again. So I pleaded nature's call, threw on these old clothes, and came here.''

A voice called from somewhere outside. ''The Prophet? Have you seen the Prophet?''

Khardan covered his face as the voice, now just outside Mathew's tent, asked permission to enter. ''Pardon, Marabout, for disturbing your rest. Have you seen the Prophet?''

''He was walking in that direction,'' said Mathew, pointing straight at Khardan.

The nomad thanked him profusely and shut the tent flap. They could hear his feet running off toward the oasis.

''Thank you, Mat-hew.'' Khardan started to rise. ''You were—as my tribesmen reminded me—going to your rest. It is the middle of the night. I am disturbing you.''

''No, please!'' Mathew caught hold of Khardan's arm. ''I couldn't sleep, not with all the noise. Please stay.''

It did not take much persuasion to convince the Calif to return to his cushions, though this time he lay sideways on them, propped up on one elbow. His dark eyes, gazing intently at Mathew, glittered in the lamplight.

''Will you do something for me . . . if you are not too tired?'' Khardan asked abruptly.

''Certainly, Prophet,'' answered Mathew.

Khardan paused, frowning. This was obviously a difficult thing he was about to ask, and he was still mulling it over in his mind, uncertain whether or not to proceed.

His heart singing with joy, Mathew kept silent, fearing the song might come to his lips. At last Khardan nodded once, abruptly, to himself. He had, it seemed, made his decision.

''You can use your magic to''—he coughed and cleared his throat—''see into the future?''

"Yes, Prophet."

"Call me Khardan, please! I grow weary of that title."

Mathew bowed.

"Then can you do so, now?' Khardan pursued.

"Yes, of course. With pleasure, Pro—Khardan."

On his arrival Mathew had carefully unpacked and hidden in a safe place the precious magical objects he had acquired during his journeys. One of these was a bowl made of polished wood he had discovered in the Hrana's camp in the foothills. Though Mathew had offered to trade a piece of jewelry for it, the owner had been more than happy to present it as a gift, following the nomadic custom of offering a guest anything in one's dwelling he admires. (Which led to being very careful what one admired.)

Mathew brought the bowl forth from its place near his pillow, handling it lovingly, delighting in the smooth feel of the wood that was a rare thing in the desert. He set it down upon the tent floor between himself and Khardan, pretending not to see the Calif's first involuntary motion to draw away from it, the stiffening of the body as he forced himself to remain where he was.

Reaching for the *girba* that hung outside the tent to keep the water cool for drinking, Mathew filled the bowl. Outside a voice had been raised in song in praise of the Prophet, reciting all his valorous acts. Mathew lowered his head, seeming to be looking into the water. But he glanced through his lashes at Khardan, who was listening with a certain amount of pleasure, yet at the same time an almost helpless irritation.

Mathew began to speak. "The visions I see in the bowl are not necessarily what will come to pass." Waiting for the ripples to fade from the water, the wizard made the standard warning as proscribed in his texts. "They will indicate only what may happen should you continue to follow the path you now trod. It might be wisdom to turn aside and try another path. It might be wisdom to keep to this one. Sul gives no answers. In many cases, Sul provides only more questions. It is up to you to ponder the vision and make your decision."

Staring almost hypnotized at the water, Khardan nodded. His face had softened into awe, fear, and eagerness. For both of them, the outside sounds had receded into the background. Mathew could hear his own breathing, the too-rapid beating of his heart. Tearing his gaze away from Khardan, he focused on the water and, commanding himself to concentrate, began the chant. He repeated it three times, and the images began to appear on the liquid's smooth surface.

"I see two falcons, almost identical in appearance. Each falcon flies at the head of a huge flock of warlike birds. The flocks meet and clash. There is fierce fighting and many of the birds fall, injured, dying."

Mathew was silent a moment, watching. "When the battle ends, one of the falcons is dead. The other rises higher and higher in the sky until he is crowned with gold and wears a golden chain about his neck and many are the numbers of birds who come and go at his command."

Raising his head, sitting back on his heels, he looked at Khardan. "Thus is the vision of Sul."

The Calif scowled, gesturing disgustedly at the water bowl. "Of what use is this?" he demanded bluntly. "That much I could have seen for myself looking into a cup of *qumiz*! There will be a battle. One side will win, the other will lose!" He sighed heavily, then—thinking he may have hurt Mathew's feelings—he cast him an apologetic glance. "I am sorry." He put a hand at his shoulder, grimacing. "I am tired. . . ."

"And in pain!" said Mathew. "let me see to the wound while I interpret this vision. It is not quite the clear crystal you make of it, Khardan," he added, carefully concealing a smile.

Shaking his head, indicating a willingness to listen though obviously expecting nothing to come of it, Khardan submitted to Mathew's gentle touch. Withdrawing the Calif's robes, the young man revealed the wound, not healed, but ragged-edged and inflamed.

"You did *not* have this attended," Mathew said severely, dipping a cloth into the bowl of water. "Lie down, that I may see it in the light."

"There was no time," Khardan said impatiently, but he lay down, stretching himself on his stomach full length upon the cushions, the lines of pain beginning to ease from his face at the touch of the cool cloth on his fevered skin. "The

women were exhausted from their use of their magic. I have
taken wounds before. My flesh is clean and knits rapidly.''

"I will do what I can for it, but I am not skilled in the art
of healing. You should have Zohra treat it—''

Khardan flinched. Mathew had his hands on the crude
bandage he was fashioning; he was not touching the wound,
there was no way he could have hurt the man, and he
wondered at the Calif's reaction. Then Mathew understood.
He had not touched the wound inflicted by steel, but another
that had struck much nearer the heart.

Resting prone, on his stomach, Khardan stared straight
ahead. Though it could not be seen, Zohra's tent stood in the
direction of his frowning gaze. "Have you ever been in love,
Mat-hew?'' was the next, completely unexpected question.

The gentle fingers ceased their calm ministration. It was
only an instant before their touch resumed, but that instant
was long enough to catch Khardan's attention. He turned and
cast Mathew a sharp, intense look before the young man was
prepared to receive it.

In Mathew's eyes was the truth.

The young man shut his eyes, too late to hide what was
there, he knew, but hoping to shut out the expression of
revulsion, anger, and contempt that he knew must contort
Khardan's face. Or worse—pity. Anything—even hatred—must
be better than pity.

"Mat-hew . . .'' came the Calif's voice, hesitant, groping. A hand touched his arm, and Mathew jerked away from
him, bowing his head, the red hair tumbling over his face.

"Don't say it!'' He choked. "Don't say anything! You
despise me, I know! Yes, I love you! I've loved you from the
moment you held the sword over my head and pleaded with
me to choose life, not give myself up to death! How could I
not love you? So noble, so strong, facing ridicule for my
sake. And then in the castle. You were in agony, near death,
and yet you thought of me and my pain that was nothing,
nothing compared to what you suffered!'' The words, bursting forth in a torrent, were followed by wrenching sobs. The
slender body doubled over in anguish.

A hand, rough and callused, yet gentle now, reached out
and rested on the quivering shoulder. "Mat-hew,'' said

Khardan, "of all the costly gifts I have received this night, this you offer me is the most precious."

Slowly, confusedly, Mathew raised his tear-stained face. A shuddering sob shook him, but he choked it back. "You don't hate me? But your God forbids this. . . ."

"*Hazrat* Akhran does not forbid love, freely offered, freely accepted. If he did, he would not be worthy of the trust and faith we put in him," said Khardan gruffly. His voice softened, and he added, "Especially love from a heart as courageous and wise as the one that beats within your breast, Mat-hew." Clasping the young man, Khardan drew him down and pressed his lips upon the burning forehead. "This love will honor me the rest of my days."

Mathew bowed as though receiving a benediction. The hands holding the wet cloth trembled, and he hid his face within them, tears of joy and relief washing away the bitter pain. His was a love that could never be returned, not precisely the way he sometimes dreamed of it. But it was a love that was respected and would be given back in trust, in turning to him for guidance, comfort, advice, in offering him protection, strength, and friendship.

Rolling over on his stomach, giving the young man the opportunity to compose himself, Khardan said with quiet casualness, "Tell me now, Mat-hew, what you make of this vision."

Chapter 14

Mathew wiped his eyes and drew a deep, shivering breath, thankful to be able to change the subject, grateful to Khardan for suggesting it.

"The vision, you remember, was of two falcons—"

"More birds," grumbled Khardan.

"—leading opposing armies," Mathew continued severely with a light, rebuking tap on the man's shoulder to remind him of the seriousness of their undertaking.

"Myself and the Amir."

"The falcons looked very much alike," said Mathew. He neatly wound the bandage around the man's wounded arm. "These falcons represent you and your brother."

"Achmed?" Worried, Khardan twisted his head.

"Lie still. Yes, Achmed."

"But he couldn't ride at the head of the army!" Khardan scoffed. "He's too young."

"Yet I believe from what I have gathered that he rides with the Amir, who is head of the army. The visions are not literal, remember. They are what the heart sees, not the eye. If you fought the Amir's army, your thoughts would be with the man, Qannadi, riding at the head of his troops. But your heart would be with your brother, would it not?"

Khardan grunted, settling himself in the cushions, his chin resting on his arms.

"Now then," said Mathew, adjusting the bandage. "Is that too tight? No? What else was there? Oh, yes. The battle. Both sides take heavy losses. There are many casualties. It will be a bloody, costly war." His voice grew halting. "One of the falcons dies. . . ."

"Yes?" persisted Khardan, though he lay very still.

"The survivor goes on to become a great hero. He will rise with the wings of eagles. All manner of people will come to his standard, and he will challenge the Emperor of Tarakan and eventually emerge the victor, wearing a golden crown and a golden chain about his neck."

"So"—Khardan, forgetting his wound, shrugged and winced with the pain—"the victor becomes a hero."

"I did not say 'victor,' " Mathew returned gently, "I said 'survivor.' "

It took a moment for the truth to sink home. Slowly, his movements hampered by the stiffness of the bandage, Khardan sat up and faced the young wizard, who was watching him with a grave and troubled expression. "What you are saying, Mathew, is that if my brother and I meet in battle, one of us will die."

"Yes, so the vision indicates."

"And the other becomes what—Emperor?" Khardan looked at him darkly, with disbelief.

"Not immediately, of course. I have the impression that many, many years will pass before that happens. But yes, the one who lives will eventually rise to a position of great power and wealth and also tremendous responsibility. Remember, the falcon wears not only the golden crown, but the golden chain as well."

Khardan's thoughts strayed outside, to his people and to those who had come to him. Only now, when the night was well past its fullness and falling off to morning, were they beginning to think of going to their beds. With the dawn the Prophet of Akhran would be faced with yet another line of men and women, bringing to him their small griefs, their great griefs, their wants and desires, their hopes and fears.

"Perhaps he can help them," said Khardan, speaking

with a shy, reluctant pride. "Perhaps, even though he is not wise or learned, he has been chosen to help them, and he cannot lightly give up that which was given him."

"It is his decision, certainly," said Mathew. "I wish I could be of more help," he added wistfully.

Khardan looked at him and smiled. "You have been, Mat-hew. He only wishes he were as wise as you; then he would know he was doing the right thing." The Calif rose to his feet and prepared to leave, winding the folds of the headcloth about his face so that he could move through the camp without being mobbed. "Perhaps, being so wise, you can answer me one more question." He halted at the entryway.

"I do not know that I am wise, but I will always try to help you, Khardan."

"Auda ibn Jad. He was cruel, evil. He cast helpless men to monsters. He committed murder and worse in the name of his evil God."

Mathew answered with a shudder.

"Yet our Gods yoked us together. Auda saved our lives; without him we would have perished in the Sun's Anvil. He saved my life by giving up his own there in the Temple of Quar. I mourn his passing, Mat-hew. I grieve that he is gone. Yet I know the world is better for his death. Do you understand any of this?"

Khardan looked truly puzzled, truly searching for an answer.

After a moment's thought, Mathew said earnestly, "I do not understand the ways of the gods. No man does. I do not know why there is evil in the world or why the innocent are made to suffer. I only know that a blanket made of thread running all one direction is not of much use to us as a blanket, is it, Calif?"

"No," said Khardan thoughtfully. "No, you are right." His hand clasped the young man's shoulder. "Sleep well, Mat-hew. May Akhran— No. What is the name of your God?"

"Promenthas."

"May Promenthas be with you this night."

"And Akhran with you," said Mathew.

He watched the Calif slip out of the tent, stealing across the compound of his own people with more care and caution than he ever took stealing into enemy camp. Seeing Khardan reach his tent in safety, noting several dancing girls in bells and silks being shooed out, Mathew—smiling and shaking his head—returned to his bed.

The young man was at peace. His decision was made.

Closing his eyes, comforted by the sound of the wind singing in the rigging of his tent, Mathew slept.

Chapter 15

Though Khardan spent a restless night pondering the vision Mathew had spread before him, he was not able to reach a decision. And thus it was his people who finally swept their Calif into the whirlwind of war.

The Sheykhs were the first to enter the tent of the fatigued and bleary-eyed Prophet, half-stupefied from pain, worry, and lack of sleep. Before Khardan could open his mouth, the Sheykhs presented their plan for battle—for once agreed upon by all present—and sat back to await his glowing commendation.

The plan was viable, Khardan had to admit this much. Reports trickling in along with a seemingly endless stream of refugees, rebels, and adventurers indicated that the forces of the Amir had been considerably reduced by the magical fog that swept over Kich. Those soldiers who survived were busy rebuilding the gate and other damaged fortifications. In addition they had to quell a near riot in the city when the rumor started that the nomads were threatening to unleash the killing mist on its citizens unless Kich surrendered.

The Sheykhs hinted that summoning the fog again might be a reasonable suggestion, to which Khardan asked them grimly if they meant to send their women before them into every battle they fought.

"Bah! You are right!" stated Majiid. "A stupid idea. It was his." He waved his hand at Jaafar.

"Mine!" Jaafar bounced to his feet. "You know—"

"Enough!" said Khardan, stifling a yawn. "Go on."

According to reports, Qannadi had sent messengers to the southern cities, calling for reinforcements, but it would take many weeks before they could be expected to arrive. A raid, swift and deadly, on Kich, and the Prophet could take control of the city, use it as a spearhead to launch attacks that would drive the enemy from Bas.

The plan mapped itself out further in Khardan's mind, though the Sheykhs never knew it. Bas would fall to him easily. The people, under his skilled guidance and leadership, could be counted on to revolt against the Emperor's troops. With Bas and its wealth at his disposal, Khardan could cut the trade route to Khandar and leisurely build his strength. Letting Khandar starve, he would march north and free the oppressed people of Ravenchai from the slave traders who ravaged their lands. He would ally himself with the strong plainsmen of the Great Steppes. The Lord of the Black Paladins would undoubtedly agree to add his own forces to the battle.

Then, when he was strong, he would attack the Emperor.

Yes, Khardan admitted to himself almost reluctantly, it could be done. Mathew's vision was not as wild and far-fetched as it had seemed to the Calif in the early hours of the dawning. It could be done. He could be Emperor of Sardish Jardan if he wanted. He would live in a magnificent palace of splendors that he could only dimly begin to imagine. The most beautiful women in the world would be his. His sons and daughters would number in the hundreds. No luxury would be too good for him. Rare and exotic fruits would roll on his tables. Water—there would be water to waste, to squander. As for his horses, all the world would come and fight to buy them, for he could afford the finest breeding stock and raise them on lush grasses and spend all his day, if he chose, personally supervising their training.

But no, not all day. There would be audiences, and correspondence with other rulers and his military leaders. He would have to learn to read, he supposed, since he would no dare trust another to interpret his correspondence. He would make enemies—powerful enemies. There would be food tasters, for he would not dare to eat or drink anything that some poor wretch had not sampled first for fear it was poisoned. There would be bodyguards dogging his every step.

He would make friends, too, of course, but in some ways these would be worse than his enemies. Couriers fawning on him, wazirs intriguing for him, nobles protesting their great love for him. And all prepared to fall upon him and tear out his throat should he show any sign of weakness. His own sons, perhaps, growing up to plot his downfall, his daughters given away like any other beautiful object to gain some man's favor.

Zohra. He saw her as head wife of a *seraglio* teeming with women, most of whose names he would not be able to remember. He saw her grow strong in her magic, and he knew that this, too, would bring him great power. And then there was Mathew—wise counselor—always near, always helping him, yet never seeming to intrude. These would be two people near him he could trust. Perhaps the only two.

A rumbling sound interrupted his daydream. Blinking, he raised eyes that burned with fatigue and saw his father glaring at him. "Well?" demanded Majiid. "Do we ride this night for Kich? Or are you going back to your bed and your dancing girls?" From his leer, it was obvious what he suspected his son of doing in the night.

Khardan did not immediately answer. He was seeing in his mind not the glorious palace or the hundreds of wives or the wealth beyond reckoning. He was seeing his younger half brother, clad in the armor of a man with a man's face and a man's sword arm, crouched in a fog-shrouded street, whispering his mother's name in a voice choked with tears.

There could be no help for it. Achmed had chosen his path, as Khardan must now choose his.

"We ride to war," he said.

Day, a week later, dawned upon Kich. The sun's light had no more than spread a blood red glow over the horizon when the cry of a tower lookout brought a captain running to see for himself. A messenger was sent to the Amir, who did not need it, having glanced out his own window and seen for himself.

His orders had already been given.

In the Kasbah below there was organized confusion as the troops made ready. Panic raged in the city, but Qannadi had that, too, in as much control as possible; men, women, and older children arming themselves and preparing to fight the invading horde.

"Send for Achmed," said Qannadi to Hasid, and the old soldier left upon his errand without question or comment.

Abul Qasim Qannadi walked over to the window—the one behind which he'd been sitting the night Feisal had died—and stared out across the plains into the low hills. A line of men, some mounted on swift, fearless desert horses and some on long-legged racing camels, spread over the hilltops. They had not yet moved but were waiting patiently for the command of their Prophet to ride down and deal death to the city dwellers of Kich. Their numbers were vast, their tribal banners and banners of other allegiances were thick as trees in a forest.

Rubbing his grizzled beard, Qannadi gazed out to the highest hilltop. He could not see him, not from this distance, but he had the instinctive feeling that Khardan was there, and it was to this hilltop that he directed his words.

"You have learned much, nomad, but not enough. Hurl your head at this solid wall. You will end up with nothing but a cracked skull for your efforts. I can stay here days, a month, if need be. By that time, my troops will have arrived from the south, and if any of your people are left—assuming they have not got bored with sitting there exchanging insults and the occasional arrow with the enemy on the walls—I will catch you between this wall and my advancing troops, and will crack you like an almond."

Satisfied with his observations, running over his plans in his head, the Amir turned back to his desk. There was always the possibility, of course, that the nomad's first onslaught would crash upon them like sea water, sweeping aside all defense and carrying the hordes of invaders into the city walls where Qannadi and his people would be cut up and fed

⊃ the buzzards. The Amir had planned for this eventuality, as
well.

"You sent for me, sir," said a clear voice.

Qannadi nodded, resumed his seat, and made a show of
sliding several pieces of folded and sealed parchment into a
leather bag. "I am sending you, Achmed, with dispatches to
Khandar. These are for the Emperor and the Commander
General. You will undoubtedly find them both in the palace,
making plans to attack Tirish Aranth. Here is a pass. You had
best leave now, in case the nomads cut the roads."

He spoke calmly, evenly, and did not look up from his
work until all was in readiness. Then he started to hand the
packet to Achmed.

The young man's face was livid, the brown eyes had
turned a smoky gray color in the pale light of dawn. "Why
do you send me away?" Achmed asked through stiff, blood-
less lips. "Do you fear that I will betray you?"

"Dear boy!" Rising to his feet, Qannadi dropped the
packet and grasped the quivering hand that clutched, white-
knuckled, the hilt of a sword. "How can you ask such a thing
of me?"

"How can you ask such a thing of me? Sending me forth
like a child when danger threatens!"

"It is your people we fight, my son," Qannadi said in a
low voice. "It is said that Sul inflicts demons on those who
shed the blood of near kin. I do not know if that is true, but I
have known men who killed those they loved and—whether
the demons came from without or within—I saw them tormented to their dying day. It was in my mind only to spare
you this. Think, my boy! It is your father, your brother you
will meet in battle this day!"

Achmed grasped the Amir's hand in his and held it fast.
"It is my father I will ride beside in battle this day," he said
steadily. "I know—I have known—no other."

Qannadi smiled and for a moment could not speak. His
hand ruffled the young man's dark, curling hair until he
found his voice. "If you are resolved in this—"

"I am," broke in Achmed firmly.

"—then I place the command of the cavalry in your
charge. You know your brother, you know how he thinks,

how your people fight. My young general," he said in a
teasing tone, regarding Achmed with fond pride, "I had a
strange dream last night. Shall I tell you?"

The young man nodded. Both men were alert to sounds
outside, sounds that would tell them the enemy was on the
move. But nothing came, so far. Khardan must be waiting
until the sun rose full and bright.

"I dreamed I found a young, half-grown falcon that had
been caught in a snare. I freed it and trained it, and it became
the most valuable bird in my possession. Its worth was
beyond measure, and I was more proud of it than certain
other falcons I had raised from infancy. Time and again this
falcon flew from my wrist and soared into the sky, yet it
always returned to me, and I was proud to welcome it home.

"And then there came the day when the falcon returned,
and the wrist it knew was still and cold." Achmed clutched
Qannadi's hand and would have spoken, but the Amir si-
lenced him and continued steadily. "The falcon spread its
wings and rose into the air. Higher and higher it flew,
attaining heights it had never before imagined. I looked up
and saw the gold of the sun touch its head, and I closed my
eyes, well content.

"I wish I could see your future, my falcon," continued
Qannadi softly, "but something tells me it is not to be. If not
this battle, then another will claim me." Or the assassin's
dagger. There were those among Quar's priesthood—not to
mention Qannadi's wife, Yamina—who blamed him for Feisal's
death. But this he carefully kept to himself. "Always remember that I am proud of you and, from this moment on, I name
you my son and heir."

Achmed gasped and stared, then shook his head, stam-
mering an incoherent protest.

"My decision is firm," said Qannadi. He pointed at the
leather case. "It is all in there, my will and testament, signed
and witnessed in proper form, legal and correct. Of course"—
he grinned wryly—"the charming sons of my loins—at least
my wives claim they are of my loins—will no doubt sit back
on their haunches and howl, then try their best to sink their
teeth into you. Don't let that stop you! With the Imam out of

ie way, I think you can handle them *and* their mothers.
'ight them and know that you have my blessing, boy!''

"I will, sir,'' murmured Achmed, half-dazed, not entirely
omprehending the gift that was being bestowed upon him.

"We will send Hasid to place my will in the Temple of
'handar. He's the only one I trust with this—my life. It will
e kept secret, of course. My wealth is considerable and
vorth the cost of a poisoned flask of wine. I know you care
othing for gold or lands now. But you will. Someday I think
ou will find a use for it.''

Rising from his desk, Qannadi picked up his helm and the
:ather pouch. Achmed helped him to gird on his sword. His
rm around the young man's shoulders, the Amir walked with
Achmed to the door.

"And now we best prepare ourselves to face this so-called
rophet of a Ragtag, Wandering God. I must admit, son, that
sometimes miss the Imam. It might be very instructive to
now what is transpiring in heaven this moment.''

THE BOOK
OF SUL

Chapter 1

All was not well in heaven.

Once again the One and Twenty had been summoned. Once again they met at the top of the mountain at the bottom of the world. Once again each stood firm upon his own facet of the Jewel of Sul, viewing the others from the safety and complacency of his or her own familiar surroundings.

Promenthas stood in his grand cathedral, his angels and archangels, his cherubim and seraphim, gathered around him. The God was looking particularly fierce, his eyebrows bristled, his lips were drawn so tightly their usual smile was lost in the snowy beard that tumbled over his cassock. The angels were in a tense state, muttering and whispering among themselves, except for one young guardian angel who sat alone in the choir loft. She seemed nervous and abstracted and kept tugging at her wing feathers as if—though knowing she must be here—she wished herself flying somewhere else. It was rumored among the seraphim and confirmed by the cherubim that the protégé of this young angel was involved in the great conflict among the humans, the outcome of which would be determined, perhaps, by this meeting among the Gods.

Uevin was in attendance, no longer fearing to leave his wondrous palace. Evren and Zhakrin both arrived, standing at opposite ends of the Jewel, eyeing each other askance, yet now according each other a grudging respect.

As the Gods came together, they spoke together, and their words were words of worry and concern, for the Jewel was still out of balance, still wobbling chaotically through the universe, and though the balance had tipped in another direction, it continued to be an unsafe and an unhealthy balance. Yet the Gods were uncertain how to correct it.

Almost all were gathered—the exception, as usual, being Akhran the Wanderer, and in this exception some saw sinister portent—by the time Quar arrived. In his almond-eyed beauty, the God had always seemed fragile and delicate. Many noticed that the delicateness had lately melted into boniness, the olive skin had a sallow, sickly yellow cast, the almond eyes darted here and there in ill-concealed fear.

Quar did not appear to his fellows in his pleasure garden but entered—in fawning meekness and humility—the dwellings of the other Gods. Those who had caught a glimpse of the God's habitation saw that the lush foliage of the pleasure garden seemed to be suffering from a drought. The leaves of the orange trees were drying up, the fragrant gardenia had— all but a few of the strongest—withered and died. No water poured from the fountains, and their pools were scum-covered and stagnant. Gazelles wandered about aimlessly, panting in thirst. Here and there lurked an emaciated immortal, peering out furtively from the parched trees and trembling whenever the dread name Pukah was pronounced (as it was, by Quar, with a curse, about twenty times an immortal day).

"Promenthas—my friend and ally," said Quar warmly, advancing down the aisle of the cathedral toward the God and, at the same time, speaking the same words to each of the other Gods, "I come to you in this time of dire peril! Heaven has gone awry! The world below totters on the brink of disaster! It is time to put aside petty differences and join together against the coming menace."

So interesting and unusual a spectacle was it to see Quar oiling his way into each God's domain that Benario hesitated a moment too long in swiping a fine emerald from Hurishta and lost his chance forever, while even Kharmani ceased, for

he moment, to count his money. The God of Wealth raised a
languid eye.

"I thought *you* were the coming menace," said that God
o Quar carelessly. The teeterings of the Jewel never bothered
Kharmani, for war meant money to somebody at least.

A nervous laughter among the younger angels greeted this
remark, to be instantly squelched by the elder cherubim,
whose serious faces reflected the grave concern in the eyes of
heir God. Quar flushed in anger but bit his tongue—and
poke in injured tones.

"I sought only to bring order to chaos, but you would not
have it so and let yourselves be duped by that desert bandit!
Now his hordes stand poised to attack! *Jihad!* That is what
Akhran the Wanderer, now called Akhran the Terrible, will
bring down upon you! *Jihad!* Holy war!"

"Yes, Quar," said Promenthas drily. "We know what the
word means. We recall hearing it before from your lips,
though perhaps in another context."

Staring intently at each God in turn and seeing them
hostile at the worst, indifferent at the best, Quar dropped the
money-coated facade. His lips curled in a snarl. "Yes, I
would have ruled you . . . you fools! But my rule in the
heavens and in the world below would have been a lawful
one—"

"*Your* laws," muttered Promenthas.

"A just one—"

"*Your* justice."

"I sought to rid the world of extremes, to bring peace
where there was bloodshed. But in your pride and your own
self-importance, you refused to consider what would be best
for the many and looked, instead, to the one—to yourselves.

"And now you will pay," Quar continued in grim satisfaction. "Now one comes to rule who abides by no law, not
even his own. Anarchy, bloodshed, war waged for sport—
this is what you have brought upon yourselves! The Jewel of
ul will crack and fall from its place in the universe, and all
up here and all down below will be doomed!

"See!" Quar, hearing a sound behind him, whirled in
error and pointed a trembling finger. "See—he comes! And
he storm follows!"

Galloping across the dunes on a steed luminous as moonlight, trailing stardust from its mane, rode Akhran. His black
robes flowed around him, the feathers on his horse's elaborate headdress glistened a bright, blood red. The God was
flanked by three tall, muscular djinn. Their golden-ringed
arms clasped forbiddingly across their broad chests, they
gazed down with grim and threatening faces upon the Gods.

Akhran the Wanderer guided his steed into the meeting
place of the Gods, and so powerful had he grown and so
commanding his presence that it seemed to the other Gods
that their domains must be blown away by the southern wind
called *sirocco*, and that they would soon wander lost and
helpless in a vast and empty desert.

Reining in his horse, causing the animal to stand upon its
hind legs and trumpet in loud triumph, Akhran slid skillfully
from his saddle. The *haik* covered his nose and mouth, but
the eyes of the God flared like lightning and those eye saw no
one, paid no attention to anyone except Quar. Slowly, resolutely, Akhran the Wanderer stalked across the sand, his gaze
fixed upon the almond-eyed, cowering God. Putting his hand
to the hilt of his scimitar, the Wandering God drew forth the
sword from its ornate scabbard. Suns, moons, planets—all
were reflected in the shining silver blade, and it flared with a
holy light.

"There!" gasped Quar, licking his lips and casting a
bitter glance around at his fellows. "There, what did I tel
you? He means to murder me as his accursed followers
murdered my priest! And you"—he glared around at the
other Gods—"you will be next to feel his blade at your
throat!"

If Quar had not been in such a frenzy of terror, he would
have noted with supreme satisfaction the growing fear and
concern in the eyes of Promenthas, the return of terror to the
eyes of Uevin, the eager gleam in the eyes of Benario. But
Quar was stumbling here and there, endeavoring to escape
Akhran's wrath and noticed nothing. There was nowhere to
go, however, and he found himself backed up against the lip
of a deep, dark well. He was trapped. He could go no farther
without tumbling into Sul's Abyss. Spitting puny curses and
baring his tiny teeth like a rat caught by the lion, Qua

crouched at the feet of Akhran, glaring at the God with unmitigated hatred.

Coming to stand before the shrinking, sniveling God, Akhran raised above Quar's head the sword that gleamed with the light of eternity. He held it poised for an instant during which time on earth and in the heavens stood still. Then, with all his strength and might, Akhran the Wanderer brought the sharp-edged blade slamming down.

Quar screamed. Promenthas averted his eyes. The angel in the choir loft buried her head in her hands.

And then Akhran laughed—deep, booming laughter that rolled like thunder across the heavens and the earth.

In one piece, safe, unharmed, Quar stood cringing before him. The blade of the scimitar had missed the God by the breadth of a hair split in two again and yet again. It stuck, point down, in the sand between his slippered feet.

His merriment echoing throughout the universe, Akhran turned his back upon the other Gods and whistled to his steed. Vaulting into the saddle, treating himself to a final amused look at the shivering, quivering Quar, the Wanderer caused his horse to leap into the night-black sky and dashed away amidst the stars.

One by one, sighing in vast relief, the Gods dispersed—returning each to his own facet of Sul, returning to their eternal bickering and arguing over Truth. Last to leave was Quar, who slunk back to his blighted garden, where he—noting that some of his plants continued to flourish—sat down upon a cracked marble bench and plotted revenge.

Promenthas dismissed the cherubim and the seraphim and all the rest back to their neglected duties, then wended his way up the narrow, spiraling stairs to the choir loft where the angel sat, her head hidden, afraid to look.

"Child," aid Promenthas kindly, "all is ended."

"It is?" She raised a face both fearful and hopeful.

"Yes. And here are some who have come to talk to you, my dear."

Looking up, Asrial saw two tall, handsome djinn in rich silks and jewels approach her. Walking beside one of the djinn, her small white hand clasped fast in his, was a beautiful djinniyeh.

"Lady Asrial," said Sond, bowing from the waist, "we know we can never take the place of Pukah in your heart, but we would deem it an honor if you would come with us and dwell among us both in the world of humans below and on our immortal plane above."

"Do you mean that, truly?" Asrial gazed at them in wonder. "I can stay with you and be close . . . close to . . . Pukah."

"For all eternity," said Nedjma, her eyes glistening with tears, her hand gripping Sond's more tightly.

"Who knows?" added Fedj with a smile. "Someday we may find a way to free the"—he was about to say "little nuisance" but, considering the circumstances, thought it best to change it magnanimously to—"great hero."

Asrial's eager eyes went pleadingly to Promenthas.

"Go and my blessings with you . . . and with the human you have so valiantly protected and defended. I think that your vigil over Mathew may now be relaxed, for—unless I am much mistaken—it will soon be shared by others."

"Thank you, father!" Asrial bowed her head, received Promenthas's loving benediction, and—giving her hand timidly to Nedjma—walked with the djinn and the djinniyeh into the desert.

Chapter 2

High on a ridge overlooking the walled city of Kich, Khardan sat on his war-horse and gazed out over the plains. It was after sunrise. The blazing orb, shining in the heavens, was reflected in the drawn and glistening blades of the *spahis*, the shepherds, the *mehariste*, the *goums*, the refugees, the mercenaries, the rebels, and all who rode with the Prophet of Akhran.

Khardan turned his attention to the walled city. It was some distance from where he and his army stood poised and ready to sweep down upon it like birds of prey. But the Calif could see—or fancied he could—the Temple of Quar. He wondered if rumors about it were true. It was said to be abandoned. The refugees had brought stories that it had been cursed—the deadly fog lingered in its halls, the ghost of the Imam could sometimes be heard preaching to priests as disembodied as himself. Whether or not this curse was true, most of the Temple's gold and jewels had been stripped from it, those who worship Benario having small respect for the curses of other Gods.

His gaze wandered restlessly from the Temple to the slave market, and his thought traveled back to the man with the cruel eyes in the white palanquin, to a slave woman with hair the color of flame. He glanced at the *souks*, the houses piled one on top of the other. His eyes went to the massive palace with its walls of thick stone that seemed to grow thicker and taller as the Prophet stared at it. He could have sworn that he saw the blind beggar seated in his accustomed place, he saw a blonde women in pink silk languishing in his arms. And here came Qannadi and Achmed, armor flashing in the sunlight, to be greeted with cheers from the soldiers, who may have momentarily lost faith in their God, but who retained it in their honored commander.

Khardan blinked, wondering at these impossible visions. Now he swore he could smell the city, and he wrinkled his nose in disgust. He decided he would never get used to it and supposed bleakly that Khandar—capital of an empire, a city containing not thousands but millions of people—must smell not a thousand but a million times worse.

And he would win this treasure at the cost of his brother's life. As a child Achmed had taken his first steps from his mother's arms into Khardan's. In those arms, according to the vision, Achmed would find his death.

The Prophet's horse fidgeted beneath him. The animal smelled battle and blood and longed to surge forward, but its master did not move. Khardan understood the horse's restlessness and stroked its neck with a trembling hand. The Calif had never in his life felt fear before a battle, but now he began to pant for breath, as though suffocating. Lifting his head, Khardan looked about wildly for some means of escape.

Escape from a battle he was sure to win.

His eyes encountered the fierce eyes of Sheykh Majiid, riding at the right hand of the Prophet and glaring at his son impatiently, mutely demanding the reason for this delay. The plan had been to strike at dawn, and here it was, nearly an hour past, and the Prophet had made no move.

At the Prophet's left hand was Sheykh Jaafar, his face falling into its customary gloomy foreboding, sweating in the brightening light, the saddle rubbing sores on his bony bottom.

To the left of Jaafar was Sayah, Zohra's half brother and the Sheykh's eldest son, who was casting looks of secret

triumph at Khardan as though he had guessed all along that
the Prophet was a fraud.

To the right of Majiid, Zeid towered magnificently over
the horsemen on his long-legged camel, the Sheykh's shrewd,
squinty eyes growing shrewder and squintier the longer they
sat here, exposed to the enemy on this ridge.

Behind the Sheykhs, muttering and grumbling with impatience, the army of the Prophet began to question among
themselves what was happening, and giving answers that
were half truths, and untruths, and no truths at all, gradually
working themselves into a state of confusion and demoraliza-
tion.

Off at a distance, separate and apart from the men, Zohra
and Mathew watched and waited—the heart of one wondering
at Khardan, the heart of the other knowing and pitying, yet
trusting.

Suddenly out of the air appeared the three djinn, Fedj,
Raja, and Sond. Bowing low before Khardan, they hailed
him in the name of *Hazrat* Akhran, who sent his blessings to
his people.

"About time, too," said Zeid loudly.

"Are these what we've been waiting for?" questioned
Majiid of his son, waving his hand at the djinn. "Well,
they've come back. Let's attack before we all faint from the
heat!"

"Yes," muttered Jaafar gloomily. "Let's get this over
with, take the city, steal what we want, and go back home."

"You"—thundered Majiid, pointing at Jaafar—"have no
vision! We will take the city, steal what we want, and burn it
to the ground. *Then* we can go home."

"Bah!" snorted Zeid. "What is this talk of taking a city?
Here we sit, slowly putting down roots into this God-cursed
rock! If the Prophet will not lead us, I will!"

"Ah, but who will follow?" questioned Majiid, whirling
around angrily to face his other old enemy.

"We will see! Attack!" yelled Zeid. Reaching out, he
yanked his *bairaq* from the hands of his standard bearer and
waved it high in the air. "I, Sheykh of the Aran, say 'attack'!"

"Attack! Attack!" The Aran echoed their Sheykh. Unfor-
unately their eyes were not on the city but on the Akar.

"I, too, say 'attack.' " Sayah leaned across his father's horse and sneered into Khardan's face. "But it seems our Prophet is a coward!"

"Coward!" Khardan turned on the young man in a rage.

Wait! Consider! said an inner voice. Consider what you will be giving up. . . .

The Prophet—pausing—considered. He looked up into the blue-and-golden sky. "Thank you, *Hazrat* Akhran!" he said softly, reverently.

"Attack!" shouted Khardan, and doubling up his fist, the Prophet of the Wandering God turned in his saddle and aimed a right at Sayah's jaw.

Sayah ducked. Jaafar didn't. The blow sent Khardan's father-in-law tumbling head over heels backward off his horse.

"Have you gone mad?" A shrill voice rang over the crowd. Zohra galloped into their midst, her horse rearing and plunging. "What of Kich? What of becoming Emperor? And what do you mean by striking my fath—"

"Get out of my way, sister!" cried Sayah.

"Oh, shut up!" Twisting in her saddle, Zohra took a vicious swing at her brother that, if it had hit, would have left his ears ringing for the next year. It missed. The momentum of her swing carried the Prophetess of Akhran out of her saddle to land heavily upon her father, just as the groggy, groaning Jaafar was struggling to his feet.

"Dog!" Sayah launched himself at Khardan and the two, grappling together, went for each other's throats.

Majiid, shrieking in fury, slashed wildly with his sword at Sayah, only to hit Zeid. The sword slit open a wide gash in the sash wrapped around Sheykh's round belly.

"That was my best silk sash! It cost me ten silver *tumans*!" Zeid foamed at the mouth. Clasping his standard in both hands like a club, he swung it in a wide arc, unseated two of his own men, and clouted Majiid soundly in the ribs.

"You know, Raja, my friend," said Fedj, giving the gigantic djinn a rude shove that sent him flying through the skies, clear across the border into Ravenchai, "I have always thought your body to be too big for your small-spirited soul."

"And I, Fedj, my brother, have always found your ugly

ose to be an insult to immortals everywhere!" snarled Raja.
Bursting back on the scene, his hands grasped hold of that
particular portion of Fedj's anatomy and began twisting it
painfully.

"And I"—shouted Sond, leaping suddenly and unexpect-
dly upon the complacent Usti—"say that you are a dough-
aced lump of sheep droppings!"

"I couldn't agree with you more!' Usti gasped and disappeared with a bang.

The hills around Kich erupted in confusion. Akar leaped
t Hrana. Hrana smote the Aran. The Aran battled the Akar.
Remnants of all three nomadic tribes banded together to turn
pon the outraged refugees of Bas.

Making his dangerous way through the flailing fists and
lashing sabers, maddened horses and screaming camels,
Mathew ducked and dodged and pushed and shoved, seeking
lways the flutter of blue silk that robed the Prophetess of
Akhran. He found her at last, pummeling with the butt-end of
broken spear a hapless Akar who had knocked out, for the
econd time, a befuddled Jaafar.

Zohra had just laid her victim low and was looking around,
anting, for her next, when Mathew appeared before her,
atching hold of her arm as she took a swipe at him.

"What do you want of me? Let me go!" Zohra demanded
uriously, trying her best to break free.

Mathew held onto her grimly and determinedly, however,
nd Zohra, struggling but too battle-weary to free herself, had
o choice but to follow him, cursing and swearing at him
ith every step.

Hanging onto Zohra with one hand, Mathew forged their
ay through the melee until he reached a black-robed figure,
ho was hacking away with a sword at another black-robed
gure, neither making the least progress, both seeming pre-
ared to spend the day and possibly the night in combat.

"Excuse me, Sayah," said Mathew politely, shoving be-
ween the two heavy-breathing, exhausted men. "I require a
ord with the Prophet."

Seeing—through a bleary haze—the *marabout* and recall-
g that this man was not only crazy but a powerful sorcerer

as well, Sayah waved a hand toward Khardan, bowed in respect for his opponent and, gasping for breath, staggered off in search of another fight.

"Come with me," said Mathew firmly, taking hold of Khardan's arm. He led the suddenly docile Prophet and the suddenly calm Prophetess back down the ridge, as far from the fighting as possible. Here, in the quiet of the vineyard where the people had hidden only weeks before with no expectation except that of death, Mathew turned to face the two people he loved.

Neither was much to look at. Zohra's veil had been torn loose—probably by her own hand—and cast to the winds. Her black hair, shining like a raven's wing, was tangled and disheveled and streamed across her face. Her best silken *chador* had been torn to shreds, her face was smeared with blood and dirt.

Khardan's wound had reopened, a patch of crimson stained his robes. Numerous other slash marks covering his arms and chest indicated that he had not found Sayah the easy match he had once scornfully considered the herder of sheep. His cheek was bruised and one eye was swelling shut, but he kept his other—dark and watchful—upon his wife.

Zohra, in turn, cast fiery glances at him from behind the veil of hair. Mathew could almost see the acid accusations rising to Zohra's lips, he could see Khardan preparing himself to catch the venomous drops and hurl them back at her.

"I have a gift for you two," said Mathew smoothly, as calmly as if he were meeting them on their wedding day.

Reaching into the folds of his black wizard's robes, Mathew drew forth something that he kept hidden in his hand.

"What is it?" asked Zohra with a sullen air.

Mathew opened his palm.

"A dead flower," said Khardan scornfully, yet with a hint of disappointment. Imperceptively, perhaps by accident since he was literally swaying with fatigue, he took a step nearer his wife.

"A dead flower," echoed Zohra. Her voice was tinged with sadness, and surely by accident as well—she took a step nearer her husband.

"No, not dead," said Mathew smiling. "Look, it lives."

Khardan, Calif of the Akar, and Zohra, Princess of the
Hrana, both leaned forward to stare at the flower lying in
the wizard's palm. Inadvertently, undoubtedly by accident, the
hands of husband and wife touched.

The crumpled petals of the flower grew smooth and shining, its ugly brown color deepened and darkened to a majestic
purple, the center bud unfolded, revealing a heart of deepest
red.

"The Rose of the Prophet!" breathed Khardan in awe.

"I found it growing on the Tel the morning we rode forth
to battle," said Mathew softly. "I plucked it and I brought it
with me, and now"—he drew a deep breath, his eyes going
from one loved face to the other—"I give it to you and I give
you two to each other."

Mathew held out the Rose.

Husband and wife reached for it at the same time, fumbled, and dropped it. Neither moved to pick it up, each had
eyes only for the other.

Khardan clasped his arms around his wife. "I couldn't
live within walls!"

"Nor I!" cried Zohra, flinging her arms around her
husband.

"A tent is better, wife," said Khardan, inhaling deeply
the fragrance of jasmine. "A tent breathes with the wind."

"No, husband," answered Zohra, "the yurt such as my
people build is a much more comfortable dwelling and a
much more suitable place in which to raise children—"

"I say—a tent, wife!"

"And I say, husband—"

The argument ended—momentarily—when their lips met.
Clinging to each other fiercely, they turned their backs on the
glorious brawl that raged unchecked on the hillside. Arms
round each other—still arguing—they walked farther into
the vineyard until they were hidden from view by the shelter-
ing leaves of the grapevines, whose entwining stems seemed
to offer to teach, by example, the ways of love. The quarreling voices softened to murmuring sighs and, at length, could
be heard no more.

Mathew watched the two go, an ache in his heart that was

both joy and a sweet sorrow. Leaning down, he picked up the
Rose of the Prophet that had fallen, unheeded, to the ground.

As he touched it, he felt a tear fall warm and soft upon his
hand and he knew, though how or why he could not tell, that
it fell from the eyes of an angel.

Afterword

We would like to acknowledge the help and support of our families: Tracy's wife, Laura, and Margaret's daughter, Elizabeth Baldwin.

We want to express again our appreciation to Larry Elmore for marvelous cover paintings and interior illustrations.

We thank Steve Sullivan for once more providing excellent visual representations of our world with his maps.

To our editor, Amy Stout, we extend grateful appreciation for her dedicated work and friendship and, yes, Amy, this time there is a happy ending!

We would like to thank Lloyd Holden, instructor for the A.K.F. Martial Arts Academy, Janesville, Wisconsin, and Bruce Nesmith, 2nd degree black belt, for taking time to assist with the fight scenes. We're still bruised.

We want to acknowledge the work of several authors we used as reference. In particular: *Arabian Nights*, translation by Richard Burton; *Arabian Society in the Middle Ages*, by Edward William Lane; *Seven Pillars of Wisdom*, by T.E. Lawrence; *Alone through the Forbidden Land*, by Gustav Krist; *In Barbary*, by E. Alexander Powell; *Land Without Laughter* by Ahmad Kamal; and *In the Land*

386 WEIS AND HICKMAN

of Mosques and Minarets, by Francis Miltoun and Blanche McManus.

Finally a special thank you to Patrick Lucien Price, to whom the character of Mathew—the wizard who leaves one world to be reborn in another—is lovingly dedicated.

Glossary

agal: the cord used to bind the headcloth in place
aksakal: white beard, village elder
Amir: King
Andak: Stop! Halt!
ariq: canal
arwat: an inn
aseur: after sunset

baigha: a wild game played on horseback in which the "ball" is the carcass of a sheep
bairaq: a tribal flag or banner
Bali: Yes!
Bashi: boss
bassourab: the hooped camel tent in which women travel
batir: thief, particularly horse or cattle thief (One scholar suggests that this could be a corruption of the Turkish word "bahadur," which means "hero.")
berkouks: pellets of sweetened rice
Bilhana: Wishing you joy!
Bilshifa: Wishing you health!
burnouse: a cloaklike garment with a hood attached

Calif: prince

caftan: a long gown with sleeves, usually made of silk
chador: women's robes
chirak: lamp
couscous: a lamb stuffed with almonds and raisins and roasted whole

dhough: ship
divan: the council chamber of a head of state
djemel: baggage camel
djinn: beings who dwell in the middle world between humans and the Gods
djinniyeh: female djinn
dohar: midafternoon
dutar: two-stringed guitar

Effendi: title of quality
'efreet: a powerful spirit
Emshi besselema: a farewell salutation
eucha: supper time
eulam: post meridiem

fantasia: an exhibition of horsemanship and weapons skills
fatta: a dish of eggs and carrots
fedjeur: before sunrise
feisha: an amulet or charm

ghul: a monster that feeds on human flesh. Ghuls may take any human form, but they can always be distinguished by their tracks, which are the cloven hooves of an ass.
girba: a waterskin; four usually carried on each camel of a caravan
goum: a light horseman

haik: the combined headcloth and face mask worn in the desert
harem: "the forbidden," the wives and concubines of a man or the dwelling places allotted to them
hauz: artificial pond
hazrat: holy

henna: a thorn-shrub and the reddish stain made from it
houri: a beautiful and seductive woman

Imam: priest

jihad: holy war

kafir: unbeliever
Kasbah: a fortress or castle
kavir: salt desert
khurjin: saddlebags
kohl: a preparation of soot used by women to darken their eyes

madrasah: a religious school
Makhol: Right!
mameluks: originally white slaves; slaves that are trained warriors
marabout: a holy man
mehara: a highly bred racing camel
mehari: plural of mehara
mehariste: a rider of a mehara
mogreb: night fall

nesnas: a legendary, fearsome monster that takes the form of a man divided in half vertically, with half a face, one arm, one leg, and so on

palanquin: a curtained litter on poles, carried by hand
paranja: woman's loose dress
pasha: title of rank

qarakurt: "black worm," a large species of deadly spider
qumiz: fermented mare's milk

rabat-bashi: innkeeper

salaam: an obeisance, a low bow with the hand on the forehead
salaam aleikum: Greeting to you!
satsol: a desert-growing tree

saluka: a swift hunting dog
seraglio: the quarters of the women of the harem
Sheykh: the chief of a tribe or clan
shir: lion
shishlick: strips of meat skewered and grilled
sidi: lord, sir
sirocco: the south wind, a windstorm from the south
souk: marketplace, bazaar
spahi: native cavalryman
Sultan: king
Sultana: wife of a Sultan, queen

tamarisk: a graceful evergreen shrub or small tree with
feathery branches and minute scalelike leaves
tel: a hill
tuman: money

wadi: river or stream
wazir: an adviser to royalty

yurt: semipermanent tent

About the Authors

Born in Independence, Missouri, Margaret Weis graduated from the University of Missouri and worked as a book editor before teaming up with Tracy Hickman to develop the *Dragonlance* novels. Margaret lives in a renovated barn in Wisconsin with her teen-aged daughter, Elizabeth Baldwin, and several pets. She enjoys reading (especially Charles Dickens), opera, and rollerskating.

Born in Salt Lake City, Tracy Hickman resides in Wisconsin in a 100-year-old Victorian home with his wife and four children. When he isn't reading or writing, he is eating or sleeping. On Sundays, he conducts the hymns at the local Mormon church.

The Darksword Trilogy marked Margaret and Tracy's first appearance as Bantam Spectra authors. They followed up with *Darksword Adventures*, a companion volume and game book set in the same world, then, the **Rose of the Prophet** trilogy. **The Death Gate Cycle**, a seven book series being published in hardcover and paperback, is their most inventive fantasy fiction yet. In addition to their collaborations, each is working on solo series. The first of these is *Star of the Guardians* by Margaret Weis.

Two Special Previews—

DRAGON WING, Volume One of
The Death Gate Cycle
by Margaret Weis and Tracy Hickman

and

THE LOST KING, Volume One of
Star of the Guardians
by Margaret Weis

On the following pages are two exciting previews of upcoming novels by premier science fiction and fantasy storytellers, Margaret Weis and Tracy Hickman.

THE DEATH GATE CYCLE

———————◼———————

Known for their innovation, Margaret Weis and Tracy Hickman reach an entirely new level with The Death Gate Cycle. *For this seven-book extravaganza they have developed four completely realized worlds. In the first four novels, a new adventure with both continuing and new characters will be set on each of the four worlds. In later volumes, the realms begin to interact, with the supreme battle for control of all the worlds in the final novel.*

———————————————————————

The following scene gives us an irresistible taste of the world of DRAGON WING, the first novel in *The Death Gate Cycle*, and the plots surrounding even the most knowledgeable of men who live there.

———————————————————————

Coming close to Hugh the Hand, the courier raised his lantern and stared quizzically into the assassin's face, inviting question or comment. The Hand saw no need to waste his breath in asking questions he knew would not be answered and so stared back at the courier in silence.

The courier, slightly nonplussed, started to say something, changed his mind, and softly exhaled the breath he had drawn to speak.

Abruptly, he turned on his heel and gestured to the assassin to follow. Hugh fell into step behind his guide. The courier led the way to a place that Hugh soon came to recognize, from early and dark childhood memories, as a Kir monastery.

It was ancient and had obviously been long abandoned. The flagstones of the courtyard were cracked and in many cases missing entirely. Coralite had grown over much of the standing outer structures that had been formed of the rare granite the Kir favored over the more common coralite. A chill wind whistled through the abandoned dwellings where no light shone and had probably not shone for centuries. Bare trees creaked and dry leaves crunched beneath Hugh's boots.

Having been raised by the grim and dour order of Kir monks, the Hand knew the location of every monastery on the Volkaran Isles. He could not remember hearing of any that had ever been abandoned and the mystery of where he was and why he had been brought here deepened.

The courier came to a baked clay door that stood at the

bottom of a tall turret. An iron key, worn on a ribbon around the courier's neck, unlocked the door. The Hand peered upward, but could not see a glimmer of light in any of the windows. The door swung open silently—an indication that someone was accustomed to coming here frequently. Gliding inside, the courier indicated with a wave of his hand that Hugh was to follow. When both were in the cold and drafty building, the courier once again locked the door, tucking the key back inside the bosom of his tunic.

"This way," said the courier. The direction was not necessary—there was only one possible way for them to go and that was up. A spiral staircase led them round and round the interior of the turret. Hugh counted three levels, each marked by a clay door. The Hand, surreptitiously testing each as they ascended, noted all were locked.

On the fourth level, at another clay door, the iron key again made an appearance. A long narrow corridor, darker than the Lords of Night, ran straight and true before them. The courier's booted footsteps rang on the stone. Hugh, accustomed by habit to treading silently in his soft-soled, supple leather boots, made no more noise than if he had been the man's shadow.

They passed six doors by Hugh's count—three on his left and three on his right—before the courier raised a warning hand and they stopped at the seventh. Once again, the iron key was produced. It grated in the lock and the door slid open.

"Enter," said the courier, standing to one side.

Hugh did as he was told. He was not surprised to hear the door shut behind him. No sound of a key turning in the lock, however. There was no light in the room but the soft glow given off by the coralite-outside. The faint shimmer illuminated the room well enough for the Hand's sharp eyes. He stood still a moment, closely inspecting his surroundings. He was, he discovered, not alone.

The Hand felt no fear. His fingers, beneath his cloak, were clasped around the hilt of his dagger, but that was only common sense in a situation like this. Hugh was a businessman and he recognized the setting of a business discussion when he saw it.

The other person in the room was adept at hiding. He was silent and kept himself concealed in the shadows. Hugh didn't see the person or hear him, but he knew with every instinct that had kept him alive through forty harsh and bitter cycles that there was someone else present. The Hand sniffed the air.

"Are you an animal? Can you smell me?" queried the voice—a male voice, deep and resonant. "Is that how you knew I was in the room?"

"Yeah, an animal," said Hugh shortly.

"And what if I had attacked you?" The figure moved over to stand by the window. He was outlined in Hugh's vision by the faint radiance of the coralite. The Hand saw that his interrogator was a tall man clad in a cape whose hem he could hear dragging across the floor. The man's head and face were covered by chain mail; only the eyes were visible. But the Hand knew his suspicions had been correct. He knew to whom he was talking.

Hugh drew forth his dagger. "A hand's breadth of steel in your heart, Your Majesty."

"I am wearing a mail vest," said Stephen, King of the Volkaran Isles and the Uylandia Cluster. He was, seemingly, not surprised that Hugh recognized him.

A corner of the assassin's thin lips twitched. "The chain mail does not cover your armpit, Majesty. Lift your elbow." Stepping forward, Hugh placed thin, long fingers in the gap between the body armor and that covering the arm. "One thrust of my dagger, there—" Hugh shrugged.

Stephen did not flinch at the touch. "I must mention that to my armorer."

Hugh shook his head. "Do what you will, Majesty, if a man's determined to kill you then you're dead. And if that's why you've brought me here, I can only offer you this advice. Decide whether you want your corpse burned or buried."

"This from an expert," said Stephen, and Hugh could hear the sneer if he could not see it on the man's helmed face.

"I assume Your Majesty requires an expert since you've gone to all this trouble."

The king turned to face the window. He had seen almost fifty cycles, but he was well-built and strong and able to withstand incredible hardships. Some whispered he slept in his armor, to keep his body hard. Certainly, considering his wife's reputed character, he might also welcome the protection.

"Yes, you are an expert. The best in the kingdom, I am told."

Stephen fell silent. The Hand was adept at reading the words men speak with their bodies, not with their tongues. Though the king might have thought he was masking his turbulent inner emotions quite well, Hugh saw the fingers of the left hand close in upon themselves, heard the silvery clinking of the chain mail as a tremor shook the man's body.

So it often was with men making their minds up to murder.

"You also have a peculiar conceit, Hugh the Hand," said Stephen, abruptly breaking his long pause. "You advertise yourself as a Hand of Justice, of Retribution. You kill those who allegedly have wronged others, those who are above the law, those whom—supposedly—my law cannot touch."

There was anger in the voice, and a challenge. Stephen was obviously piqued, but Hugh knew that the warring clans of Volkaran and Uylandia were currently being held together only by a mortar composed of fear and greed and he did not figure it worth his while to argue the point with a king who undoubtedly knew it as well.

"Why do you do this?" Stephen persisted. "Is it some sort of attempt at honor?"

"Honor? Your Majesty talks like an elflord! Honor won't buy you a cheap meal at a bad inn in Therpes."

"Ah, the money?"

"The money. Any knife-in-the-back killer can be had for the price of a plate of stew. That's fine for those who just want their man dead. But those who've been wronged, those who've suffered at the hands of another—they want the one who brought them grief to suffer himself. They want him to know, before he dies, who brought about his destruction. They want him to experience the pain and the terror of his victim. And for this satisfaction, they're willing to pay a high price."

"I am told the risks you take are quite extraordinary; that you even challenge your victim to fair combat."

"If the customer wants it."

"And is willing to pay."

Hugh shrugged. The statement was too obvious for comment. The conversation was pointless; meaningless. The Hand knew his own reputation, his own worth. He didn't need to hear it recited back to him. But he was used to it. It was all part of business. Like any other customer, Stephen was trying to talk his way into committing this act. It amused the Hand to note that a king in this situation behaved no differently from his humblest subject.

Stephen had turned and was staring out the window, his gloved hand—fist clenched—resting on the ledge. Hugh waited patiently, in silence.

"I don't understand. Why should those who hire you want to give a person who had wronged them the chance to fight for his life?"

"Because in this they're doubly revenged. For then, it's not my hand that strikes the killer down, Your Majesty, but the hands of his ancestors, who no longer protect him."

"Do you believe this?" Stephen turned to face him; Hugh could see the moonlight flash on the chain mail covering the man's head and shoulders.

Hugh raised an eyebrow. His hand moved to stroke the braided, silky strands of beard that hung from his chin. The question had never before been asked of him. It proved, so he supposed, that kings *were* different from their subjects—at least this one was. The Hand moved to the window to stand next to Stephen. The assassin's gaze was drawn to a small courtyard below them. Covered over by coralite, it glowed eerily in the darkness and he could see, by the soft blue light, the figure of a man standing in the center. The man wore a black hood. He held in his hand a sharp-edged sword. At his feet stood a block of stone.

"The only things I believe in, Your Majesty, are my wits and my skill." Twisting the ends of his beard, Hugh smiled. "So I'm to have no choice. I either accept this job or else, is that it?"

"You have a choice. When I have described the job to you, you may either take it or refuse to do so."

"At which point my head parts company from my shoulders."

"The man you see is the Royal Executioner. He is skilled in his work. Death will be quick, clean. Far better than what you were facing. That much, at least, I owe you for your time." Stephen turned to face Hugh, the eyes in the shadow of the chain mail helm were dark and empty, lit by nothing within, reflecting no light from without. "I must take precautions. I cannot expect you to accept this task without knowing its nature, yet to reveal it to you is to place myself at your mercy.

I dare not permit you to remain alive, knowing what you will shortly know."

"If I refuse, I'm disposed of by night, in the dark, no witnesses. If I accept, I'm entangled in the same web in which Your Majesty currently finds himself twisting."

"What more do you expect? You are, after all, nothing but a murderer," Stephen said coldly.

"And you, Your Majesty, are nothing more than a man who wants to hire a murderer." Bowing with an ironic flourish, Hugh turned on his heel.

"Where are you going?" Stephen demanded.

"If Your Majesty will excuse me, I'm late for an engagement. I should've been in hell an hour previous." The Hand walked toward the door.

"Damn you! I've offered you your life!"

Hugh didn't even bother to turn around. He sounded weary and exasperated. "The price is too low. My life's worth nothing. I don't value it. In exchange, you want me to accept a job so dangerous you've got to trap me to force me to take it? Better to meet death on my own terms than Your Majesty's."

Hugh flung open the door. The king's courier stood facing him, blocking his way out. At his feet stood the glowlamp and it cast its radiance upward, illuminating a face that was ethereal in its delicacy and beauty.

He's a courier? And I'm a Sartan, thought Hugh.

"Ten thousand barls," said the young man.

Hugh's hand went to the braided beard, twisting it thoughtfully. His eyes glanced sideways at Stephen, who had come up behind him.

"Douse that light," commanded the king. "Is this necessary, Trian?"

"Your Majesty"—Trian spoke with respect and patience, but it was the tone of one friend advising another, not the tone of a servant deferring to a master—"he is the best. There is no one else to whom we can entrust this. We have gone to considerable trouble to acquire him. We can't afford to lose him. If Your Majesty will remember, I warned you from the beginning—"

"Yes, I remember!" Stephen snapped. He stood silent, inwardly fuming. He would undoubtedly like nothing better than to order his "courier" to march the assassin to the block. The king would probably, at this moment, enjoy wielding the executioner's blade himself. The courier gently drew an iron screen over the light, leaving them in darkness "Very well!" the king snarled.

"Ten thousand barls?" Hugh couldn't believe it.

"Yes," answered Trian. "When the job is done."

"Half now. Half when the job is done."

"Your life now! The barls then!" Stephen hissed through clenched teeth.

Hugh took a step forward toward the door. The young man, still blocking his way, shot a warning glance at the king.

"Half now!" Stephen's words were a gasp.

Hugh, bowing in acquiescence, turned back to face the king. "Who's the victim?"

Stephen drew a deep breath. Hugh heard a clicking, catching choke in the king's throat, a sound vaguely similar to the rattle in the throats of the dying.

"My ten-year-old son," said the king.

STAR OF THE GUARDIANS

———■———

Volume One
The Lost King
by Margaret Weis

Even before Margaret Weis teamed up with Tracy Hickman, she had several writing projects in the works. Now, more than ten years in the making. **Star of the Guardians** *is finally publised. It's the page-turning tale of the man known as the Warlord and his search for the lost heir to the galactic throne.*

"Ah, Dr. Giesk. I was beginning to think you might fail ʲe."

The deep baritone voice was emotionless, almost pleasant ꞁd conversational. But Dr. Giesk shuddered. *Failure* was a ʲord the Warlord never spoke twice to any man. The doctor ʲuld not remove his hands from the controls of his delicate ʲquipment, but he managed to give the Warlord a beseeching ʲok.

"The subject proved unusually resistant," Giesk quavered. "Three days, my lord! I realize he was a Guardian, but none of the others held out that long. I can't understand—"

"Of course you can't understand." The Warlord stared down impassively at the man on the table. He laid a guantleted hand upon the quivering chest of the man with as little regard as he would have laid that same hand upon the man's coffin. Yet, when the Warlord spoke, his voice was soft, tinged with a sadness and, it seemed, regret.

"Who is there left now who understands, Stavros?"

The gloved fingers touched a jewel the man wore around his neck. Hanging from a silver chain, the jewel was extraordinarily beautiful. Carved into the shape of an eight-pointed star the gleaming jewel was the only object worn by the naked man, and it had been left around his neck by the Warlord's expressed command.

"Who knows of the training, the discipline, Stavros? Who remembers? And you. One of my best."

The man on the table moaned. His head moved feverishly from side to side. The Warlord watched a moment in silence then bent close to speak softly into the man's ear.

"I saved your life once, Stavros. Do you remember? It was at the Royal Academy. On a dare, you had climbed that ridiculous thirty-foot statue of the king. You were what—nine? I was thirteen and she . . ." the Warlord paused, "she would have been six. Yes, it was soon after she came to the Academy. Only six. All eyes and hair, wild and lonely as a catamount." His voice softened further, almost to a whisper. The man on the table began to shiver uncontrollably.

"Fascinating," murmured Giesk with professional interest monitoring his instruments. "I haven't been able to illicit response that strong in three days."

The Warlord moved his hand up to the man's head, th

gauntleted fingers stroking back the graying hair almost caressingly. "Stavros," commanded the Warlord, his helmeted visage bending over the man. "Stavros, can you hear me?"

The man made a slight moaning sound. A froth of blood appeared on his ashen lips.

"Be quick, my lord!" cried Dr. Giesk, "or you will lose him!"

The Warlord brought his face so near to that of his victim that his breath touched the man's skin, displacing the bubbles of blood and saliva on the gaping mouth.

"Where is the boy?"

The man shivered, fighting with himself. But it was useless. The Warlord regarded him intently. The guantleted hand moved to rest upon the cold white forehead.

"Stavros?"

In a wild, tortured shriek, the man screamed out words that made no sense to Giesk. He glanced at the Warlord uncertainly.

The Warlord slowly rose and straightened. "Well done, Dr. Giesk. You may now terminate."